# Life

By Leo L. Sullivan

Compilation and Introduction copyright © 2004 by
Triple Crown Publications
2959 Stelzer Rd., Suite C
Columbus, Ohio 43219
www.TripleCrownPublications.com

Library of Congress Control Number: 2005930724
ISBN: 0-9762349-9-8
Cover Design/Graphics: www.MarionDesigns.com
Author: Leo Sullivan
Associate Editor: Cynthia Parker
Typesetting: Holscher Type and Design
Editor-in-Chief: Mia McPherson
Consulting: Vickie M. Stringer

Printed in the United States of America

# ACKNOWLEDGEMENTS

First, I would like to thank God. To my loving mother, I am your only child – I know that I have taken you through hell and back. One day you're going to answer the door bell and I'm going to be standing there with open arms. I promise I'll never leave you again. I love ya Ma!

Taya Baker, my confidant. You held me down. Every Black man is given one ebony angel in his life time, you are mine. You showed me that every real brotha has to have a strong sista in his life, that balance like some rite of passage to manhood. First you must learn how to love a "Black Woman". Love ya Booboo.

To my nigga Lateef Varo, trapped behind enemy lines on Fed. We will continue to engage the enemy for our freedom. Keep yo head up!

To my sista Assata Shakur, Sundiata Acoli, Marilyn Buck and all the other comrades who dedicated their lives to our struggle, peace and blessing with God's speed. Afeni Shakur, thanks for keeping Tupac's legacy alive. Not to forget about dem Chi-Town 47th street G.D.'s my ole stumping grounds. Sarasota, Florida, the home team. Big props go out to dem niggaz in that 'trape' in Opa-Locka, Florida. Twon, wuz up!

Hellema publications, girl you ass in just too busy, thanks for being there. Tajuacla & Jack Parker and their book club. I would be remiss if I forgot to give mad love to my nigga Marvin Johnson, aka Blazack. May we never have to take a trip up that road again for dem 'chips'. Iras in Hot Atlanta FM 89.3 get at me. To my partner Wayne Stone and his family and his son Jr. Communications is the key to winning any war. S. Lindsay, exhale and let it go. To my daughter Desire Monae Harvey that I have never had a chance to hold, I love baby girl. Ashley McMillion and Dwight Williams II thanks for your support.

To my dude Clifford Senter a.k.a. "Fateem" and his sis Laurita, also Professor Akinyele at Georgia State University African studies – y'all missing in action. To my dude Gucci out the bottom in Miami. To Phyllis Murphy, my baby mama, it ain't over yet!

Fo-real fo-real, Vickie Stringer and her side kick Tammy are the real Gangstaz in this industry. To my editor, Cynthia Parker and to Mia McPherson and the entire TCP family, thanks for letting me shine. I came so close to signing with another company that I just found out that did not have my best interest at heart. Leon Blue, it was you that sparked the flame for this joint. Good luck with your company, "InfraRead". Also, to Victor Martin and Jason Poole, thank you for paving the way.

Most importantly to my readers: Thank you! In this book I am giving you my very best. This was the closest I could take you into "that world" and keep it gangsta without catching another federal indictment. Also, it was important for me to make a statement in my writing, to be conscious and with a message. To those I forgot to mention on paper, don't worry, you're in my heart.

Visit my website at: WWW.LEOSULLIVAN.COM. Tell me what you think, or you can write me directly at: P.O.Box 725 Edgefield S.C. 29824.

# Dedication

This book is dedicated to my mentor and best friend in memory of his son Tupac Shakur (God bless his soul). Mutulu, there aren't enough words in any language to express my love for you, my teacher, my mentor, the father that I never had. You treated me like I was your own son. For me it was a blessing to have spent nearly ten years of my life under your diligent guidance. You forced my mind to go to another level, to a plateau outside the mundane box of limitations that unconsciously some Blacks have been trained to place on our minds. You embraced my writing, nurtured it. Had me writing lengthy essays and treatise. You had me on the radio doing poetry, speaking in front of packed audiences. I was scared to death! Remember? You told me that they had to let me in the door. We would argue, people would walk by and see us yelling at each other. I'll never forget the day they moved me to another plantation (prison) after all those years of being around you, I was crushed! One day I set down to write you a letter and I just cried…and cried…well, finally, I'm here at the door just like you said, "Knock! Knock!"

Dr. Mutulu Shakur, I love you my nigga. I hope we meet again!

The author regrets the vulgar and degrading language used to depict the characters in this book. Especially those made in reference to Black women; however, he feels that it is a true and accurate account of the plight of Black life in terms of the vernacular and how urban impoverished Black Americans view themselves. Unfortunately, this book may be viewed as socially incorrect by today's standards, thus tarnishing the rose colored glasses that most of today's Black writers write from. The reality is men abuse women, and like it or not, Black America is caught up in the yoke of a severe AIDS epidemic.

How can America be the richest, industrious nation in the world, but yet choose to spend more money incarcerating young Black men than on the entire educational budget? Only by examining ourselves realistically within, will we be able to find a viable solution to help ourselves. Since time immemorial, someone has been determined to destroy us! Humanity.

"...I'm speaking as a victim of this American system. I see America through the eyes of the victim. I don't see any American dream; I see an American nightmare..."

- Malcom X, April 3, 1964

# Chapter One

## "The Set-up"

### *1992*

I watched her as she slept. The rise and fall of her brown succulent breasts beckoned me. A beacon of light shined through the worn out curtains, illuminating the pellucid curves of her beautiful body. Nubile femininity captured on the cinematic screen of my mind. Once again I thought about rolling off into her, burying myself in her moist womanhood. The mounds of her sensuous flesh I could molest as from a mental escapism, she could be my sanctuary, at least for that infinite moment in time.

I was 26 years old, not even four months out of the joint and was back to throwing bricks at the chain gang as the old folks used to say–meaning, I was hustling with little regard for the law.

As I lay in bed, in a fleabag hotel room, with a broken air conditioner and no immediate plans for the future, I dreamed as all hustlers do. If I could just hit that one big lick, I would get out of the game.

On the dresser was my best friend–my gun. A big ole .44 Magnum named Jesus. Actually, it wasn't me that named it Jesus, its victims did when they were forced to look down its long intimidating barrel. Next to it laid eighteen cocaine rocks and about three hundred dollars–my entire life savings–and the keys to Lil Cal's tricked out Chevy, along with a pack of condoms. Cal was out of town and I was responsible for his ride.

Lying next to me in bed was Kim, a bonafide freak. I reached over and caressed her nipples. She stirred in her sleep lassoing a long leg on top of me. Her elbow came to rest on my morning erection. She crooned groggily.

"You asleep?"

"Naw, I was just lying here thinking."

"Thinking 'bout what?"

I felt her fingers walking across my thigh toward my morning glory. It was hot, stuffy and we were nude. The bed sheets stuck to our bodies. Her hand found its destination, stroking me with a determination, trying to rekindle an ember of passion from the night before. The gold bangles on her wrist jangled, signaling in chimes, her urgency. In one quick motion she climbed on top of me positioning herself to take me in. Her sultry breath a whisper against my cheek.

"Want me to serve you?" she flirted—meaning oral sex.

A hot, salivating tongue trailed my chest as she lowered her head. You see, at 30, Kim could do things with her mouth that made men curse God in ecstasy. She had a gorgeous body with generous curves, a small waist and a plump behind. She was light skinned, with a smooth complexion and a slight Bugs Bunny over-bite that somehow gave her beauty an alluring sexual appeal. However, she was the kind of broad that made a brotha appreciate tinted windows, cheap hotels and late night creeps. Kim had one major flaw—she was a powder head. Over the years it looked like the more cocaine she snorted the finer she would get. What made her so interesting to hustlers was the fact that she had a college degree, a good job and she knew how to talk proper like white folks with all them big words. She ran through all the dope boys like water. She had two vacuums that could suck you dry, the one in her mouth, and the other one in her nose. Both were lethal.

So I guess by now you have figured it out, I was in this sleazy ass hotel room tricking with Kim. She was about to gobble me up, her vacuum was on my stomach. There was a knock at the door. I had to wrestle her off of me as I got up, grabbing my gun while putting on my pants. I padded over to the door and looked over my shoulder placing my finger over my lips to quiet Kim. No one was supposed to know I was here. A large cockroach labored across the door as I looked through the peephole. Dre' and some other dude were standing outside the door. I removed the chair from underneath the doorknob, and then I remembered to put on my shoes and shirt. Placing the gun in the spine of my back, I opened the door. I had not seen Dre' since I went to the joint, and from the look on his face, he was not happy to see me. He owed me a few grand.

"Wha …What …What's up L?" he stuttered. "I saw Lil Cal's car out front. The lady at the desk said he was in here."

"Naw, Lil Cal gone out of town. I'm keeping the car," I said, sensing something. I stepped to the side as I invited them in. Dre' was hesitant. I noticed the big dude nudge him in. He had on some jewelry, too much for this side of town. Dre' read my mind as he fidgeted.

"This is my cousin, Big Mike, from California." The platinum chain on his neck must have cost a fortune. Mike looked like a dark skinned version of Suge Knight, only taller and with an athletic build like the kind of man that works out a lot. I couldn't read his eyes because he was wearing dark shades. That disturbed me. One thing was for certain, dude had cheddar. He stroked my curiosity, Kim's too. She could smell cocaine and money like a police K-9. From the look in her eyes she was on to his scent. Her greedy eyes flashed dollar signs as she got up from the bed wearing only the sheet like a sexy toga. Giving them an "I go good with coke and a smile" pose, she stood, standing back on her legs displaying a lot of peek-a-boo cleavage and the flaming red hair on her crotch left little doubt in anyone's mind as to what was what. As she sashayed to the bathroom, there was a moment of silence, the way men give homage to a nice round ass.

"Yo, wuz up," I said, trying to get a feel for what was going on.

"Nuttin'. I was lookin for Lil Cal," Dre' said. It looked like his eyes were trying to tell me something. The thought of money made me ignore him. Big mistake.

"Ya'll trying to get some yae?" I questioned, meaning cocaine.

"Yes," the big man replied.

"No," Dre' said simultaneously.

The big dude took the lead with Dre' looking as uncomfortable as a nigga at a Clan demonstration. I was thinking of the five grand he owed me and now I got his ass trapped in a raggedy ass hotel room. Wasn't it Tupac that said, "Revenge is sweet as pussy." A lot of nights I used to lay up in my cell in the joint thinking about all the niggas that had crossed me. Dre' did not even send me a dime. The more I thought about it, the angrier I got. The Suge Knight-looking cat fired up a blunt. Between puffs he said, "We trying to cop a couple ounces of crack."

"Crack?" I repeated incredulously because real hustlers never refer to dope as crack. Dre' just rolled his eyes up at the ceiling. I thought I had it figured out; Dre' was about to take this lame for his scratch and did not want me in on it. Just then, as if on cue, Kim strutted out of the bathroom. Her hair and makeup were immaculately done as if she were ready to pose for one of those glamour magazines. She was scantily dressed in a black sequined miniskirt and high heels. She was the poison to the dope game.

Money, whores, cars and clothes are all accentuates that lead a brotha to prison or worse. Kim's perfume fumigated–all eyes were on her as she sat on the bed, crossing her long legs seductively. In the back of my mind, I was plotting on how to relieve Dre' and the big lame of their cash. Kim was working her charm on the lame like a boa constrictor charming a bird. His eyes were glued to the meaty exposure of her thighs as she gave him that "pussy for hire" smile. The whole time Dre' was looking at me with something in his eyes, something that later on, I would regret that I did not recognize.

I walked to the door opening it wide. "Kim, I'll holla at you later."

Her brow frowned at me as if to say, *I know that you can't possibly be talking to me.* She opened her mouth to speak, but thought

**4**

better of it. With hands poised on her hips, she just looked at me.

"I'll be down in a second, wait for me in the car."

Her nose was running, she needed a snort. She took one last look at the big dude, did her mental telepathy thing that whores do when they are trying to catch a trick. She turned to me, "L, don't keep me waiting," and spun on her heels. I shut the door.

"How much money you got?" I asked, talking to no one in particular. The big man shifted his weight uncomfortably. Dre' knew what was about to go down. I had blood in my eyes.

"Yo, L, man I stopped by your mama's crib and wasn't no one home. In fact, I did not even know you were out until just now." He tried to smile, but all his face unveiled was a mask of fear. There was an adrenaline like raw energy, it started with the heart-beat, sweaty palms and it completely seized control of a man as well as his victims. The kind of power that only a gun can bring.

Power, I was feeling it. I reached into the small of my back pulling out Jesus, the savior. For the first time, big man removed his shades. He was severely cockeyed. I couldn't tell what the fuck he was looking at. Dre' mumbled something about he thought we were tight. I started to smack his ass upside the head with the barrel of the gun.

"Just let me get them chips you owe me, it should be about five grand with interest," I said with a menacing scowl on my face.

Dre' dug into his pockets removing a large wad of cash.

"Where is the rest of it?" I asked, pointing the gun in his face.

"Swear to God, that's all I got."

"Nigga get flat on the floor," I barked. Dre' did a belly flop. If there had been any water I would have given him a ten. I turned to the big man. I still don't know if he was looking at me, the floor, or what. Beads of sweat were cascading off of his forehead. "Let me get that up off of ya big man."

"Noooo!" Dre' screamed. I thought he was more worried about the big lame than he was about himself. I thought that was strange. Everything was moving fast and this big nigga looked like he was thinking about bucking, so I cocked the gun.

He flinched, then slowly he reached into his pants and removed a pouch. Casually, I took a step back as he tossed it to me just in case this Suge Knight-looking nigga got any bright ideas and I had to bust a cap in his fat ass. I looked inside the pouch, bingo! Nothing but hundred dollar bills.

Dre' was still on the floor whimpering, "No, no, L! Cal, not you! Cal, not you!" His jabbering was inaudible to me because I was focused on the lame with the fat chain on his neck.

"Big man, let me get that ice off of ya," I insisted, pointing with the gun. His eyes shot daggers at me.

"I'd beat your little ass if it wasn't for that gun."

He took a step forward.

"Yeah, and my aunt would be my uncle if she had balls. Save the rap and un-ass that ice."

He took the chain off, a little too slow for my liking, but I stripped his ass like a stolen Chevy and made him lie on his stomach on the dirty-ass carpet. I heard tales where dudes got killed doing robberies for failure to search the victims during a hasty getaway. While I was patting big man down, I found a loaded .380 pistol in a holster strapped to his leg. The last thing I needed was to get shot in the back. While I was searching Dre' he was shaking like a leaf on a tree. I felt something taped to his body; it ran from his back, around his stomach and taped to his chest. A police wire. Dre' turned informant and I was being set up. My heart skipped a beat. Alarmed, I panicked as Dre' began pleading.

"L, it wasn't meant for you, they want Lil Cal ... Lil Cal ..."

My life flashed before my eyes. I was going back to prison, big time. I could visualize cell doors slamming. I had just robbed an undercover Narc Agent. Shit! In a fit of rage I kicked Dre' in the face, threw the wire across the room and ran over to the window and looked out. Sure as hell the police were everywhere. I felt like a trapped animal. With only one way in and one way out, my mind raced in a million different directions. Quickly, I grabbed the old oak dresser and dragged it in front of the door creating a barricade between my destiny and me. As soon as I turned around the cop was getting off the floor in an attempt to tackle me. I pointed the gun at him. "Don't make me kill you!" He got back down on the floor. There was a thunderous noise at the door. A battering ram.

"POLICE!" came the shout from behind the door.

Wood was flying from the door like sharp metal. I ducked down and suddenly remembered the bathroom. I ran in there and kicked the door behind me. There was a small window over the toilet. I could hear footsteps as the front door came crashing down. Police were screaming, "Stay on the floor, stay on the floor!" to Dre' and the Narc Agent. I broke the window, and cut my hand in the process. The police were at the bathroom door. I was moving fast. It was a two-story drop in a small gangway with a spiked fence at the bottom. Just as I got out of the window the bathroom door burst open. I jumped, descending downward. I fell inches from the fence and injured my ankle, as shots rang out, ricocheting above my head. As soon as I cleared the gangway I saw an elderly white man cleaning the windshield of his car. A platoon of cops turned the corner heading straight for me. I bum rushed the old man and knocked him down. I dipped into the car, which was an old Caddy, but in mint condition. The tires screeched a complaint as I pulled out, pedal to the metal. In the rear view mirror I could see a cloud of smoke and angry cops running behind me as I distanced myself, heading for Highway 301, doing a hundred miles an hour.

It was Friday, about 8 o'clock in the morning and the traffic was dense. White folks in their cars gawked at me in horror. In the distance behind me I could see an array of police cars—their lights flashed as they all trailed behind me. It looked like a scene from the O.J. Simpson chase. I turned a corner on two wheels, and drove across the grass on 27th and Martin Luther King Park. I was driving like a bat out of hell, looking for a place to get rid of the car and run. I made another sharp right, then a left, driving in the wrong direction on a one-way street, traveling over a hundred miles an hour. I was not wearing a seat belt so I could make a quick exit. In most high speed chases the police are notorious for causing wrecks that end in fatalities. I slowed the car down pulling into a driveway of a house and shifted the car into park. I had lost the police. With my hands on the steering wheel, I watched both ends of the street. My hand was bleeding, but I could not feel a thing. I was numb as my heart pumped ice water into my veins. Running from the police has always been like dancing with the devil. Getting away was like escaping from hell.

A dark cloud that hovered over me reverberating a mighty roar shattered the lull of the morning silence. A police helicopter had located me. I did not panic. In fact, I just sat there thinking, *there is no way in hell I am going to out-run a police helicopter*. Then I thought, *fuck 'em!!!* I was facing a thousand years in prison! I stepped on the gas and the car fishtailed out of the driveway hitting a parked car. If I was going back to the joint, they were going to have to catch me. It was on. This was some "ride or die shit" and the gas tank was full. I headed back to Highway 301 with the helicopter still on my ass. The wind wooshed around my ears as I continued to disobey the speed limit. Fuck it! The Bradenton City Limit was about five miles away and I knew there would be a roadblock full of rednecks and trigger-happy police. I watched too many episodes of "Cops" for this not to be true. I found a Pall Mall cigarette butt in the ashtray, lit it and inhaled deeply. The wind whooshed around my ears–I was driving at a hundred miles an hour. Up ahead police cars were coming from the opposite direction, on the other side of the highway. I zoomed past them. They would have to turn around to follow me.

A sign up ahead read, "Bradenton County" and I saw the famous roadblock. Hell, they were using eighteen-wheelers and police cars. High-powered rifles were aimed at my tires. I stepped on the brakes, the tires screamed and sent me sliding … sliding … out of control near the steel spikes they placed in the road to bust my tires. I made a ninety-degree turn and that old Caddy did the unexpected and leaped over a ditch, plowed over the guardrail, and up a steep hill. As I looked toward the sky, I squinted at the bright sun as sweat burned my eyes. I could see that damn helicopter was still on my ass.

I turned right on a mean thoroughfare. The traffic was heavy but managed to part like the Red Sea for a Black man driving like a maniac with a police helicopter on his ass. I could see some of the expressions on them white folks' faces as I zoomed in and out of the traffic changing lanes like I was in the Indy 500. I turned, entering the Bradenton Shopping Mall, nearly hitting an old lady pushing a shopping cart. The damn helicopter was so low now that it looked like it wanted to land on the car. I parked the car in the lee of a carwash, hopped out and walked briskly toward the mall's entrance.

Inside, the cool air hit my face and I had to adjust my eyes from the ardent sun. As I walked, no one appeared to be paying much attention to me. I passed a jewelry store; next to it was an ATM machine, and a Burger King restaurant. My mind was churning. *Think fast! Think fast!* I told myself. I knew any minute the mall was going to be flooded with irate cops that wanted to beat my ass. Pedestrians traversed the halls; it was semi-crowded so I blended in. Across from the movie theater was a clothing store called The Gap. I got an idea and walked inside. I swore to God, I had never been so happy to see another Black man in my entire life. The brotha greeted me with a warm smile as his eyes held me, giving me a once over. I looked like hell. There was blood on my shirt and pants from where I cut my hand. I dug into my pocket, pulling out two crumbled one hundred dollar bills.

"I need a pair of size thirty-six pants and a large shirt. I'm in a hurry. Oh, and you can keep the change," I told the sales clerk.

A few other people came into the store. I looked up, startled. The clerk sensed my apprehension, but the money motivated him. The brotha gave me a shirt and a pair of pants. I turned and saw the police through the window. The clerk did, too. I ducked inside the dressing room. They arrived in full force. I thought about a shootout as I took the guns out of my pants while changing. I felt my heart pounding in my chest so hard it felt like it was going to

**9**

come out. The dressing room was about the size of a small closet with one of them partial doors with slants. I watched as a Black girl entered, she was tall and regal in splendor. I needed a way out from the store. As soon as I stepped out of the dressing room and placed the bloody clothes in a trashcan, the police rushed in. The girl was about two feet away from me. A honey toned sister with hazel eyes and long silky brown hair. She watched me intensely as if she knew me or something. The police headed straight for me. Something dawned on her, it registered in her eyes and I could see it on her face. Her delicate lips formed a tight, thin line across perfect ivory teeth with her jaw clinched in a contemptuous Black woman's scowl. To this day, I don't know what made me do it; fear and desperation will make a man do strange things. I grabbed her. She screamed, I laughed and played it off as if I knew her. I whispered in her ear, "Please, please Shorty help me!" I just knew that she felt the gun in my pants.

Surprisingly, this Black woman that I did not know, embraced me tightly. Her euphonic laughter was the barrier that shielded me. Four heavily armed police officers with bulletproof shields and helmets walked right up to us. The clerk in the store looked as if he were going to shit in his pants. I could hear dogs barking like they were on to my scent, but through the crowd that had gathered, their barks went unnoticed.

"Have you seen a Black man wearing black pants and a gray shirt?" the police questioned as they looked around the store.

The clerk looked at me as if he were weighing his thoughts between the money I had given him or telling the officers I was right up under their noses.

"No sir," he finally answered.

I felt the girl shake in my arms as the cop in the front of the store announced, "He ain't in here." They stormed out of the store. I realized that I had been holding my breath. The woman untangled herself from me and took a step back. It felt like her piercing hazel eyes bore right through my soul, and then somberly, she closed her eyes and shook her head. The expression on her face said I can't believe what I have just done.

A customer asked the clerk for help, causing him to snap out of his daze of watching us, two complete strangers and the upheaval of the police. The girl turned and walked away. I could sense that she was troubled by her actions. I followed behind her like a lost puppy. On my way out of the store, I grabbed a Lakers hat and a pair of dark shades.

All hell broke loose in the shopping mall. The woman was walking fast and the place was crowded. The police scurried about, in what looked like a mad frenzy, searching for me. Outside the sun was bright and there was not one helicopter in the sky now, but two. The other one had ABC News 40 stenciled on it. The mall parking lot had taken on a festive atmosphere with hundreds standing around gawking at the herd of police. I was able to blend right in as I followed the woman. She walked to the raggediest car in the lot, a rusted old Ford Mustang. Abruptly, she turned on her heels doing a half pirouette.

"Go!" she pointed. "I've helped you enough." She couldn't look me in my eyes.

*****

# Chapter Two

## "A Black Woman's Love"

### — Hope —

I sat in my car reading the letter for what seemed like the umpteenth time. It was a letter from my brother, Bryant, on the lockdown. In the letter, he stated that he was a Muslim now and that he changed his name to Malik. Painfully, I thought, *how was being a Muslim going to get the life sentence off of him?* My eyes started to water as I fought back the tears. In his letter, he vented his frustration, blaming it on the white man. As usual he went off on Black women, saying they were never there when a brotha needed them. He said I abandoned him when he needed me the most—when he was going through a severe drug addiction. In some ways he was right and his maudlin words hurt me to my core. Between going to college and working a full time job I neglected him. His poignant words, *you never helped me,* would forever be embedded in my mind. The white folks gave my brother a life sentence for eighteen rocks of cocaine. I have another brother, Marvin. He was on the run from the law at the same time. My father was in mourning. Daddy, he's a good man, who has been working for the post office for as long as I can remember. My mother passed away from cancer when I was 6 years old.

The noise from the helicopter disturbed my reverie. I looked up to see it hovering over the parking lot like some evil vulture about to pounce on its prey. That's when I saw a car come to a screeching halt inside the car wash and this fine chocolate brotha came walking out. I swear to God he looked identical to my oldest brother. I just had to do a second take. The resemblance was uncanny. Nervously, he looked up at the helicopter and entered the mall. For some reason, tears spilled over the brim of my eyes like a dam that suddenly burst. I was propelled into another time, another place. Black men being lynched and killed. They took my brother's life for eighteen rocks of cocaine. It seemed like from the beginning, or as far back as I could remember when I was a young girl, Black men were always running. Running from life and running from their responsibilities. I exited my car in a daze and then the police showed up in throngs. Too many white faces, all of them police, lawd-have-mercy. It hurt a sister to her heart to see so many Black men locked up. Six percent of the population, 90 percent of all incarcerated. Until this day no one could convince me that this was not genocide, especially when the majority of the people that commit crimes are white. In my heart I really thought I could change the world. Maybe it was because I was young and naïve, just 21 years old. Anyway, that was why I was going to college to become a criminal lawyer. And one day, I planned to present my case to the United Nations just like Malcom X wanted to do.

Police raced past me with police dogs. I tried to shrug the sight from my mind, but even as a little girl growing up in the ghetto, ever since I saw the movie *Roots*, white men in blue suits, chasing Black boys–well to me they always look like slave catchers. It was pure pandemonium as I walked. The police were everywhere. It unnerved me. I stepped inside of a clothing store, more for mental refuge than to shop, and that was when I saw him again. The fear in his eyes sent shivers through me. He changed clothes. His handsome face was angular with dimples. He was frightened and his desperation was palpable. I was only a few feet away from him now, I couldn't take my eyes off of him. I walked right up close to him, and then all hell broke loose. The police stormed in and headed straight for him. He looked at me with my brother's eyes

... the police neared ... he grabbed me. I screamed like I was his damn hostage and although he laughed in a mock show of affection, I let him hold me. In fact, I sunk right into his arms like they were the waters to my bath. He whispered into my ear, his lips brushed across my earlobe, I felt the two day old stubble of his beard to my cheek. His raw masculinity seeped inside my soul.

"Please, Shorty, help me!" he pleaded.

I was sure the police were about to arrest him. They walked right up to us and the clerk was startled, like he was watching a horror movie. When one of the officers asked him something, I wasn't paying attention to what was being said, I just kept hearing my oldest brother's voice, *you never helped me.* Somehow these words shattered my resistance. As I watched the police walk out of the store, I was suddenly filled with trepidation. What if I was helping a maniac, some hardened criminal on the loose from some insane asylum ... with a gun! I turned and walked away. I had done some stupid things in my times but this took the cake. God, the man could be a murderer or a rapist with those damn sexy eyes.

Finally I made it to my car but to my utter shock, he was still behind me. Unable to believe he actually followed me out of the mall, I turned toward him and in a brusque manner, I yelled, "Go!"

He cringed. The mere sound of my own voice emboldened me. I fumbled with my purse removing my key chain with the can of mase attached to it. We were starting to attract attention. Darkness temporarily shielded me from the sun. I looked up and saw two helicopters in the sky.

"Shorty! I swear to God I have not done anything wrong, you gotta believe me."

One of the helicopters lowered, it looked like it was taking a picture of us. It was damn sure filming the mall. I panicked and quickly walked around to the passenger's door because my old car, which I had named Betty, only cooperated with me when she wanted to. The man must have thought I was opening the door for him because he sure as hell hopped his ass in, and to this day, I don't know why I let him get in. I walked around to the driver's side and he opened the door for me. He reclined all the way back in the seat. I prayed old Betty would start. This became a ritual, I turned the ignition, pumped the gas and she coughed and sputtered to life. I drove out of the parking lot scared to death. Once I hit the highway, I turned to him.

"You can get up now."

The wind tossed my hair. He popped his seat up shielding his eyes from the sun with his hand.

"Thanks Shouty," he said with too much hubris for my liking.

"My name is Hope Evans. Please don't refer to me as 'Shorty' or 'Shouty' or whatever it is. You can call me Ms. Evans. Now where do you want me to drop you off?" I was trying to sound stern and unafraid. I felt the corners of my mouth saccade. Hell, he had a gun. He could take whatever he wanted. I felt his eyes roaming, leering at me. I wasn't wearing a bra for the long trip. I wanted to be as comfortable as possible. Every time I hit a bump my breasts would bounce; I could feel him looking at them. I was wearing a FAMU T-shirt. Furtively, I looked down at my breasts and noticed that my nipples were protruding. I tried to hide them by rubbing my feet thereby placing my arm to obstruct his view. And then my worst fears came true. He pulled out, not one but two guns, and pointed them right at me. I almost pissed in my panties as my entire life flashed before me.

"Where can I put these?" he asked.

My mouth moved, but my tongue refused to oblige. I pointed to the glove compartment. I swore to God, one of those guns was so big it wouldn't fit so he placed it underneath the seat.

"Where ya headed?" he continued, trying to make conversation.

"Tallahassee." The word came out of my mouth strained. I hoped that he didn't notice. "I am a Senior at FAMU."

"You in one of them crazy sororities?"

I don't know about crazy, but I am a Delta." With that, I

glanced over at him, I was curious as to why he asked me that. He smiled sheepishly answering my curiosity.

"I saw the bumper sticker on your car."

I took advantage of his laxity. "Why are all those police looking for you?" Silence, in the form of a pregnant pause filled the air, and I instantly regretted asking. He turned to me, his words slow, deliberate, his brow crest and eyes distant.

"This morning when I awoke, I was seriously thinking about getting out of the game, stop selling dope, no more hustling … then this nigga and his supposed-to-be-cousin came by my hotel, dude and him were looking for some hard …"

"Hard?" I interrupted.

"Crack cocaine!" he said, giving me a look, somewhat annoyed.

"Uh huh." I nodded my head like I got it.

"This dude owed me money, and I'm figuring if I take what belongs to me really ain't a crime, besides who he gonna tell? And if he don't like it he can get it like Drac!"

"Who?" I couldn't understand his lingo.

"Drac, Count Dracula, the vampire got his in blood."

"Uh huh." I nodded my head. Just then an eighteen-wheeler flew past us.

"I hate them damn trucks. My hair flies everywhere," I said out loud.

"I took my money from dude and his cousin. Come to find out his cousin was really an undercover cop. After I realized that I was being set up, I jumped out a window, stole a car and here I am." He gestured by waving his arms.

More silence—the kind that comes when two strangers are considering each other. I honestly felt that he was being sincere, even though he was in big trouble, it could have been worse. He could have been a killer or coochie-taker. I felt somewhat relieved. Now all I had to do was get his ass out of my car.

"Where do I drop you off?" I tried to sound nonchalant.

"Tallahassee."

"Talahasseeeeee?" I quipped.

"The same place where you headed." He tried to say it with a straight face but then added, "Don't worry Shouty, as soon as we get there, you can drop a nigga off at the mot."

He meant motel. I watched as he primed his lips with his tongue. His eyelashes were long like a girl's and pretty, too. I couldn't help thinking, so handsome, yet he was so damn dumb. He was just wasting his life, headed in the same direction as my brother, and his language was foolish. He actually thought he was sounding pimpish, trying to impress me, but there was something about him, his character and its aloofness. He wore his thugness like a black panther; it was all a natural part of his aura. I could, for the first time, see how a sister could be attracted to a thug. Not me, of course, or so I thought. I thought that he was the same kind of brotha that hung out on the street corners drinking out of brown paper bags, saying slick flirtatious remarks about girls' asses when they passed to go to school.

I knew that I was on fragile ground, but I had to take control. "Listen," I said with more venom than I actually had. He turned and stared at me with those big old pretty eyes. I almost drove off the road.

"The name 'Hope' has a special meaning for me. My mother named me that and she almost died while giving birth to me. She passed away later, when I was a small child." I heard my voice crack. "And another thing, I would appreciate it if you would not use that word 'nigger', ever in my presence. Too many of our ancestors have died and sacrificed their lives just to be treated as human beings. The word 'nigger' serves no other purpose but to dehumanize and degrade Black folks." I turned to look in his direction and noticed that his mouth had formed in an O like shape, like I had just berated him or something. "And another thing –" I was on a roll and felt like getting everything out of my system. "What I did back there was wrong, and you were wrong, regardless of how we try to sugar-coat it. You have issues that I cannot be involved with. Where do you want me to drop you off

**17**

and boy, don't say Tallahassee!"

I was winded like I just delivered a speech. He dug into his pocket removing a large roll of cash, peeled off some bills and placed them in the ashtray I used for loose change. I spied the money, hundred dollar bills.

"Dig Shouty, I mean Hope." He minced his words miserably. His voice was pungent, pleading with sympathy. "Hope, you gotta help me! I gotta get out of this town, please."

As I drove through the country roads listening to this brotha's voice, sounding like a melancholic song, the woes of Black men confiding in a sister, asking them to help them get away, I wondered if men use the word "help" on women knowing that, by nature, we are often powerless to turn them down because it tugs into our God-given maternal instincts. He must have seen something in my eyes, or my demeanor, because the cadence in his voice perked up as he said.

"Hope, I promise you as soon as we reach Tally, I'll buy you anything you want." With that, he leaned the seat all the way back and closed his eyes. I watched him thinking it couldn't hurt much having him along for the drive, and I can't lie, the three hundred dollars he placed in my ashtray I could really use.

After crossing a scary-ass bridge in Tampa Bay, I notice the red emergency light in my car come on, which was not normal. I reached my favorite landmark, the toll booth. I had been driving for over six hours and was tired. Moments later I pulled into a Shell gas station to fill up and stretch my legs.

"Hope." He called my name like it was a tester to see how it would sound rolling off his lips.

"Yes," I answered.

"Let me pay for the gas, you look tired. I'll get us something to eat and you can get some rest. Let me drive the rest of the way." He smiled, exuding a charm that I am sure he knew made women weak, or at least it did me. His dimples were so deep I could sink my baby finger in them. I watched him walk off looking like any average male student on FAMU. Too bad he was a thug.

I went to the restroom to pee. Afterward, I checked myself in the mirror. I looked like shit, I had dark circles under my eyes and my hair was a mess. As I fixed my hair in the mirror, I reflected on my life. Between going to college and working full time, life was extremely hard. There were times I thought about just giving up. I stayed broke all the time. I had just over one hundred dollars to my name, besides what was in the ashtray, and I was going to send my brother most of that. Fortunately, I lived on campus. After college, to help me get through law school, I was going to get a job at a law firm as a clerk and get some hands-on experience.

I returned to the car pretending not to watch him as he came back with some food. Fried chicken, french fries, corn on the cob and a side dish of hot apple pie. My taste buds were doing the "bomb" thing with that delicious aroma which made my mouth water. As he ducked in the car, placing the food in the seat, I began to notice that he never really paid me much attention the way men normally do. I sat back in the seat, munching on fries, watching him do the manly thing, checking under the hood of my car, checking the oil, adding water and inspecting the motor. At that moment, I couldn't help but be thankful for having the brotha with me. Lord knows a woman needs a man around to do those kinds of things.

He returned with a grim expression on his face like he wanted to charge me with vehicular homicide, for the attempted murder of my own car.

"Your radiator has a hole in it the size of 95 South and it's leaking."

The man was telling me nothing I did not know. At the time I just did not have the money to have it fixed.

"I was told as long as I keep antifreeze in it, it would hold up."

"How long ago were you told that?" he asked, eyebrows knotted up together like he had an attitude.

A yellow school bus pulled up beside us in the next lane. Kids screaming and just having a jolly time. I played dumb and shrugged my shoulders. I answered his question carefully because

I did not want to incriminate myself.

"I don't know, maybe a year, or so." Actually, the mechanic told me that it would cost over three hundred to get it fixed, hell, my car didn't cost that much.

"Scoot over!" he said curtly.

I looked up at him as if to say, *I know you ain't talking to me with that tone in your voice.* I could tell he was a brotha that knew how to take charge and for some reason I let him. I slid over to the passenger's side and watched, feeling like a scolded child as he got into my car with his oily, filthy hands on my steering wheel.

"There is no way we can make it to Tallahassee unless we drive real careful and not let the car overheat." As he drove off he pointed to the red light on the dashboard.

"See this light right here, how long has it been lit up like that?" His tone was like my father's and I was not liking it.

"I never paid it much attention," I answered nonchantly. I just wanted to piss him off some more.

We rode in silence for a while. The food was starting to get cold and Betty started to act up, nothing bad, I just knew the sounds of my car. That was one thing I knew better than he did. Moments later we pulled into a rest station. Dusk was starting to set and the air felt cool on my skin. We parked next to a huge camper with a boat hitched to it. White folks with money, vacationing because they could. I admired their vehicle and waved at the old lady inside. She took one look at me with disdain and closed her window like I was contaminating the air.

He returned to the car, looking under the hood. I watched as he added water and did some more things. Occasionally, he would glance at me and shake his head, like he could not believe how dumb I was. And now that I think about it, it was kind of dumb of me. In a way in knew I appreciated having him with me. Just thinking about being out here all alone with my car broke down gave me the creeps.

He returned after he washed his hands and we tore into our food. Picnic on wheels. I sat sideways with my back on the door facing him. In between bites he stopped eating and stared at me. It was the first time he really looked at me. He had oily chicken crumbs around his mouth but I resisted the urge to wipe it off.

"Hope ... I like that name, it's beautiful, like maybe you can be trusted ..."

"Mr. Anonymous, I'm glad that you mentioned that," I said, placing my chicken breast down looking at him intensely. The atmosphere changed to a mental standoff between man and woman.

"You never did tell me your name."

He looked at me as if to say, *I had no intention of doing so*, so I continued in a Black woman's threat, talking with my hands in the air.

"Since I am aiding and abetting a fugitive, and the fact that you're driving my car, it would be mutual respect if I at least knew who you are."

He had the nerve to smirk at me with those shimmering brown eyes. I could tell he was thinking if he should tell me his name. Finally he sighed, exhaling deeply, the way people do after weighing their thoughts.

"My friends call me 'L'. I was born in Chicago. My dad and step mom moved to Sarasota, Florida when I was about a year old."

I watched as he took a big swig of his Coke. I took the opportunity to pry further.

"You still have not told me your name."

He smiled at me, shaking his head with a sly expression that I had seen many times before, acknowledging my wits. I resisted the urge to smile back. It was important I knew everything I could about this man.

"OK, my real name is Life Thugstin. Everyone calls me 'L' for short, and before you ask, my father named me Life because my mother died while giving me life. It was a painful death of childbirth."

When he said that, something deep within me tugged at my

heartstrings. My mother died while I was a small child, at least I did have fond memories of her. Life had none. Right then, in my own strange way, I bonded with him.

"My father is the famous preacher, Reverend Freddy Thugstin. You heard of him?"

I was completely speechless. Damn right I heard of him, and just about everybody in America has heard of him, at one time or another. The man had a radio show and his own television show on cable. This brotha was truly puzzling me now. Most children were forced into a life of crime due to economic and poor family structure. If what I was hearing was true, Life's family was doing pretty well financially. I could not help it, I delved deeper.

"Your father is the Reverend Thugstin? I've seen his service on television many times on Sunday mornings … what happened to you?"

"What do you mean, what happened to me?" He made a face that would have scared a small child.

"Your dad has that big old church with all those people attending." I wanted to say all that money too, but I didn't because it would not have sounded appropriate since his father was a religious man.

"My dad is full of shit, a pussy-ass nigga. He could drop dead as far as I'm concerned."

"Don't say that!" I said scornfully.

"You only see what the lights and cameras show you. I got so many bastard brothers and sisters, I can't even keep count of all of 'em. That church for him is nothing but a harem."

I decided not to pry any further; it was clear that Life and his father had major issues. Now that I looked at him, he was the spitting image of his dad, with the same handsome features. You could tell they made beautiful babies. Tactfully, he changed the subject, or so he thought.

"So you're studying African studies?" he inquired as he turned to look out of the window. I could sense that his mind was somewhere else, probably at his daddy's church in Sarasota. A woman has to be careful with digging up old wounds, the hurt was still there.

"Yea, I'm taking a course in African Studies. I'm majoring in Criminology, Sociology and some more ologies. I'm going to be a lawyer." With that, I held my chin up, those were like magic words to 'em. Hell, I was halfway to achieving my dreams. I thought about my brother in prison, heard his remark every time I said I was going to be a lawyer he would joke and say, "And get you big bro out of prison." The only thing was, I knew it wasn't a joke.

The car was quiet, like too many thoughts being churned out at the same time. I did the woman thing, and began to clean the mess up that we made. I got out of the car with bags of chicken bones. Somehow I felt that Life could use the solace of being alone with whatever it was that was troubling his mind. The old bat in the camper rolled her eyes at me. As I approached the trashcan a mangy dog sat about three feet away licking his chops like he had been expecting me. I tore open the bag and threw him a bone. He just cocked his head sideways like maybe he was debating if I could be an undercover lady dogcatcher. As I walked back to the car, I noticed the chill in the air. Night was falling, turning the sky a beautiful shade of blue.

When I got back to the car, Life was inhaling deeply on a Newport cigarette. I don't know what white folks are putting in them smokes, but I swear sometimes people look like they are making a television commercial when they are inhaling them. Normally I don't let people smoke in my car, and I have been cursed out a lot for that, considering how ragedy my car is but there is always that one exception.

*****

# Chapter Three

## "Flirting with Death"

### *— Hope —*

After about two hours of driving we were just about two hours outside of Tallahassee. I don't know why everything always looks so spooky on the highway at night when you are traveling across the country.

I was listening to my tunes. Anita Baker was crooning about sweet love and the heat felt good on my feet. The whole time Life was quiet, the way men are when they have something on their mind. I cannot stand an overly sensitive man, but I did kind of want his conversation. He showed me nothing less of that of a gentleman. I still was not sleeping on him.

Betty suddenly started to show her ass. The car lost power, the lights dimmed and the motor cut off. Life slammed his hand into my dashboard, like he had lost his damn mind, scaring the shit out of me. The car coasted. I sat up in my seat, eyes bulging out of their sockets. Life got out, slamming the door behind him. It was so dark outside I could barely see my hand in front of my face, and once again I was thankful I was not alone.

Life got back in the car and tried to start the motor. Nothing.

"We are going to have to let the engine cool off," he said, frustrated. Still, I was happy to have him with me. And then he added, "If that doesn't work, we'll just have to walk."

"Walk?" I repeated like I was just learning to speak English.

After an hour my feet were cold and I sat balled up in the car shaking. Occasionally, Life would dash out of the car and try to wave down a car for help, flailing his arms. After a while I was beginning to think it was a waste of energy. A Black man at 10 o'clock at night, waving at cars, must have looked like a robbery about to happen to white folks. I knew one thing for sure, every time he opened the door, he let out the little warm air our bodies produced. My feet felt like icicles.

"I'm cold," I said more to myself, as I changed positions from one side of my buttocks to the other. "My feet are freezing." I was trying to give him a hint to keep the other door closed.

"Give them here," he said as he rubbed his hands together.

"What?"

"Give me your feet."

I lingered on that thought a moment or two. I thought it was a cute gesture, but it would be inappropriate with this brotha, besides my ashy feet looked like I had been kickboxing with Bruce Lee. To my utter surprise, this man reached over and grabbed my feet. I figured what the hell, so I let him. He placed my feet on his lap removing my sandals. His big hands were so gentle and warm, they felt like hot butter caressing my skin. Skillfully he rubbed the arch of my foot carefully placing pressure at all the right points. The feeling was completely tantalizing. I moaned out loud. I swear to God it felt like he was massaging my clitoris. I closed my eyes, "hmmmm yeah." I went to thinking that this is feeling too damn good, too intimate. I wiggled my toes.

"Ok therapy man, where did you learn that?" I asked playfully. He stopped and placed my feet under his shirt. This man was really trying to keep my feet warm.

"My stepmother, Brenda. She raised me after my mother died. She taught me a lot."

I learned there is always a Black woman in a man's life somewhere at some time, even if it is only her prayers, and from the smoldering look in Life's eyes, I could tell this was the woman.

I wiggled my feet on his washboard abs. His belly rumbled in an attempt to suppress a laugh. I had to admit, homeboy got major points for being a complete gentleman. Once again though, I had the feeling he was treating me like his little sister, not a woman. That was cool with me. After all, he was a thug.

We both fell asleep to the murmur of crickets and an occasional passing car, the sounds of the night.

I awoke with a startle to the cataclysmic sound of what I thought was an earthquake. I couldn't get my bearings straight. Lights blared in my face and the police had the car surrounded. Someone was pounding on my window so hard I was sure they would break it. This was it. My stupidity had caught up with me. Everything I gained would be lost. Here I was about to go to prison and possibly get shot in the process. *Oh-lawd!* I thought. I had a loaded gun under the seat.

I watched as Life rolled down the window in what looked like slow surreal motion. A gun was pointed at his head. On my side, I could see little beady eyes staring at me. A face smeared the window with breaths of sinister fog, as a bright light continued to shine in my face. I was shaking so bad I did not know what to do.

I heard a formidable voice bark out in a southern drawl.

"Boy, wha ya think ya doing herah?"

I could smell the faint scent of alcohol. I knew at that moment that something was drastically wrong! I peered out of my passenger window. There were now two pairs of eyes, fiendishly staring back at me.

"Jimbo, derra niggrus in dis herah car," the ominous voice announced.

The faces on my side of the car hooted in a kind of laughter that wasn't filled with the pleasure of kindness. It made my flesh crawl. I realized then that they couldn't be the police. This was worse, much worse!

"Boy, yea know yous in Steam Hatch," the redneck said, pressing the gun against Life's temple. It was then that my vision cleared and my brain snapped into overdrive. The lights that I mistook for police lights were actually shinning from a large four-wheel truck that looked like it was two stories high. Its fog lights shined bright like the morning sun.

Oh God! I felt Life's hand trying to reach underneath my seat for the gun. I was paralyzed with fear.

"Boy, wha yea doin?"

"N-N-N-Nothing sir," Life stammered.

"Place yo hands where I can see 'em!"

"Elmo, go to dah truck and get dah rope and crowbar, we's fixin to hav-ow-selfs some fun."

I felt Life nudging me to pass him the gun. I did what white people usually do in them scary movies, stand motionless when they were in danger. I literally just sat there unable to move while the white man had that gun to Life's head.

"Hope! Hope! Hope!" Life whispered my name like sips of a dying man's last breath. Lawd have mercy, I was afraid to move.

The car door flung open and a malodorous smell of unwashed bodies and whisky filled the air. A glumy face with rotten teeth and manes of dirty blond hair and blue eyes stared at me with the look of the devil. The other face was hulkish, with a large bulbous nose and a shaggy beard. Their lupine laughter echoed in the night like crazed hyenas on a frenzy for the hunt about to kill. A white man's sport.

"You sho'll is purdy," the white man with the blond hair said as he tried to caress my hair. I moved my head.

"Elmo, lookahera. She's a purdy black gurl. Nah all we wanna do missy is tie ya'll up and have ourselves a lil fun," he snickered and scratched his privates.

Life's hand was under the seat now and I really thought he was going to be foolish and grab the gun.

"Put yo hands up and get out da car. Jumbo, tie the gurl up first."

"Hold up! I have money. Lots of it, just don't hurt the girl."

"Huh?" The gunman peered closer to Life as if he were examining some fine specimen of a nigger. The word money had his attention.

As I looked on, to my horror in what looked like blazing speed, Life grabbed the gun. A tussle ensued and the gun fired. I screamed, shattering the lull of the night. Life hung onto the old man with a death grip. The old white man must have been as strong as a bear, because he pulled Life through the window like he was a little rag doll. The other two men ran to the other side of the car to help their partner. Vaguely, I thought I heard Life yell for me to get the gun, but I was scared to death. I couldn't move.

Though blinded by the high beam lights, I watched the silhouette of bodies ensconced in the throes of death's struggle, as Life Thugstin fought for his life. The other two men were now pummeling him with blows and somehow, amazingly with the brute strength of determination, he held on to the gun. I watched as one of the white men drew back hitting Life with an iron crowbar. He cried out in pain. To me, at that moment, at that time, his cries sounded like the vociferous shrieks of a million dying Black men being tortured. They were going to kill Life, just as sure as I sat there in the car doing nothing, just as sure as the moon and the stars would bear witness once again to the senseless atrocities waged against a human life.

In the torrid passion of insurmountable fears, something loomed in me that I have never felt before, it seized my body, pushing me forward. Rage! The kind of rage that made me lash out without caring. I grabbed the gun from inside the glove compartment. It was heavy. I staggered out of the car into the dreary night. Something possessed me. The white man that tried to touch my hair was about to wack Life in the back with the crowbar once again. I fired the gun. The sound was deafening. A blast of orange exploded around my head. I was nearly knocked to the ground but somehow I managed to keep my balance.

"Muthafucka, get the fuck off of him! Now bitch, or I'll blow your muthafuckin brains out!" I yelled as spittle dribbled off my lips like a deranged maniac on drugs. My hands trembled as I aimed the gun. Tears streaked my cheeks. They all backed up off of Life, leaving his lifeless body lying in a heap in the weeds and dirt. I called his name, "Life … Life!" He did not move. One of the men was holding a knife in his hand. Oh my God! My eyes darted to the knife and back to Life. A lone car passed. Three pairs of eyes stared at me.

The leader spoke as he inched toward me. "Naw, Missy give me dat dere gu–"

*Pow!* I fired the gun at his head.

"Get on the ground now!" I heard the crowbar hit the ground. They all tried to get as flat as the dirt.

"Please don't shoot, lady," I heard one of them cower.

As if being awakened from the dead, Life moved and sat up rubbing his head the way people do when they are trying to get over a hangover. I watched as he slowly rose and walked over to me. There was a cut above his eye and his mouth was bleeding. I swear to God I wanted to hug that man, that thug. There was no doubt in my mind he would give his life for me.

"Give me the gun!" he said with a tone in his voice that let me know he was in control.

At that moment, I just fell apart, a fragile husk of myself. I fell into his arms. He whispered in my hair for me to go sit in the car.

I walked to the car with legs that felt like rubber with weights attached to them. Once inside the car, I looked at my watch–1:48 a.m.

Life now held a flashlight and rope he had taken off the men. At gunpoint he made them all strip naked and walked them into the woods. Fear danced with death's flirtation as I sat in the car praying to a god that not even I was sure of.

It seemed like Life had been gone for an eternity when I heard the shots ring out, and then Life came running from out of the woods. I noticed that he was limping badly.

"What did you do?" I asked as soon as he entered the car. He ignored me.

"See if the car will start," he said out of breath. His body omitted an odor. I wondered if it was death. Another car passed and I couldn't help thinking I just wanted to get away, safe.

I turned the key, praying with all my heart, that Betty would start. Please baby, please start for mama. The motor turned over. I knew the sound like I knew my own voice. She sputtered and then died with a cough. Life watched me like I was a judge about to decide his fate. I turned the key again and she started like a brand new motor. "Thank you Jesus," I mumbled. Life hopped out of the car, picked up the hunting knife off the ground, sliced all the tires on the truck and ran back to the car.

"Let's go," he said with emotion in his voice. I eased the car onto the road. I did not realize I was that cold until I felt the heat on my feet. Life was jabbering away with the adrenaline rush of a man who had just received a last minute reprieve from the electric chair.

"Goddamn, Hope, that was some gangsta shit you pulled back there. I just wished you hadn't taken so damn long. Them crackas was tryin to kick the bone outta my ass-."

We passed a sign that read "Kissimmee, Florida." 176 miles to Tallahassee. My mind was all over the place.

"Life what did you do to those men? I heard shots." My voice cracked, like too much pressure on a dam.

"Girl, do you know what them crackas was gettin ready to do to us … to you?" His eyes finished the statement when he looked at me saying that they were going to rape me. He fired up a cigarette as I drove through the night wishing the car would go faster. I turned on Route 19, a thoroughfare that goes through the hub of the city. The town looked rural and antebellum; still I found it comforting to be back within city limits. The streets were lined with stores and small businesses, hotels and restaurants and the speed limit was 35.

I passed through the toll booth and paid a dollar. On both sides of the streets were police cars. "Smile," Life told me. For the benefit of the police, I spread my weary lips across my teeth and displayed a smile as fake as the plastic fruit Grandma kept on her dining room table. After what I had just experienced back there, mentally and physically, I was exhausted. We drove in silence, and then it happened, the car slowed, kicked and sputtered. The motor died. I coasted into a parking place on the side of the road. Once we stopped, the reality of my grim situation pushed me over the edge and I completely lost it!

"Nooooo! Nooooo! Noooo!" I wailed, pounding my fists on the steering wheel. The last twelve hours had been too much for me to handle. It felt like I was having a nervous breakdown.

Slowly, I turned my head, and glared at Life. He was looking at me with shock written all over his face, the way a person does when they are trying to decide if you have lost your damn mind.

"You!" I screamed at him, pointing an accusing finger in his face. "Ever since I laid eyes on you, everything that can go wrong has." I felt tears brimming on the rim of my eyes. "I want to go home. I don't want to be stranded with you, and God please tell me, what did you do to those men back there?!" My voice pleaded. I was winded. The police cruiser that was at the toll booth, passed.

"Smile," Life said.

"Shiiit," I hissed, showing my teeth for a different reason, looking like an angry possum about to attack his ass.

"Listen Hope," Life said. His voice was diplomatic, but I could tell he was fighting for self-control. We were two people getting on each other's nerves.

"You should have never attempted to make a trip in this car. The radiator leaks, the motor is bad and some mo shit." The cadence of his voice changed almost as if he were talking to a small child.

"Hope we're just about two hours outside of Tallahassee. We can walk, sleep in the car, or we can get a few hours of rest at a hotel while the car is getting fixed. I saw a Holiday Inn a few miles back. I'll call a tow truck and we can leave first thing in the morning."

I slumped over the steering wheel placing my head over my arms. I was exhausted, my head hurt and just the thought of a long luxurious bath was tempting.

"We'll sleep in separate rooms," he assured. His words a gambit. I figured, what did I have to lose? It was 2:00 a.m. and I was tired. Spending the night in my car just did not appeal to me. So I agreed under those conditions.

About thirty minutes later a tow truck was being hooked up to my car. I grabbed my meager luggage and the three one hundred dollar bills in the ashtray. Ever since I was a little girl, there had always been something about hotels that I found alluring. They made me feel like something I have never enjoyed, a vacation. At the Holiday Inn we got separate rooms with an adjoining door. I kept mine locked.

As soon as we got our rooms, he walked me to mine like a complete gentleman, and then went to the bar to get something to drink. I took a long, hot luxurious shower that felt so good I did not want to come out of there. Afterward, I put on my nightie and crashed underneath the covers, but I could not sleep. Life's face kept appearing on the screen of my mind.

OK, I can't lie, curiosity was killing me. It also killed the cat, or in my case, I should say kitty.

*****

# Chapter Four

## "Fahrenheit of Lust"

### — Hope —

Curiosity got the best of me and I made the second biggest mistake of my life. The first one was helping him and now this.
I tiptoed to the door, unlocked it and then tried his door. It opened. A single dim light shined in the room. Life sat perched in a chair in front of a large picture window with the blinds opened wide. He wasn't wearing a shirt. The gleaming swimming pool in front of his room reflected a kaleidoscope of colors off of his body. A cigarette dangled from his finger as gray smoke ringed his head.

On the table was a bag of ice, a fifth of Hennessy and a shot glass half filled. For some reason I just watched that man as the smoke curled out his mouth, the stolid face of a Black man impelled by his thoughts. Lord knows he had a lot to think about. Again I wondered if he killed those men. I also wondered was I attracted to him, a thug.

He took a sip of his drink, pinky finger extended, then he made a face the way people do from a drink of strong liquor as he stared at something out the window. Whatever it was held his attention. Moments passed and he had me looking too, and suddenly it dawned on me what he was looking at—Me!!

"Do you always creep into people's rooms spyin' on them when you think they're not watching?"

I was cold busted. The entire time, he was looking at me through the reflection in the window. Slowly he turned toward me and I could see the scar underneath his eye. Something was missing, something was wrong. This was the intimate part of the man without his mask, hurt prevailed on his face and instantly I regretted coming into his room. His eyes roamed my body for a fleeting second and then looked away, as if he were dismissing me.

"Go and get some rest. We got a long day tomorrow with the car and all." His words were languid, he sounded tired. I just stood there, lost for words, not able to describe what I was feeling for this man. Maybe it was sympathy wrapped up in a big ole ball of sorrow.

I was wearing practically nothing. My nightie was very transparent. It was made of sexy satin and lace, cut short way above the thigh. The cleavage was more than an eyeful since I wasn't wearing a bra. I was about as nude as a woman could get except for my panties. Talk about a girl's pride. "Can I have a drink?" I heard my voice say, husky with a feminine timber of boldness.

"Hope, I got a lot on my mind," he said running his hand over his short cropped hair. "Get some rest, I'll have breakfast waiting for you when you wake in the morning."

He just stared at something in the window. Something only he could see. I recognized the hurt on that man's face, the way only a woman can. Barefooted, I padded across the shag carpeting and fixed myself a drink. He turned and looked at me annoyingly.

"Didn't you hear what I just said, girl?" His voice was slightly slurred. I ignored him and bent down to retrieve a piece of ice that I intentionally dropped to the floor. I flirted just to get his attention, to see his reaction. Ever since we met, he treated me like his little sister. The man never paid the slightest bit of attention to me. I wondered if there was such a thing as a gay thug. I sat down right in front of him, crossed my legs ladylike and took a swig of my drink. It burned in a nice way. Quiet engulfed us like a gentle storm. I was lost for words. *What am I doing?* I continued to ask myself.

"So what are you going to do when you get to Tallahassee?" I asked.

"I dunno … I dunno …" he shook his head somberly. "Maybe find a job and save up some money to go to night school, get me a lawyer."

"Yeah, that would be a good idea. You could use a good lawyer, because you damn sure know how to find trouble. You are a jinxy-ass man." With that, he erupted in hilarious laughter, full and vibrant. The kind of hearty laughter that would stand out in a room full of people, loud and jovial. It reminded me of Eddie Murphy's singsong cackle. Masculine and strong, I couldn't help but smile, too as tears rolled down his cheeks as he continued to laugh. I poured myself another drink, a nightcap I told myself. I already had a buzz. I took a sip and raised up to stand, I slightly staggered but he did not notice. "I'm going to get some rest. Check out time is 11 o'clock and it's just about 4 o'clock." He just looked at me, his ebony eyes opaque slants, eyes that I couldn't read. He stood. His bronze body was sculpted like one of them African statues of a warrior. His stomach was chiseled. His brawny chest was big and hairy. He wore a large platinum chain.

The light from the swimming pool shimmered off our bodies. I bit down on my bottom lip as he walked toward me. No one can convince me that a man and a woman, in the solitude of the night, confronted by their riveting intimacy, do not produce a kind of celestial energy that holds them bound to the laws of nature. It's fervid heat of unquenched passion. I felt my body tingling as if I were on fire. I knew that if he touched me we would both burn in a fahrenheit of passion. The Hennessy, mingled with his manly scent, was like an aphrodisiac to my feminine loins.

"Hope I'm sorry for everything that I've put you through. I can't thank you enough for what you've done, and to be truthful with you, I'm really not a …not a …" he stammered and for some reason I felt my body leaning toward him like how gravity pulls.

"I'm really not a jinx," he said awkwardly. This time I burst out in laughter spraying his face with spittle. For some reason, I was feeling giddy. I wiped his face with an affectionate hand. He kissed my fingers and then pecked me on the forehead like I was his little sister and gently pushed my shoulders.

"Get some sleep Shouty, I'll wake you in the morning," he said, as he smiled displaying that dimple. Just as he was about to turn away, I flung my arms around him, lassoing his neck, kissing him fully. At first he did not respond. So I kissed him with everything I had. I grinded my torso against his manhood and then I felt him respond as his hands went under my nightie palming my ass. The fire was ignited. The torrid passion of flames roared. His lips found their way to my neck as his hands pulled my gown down exposing my breasts. My nipples were erect. He squeezed and sucked them greedily. I moaned. I could feel his stiff erection running down my thigh. His lips and tongue trailed my flesh, licking me like I was sweet molasses. I was moist and getting wetter with every touch. Then something panged in me. This was not right. Through the fog of alcohol and fervid lust, clarity began to crystallize. *This is not right! What am I doing? What am I doing?* I thought to myself, finally I shouted, "Stop!" I placed my hand on his chest in an attempt to push him away, but he just kept pulling on my panties, tugging.

"No, please!" I begged. It was as if I awakened something dormant in this man. Something bestial. He was not listening to me. He had my panties around my thighs and then pushed me against the dresser, pinning me there. I felt my panties being torn. There is a name for this and I couldn't believe this was happening to me. In one quick motion he slid out of his pants. His erection was enormous and crooked, leaning to one side. It felt like he carried me on it as I was being picked up and taken to the bed.

"No," I whimpered, but even to me it sounded like "yes" and I wasn't putting up much of a fight. Even as he climbed in between my legs placing on a condom, my futile resistance seemed to only excite and arouse him more. "Noooo ..." My words were silenced with his kisses. He was in between my legs and his touch was as gentle as a feather. I was still saying "no" as he entered me slowly. The pain was excruciating. I never knew that hurt could feel so good.

"Hope," he called my name like I was his goddess. With that, my legs spread and invited him into my kingdom—open sesame.

"Hope, I just want to make love to you." His words a murmur against my hot flesh as I moaned out loud in ecstasy. Slow and passionate were his loving strokes. He has not entered me fully as if to see if my body could withstand the length of his manhood. His short strokes were driving me crazy.

"Hope, do you like this?" He eased deeper inside of me.

"Yes! Yes! Yes!" I lamented praising Jesus, cursing out God as I road the ebb and flow of the torrent tide of his skillful lovemaking. He thrust deeper, testing my womanhood. I felt him going where no man had ever gone before, impaling what felt like my chest cavity. His strokes, even tempered, like he was measuring just how to love my body. As he reached his destination, I felt my body shake and shiver in uncontrollable convulsions that sent me into fits. I was out of control as Life road my body like I was a wild stallion and he was a Black cowboy. I had an orgasm that made me scream. The whole time his lovemaking never stopped. He devoured my body like lovemaking was an art to be crafted and practiced solely on me. Twenty or thirty short strokes and then one deep stroke. Ten short strokes and then one painfully deep long one, and still he was not even halfway inside of me. I reached another orgasm with one of his deep stroke maneuvers as my fingers clawed his back. He spread my legs wider grabbing my ass, pushing deeper inside of me causing the throes of desire to explode. Showing me yet another facet of my sexual identity that I did not know existed. "Ohmygod!" I moaned in ecstasy. He stroked me with a rhythm so intense that our bodies were saturated with sweat.

Over an hour had passed when he grabbed one of my legs and held it high in the air asking, "Hope, do you like this?" His raspy voice breathed on my erect nipples. Each part of my body that he touched, he made love to as if his only mission were to please me. I could not talk, I was in another zone. I was about to reach another orgasm, that one was being summoned from somewhere deep within me and caused my head to thrash back and forth. Life was driving me up the wall. Then suddenly he stopped … labored breathing echoed like two fighters engaged in battle, damn, just as I was on the brink of another orgasm.

Slowly, he eased off of me, his tongue making hot trails on my breasts as he pulled out of me. He sucked on my body, loud, with slurping sounds that teased and tingled me with ecstasy. Lower and lower his hand went. He stuck a finger inside of me, then two, which stirred my passion. His tongue traced my navel … my pubic area … my thighs. I was pulling my hair out. I had never had a man go down on me before.

"Ooh shit! What … ah … are you doing?" The timbre of my voice broke. He had taken so much from me, yet giving too much. His deft tongue molested my clitoris, sucking on it like it was the sweetest candy in the world.

"Hope, do you like this?" I just nodded my head, and for the first time, I tried to scoot toward the headboard, away from him. This was the best torture that any woman could endure.

"Hope."

"Ye … ye … yessss!"

"I'm cheating …" lick, lick, lick, lick, "… it takes a thousand strokes to please a Black woman." With that he spread my lips and buried his tongue inside of me. His tongue acted like it had a license to seduce me. He drove it down south licking my ass. After about another hour of him loving me, I thought I was going to cry from ecstasy. I had never been made love to like that before. I reached yet another orgasm. We broke the record for the number of orgasms I have had in a single night. We changed positions. He placed me on my stomach and put pillows underneath me and took me from the back. This was the most painful position. It felt like he was stretching the elastic out of my stuff. I tried to squirm away as his once gentle loving became brutally rough. Over and over he thrust deeper and deeper. I cried out in pain. It only seemed to increase his lust. He was past the thousand strokes of loving me. Finally, his body jerked and shivered, saliva dribbled from his mouth onto my back as he came inside of me. Satisfied, he keeled over off me onto the bed, panting, I was exhausted. Perspiration glistened off of my body. I was lying in a puddle of our love juices too tired to move.

Predawn had peeked over the starry horizon. Everything looked murky, like a mirage. It was hard to tell if I was awake or asleep. I was in a sexual daze. I touched myself. My coochie was swollen and sore. This man beat it to death. I watched as Life removed the torn rubber from his still erect penis. I couldn't help thinking, every woman should try a little thug love in her life.

Nude, except for the one sock he had on, I watched Life walk to the window and close the blinds ending our freak show. He came back, sat on the bed, propped his leg up, the one with the sock on, and lit a cigarette. He watched me intently as he blew smoke right in my direction. I would have given the world just to have read his mind. What really goes through a man's mind after a woman gives him her body? Well actually in my case he took it, kinda.

For some reason, I dozed off to sleep thinking about Marcus, my fiancé. I was guilt ridden. He was the love of my life, but sexually, there was no comparison between he and Life. Marcus wasn't into oral sex nor was he half as endowed as Life was. I went to sleep with my hands between my legs, thinking how that thug had put it on me.

At 11 o'clock, I was awakened to the sound of the phone ringing. Disoriented, I couldn't remember where I was. I finally remembered to speak. "Hello?" I was informed that it was checkout time. Still I could not get my bearings. I lay back down on the pillow. Then it all came back. I was in a hotel room with a man I hardly knew, he had taken my body. Oh, shit! I thought about the guns, the police and those evil white men that tried to abduct me. I sprung from the bed, my torn panties lay on the floor as a reminder of the conquest of my body. And Life was gone. I did not know if that was good or bad considering all that he took me through. My mind raced a mile a minute. I went into the adjoining room. He wasn't there. I ran my fingers through my hair. The phone rang, startling me.

"Hello?"

"Wuz up, Shouty!" From the sound of his raspy voice, he had been drinking. "I got the car fixed. You ready to bounce to Tally?"

"Yaaa!" I was excited for some reason as I answered. "I'll be down in a sec." I hung the phone up and walked over to the window; children were playing around the pool, it was a beautiful day. As I took a shower, I had to admit, even though Life Thugstin was a thug, he handled his business. I shuddered at the thought of what would have happened to me if Marcus would have been there when the white men tried to abduct me. I rubbed my swollen private thinking once again how every woman from time to time needs a thug in her life. Once thing for sure, once we made it to Tallahassee I was going to get rid of his ass like a bad habit.

I walked out into the hotel vestibule with my luggage in hand. I was wearing white slacks with a pink blouse made of soft cotton. Life, nor my car, were anywhere in sight. I looked around, the sun still bright and I heard my name. Life was all the way at the end of the parking lot. He came strutting toward me with all new clothes on. A gold Nike sweatsuit with a brown Kangol hat and a pair of the new Jordans that had just come out. Once up close he tried to kiss me while speaking, "Hi baby!" I ducked. He reached for my luggage making a face, a knowing grin. I took off walking. I smelled his cologne.

"I have a surprise for you." I continued to walk. Betty was still nowhere in sight. I stopped, looked behind me and saw that he had stopped, placed my bags down and was pointing at a car. I knew I was right earlier, the man had been drinking. "Da–dahhh-hhhhh," he droned, gesturing at the car, palms open pointing. It was an older model candy apple red Honda Accord with a sunroof and rimmed expensive tires that cost more than my old car.

"Boy! Have you lost your damn mind? Where is my damn car?" I said walking up to him. Again he tried to kiss me. I moved out of the way.

"This is your car!" he beamed.

"No it ain't." I scoffed. "I own a blue 1973 Ford Mustang."

"Not no mo, I sold it to the junkyard for $75.00."

"You did whatttt? I know damn well your jinxy ass ain't sold my car!" I was all up in his face. His eyes darted to the ground as he dug into his pocket passing me my ID with the title and registration in my name. "You went into my purse while I was asleep and stole my ID, sold my car and bought this car?" I asked trying to control my temper. My jaws were clinched so tight it felt like I was going to crack my teeth. He looked away. "Why?" I asked. I found it amazing how men could turn into little boys. He mumbled something about last night, and me saving his life. I could see that I hurt his feelings, yet he tried to mask the pain with a facial expression that returned my question with, *why can't you accept my gift?* Dope boys were notorious for buying college girls cars and nice things, but as I found out, it often came with a price. I was not trying to get involved with him, or fall into one of his traps.

My tone softened, "You have got to take this car back, you shouldn't have –"

"Hope, there's a lot of shit a nigga should not have done!" he interrupted, taking a step back from me. This was our standoff, but this was his world, I was just a visitor trying to get out.

"I don't know how I will ever be able to pay you back," I said with more innocence than I had intended. He took a look at my body and smiled brightly.

"You already did, last night, a brotha be loving that wild shit!"

That was not what I wanted to hear. Then he tried to take my hand but I pulled away. His handsome face scowled into a look of confession. "Um … about last night. I did not mean for it to go that far." He grabbed me by my shoulders and pulled me up close to him. I did not know if he was going to kiss me or hit me. His breath was hot on my face, as hot as last night's passion. I was powerless to move. A couple stared as they passed by. In the distance I heard a fire truck. This closeness and energy from this man seized me completely. If he told me to go back inside the hotel and take off all my clothes again so that he could make love to me, I probably would have. Some men possess overwhelming energy that is just that powerful over women. Life Thugstin was one of those men.

"Hope, you cannot tell me that you didn't enjoy last night as much as I did." His words seeped inside of me, nuzzling in a place that I wanted to keep him forbidden. I attempted to speak but the words just froze in my throat. I tried to look away, but his eyes would not let me. They pleaded for an answer, an answer that he and I knew the truth to. He squeezed my arm until it hurt. "I … I … I'm engaged to someone." My words came out on his face and washed down on him. For a fleeting second, I swear I saw anger in his eyes. I thought for sure he was going to knock my ass down. He released me like I just told him I'd tested positive for some virulent plague. He reached into his pocket and handed me the keys to the car. They were on the same key ring that my old keys were. I walked around to the driver's side, wishing there was something I could say, something to comfort him. I felt like shit. As soon as I got in the car I noticed the bags of clothes he bought me from Macy's. I saw an expensive Dooney and Burke purse, it was gorgeous.

For the next half hour or so neither of us spoke, but I could read his thoughts. He wanted me, and it shamed him. He gambled on me and lost. I needed to speak my mind, for the longer we remained silent, the more pent up frustration I felt with each passing mile. Hell, no one told him to spend his damn money on me! I turned to him, "What I did last night was so wrong and I'm sorry. Things just got out of hand," I said as I drove. I was so full of anger that I saw veins in my hands as they clinched the steering wheel. "I made a bad judgment … no, horrible judgment … twice. I'm 21 years old." He shot me a look that said what's that got to do with it. I continued, "I was not trying to take advantage of you. I promise I'll pay you back. How about fifty dollars a week until I get this car paid off. Can we just be friends?"

"Yo, check this out Shouty, all of my friends chase cats, eat shit and bark at the moon," he said so coldly that I had to turn and look in his direction. This was a side of him I had never seen before. I watched as he casually took a cassette tape out of one of the shopping bags and placed it into the deck. Jodeci crooned, begging a woman to stay for a little while. The music was very nice, melodic. I swayed into the rhythm of my emotions like Life was using that song to talk to me.

I drove eighty five miles an hour, my mind racing, guilt ridden. In History I read that lust, in the form of passion or pussy, had been known to start wars. As a young woman I was just beginning to learn, a lot. A man would actually go to great lengths to impress a woman. And I had never been sexed like that before. *Hope, can I lick you here … touch you there … it takes a thousand strokes to please a Black woman,* I remembered him telling me. I heard my mouth blurt out, "If you like you can call me at the station. I host a show on campus radio. It's called The Panther Power Hour. We deal with issues like Affirmative Action, Police brutality —"

"Listen, dig," he interrupted. "I ain't finta start nuttin wit you I can't finish. You don't owe me nuttin, aight?" Then he turned and looked at me, "Besides you wasn't all that anyway."

I turned up the volume so high on the stereo it sounded like it was going to bust the speakers. He cringed and looked at me like I was crazy. We drove the rest of the way not speaking and me still not believing the last twenty-four hours of my life.

I finally reached Tallahassee and I drove down Tennessee Street. There is so much human electricity in this college town that it pulsates. You can actually feel it, like your own heartbeat, that is if you are young, 21 years old and hungry to succeed like I was. I was happy to be back on my old stomping grounds. Life was looking out the window like a kid in a candy store. Women of all ethnicities walked the streets. I pulled into the new Holiday Inn that had just been built. Life turned and watched me. For some reason I thought of an old saying, *penny for your thoughts.*

*****

# Chapter Five

## "The Land of Milk and Honey"

### – Life –

I was watching this broad Hope, she done played a nigga like a piano. I could see she felt like shit, guilty conscience and all. I wanted her to marinate in it. I knew she felt bad about having to accept this car plus me selling her old piece of junk. She thought this car cost a lot of money. Hell, I hacked off that much money in a strip club, besides, I could make it back in an hour hustling. Now, as I looked at her, I was filled with envy, lust and some more shit. I couldn't believe she gave me that lame ass excuse, talking 'bout she got a man. Fuck her! I was a playa. I needed a bitch about as bad as a fish needed a raincoat. I was forced to admit, that was some gangsta shit she pulled at the mall, rescuing me from the police and her sex was sweet and pure like it was the first time I ever made love to a woman. Afterward, I had to smoke a cigarette and watched her as she slept, thinking how God knew what he was doing when he created Woman.

She pulled up at the hotel. Sadly, it kind of disturbed me. I knew it was the end of the road for us but it was all-good. I knew that I was going to take over this town, little by little, this was what we hustlers called fertile land. A nice-sized city with plenty of money. My plan was to make a couple million, build a small bankroll and get out of the game, so I thought.

I reached into my pocket and put on my two chunky

bracelets, and the fat iced-out chain I took from the police back there at the hotel. As I pulled out my bankroll, I could see Hope watching me through the corner of her eye. So I stunted for her doing what playas do. Money, hoes and clothes is all a brotha knows. Then I gave her my best Mack pose, leaning against the car door, I took of my Kangol and caressed the waves on my head like I was blessing myself. I just transformed right before her eyes.

"Here." I passed her two crispy one hundred dollar bills. "Go get me a hotel room, the biggest room they got with a view of the pool," I said just like I intended, a command, showing no respect for her. Hope sucked her tongue as she turned and glowered at me. If looks could kill, her fulgurant eyes would have done a drive by. She opened her mouth to speak and suddenly thought better of it. She got out and slammed the car door. I watched her as she walked away angry. I was sure she was unconscious of the sensuous sway of her hips. Her struts forceful like she could take out frustration on the concrete. I've always wondered what their mommas gave them. Moments later she returned. I could not help admiring her walk.

"Here," she said passing me the keys along with a slip of paper. Just then a car drove by, music bumping. It was a sleek, sky blue Lexus SC430, full of shouting females. The car made a U-turn in the middle of the street. There was always something about college females, they're always hyperactive, like where is the party at. I watched Hope as she watched the car. "No, this can't be happening to me," she mumbled. The car pulled in right next to us. Females were five deep. They were loud and excited to see Hope. I stood outside to get an eyeful of diamonds glistening. I felt like a pimp on a hoe farm. All eyes on me.

"No it isn't! Not the good sister Hope. On the smooove creeeep," the driver droned. The rest of the girls cracked up in giddy laughter. Hope smiled painfully like she was getting a tooth pulled. The driver was mixed with something. If I had to guess, I would say Spanish. Her complexion was amber, like she was kissed by the sun. Her deep green chatoyant eyes were stunning, they could hypnotize a man. She had me spellbound. She had long silky black hair that cascaded down to the middle of her back, like she had just brushed it and let it flow. She stepped out of the car wearing a white halter top and tight-fitting blue jeans. Her walk was provocative, like the purest essence of a woman's femininity. The pussy print between her legs was balled up like a fat fist on both sides. Damn she was wearing them jeans. I bit down on my knuckle and Hope rolled her eyes at me. The driver never took her eyes off of me. Not even one second. It felt as if I were being inspected.

"Trina, this is L."

"Heeeey L, with your fine self," cooed a girl in the car.

I tried my damnest not to blush and then they all joined in harmously, "Hi, L." I was cheesing like a brotha posing for a toothpaste commercial. Then someone yelled, "look at those cute dimples." The whole time Trina was checking me out, my jewelry and my clothes. There was something uncanny about her. Like she knew me from somewhere.

"Damn, ain't you and Marcus still together?" Trina asked, slinging the words in Hope's face.

"I'm on my way to his house," Hope retorted, with her lips twisted to the side accompanied by a tilted neck. I could tell there was friction in the air. Women have a strange way of communicating. They use body language like chickens that used to have arms.

"Trina is my Sorority Sister," Hope said to me. As if on cue the girls in the car made a noise, I guess it had something to do with their sorority. They all erupted in jovial laughter.

"She's from the Bronx."

"Wuz up Shouty?" I said, giving her a nod like I hardly noticed she was there. One of the girls said, "Ask him if he has any friends fine like him." They all laughed, everybody except Hope and Trina. I watched as they talked in generic chatter while the sun beat down on us. I felt a trickle of perspiration cascade down my spine as I looked at all of the beautiful sistas. It was like I was in paradise.

"What room are you staying in?" Trina asked, completely catching me off guard.

"Who, me?" Dumbfounded. I looked at the key in my hand and answered "A-4."

"We're going to get something to eat, you want to join us?" Trina asked like it was a challenge. The whole time she just looked at me.

"No, I was dropping L off. I gave him a ride from Sarasota yesterday. We had car trouble and just made it into town." I listened as Hope made excuses that sounded like lies.

Trina frowned at her, and then asked me, "What brings you to Tallahassee, L?" I thought I detected a trace of an accent.

"I'm here on business."

"What kind of business?" she asked placing her hands on her round hips. I noticed somehow she had inched up closer, the wind blew her hair. A car passed, some brothas hollered at the girls and the girls hollered back. I smiled like a sly fox, the way men do when they're lying to a woman and they both know it.

"I'm in the import and export business," I said turning the gold bracelet on my wrist. Something about Trina pounced on me, perhaps it was her eyes, the way she looked at me, bold, aggressively. She made no secret about it. She was trying to get with me, and when she walked away, she showed me more. I watched for a moment, placing her index finger over her temple like she was contemplating the plot.

"Gee, Hope. You say that you left town yesterday, but your paper tag has today's date on it."

"Ummm, that was a mistake they made at the car lot," Hope stammered.

"Yea, right. You better be careful Marcus doesn't learn of your mistakes," Trina said, like a threat, and then winked her eye at me. "I'll be seeing you around L." She pointed at me like she had just staked her claim on me. I raised a brow thinking I just witnessed a cat fight. Trina jumped in her car. The girls clamored. The system in her car was turned up loud, thumping so hard I could feel it vibrating. Mary J. Blige's song "Real Love" filled the air as they drove off.

"Bitch!" Hope cursed giving me the evil eye. "Listen Life, you got to stay away from her. Trina is bad news. Her family, or somebody is heavy into drugs. Her last boyfriend was a baller, now he's doing life in the feds."

"Why are you telling me this?"

A car pulled up and two gorgeous women got out. They were holding hands.

"I don't want you to get into any trouble. That's all."

She looked at her watch, a signal to me that she was about to go. She turned and opened the car door. As I placed my hand over hers, she gulped air, and took in a deep breath. So much more innocence exuded from her. In the sunlight, I watched the wisps of baby hair cascade down her delicate forehead. I noticed that she did not remove her hand, nor did she blink for that moment in time. Our eyes locked and I knew if there were a way to check her heartbeat, it would be in the same rhythm as mine.

"Life, you know I'm the kind of girl that believes in speaking her mind. I'm very much attracted to you ..." I watched as her tongue moistened and primed her lips, lips that I wanted to kiss, preparing to tell me what I did not want to hear.

" ... and ... and last night you made love to me like I had never been ... been touched, made love to before." She then took my hand off hers, and looked away, breaking our physical communication.

"We're from two different worlds." Her voice now sounded harsh and cold. "Your world is where I am running from. Poverty and pain fills us with greed and envy. Money can't buy love. It can't buy me." She shook her head like she was trying to chase away some evil demon. "You'll end up dead or in them white folks' prison."

Her words stung me like a premonition. One of my knees felt like it was going to buckle. A Black woman's premonition is the closest thing to God, my stepmom taught me that. Somehow, I know that Hope's words held the truth. The kind of truth that no hustler wanted to take heed to.

"For you, Hope, I'd hang up my scale, no mo dope game, place my pistol, Jesus, in the closet. If you help me, I'd go straight," I said, dead serious not knowing or caring where that voice was coming from. I knew that it just felt good talking to her. Silence. I looked over her head. There was a Goodyear blimp in the sky. Her rejection of me was written all over her face. It answered my question in a way she could never have. Time was of the essence. What I just said even sounded whack to me, that was my weak heart talking. I realized I needed to spit game like flavor in her ear. "Tell you what, give me something to read, something conscious." I watched her delicate eyebrows furrow like she was trying to read my brain to see if I was lying. I know that all them people with that fake-ass "Black Man" talk were suckers and wanted to try to get people to read like it was going to kick start a revolution. Her eyes softened, maybe she saw potential in me. I damn sure did, enough to want to sell bricks and buy a villa in Manila, smoke trees while getting my dick sucked by one of them exotic-looking bitches under a palm tree.

"Life, there's a book titled, *The Destruction of Black Civilization*, written by a man named Chancellor Williams and another book, *Miseducation of the Negro.*"

I could have won an award for best actor the way I feigned interest. She went on to talk about some cat name Marcus Garvey. Her faced beamed, like she really enjoyed the topic. Boring. I was trying to remember how far the Black section of town was that we passed. I knew it was called Frenchtown. I heard talk about it while I was in the joint. I needed to know what size their dime rocks were. I was making plans, like a general, about to mount an attack, to take over them Tallahassee niggas turf.

"Life! Life! Boy, you ain't heard a word I've said." She got into the car.

"I heard ya." I made a face, my best impression of don't go.

She reached in and placed each one of the bags that I bought for her on the curb. "I'm sorry, but I cannot accept these. Call me at the station tonight, we'll make arrangements to pay for the car."

As she pulled out, I shouted, "Bring the books when you come back tomorrow."

"Come back?" she mouthed the words, looking at me strangely. I thought to myself, *you'll be back as soon as you find Jesus under your front seat.*

I went to my room. It was nice and comfortable with a scenic view and a king-sized bed. It even had a kitchen with a stove and fridge. I counted out my cash, a little over eight grand. I cut a hole in the mattress and stashed it there for safe keeping. I placed my jewelry under the pillow and changed clothes, a simple pair of jeans and a large white T-shirt. I was about to make my first foray into the Black section of town. There was a risk involved. I needed to look as inconspicuous as possible. I easily concealed the .380 in my pocket and only took eighteen dollars and some loose change with me.

I walked a mile or so taking in the sights. This city was alive. The Florida State campus was huge. White broads walking around, scantily clad, teaming with other vibrant ethnicities. I blended right in, and even though it was hot as hell, I enjoyed the sights and sounds. To me it was like being in a foreign land. I passed a car lot, across the street was a Popeye's Chicken, and down the street from that was Netherworld, better known as Frenchtown. I've often wondered how the Black section of town was always placed in the middle of white folks' areas so that they can conveniently drive by with their expensive cars, windows up, doors locked and scorned expression on their faces at the shock of the plight of Black life.

I was definitely approaching the Black section. I could tell because the value of the land looked dilapidated. I strained my eyes to the glare of the sun. I saw it up the street. To the casual eye it would not have been detected. I spotted what looked like a lookout man or woman. Any trap that is making any money has one. The best lookout in the world is a dope fiend. They stay paranoid, on perpetual alert. That is, if they're not getting high.

As I continued to scan the streets, I walked gingerly as I passed a drugstore. Little kids were inside buying candy. Then a barbershop. On the corner where I stood was a soul food restaurant. My pace slowed. Across the street was a pool hall, a sleazy tavern and a liquor store all right next to each other. People were gathered out front. It felt like a thousand pair of eyes stared at me as I waited for the light to change. One thing was for sure, whenever you make an excursion into someone else's hood, they know that you are not from there and that's where the problem starts. Like walking into a lion's den. I crossed the street. In the abandoned lot there was a big commotion. A tall goofy-looking white boy was walking backward, palms in the air. His eyes darted back and forth and he wasn't wearing a shirt. He kept wiping the dirty blond hair from his face. His glasses were so thick that I wondered if he could be legally blind without them. About ten teenagers had him surrounded. They had baseball bats, two-by-fours and iron pipes.

"Give me dat money, cracka," one of them shouted. I watched as all hell broke loose. *POW! CRACK!* They tore off into his ass like he was responsible for slavery. One thing I can say about that white boy, he never fell to the ground, nor did he give up that money. He made the crucial mistake of coming to buy a rock without the aid of a Black person he knew, a mistake that has caused many a white man his life, trying to buy dope in a Black neighborhood. Someone hit him in the back and the sound exploded like a cannon. That white boy found a small crack of daylight and took off like a racehorse. As he attempted to pass me I stuck my foot out and tripped him. He fell flat on his face and slid across the worn out concrete. His glasses went one way while he went the other. I ain't never liked a cracka. Never! Ever since my stepmother told me the sad story about how they stole my granddaddy's land and killed him. That was one of the reasons why my father lost most of his mind.

The crowd of youngsters moved on him again. This was pure

recreation for them. Black boys have so much pent up energy, for them this was almost a daily occurrence, and it wasn't just white boys asses they whipped either. They didn't discriminate. I know just as sure that if they knew I was from out of town they would have rat packed my ass too.

They continued to kick his ass. This was all done in broad daylight. White people passed in their cars with the look of horror on their pink faces. Talk about the natives being restless, this was turning into some kind of sport. One thing was for sure, it was going to draw a lot of heat. *Whoever's trip this is, they're not doing a good job of managing it,* I thought.

I watched as this woman ran into the melee, arms flailing, screaming and pushing, shoving people off the white boy.

"Ya'll leave 'em alone! Leave 'em alone!" she screamed. For some reason they obeyed her. She helped the white boy up and brushed off his pants. Someone threw a bottle that whistled past his head. Punched, drunk and bleeding, he staggered around like he just went a round with Mike Tyson and miraculously survived. The woman found his glasses and gave them to him. They had been stomped on and were badly cracked. Staggering, he placed them on upside down. He went into his mouth and took out a wet and bloody twenty dollar bill. "Here, Nina Brown, all I wanted was a rock," he whined. Crackheads never cease to amaze me. This white man risked his life just for a rock, and now he acted like it was just another day in the death defying life of a rock star. The lady dug into her bosom, retrieving a matchbox, and gave him a small rock. His tongue moved around his cheek like it was searching for something, then he spit out a tooth, smiled gleefully through swollen lips and took off into a trot, only the trot resembled a hobble like he had just been hit by an eighteen wheeler.

I recognized the woman they called Nina Brown. The other cats were checking me out now, especially them youngsters. I played it off and called Nina Brown's name like I knew her all my life. "Yo Nina! I got eighteen dollars." I patted my pockets. "Where can I get a dime bag of weed at?" Actually, I was letting niggas know, I ain't got no money. As Nina entered the store she shot me a look like she was trying to figure out where she knew me from. The air conditioning in the old run down place felt cool on my face. My shirt was sticking to my back. The tile floor cracked under my feet. I noticed a nice looking pecan woman with breasts so large they made me smile. She was older than me. Something about her hair reminded me of a straightening comb, it shined like the little girls' hair that I used to see when I was in grade school. I requested a quart of beer, Olde English 800 and a pack of Newport cigarettes.

Nina Brown counted her money and watched me. She had a Bulls cap on her head cocked to the side. Her skin was dark. I guessed her age to be anywhere between twenty-nine and forty-nine. As hot as it was, she had on a black jacket with what looked like a hundred zippers on it. She walked right up to me, smelling like a small mountain goat. From the look of her weary, blood cracked eyes, she had been up for days, possibly weeks. She craned her neck at me, popped her lips, a prologue to speak. For some strange reason almost all rock stars do this.

"Whoisyou?" she asked, frowning at me. I took a step back and tried not to smile. Rock stars have this thing they do with their necks. It's sort of like a curious rooster.

"They call me L," I said as I smirked at her.

"How did you know my name?" she asked, placing some crumbled bills in her worn out jeans.

"Hi, Nina Brown," the cashier said, passing me my change.

"Hi, Ms. Atkins," Nina Brown responded politely.

The bell above the door chimed, as a runt of a woman walked in. She looked to be about 22 years old or so. She wore a hair weave that looked like she had cut it off of some poor poodle dog, and red lipstick that would have shamed a clown. The woman looked like a misfit, which is something very hard to do in the ghetto.

She walked right up to Nina and started whispering in conspiratorial tones. I eavesdropped.

The girl's name was Shannon. She was known in the hood as what is called a Regulator. They are hustlers that can skillfully break down a cocaine rock to its lowest form if need be, to make a profit. They hang around junkies religiously, like a vulture that waits on its dying prey. No matter how much dope you give them they'll find a way to go bad. Get them in the back of a police car, and somebody is going to jail, and it won't be them.

"Ain't nobody got none," Shannon was saying, panic stricken, like she was going to cry. Nina thought for a minute at whatever the riddle was.

"Tell them to go around the block, I think I know where we can find some at." That's why Regulators like to hang around rock stars. In theory, a rock star was a genius, at least at plotting to get money and finding a cot in jail. Nina Brown still commanded authority. You have some rock stars like that. Always a reflection of their former selves, the last thing an unsuspecting victim should do is listen to them talk. A real junkie can talk a starved cat off a fish truck if that's what he has to do to get high.

She turned to me. Looked me in the eye with a "man don't lie to me" expression.

"You got some dope?" she asked.

"I don't sell dope." I lied.

Her experienced eyes were looking at my two hundred dollar pair of Jordans. She sized me up.

"Look, boy, you either got some dope or you're the Po-Po." Nina Brown was a true street veteran. My shoes gave me away. Plus, the expression I wore on my face did not help none. Some junkies are just a ball of fun. I kind of liked Nina Brown from the start.

I walked out with her on my heels. She was onto my scent like a camel to water. As soon as I stepped onto the sidewalk, it was pure pandemonium. The police had people like they called in the riot control. Vans, cars, dogs. I had the .380 in my pocket. The one that I took from the police at the motel. Dumb.

"You!"

A policeman pointed at me. "Get your ass over here!" He was talking to me. I had no place to run. I was trapped. For some reason, Hope's face flashed before my eyes and I heard her voice, *you'll end up dead or in prison.* Nina Brown grabbed the back of my pants and snatched me back in the store.

"Hurry! Give me everything you got, I'll keep it for you."

That was the oldest junkie ploy in the world, but very effective. If I would have deposited all my dope and money to her in order to be saved from the police, her and her rock star friends would have had the great smoke out, smoking all my dope and spending money like it grew on trees.

I passed her the gun. She took one look at it like that was the last thing in the world she wanted to trick me out of. She tossed it into the trashcan like it was a hot potato. The police came in the store, snatched my ass out of line, and lined me up with the other fellows. I gave him a phony name and address and prayed like hell that the computer didn't find anything wrong. Once before I had done that and the name I gave them came back with a warrant on it and they took me to jail.

One by one, they locked some up, let some go. When they got to me, they let me go. The cop poured out my beer, faked like he was going to kick me in the ass. I walked off into the ardent sun feeling like someone somewhere was praying for me.

Nina Brown followed me like a lost stray dog.

"Well, you ain't the police, that's for damn sure."

I thought I heard her snicker. She saw my fear and somehow found it humorous how I stumbled around back there. The police have a way of scaring the shit out of a nigga, especially when you're on the run.

She ran to catch up to me. I was trying to distance myself from the police as quick as possible.

"Here." She passed me a brown bag. "You owe me big time."

"Nigga, I know you was servin', cause I can tell. What you carrin a gun fo?" She had to struggle to keep pace with me. Once again I was thinking, hot as it is this woman got on a jacket. "I ain't stupid." A police cruiser was headed our way and I was carrying this gun in a brown paper bag like a loaf of bread. The police cruiser slowed. I already made up my mind to run like hell if they tried to pull me over.

"Nina Brown! Take your skinny ass home before I lock you up!" the police bellowed over the loud speaker in the patrol car. He laughed at her and she threw up the finger at him. The officer laughed and drove off.

"Asshole! His name is Spitler. I went to school with his punk ass. We were on the same track and field team. He works in the Vice Squad now. You got to watch him, he's dirty."

We continued to walk. Frenchtown reminded me of the old days. Some of the houses were set up on bricks, mingled with a few modern homes. There were a few vacant lots, worn pavements and dusty roads, like Black folks in poverty trying to survive.

"Look, man, 'L', where you from?" The tone of her voice was agitated.

"Miami." I lied.

Her bloodshot eyes lit up like Vegas slot machines. Everybody knows that niggas from the bottom are considered as having been born with a silver coke spoon in their mouths. Like a cocaine cowboy.

Now Nina Brown was talking a mile a minute about a cocaine drought, how there wasn't no coke nowhere in town and how she just sold a white boy a piece of soap. "The white boy that was getting his ass whooped back there?" I asked.

"Yep," she answered somberly nodding her head like one of them bobblehead dogs that people keep in their car on the dashboard. I erupted in jubilate laughter. She continued like it was her sales pitch. "Everybody waiting on Stevey D to come back from Miami, they went to cop some dope. Just let me hold something." Just then a blue BMW on dubs pulled up with three people sitting inside, including the girl that Nina was talking to in the store, Shannon, the Regulator.

"They from Carolina and they want to buy some dope," Nina

whispered. I guess these were the dudes they were whispering about in the store.

"Yo, Nina! Stevey D and them ain't showed up yet?" the driver asked.

"Wuz up playa?" I said, ducking down talking to the driver. He gave Nina a look, like who the fuck is this nigga. I continued, "I'm Stevey D's people. I'm from Miami." Nina took one look at me and caught on. That's the brilliance of working with a junkie, they got more game than Toys R' Us.

"What ya'll looking for, he got it." She was the sales representative. The Regulator was in the back seat squirming around like she was going to blow up at any minute, seeing Nina Brown steal her sales commission. I detected trouble from her as she cut her eyes into slants of optic disdain at us.

"How much you charge for an ounce?" the driver questioned placing his arm out the window showing off his Rolex. He was young, barely into his twenties. Light skinned. I could tell he was a ladies' man. He had diamonds on his fingers.

"I charge a grand a piece," I said and looked around like I was into big things and wasn't trying to get caught. I continued, "I'll give you six ounces for five grand."

The Regulator in the back seat started nodding her head like she was going to try to blow the whole thing.

"Is the dope good?" the driver asked.

"I dropped twenty eight ounces in the water, got back twenty seven."

Someone in the car droned, "Damn!" in approval.

"You sho this Stevey D dope?" the driver asked. For the first time I could see the youth in his face.

"Look man, I ain't got all day. All I got is six O's left. You want them or not?" I said like he was starting to get on my nerves.

"Lemme see."

"Meet me back here in an hour. The spot is hot."

He placed the car in gear and looked at his watch. I pointed my finger at the runt in the back seat. "Shouty, let me holla at you for a minute, I got something for ya," I said digging into my empty pocket. She got out of the car like it was on fire. Thus went her allegiance to them Carolina niggas. As the car drove off, my mind was formulating a plan, mind racing in meticulous thought how I was going to relieve these busters of their bankrolls. I looked up to see Nina Brown, and the runt Regulator, watching me like I was about to perform some great feat, like go into my pocket and break them off something. I hadn't been in town a minute, and here I was plotting like a disbarred member of the Forty Thieves. The sun suddenly felt hotter on my face, or was it the two pair or beady eyes staring at me?

"Like, I'll give ya'll an ounce to split when I get back," I said, not knowing where I was going to get dope from.

"Naw you ain't!" Nina Brown said with an attitude looking at the runt making her intentions known. "You gonna give me the dope and I'ma give her what I think she should have. Them my customers."

"Ninaaa!" the runt shrieked indignantly stomping her feet. Nina balled up her fists. The expression on her face was "take it or leave it." The runt had no choice.

I know that if Stevey D and his crew showed up I was as good as dead. Here I was, breaking the law of the land, at least the ghetto's code of ethics. And believe it or not, the ghetto has one. Never sell dope on someone else's turf. Not only was I selling dope on someone's turf, I was using his name. Talk about being on a mission. I loved doing this kind of shit but to make matters worse, I didn't even have any dope.

"Meet me here in forty minutes," I yelled to Nina Brown as I took off walking.

The Regulator answered "OK" like I was talking to her.

I remembered seeing a drug store at the corner. I went in and bought six tubes of Oral Gel, some sandwich bags and some candles. I also bought one of them five-dollar scales. They did not have any cooking flour so I found some at the Winn Dixie down the street from my hotel. By then, twenty minutes had already passed. Shit! I was behind schedule.

In the hotel, I mixed up the ingredients. Melted down the candle wax, carefully blending it with the flour to give it that cocaine texture and added the Oral Gel that would numb the mouth, just like cocaine, if someone wanted to taste the dope. However with a large amount of fake dope like this, there was risk involved. It was too big to stand a taste test. *Maybe*, I thought. I knew cats that sold keys of this stuff to the feds for major money.

I liked the fake dope, better known as Dream. It looked good. Good enough to sell these suckers a Dream.

I changed clothes. Played the part for the occasion. Put on a pair of jeans, and a Tommy Hilfiger shirt, dug into the mattress and removed five hundred dollars. I put on the big platinum chain I took from the cockeyed Suge Knight-looking lame and looked into the mirror. I felt my heart racing in my chest and heard one of the voices in my head pleading with me not to do this. I smiled and called myself a coward and raced out of the door. I was running late by five minutes.

As soon as I stepped out into the hotel lobby, I was fortunate a cab was waiting at the entrance. I told the driver to take me to Frenchtown. He turned up his nose, and was about to complain until I shoved a hundred dollar bill in his face and told him all he had to do was drop me off at the gas station and wait for me. If I was not back in fifteen minutes he could keep the money, but if I did come back, there would be more where that came from. He nodded his head like my new partner in crime. Money has a way of doing that to people.

My palms were sweating, I had the jitters and for a moment I thought about the dangers of what I was doing. You normally do this kind of shit on your own turf, so in the event if something went wrong, you had back up, or at least knew where to run. I was completely alone. My only back up would be my wits and the ability to talk fast and stay calm.

The cab driver dropped me off. I believe that old white man could sense that I was up to something. I was trying to shake fear like tiny raindrops off of my Black skin. This was some gangsta shit with an adrenaline rush so high I could feel the blood running through my veins like ice cold water.

Nina and the Regulator were still posted up like watch dogs as I approached.

"Dude in the BMW been back yet?" I asked.

"No but Stevey D and his boys back. They driving around like they looking for somebody. I think they're looking for the BMW," Nina said fidgeting. I did not know if she was nervous or needed a hit. Probably both.

I looked to see the black BMW easing up the street, Tupac's song was blaring from the system, "I Get Around." I felt the six ounces of Dreams in my underwear in a bag and the gun right next to it, in case I needed to get to it fast.

The car came to a halt right in front of us.

"Yo, my man, you straight?" the driver asked. I thought I detected some urgency in his voice, like when you drive from state to state looking for dope and can't find none.

I went right into my act.

"My nigga, check this out!" I peeked into the car, like I was suspicious or something, at the same time I was flaunting the big chain on my neck with the iced out crucifix on it.

"It's too many niggas in this car. It's been some cats from out of town going through here robbing muthafuckas," I said, with my eyebrows knotted up like they was the niggas. I was making them look like the crooks trying to scheme me. I took a step back.

"Nina go get my shit!" I was talking about a gun. Nina walked off with a purpose.

"Noo, noo, it ain't like that," the driver said, throwing up his hands in frustration at seeing a sure deal suddenly go bad.

"Get out!" I heard him demand to his passengers. He also said something about he'd meet them up the street at a gas station.

I sat in the car, passed him the six ounces and tried to start up a conversation about the police busting cats from out of state. I talked fast and watched as he examined the dope. Six of the prettiest ounces of Dreams you've ever seen. He took one out and looked at it closely, too close. Think fast! I had to rely on my mouth and cunning wits.

"Give me $5,500 for all of it."

"Whaaaat!" He snorted, turned from looking at the dope and looked at me. "You said five G's at first for all six of them."

"It's a shortage of dope, I thought we had more," I said and watched as he took the dope out the bag. I held my breath. A police car cruised by and we both saw it. It passed us. He continued looking at it, wearing my patience thin.

"Man, this shit ain't right!" he screeched. I felt for my gun. "I'll give you $5,300."

I sighed a sigh of relief and looked around and reminded him that the police was hot. I told him to give me the money; said it like he was taking advantage of me.

He went underneath his shirt and I noticed he wore a money belt. I hadn't seen one of those things in my life except in the movies. He counted the money and weighed one of the ounces. I peeped the chrome plated Beretta in his waist when he was taking money out of the belt.

He passed me the money and I put it into my pocket. The only thing I was concerned with was getting out of that car as fast as possible.

"You didn't even count the money," dude said, looking at me suspiciously like maybe a light was going on in his head.

"I trust ya," I said, about to get out of the car.

"Hold up a minute," he said and reached out and touched me on the shoulder. From then on everything moved in super slow surrealistic motion. Like the world slowed to a small pace. I watched as he went into the bag, broke off a big piece of what was supposed to be dope, bite off a big piece, spit candle wax and flour onto the windshield.

"Gimme back my muthafuckin money nigga!" The scowl on his face was menacing like he wanted to inflict so much pain on me. I wish that I could have stopped him. I listened to that coward voice in my head that said, *I told you not to do it.* I shot him. Again … and again … and again. He was not trying to give up his grip. Finally, he stopped moving. There was a gray cloud of gun smoke in the car shimmering. I took his Rolex, money belt and gun. His blood was on my hands, it smoldered in my brain like the stale odor of death in my nostrils. God, I was moving on instincts. The silent rules that were handed down to me in the ghetto, kill or be killed, rang loud in my head. There was no halfway mark. I exited the car in a brisk pace, trying not to draw attention to myself. As I walked across the street, I was nearly hit by a car. I saw an old lady looking out of her window like she knew what I had done. Nina and the Regulator looked at me like I was the Devil himself, cut loose in Frenchtown. I ran across a vacant lot.

The two dudes that were with the cat that I had just robbed were standing in front of the store. They watched me with dread on their faces. I had blood on my shirt and hands. "Yo, your homeboy said he's ready to go. They took off running in his direction. I jumped in the cab. That's when I noticed the police car parked behind the dumpster, the same one that Nina Brown said was a crooked cop. I could have sworn he nodded his head and smiled.

The cab drove through Frenchtown. It was eerie. The old lady that saw me was now standing outside her apartment watching as people tried to revive the body. Nina Brown was the only one who saw me as the cab passed. Our eyes locked. She mouthed silently, "You owe me."

On the way back to the hotel, I had the cab driver stop at a local Radio Shack. I bought a boom box with a cassette player. I got back to the hotel with a feeling of triumph that only a hustler can describe. I counted out my cash, including my stash. I had a little over nineteen grand. I was elated. I had to get mines from the muscle. Lived off the fat of the land, coming up from the dirt. Every day in the news, you hear about barons, rich white men stealing billions from corporate America, people's life savings and almost never went to prison. I took mines, but it only added up to thousands. I knew if I ever got caught, they would try to take my life. But still, I shared one thing in common with those white men, the elation of greed. To us, a crime wasn't a crime until you got caught.

With the money spread out on the bed, I smiled to myself and walked over and turned on the television. There was footage of a high-speed chase, a car driving recklessly with abandon. It was being shown from a police helicopter. I watched, fascinated. It was me, driving like a madman. The newscaster was asking for any information that could help lead to my arrest. For me, that was good news. It meant so far they did not know who I was. Maybe Dre' did keep his mouth shut and the bust was really meant for Lil Cal. My heart dropped in my chest as the camera showed a snowy picture of Hope and I exiting the mall. The picture had come from a surveillance camera captured from a bank that we passed. It wasn't a good one, but I could see Hope's face. Luckily I put on a hat. Shit! I turned off the television just as the station was talking about a shooting in Frenchtown.

I took a shower and fell asleep listing to the radio. I had not slept in the last twenty-four hours. I dreamed about Hope. She was right there in bed with me.

Someone was knocking at the door. Soft raps like a bird pecking. I awoke with a start, my mind adjusting to my new environment. I got up, staggered over to the dresser and got my gun. I peeked through the peephole, it was Hope. I flung open the door, half hoping she would jump into my arms. To my surprise, it wasn't Hope, it was her friend Trina. I guess she could tell by the expression on my face that I was not expecting her. She wore a black minidress that clung to her voluptuous figure like the skin on a potato. She was stacked like a brick house and knew it.

"May I come in?" she asked, smiling seductively, displaying perfectly even white teeth.

I peeked my head out of the door, looking both ways. Bitches were notorious for setting niggas up from out of town. I touched too many niggas that way on the jack tip like that, wasn't about to let it happen to me.

"I'm harmless, wanna frisk me?" she cajoled making a mock show of searching herself as her hands manipulated her flesh pushing up her breasts. She wasn't wearing a bra. Her soft cotton dress with its thin lace shoulder straps and low cut neckline revealed just enough to capture any man's imagination. Quarter-sized nipples pointed at me.

"Come in," I said reluctantly, grilling her with my eyes like she was in violation of something. She pranced in, her plump ass bouncing to a rhythm of its own, straining against the soft fabric of thin material. I could not remember seeing a woman as fine in my entire life. She sat in the chair next to the bed and crossed her long legs, one over the other. Her curvaceous thighs spread for me like an hourglass, accentuated by a small waist. I tried not to stare but couldn't help it. Her cat eyes dared me. If I had to guess, I would say she was wearing red panties. I saw the tattoo on her right breast. It read, "Thug Misses" in purple and red letters.

"Wuz up?" I said and walked over and peeked out of the window into the darkness. If she saw the gun in my hand, she paid it no attention.

Ice Cube once said, "Never trust a bitch with a fat ass and a sexy smile." That was a song that now held meaning to my life.

"I thought maybe I could be of some service to you." The timbre of her voice was melodious like a song.

"Service?" I quipped, thinking about how much I would pay her to let me cut. Sex that is. With sure sophistication, I watched as she went inside her purse and removed a Black & Mild and freaked it on the nightstand. I continued to occasionally look out the window and at her round thighs.

"Papi, you pop up in town with that square-ass bitch, Hope. I saw the date on that car tag, I also saw how she looks at you. I got enough sense to recognize a playa. Hope is on some conscious, intellectual bullshit, besides, she got a man," Trina said as she freaked the Black & Mild, talking to me like she trying to save my life. She continued, "You came here running from something. You want to open up shop. Bleed this town for all you can get and then get the hell out."

She completely caught me off guard. I was now looking at her from a totally different perspective. Her voice was laced with some kind of accent, maybe Spanish. It dawned on me that it matched her hypnotizing cat eyes and enchanting beauty. After she finished with the Black & Mild she removed a blunt from her purse, busted it open with a long manicured fingernail. She placed the weed in the blunt. Licked it while looking at me with a face that said, "this is how I would love to do it to you."

"You know that's bad for your health," I said for the sake of conversation.

"So is this town to niggas that come in here shooting people up and selling fake dope," she retorted, causing my mind to stagger on the red alert. She had me on my toes against the ropes. My mind racing, *how in the fuck did she know that?*

She fired up the blunt with a gold lighter. I could sense that she was amused with our cat and mouse game. She inhaled deeply on the potent weed. It was hard to believe I was looking at a college student. What the fuck were they teaching in school?

"I'm that bitch, Papi. Ride or die bitch." She uncrossed her legs and leaned back in the chair, like hot pussy on a platter. I looked out the window again, but this time I was checking for my own composure, trying to restrain myself. I placed the gun in my pocket, grabbed the Hennessy off the table and drank out of the bottle. It burned like the suspicion I had for her. I set my buttocks on the edge of the table, ogled her luscious body as smoke curled from pure lips making a halo around her head, giving her an angelic appearance or perhaps a devilish one. In the fog of smoke she said, "Nina Brown told me about your little caper." She smirked knowingly. I almost choked on my drink, but I should have figured that. Talk about a small town. She had my attention.

"You can get twenty for a brick and a grand for an ounce as you already know." I took another swig from the bottle, nodded for her to keep on talking, since she seemed to be enjoying herself.

"My last lover is in the feds. He made over a million dollars, mostly due to my connections. I never got credit for it." She stopped and took a long drag off the blunt. "I can get a brick for ten thousand, cook it, break it down to dime rocks and make over a hundred thousand dollars." I whistled out loud at that. Either she was lying, or was a bad bitch for real. She was starting to look like a sexy dollar sign. All real hustlers recognize the potential for making money, and in a new town, a female is always the first real option.

She kicked off her heels, wiggled her pedicured toes in the carpet and yawned like a feline. I watched the swell of her breasts as her nipples pointed skyward and her thighs spread across the chair. Her perfect body alluring. I was fighting this urge.

She looked at the ashes on the blunt as if contemplating a thought. And then she spoke, her cat eyes narrowing as if she couldn't put enough emphasis on what she was really trying to relate to me.

"Papi, I want to do the Bonnie and Clyde thing … you and I. Stake some chips, get rich, leave this town. You know what I mean?" Her voice was sultry, eyes dreamy. That black dress eased up her thighs. I could see red lace panties, red like I imagined her venom was. If she was poison, I was about to OD on her. No real playa is really immune to the whims of a woman. You just go on guts and instincts. She padded over to the radio. I watched her ass bounce for me. She turned the radio to the college station and I heard Hope's voice. I got the feeling she was doing this to read me. Just to see how much I cared for Hope. They debated, I listened, and Trina watched me the way a woman does when she is trying to read a man. Finally, music came on and Trina snapped out of her reverie.

Slowly, sensuously, her body came to life. Her lower torso grinded back and forth in a dance as if she were making love without me. She eased right up close to me. Her perfume, mingled with the weed, was like an aphrodisiac to my loins. Trina was coming on strong, strong like a woman that was sure of herself. A nimble finger walked down my thigh. I could feel the heat from her body. Trina was bold. I liked that in a woman, but under these circumstances, I was not too sure of her motives. The only thing that I was certain of was that she set me on fire, and her passion stroked the flames that went on to the furnace of my body. I stuck my hand under her dress and palmed her plump ass. She was soft and firm. I used the other hand to squeeze and spread her cheeks. I was rewarded with a soft moan that could have passed for a purr.

"Hey Shouty, I really ain't into the bump and grind. Just put a price on the damn thang and lemme hit it."

She pulled away from me. "Why buy the cow when you can get the milk for free, Papi?"

She then unzipped my pants, stuck her hand down my leg and pulled out my joint. "Ooohh weee," she droned. "You're Mr. Big for real, huh?" Her voice breathy. She licked my neck … my chest … stomach … down … down … took me in both hands, primed her lips, stroked me and talked to me at the same time. "Papi, you like this?" I nodded, took my hand and tried to force her head down on me.

"Um, um, um. I'm gonna make love to you like no woman has ever done before." The cadence of her voice was raspy. Her tongue left a trail of hot saliva. Some women thought that the way to a man's heart was through his stomach, but Trina knew better. She eased me into her hot mouth, slow as if savoring the taste like she was a real head hunter. She went inch by inch. In the background I could hear Hope on the radio. I looked down and saw her face just as Trina deep throated me. I gasped, gulped air holding onto the edge of the table as if it would prevent me from drowning myself in her as her mouth went up and down masterfully as she manipulated the juices in her mouth. I was losing control. She was going too fast. Her hands gently caressed my balls. I groaned in response as my hands held her head. She was moving too fast. She was about to make me a minute man. My toes curled as I felt my back arch. I was in that place of no return. The spoils of her virtuosity were stronger than my masculinity and she took what I wanted to deny, at least wait. I came in jets of milky white, just as she pulled her head away, aiming my semen on her chest.

She looked up at me and I saw something in her eyes, it wasn't love either. Maybe it was the same thing Samson saw in Delilah before she cut his hair. She rubbed my juices on her erect nipples and then my dick. I reached down and pulled her up. She wiggled out of her dress, and then her panties. Pussy juice glistened between her thighs. Trina had one of them bodies that just made me want to stare. She touched herself and continued to rub her nipples like it really turned her on. I took off my clothes like they were on fire and we got in bed.

"Wait, wait!" she halted. "We need a condom. A hard dick ain't never had a conscience." Her pleas fell on deaf ears. There was no way in the world I was going to ruin all this good pussy with latex. She reached over and fumbled with her purse. I placed two fingers inside of her, then three. She moaned like a bad song, a silent surrender as I went deeper and stirred her passion.

"Don't do this ... to me. I don't have any rubbers," she squalled. That was her problem. I rolled on top of her, dick in hand, like a battering ram. She resisted, and made some kind of move with her hand, curled her spine, did some kind of leg lock shit like they do while wrestling. It worked. She effectively put the coochie on lock down. I bit down on her breast. "Ouch!" she shrieked. "Please don't do this to me," she whimpered as she unwrapped her legs. I found the entrance of soft silky pubic hairs. Her eyes matched mine. She was tight and wet. The sensation felt so good that I fought to keep control. Then she kissed me with a fervor that almost sucked the juices out of my mouth. My hands roamed her body. She spread her legs wider for me. She spoke in Spanish. "Make love to me, this is your pussy."

I was barely inside her and she began to cum. She quivered and moaned. I went deeper. She dug her nails into my back. "You're hurting me, go slow," she stammered. She stroked my ego and didn't even know it. I found a rhythm, rode the wave of her body like she was the last woman in the world. This wasn't making love like what I did to Hope. We were fucking, wildly. I plunged deeper. She made a noise like I was torturing her. She panted. I was in a zone, like a runner with a fast pace. Her teeth snarled at me with an expression that she was determined to match each one of my thrusts. Our bodies were covered in a sheen of sweat. I was pounding so deep within her that it felt like I was about to lose myself. She was now making enough noise to wake up the dead, and then she reached another climax, one that made her shudder into uncontrollable convulsions. Her eyes rolled in the back of her head like she was possessed with something. As her head bumped against the headboard and long legs wrapped around my waist, I took one of her legs and placed it on my shoulder. Her eyes showed a hint of fear, for she knew what was next, and in one long thrust, for the first time, I drove all the way into her and she screamed as her talon fingernails raked my back. Our breathing was heavy and sweat cascaded from our intertwined bodies. Her cat eyes exerted robust energy as she looked up at me and squinted. She bit down on her lower lip in a painful show of a woman's determination. Her voice screeched like chalk on blackboard and she lamented, "I have not been with a man in almost a year ... you're ... trying to hurt, meeee ... with that thing." Her seductress Spanish was thick. "Pa...pi...let me suck iiiiit!" In mid stroke, I stopped, and burst out laughing.

"What's so funny?" she pouted. Her eyes smiled up at me. Even with her hair half matted to her face, with sweat and the painful wrinkles in her eyes, she was still one of the most beautiful women I had ever seen. I took what I could get and then some. Afterward, I rolled off of her and lay there satisfied, depleted. She looked over at me with a knowing grin, the kind lovers share when they have both been satisfied by the other, only I kept seeing something else. I closed my eyes because the game can make a nigga paranoid. For some reason the faces of Dre', and the nigga that set me up, popped into my mind. I cringed like I had just been shot. Shot by the reality of my own stupid blunder. Dre' was looking for Lil Cal. Lil Cal was from Miami, a spot called Opa Locka. It was infamous as a dope hole for young thugs, better known as the "Triangle," where you could walk in and never come out. I would never go in there without Lil Cal with me. Shit! All this time I forgot to warn my nigga Cal about what Dre' was up to. I leaped from the bed and startled Trina. So much had been going on in the past two days. I paced the floor thinking. Dre' had family in Tallahassee, or was it Jacksonville? Orlando? I forgot and we used to hustle together. My mind was really congested. I paced the floor naked while Trina looked at me with the covers pulled up to her chin. I picked up the phone, dialed 305 area code. The phone wouldn't let me call out long distance. I slammed it down, cursed Dre' out and paced some more, rubbing the waves in my head absent-mindedly.

"Pass me my purse," Trina said, reading my mind. I grabbed her purse, rummaged inside and found a phone and a tiny two shot derringer .38 pistol, powerful enough to put any man down.

Livid, she sprung up in bed and screamed at me, "Gimme my damn purse!"

I did what playas do, I ignored her, dialed the number and watched as she stormed toward me. She snatched the purse out of my hands and came close to getting her first ass whoopin too.

Someone answered the phone on the third ring. It was Blazack. Before I could tell him what happened, he told me that the Feds got Lil Cal as soon as Dre' walked out of the house. Cal sold him a brick. Heavy hearted, I sat down in the middle of the floor. Blazack went on to say that he felt like my boy Dre' had something to do with the bust. Blazack was one of the most dangerous men that I had ever known. It was like he had been born in the wrong era. He was a cold-blooded murderer, who went at life like it was his mission to die. He was the only man I knew that beat three murder raps. He really didn't have to sell dope. If he walked up to you and asked for something, like an ounce or two, it was best to give it to him or risk getting shot, or have a loved one come up missing. Every real crew had to have a Blazack, he was the enforcer, the man that went into the trenches and did the dirty work. He didn't aspire to be rich, just enjoyed staying true to the game. Reluctantly, I told him what happened. I could hear his breathing on the phone, a silent threat to wreak havoc on whomever he felt was responsible for setting up Lil Cal. This included me. I felt my heart racing in my chest after I'd finished telling him what happened.

"What took you so fucking long to warn us?" he yelled on the phone.

"Man, I've been caught up in all kinds of bull –"

"Fuck that nigga!" he yelled. He wasn't even tryin' to hear about the shit I had been going through. "I know where yo old man live at with that big-ass church down there in Sarasota, if you tryin some funny shit –"

"Hold up!" I interrupted. "Don't go there, don't go there." I was tryin to calm him, at the same time, let him know I ain't nothing nice either when it comes to gunplay.

"Man I've been in all kinds of dumb shit. Peep CNN, that's me running from the police. I would never set ya'll up."

"Nigga where you at?" Blazack asked. I didn't like the tone of his voice. It took a few seconds to answer, I'm sure he noticed. Trina made a face at me as I answered, "I'm in Tallahassee. It's sweet. I've already hit a lick for some grands."

"Fuck that nigga, you was the one that introduced us to that hot-ass nigga." Blazack was on some serious death before dishonor shit. That was cool unless the wrath of his anger was directed at you. Trying to stop him was like trying to stop a suicide terrorist. He simply did not care.

"Dre's grandfather lives in Sarasota," I blurted out.

"Let's kidnap that fool!" Blazack said coldly. I didn't answer, Blazack was crazy like that. One thing was for sure, someone's family would be receiving an unwanted visit from him.

"Look man, the spot is hot as hell here. Let me come down there until shit cool down and together we can look for that nigga Dre'. You know what they say, three can keep a secret, if two are dead," Blazack said.

I pondered over his riddle, the math did not come out right, but I owed an allegiance to my nigga Cal. Blazack was his own man, which by code would make him my man, too. At least help him get out of this mess, that I felt responsible for getting him in. We made plans. I was to Western Union him the money to come to Tallahassee. One of the biggest mistakes I ever made in my life.

I walked back to the bed with the feeling a man has when he knows he has just fucked up by not following his first mind.

Trina sat up in bed and the covers fell to her waist. Suddenly, I had an urge to beat in her guts again. She fired up the roach and took two pulls which almost choked her. "Smoke this, it will make you feel better." I took it, and watched as she padded to the bathroom. Her ass looked like Serena Williams', only finer. She closed the door, at least I thought she did. I counted out my stash and hid it under the carpet.

She returned smelling like soap and something else sweet. We had an idle conversation as she made the bed, until I suddenly remembered about Dre', and the likelihood that he had family in Tallahassee, which meant that he could have possibly been hustling there, too.

"You know a nigga named Dre'. Drives a sky blue caddy on dubs?"

She stopped making the bed momentarily as if to think. I admired the gap between her legs as she bent over. She shrugged her shoulders no, but I kind of got the feeling she was lying. We got back in bed. It was a quarter after four in the morning.

After we got cozy, she snuggled up close against me and whispered in my ear like she was still hot and horny.

"Have you ever tried a sixty nine position?" she asked mischievously. Her hand went under the covers on a mission. I resisted the urge to laugh. Trina was trying to beat me for my head. Oral sex that is.

"I don't eat pussy." I lied. I felt her body stiffen and then relax. "You want me to do you again?" She said it like a dare. She held the hard response to her question in her hands. Then she closed her eyes and went into that utopia where women go when they're being sexy and sweet and it's as natural for them as breathing. With her eyes closed, she took me on a trek down memory lane.

"I was born in New York. I'm the youngest, and only girl. My father has been dead now for about eight years. When he died, my world came crashing down. My mom is African American, and dad Cuban. Word is bond, he taught me so much." Her eyes popped open, she looked at me as if she were pleading. She continued, "I can cook dope, cut, weigh and sell it. That's where Nina Brown came in at." She removed a lock of hair from her forehead, adjusted her pillow and leaned toward me. I had to strain my ears to hear her. While talking, her mind was distant, giving me a piece of her past.

"My father left a trust fund for me after he died. It's over a quarter of a million dollars. I receive the money annually, but only if I'm in school. My daddy was smart like that. He said, life's education didn't guarantee a thing. He wanted me to be street smart, too. He died from AIDS." She said this somberly as the timbre of her voice changed. "Now my oldest brother has it, and to think we just finished playing Russian Roulette with a loaded dick." I felt like I had been hit with a low blow. Moments passed and the silence was uncomfortable. As she looked at me, something about her moved me. And now, caught up in the liaison of raw sex, fervid passion and the intimacy of pillow talking, I found myself looking at her the way a man does a woman. I was feeling her like she had just jumped on my chest with spiked heels.

She huffed, "I'm tired of these fake-ass hoes too. Fronting like they down with me just to be seen in my whip." Just that quick, her mood changed. Her eyes sparkled.

"Once you've been exposed to the game, money and power, nothing else will do! My daddy taught me a lot. He also said ain't no drug dealer got no business in the game over a year. Ain't no future in fronting. People that sell get hooked just like the people that buy." She stopped talking to catch her breath. I was admiring her brain like she just submitted a verbal application to me, "Gangsta Bitch For Hire." She bragged, resting her head on my chest. "Papi, I'm claiming you." Her head went under the covers and she took me into her mouth. Trina could suck a dick. As her tongue worked its magic on my body, I wondered, *is she just one of them bitches sweating me for my cheddar, thinking I can make her life better?* I ran up in her after she finished giving me head. We did it until the sun came up. She paralyzed me with her body and afterward, she rested her head on her elbows and watched me until I fell off to sleep.

\*\*\*\*\*

The next day I was awakened to the sound of someone pounding on the door. Trina was gone. Instantly I knew that something was not right. I stared into the darkness and called her name. The knock continued. Groggily, I got out of bed, hit my big toe on the chair, "Shit," and stumbled to the door. "Who is it?" I shouted rubbing my sore toe.

"Hope," the voice answered back.

I opened the door, and the ardent sun electrocuted my blood cracked eyes, blinding me. I was standing in my boxers with a morning erection. Hope looked at me pathetically and stormed past me. She was wearing some kind of African garb of floral colors of picot yellow and brown. It was long with a matching hat. She looked like a Princess. I remembered hearing her voice on the radio, but couldn't recall a thing she said. In her arms she was carrying books. I closed the door limping toward her. "Life, Boy! Did you see the news?" I had not really paid any attention to anything she had said. My attention was focused on the carpeting on the floor pulled up. I walked over to it, bent down and examined it. My money was gone. Never trust a bitch with a fat ass and a sexy smile. Trina had beat me for my stash.

\*\*\*\*\*

# Chapter Six

## "Thug Love versus Old Love"

### *— Hope —*

I drove away from that hotel with the residue of Life Thugstin in my skin, and in my flesh. I felt humiliated and ashamed. The car I drove was the evidence of my sins, my betrayal to the man I love, my boyfriend Marcus, and yet, I thought about Life and what happened at that hotel. The way that man made love to me, I had never experienced nothing like that before. He had sexed me to the point of tears. As a young woman, I did not even know that was possible. Ecstasy! I thought about his soft touch, how he spread me apart, placed his lips on my privacy, devouring me. Yes, I knew it was so wrong, but for that moment in time it felt so right. I could understand why women cheat, but I was so wrong, morally wrong, or was I? *Hope can I lick you there?* Shit! I cursed the diction in my mind, changing lust over reason, infidelity over love. I was so wrong! Life and Marcus were as different as day and night. Marcus just graduated from college with a degree in Structural Engineering. He came from a middle class family. He was high yellow with curly hair, a real "Pretty Boy." We had been together for over two years and he was the man that I gave my virginity to. I almost never enjoyed making love with him. He just never satisfied me, and oral sex was out of the question. There was so much I wanted to learn. I asked him to experiment and he then accused me of cheating on him because of the things I wanted to

**75**

do with his body. So I decided long ago that sex was not everything. Now I wondered about all the things that I had been missing. Life taught me a lot but Marcus ruled my mind. As I pulled up in his driveway, I had a lot of explaining to do and I needed to do it before Trina saw him. The trepidation of it wore me down like a ball and chain. I knocked on his front door. His front porch was decorated with all kinds of exotic plants. The summer breeze felt good on my face. There wasn't a cloud in the sky. I pawed at my hair. The door opened. Marcus Green was dressed in causal black slacks and a Tommy Hilfiger shirt. He took one look at me and smiled, taking me into his arms.

"Girl, I missed you," he said dearly, planting wet kisses on my face and neck. He pulled me inside. He was unusually vibrant and beamed. "I've found a job!" Animated, he carried me through his small apartment with the excitement of a man that had just accomplished one of his biggest dreams and he wanted to celebrate. In my mind I wished that I didn't come; the generic smile on my face was as plastic as a storefront mannequin. He sensed my discomfort. "Baby are you OK?" he asked, while taking my hand and cocking his head sideways, affection written all over his face.

"I'm just tired from the long drive," I said and kissed him on the cheek, feeling so guilt-ridden that I wanted to run out of the door.

Marcus watched me intently. "Let me get you something to drink. Want a beer to celebrate?" he asked as his eyes roamed my body in a way that I knew so well. I nodded my head yes and watched as he danced away with a look in his eyes. I had the uncanny feeling that something was not quite right.

I sat on the couch and the television was on the news. I watched absent-mindedly as a litany of voices chanted in my head. All of them chaos of my guilt. Suddenly on the screen, three white faces jumped out at me. Startled, I felt my heart racing as I sat on the edge of my seat. The newscaster began to announce that three men had been shot. I covered my mouth with a trembling hand. My question was finally about to be answered.

"Last night, three men were robbed at gun point and shot in the buttocks. The victims stated that they were robbed by five heavily armed Black men driving an older model Ford Mustang."

Marcus returned with drinks in his hand. My eyes were glued to the television set like I was in some kind of trance. He sat down, passed me my drink and placed his arm around me just as a commercial came on. I was trying to decipher what I had just heard, and yes, it was tragedy that those men had been shot in the ass, but thank God they were not dead. And then it dawned on me what the announcer said, "... five heavily armed men ... shot in the buttocks." I couldn't help it, I laughed out loud, maybe from the relief that the thug, Life, had not killed those men.

Marcus was talking a mile a minute, and I never heard a word he said until he turned to me and looked at me strangely, and asked what was I laughing at. I turned and kissed him fully. In return, he responded in a way that caught me off guard. He acted as if he were starving for my body. His dexterous hands found their way under my blouse, unhooking my bra with the snap of a finger, releasing my breasts. My nipples were still sore from the night before. I didn't know why. I had no intentions of having sex with him, but my conscience needed to relieve the guilt of my debauchery. His mouth found my nipples and he gently nibbled on them in a way that almost drove me crazy. His body language was urgent, a man's desire that he needed me, it felt almost primitive. And in the cramped chamber of my mind, where I had wronged him, I needed him, too. Needed him to forgive me. In my heart I loved him. I would not deny him, not today, not ever, I needed his forgiveness. My love was all I had to offer. I pulled away from him. He opened his mouth to complain but I silenced him by putting my finger over his pouting lips, and stood, giving him a look with the promise of the world I was offering as I disrobed down to my bare essence. With no inhibitions, no restraints, I gave him my sinful body to do with what he pleased. He laid me on the couch gently, entered me slowly. I closed my eyes and Life's handsome face appeared. I spread my legs wider, whispering epithets into his ear. I wanted him to punish me, purge me from my sins. But all Marcus could do was poke me, and eight minutes later we were finished. He lay on top of me spent, panting like he had just got finished running a race. We didn't use a condom. My mind was so full of guilt that I forgot, but Marcus on the other hand, was a stickler for birth control.

"Hope, I love you." Marcus slobbed on my face with wet kisses, his weight was starting to hurt, and to be truthful, I was very disappointed in his lovemaking skills again. It numbed my guilty conscience considerably. Marcus then asked, in what sounded like practiced tones, "Hope, will you marry me?"

His timing was horrible! I did not answer, but in the back of my mind, I wondered if he intentionally didn't use a condom. He was still lying on top of me, his weight still uncomfortable. Just as I was about to complain, avoiding his question, in my peripheral vision I caught a glimpse of something on the television set. It was a police chase shown from a helicopter, Oh my God! It was Life Thugstin in a car chase running from the police. The camera showed him driving down one-way streets, over guard rails up until the point he exited the car at the mall. Now the reporter was showing footage, a couple exiting the mall. I could vaguely see myself walking with Life. Our figures showed up as only darkened shadows. The reporter was asking for any help that might lead to any arrest of the suspect. I thought my heart was going to explode in my chest. Suddenly, Marcus's weight on top of me was too much to bear. He was still whispering lilting affections into my ear. "Hope be my wife." I could feel his little erection on my thigh prodding now with anew vigor, but all I could envision were prison bars. It felt like he was suffocating me. *You'll be back in a hurry, trust me!* Life's words resonated in my brain like a bomb being detonated. I shoved Marcus off of me and he nearly fell on the floor. "Hope! What's wrong with you girl?" he screeched. I sat up, flustered, running my fingers through my hair. Now I was wondering if Life left something in that car, something to make me come back to him. Oh, God! And the police were looking for me, too. I untangled my body from Marcus' and began to quick-ly dress. Marcus was pleading for all the wrong reasons. "Hope, I love you. You know that I do. Talk to me."

My mind was racing a mile a minute. I touched his arm. "I love you too, but we're rushing things. I still have four years of law school and you still need to get situated," I said, gesturing with my hands emphasizing on his small apartment.

Crestfallen, Marcus casted his eyes to the floor. I couldn't help thinking to myself, *men are like little boys when it came to rejection.* Even though I loved him, I was not trying to marry him, not now. Plus there was something else about him that I just could not put my finger on. "You did agree to move in with me after you grad-uated from college, and if I'm good enough to shack with I'm good enough to marry," he spit defensively. Sometimes when Marcus was ill tempered he acted peevish and now he was starting to piss me off as he stood with his bird chest stuck out, eyebrows knotted together in contempt.

"First of all, I never agreed to move in with you. I said that I would think about it and that was only because I felt that it would be good for us financially."

"Now I have a job, a good one. We can get married, have some babies —"

"Marcus!" I screamed his name so loud I thought the vein in my neck was going to burst. "There will be no babies! I can assure you of that!" I slid that in to let him know that I was on to his lit-tle move that he made by not using a condom. "And no marriage." Now it seemed like my tongue had a mind of its own, and the more I talked, the smaller Marcus got. "I am not going to be dependent on no man. What part of this don't you understand? I fully intend to be a self-sufficient, independent Black woman doing her own thang. And until I am ready to have some babies, there will be none!" I rolled my eyes at him. Marcus looked at me as if I had just doused him with cold water.

"Fine! If that's the way you want it, Miss Independent Black Woman." And then he did something that struck a serious nerve.

He stood and pointed his finger in my face. "You're 21 years old. You need to first understand, this is a man's world." He said it like he was taunting me, and the reality of it sent chills down my spine. I knew that it held some truth, but I was not going to back down. "Girl, I'm trying to take care of you."

"Shit." I hissed standing akimbo wearing the wrath of my anger, "That's just what I don't want you to do, take care of me." I shot back at him. "Yeah, you would wanna keep me barefoot and pregnant, and after I have all your babies, trade me for a younger version, I think not!" I pointed my finger in his face shaking my neck. We were standing too close for comfort now.

"Do what the fuck you want to do!" he yelled, grabbing me by my shoulders. "I am not putting my life on hold for your women's liberation bullshit dream."

I pulled away from him. This was our first real fight.

"Don't you ever put your hands on me!" I lamented with my little fists balled up ready to tag his ass. He opened his mouth about to speak and thought better of it and stormed out of the room. I continued to get dressed. I noticed a few of my things around his apartment and wondered if I should take them. I knew in doing so what the implications would mean. I don't care what anyone says, life is the hardest for a Black woman. Not only was I discriminated against for being a woman, but for also being a Black woman. And for some strange reason, brothas found me intimidating when they learned my aspirations.

I headed for the door. My anger was starting to quell. Maybe I did go too far. I was trying to be a woman dealing with a man in a relationship.

"Call me. I'll be on the air tonight," I said swallowing my pride. "We need to talk."

Marcus appeared from the shadows of the doorway down the hall. I could not read his continuance, didn't want to either. I closed the door to our lives and meandered to my car. I glanced up at Marcus' window to see him standing there watching me. *Good for his ass,* I thought. Make a brotha sweat, let him see me in my new ride. Let him know I wasn't doing all that bad. For the first time in my life I had no regrets about accepting the car from thug, Life.

I put on my dark shades, turned up the volume to my booming car system. My girl Mary J. Blige was crooning, "Not Gon' Cry." I drove out of the parking lot bouncing to the rhythm. That was my song, haay! Now it held special meaning. There's something about a break up that can either zap your strength, or be very empowering, if you're determined to be an independent Black woman like myself. I drove all the way to the campus with a new-found resolve for myself.

It was like being back home after being gone for so long. FAMU campus is like one big happy family. I was suddenly filled with a feeling of euphoria as I watched students perambulate the campus grounds. I was scheduled to graduate that year.

I pulled into the student parking lot, waved at a few of my friends and chatted with some. As I was unpacking my things from the car, I thought about Life's words, *you'll be back.* I searched the car for something he might have left. I could find nothing. I sighed in relief, and then something told me to look under the front seat. I stuck my hand under the seat and felt that big-ass gun that he called Jesus. I slumped in my seat. That's when I noticed the trashcan. I thought about dumping the money and gun into it, but ain't no sister I know gonna throw away money. Especially me, as bad as I was doing, trying to make it through college. If they would have had a student welfare line, I would have been the first to sign up. I decided right then and there, I was going to give him back his money and big-ass gun, as well as a piece of my mind. In doing so, I realized I was falling right into his trap, and I kind of wanted to. Life Thugstin was an intriguing character. That much I had to admit.

I needed to get some rest for the show that night. Me and my girl, Nandi, hosted a show together called, "The Panther Power Hours." She was from California and graduated from FAMU a few years before. Now she was going to Florida State University to earn her Doctorate Degree. For years the show had been a big underground hit. We played nothing but conscious Rap and old R&B back when the music was good. Nandi would mix in sound bytes of Malcolm X and Farrakhan. She was also real heavy into poetry. Often, she and other poets would perform—that's what gave the show its flavor. On a few occasions, a famous rapper would come by.

As I carried all of my meager luggage to my room, I spoke to all my friends. I checked out all the new hairdos and designer clothes that I could not afford. FAMU could be like a Black fashion show teaming with Black folks of all social status.

Once inside the room I shared with my homegirl, Shanana, I took a long hot shower. Afterward, I slept faithfully until my alarm clock went off at 9:00 p.m. I called Nandi from the payphone down the hall. As usual, she was excited and upbeat to hear from me. Talking was her natural forte. Her tongue was a double-edged sword. Nandi Shakur was the first conscious person that enlightened me to the plight of Black life in a way that opened up something deep within me. Black people were dying from genocidal acts at a rate so high that, if it had been any other race of people, there would be a blood bath. Between the AIDS epidemic affecting the world, especially in Africa, and the rate that the government was illegally imprisoning our Black men under the disguise of a war against drugs, we were on our way to becoming nonexistent. We had more Black men in prison than colleges and universities. She asked me to think, if America had more white men in prison than colleges, what would they do? I knew the answer to that.

When I first met Nandi she was in my Political Science class. She always stood out, not just that she was beautiful, but the way she dressed and her long locks of hair. On this particular day, she was arguing vehemently with a white professor, a man that I held very high respect for. The subject was, "Should Black people be given reparations for slavery?" Most of the students in the class felt that Black people should not receive it. I felt that they were just agreeing with the professor's logic in that color did not matter, and that white America suffered due to slavery, too. Nandi was livid! She argued to the point of tears. Said she owed it to her ancestors to hold white people accountable for the atrocities of over one hundred million people killed or enslaved. I just sat behind my desk and watched the heated exchange of words. The class tried to ridicule her. I was sort of against her too because as far back as I could remember, I had always been taught that it does not matter what color you are, and like the professor was saying, reparations would establish a new color code. Nandi was on her feet, "Why ain't there any Black men in this class?" I looked around, and to my surprise, there weren't. Normally there were three brothers in the class, but I had not seen them in a while. "You teaching it shouldn't matter what color you are, but it does, and racism still exists as an institution exploited by whites!" Nandi's words were filled with hurtful overtones that compelled me to look at it from her perspective.

The professor was offended by her statement. His right hand trembled as he pointed at the door and asked Nandi to remove herself from class. To my surprise some of the students applauded. Nandi was an outcast because of her liberal views and her African style of dress. I'll admit, at first I was taken aback by her unique style, but as I watched her hold her head dignified with tears streaking down her beautiful ebony cheeks, something gnawed at my heart. Nandi picked up her books and walked to the door. I stood too and followed her. She looked over her shoulder at me as I placed a reassuring hand on her shoulder and we both walked out the door. She had been my girl ever since.

*****

I arrived at the station and Nandi was already there, which wasn't unusual for her. She was a perfectionist. As soon as she saw me, she stood and embraced me. Nandi Shakur was what men called a stunner. Her beauty reached out and grabbed you. People openly stared at her. Her cinnamon complexion, combined with her long golden locks of hair, seemed to make an entire room radiate in her splendor. On each of her fingers she wore rings, Ankhs and trinkets of Africa's antiquity. At 23 years of age Nandi was still a virgin, and made no secret about it.

"… three … two … one … WRXB The Panther Power Hours is on your urban conscious radio station 89.3. This is your girl Nandi Shakur and Hope Evans coming to you live from the campus of FAM-U," Nandi said. Her voice was so vivacious and full of energy she could pull people through the speakers. Public Enemy played in the background and the small radio station was alive. The topic was supposed to be on Affirmative Action, but to my surprise, Nandi flipped the script on me when she announced that the topic was going to be, "Where have all the good men gone?" I furrowed my brow with a quizzical expression and just listened while she unveiled another facet of herself. As always, like the audience, I enjoyed listening to her talk.

"The reason that I have abstained from sex is because when I do decide to give a man my body, it has to be a brotha that I want to spend the rest of my life with. He has to be very special; my King. So until then, I choose to remain celibate. Unfortunately, there's a shortage of good men."

I watched as Nandi talked, and noticed how her brown eyes sparkled as she held a mug of herbal tea in her hand. And for the first time I saw hurt in her eyes, as I gazed at this beautiful ebony Queen. Then she said, "So far all of the Black men that I have dated ain't shit …" Nandi lambasted that over the air. I almost fell out of my chair. The Dean of the school already threatened us once to cut down the language. I played a record by Gil Scott Heron, titled "The Revolution Won't Be Televised" and watched as the phone lines lit up like a Christmas tree.

One sister by the name of Regina called in, and we went live on the air with her conversation.

"Yeah, you're right girl! Black men act like they're scared of commitment, and sista, you ain't wrong for keeping your stuff on lock down. Once you give them some, they start act'in disrespectful. Give a brotha some cat, and he will turn into a dog," the caller said, causing us all to erupt in jubilant laughter.

Another sister called in. Her boyfriend of four years wanted to be a rapper. She said that he never had a job, but hustled to support her. She loved him immensely, but was ready to settle down, get married and have some babies. He wasn't. Our advice to her was to let him know, and if he did not approve, let his ass go!

Another woman called in. She refused to give her name. Her voice was sad and full of pain.

"My boyfriend is sick … he has AIDS." We could hear her breathing on the phone like she was struggling with her voice. I leaned forward in my seat trying to catch each and every word.

"He is a very heavy … drug user. We have been together for over five years –"

I interrupted.

"My sista, have you been tested for AIDS?"

"Yes … No …Well, sort of," the caller stuttered.

"Sorta? What kind of damn answer is that?" Nandi chirped in.

"A few years ago I was tested, but my boyfriend seemed to get upset with me." She began to cry. Nandi and I just looked at each other.

"It's as if he wants me to catch it too. We have been having unprotected sex." Nandi bolted straight up in her seat spilling her tea.

"I have a 7-year-old daughter from another relationship."

"Listen! Listen to me, my sista. You gotta protect yourself as well as your child. Ain't no man worth your life, not to mention your child's life too. AIDS is serious! It's a biological warfare designed for population control to kill off Black folks –"

"But I love him," she interrupted.

"Do you love him enough to die for him?" Nandi yelled into the phone, I cringed in my seat.

No answer. The line went dead. Nandi just looked at the receiver shaking her head.

The next caller was a man. I recognized his voice instantly. It was my boyfriend Marcus. I perked up and mouthed to Nandi that it was Marcus. Adamantly, she waved her hand to let her handle him. There was no secret about it, she thought he was too feminine. Too pretty. A real momma's boy, which he was.

"Ya'll sistas talk all that yippity yap about men being dogs and whatnot, but when a real man steps to you, ya'll don't want to acknowledge ya'll's place."

"And what place is that?" Nandi asked dryly.

"Ya'll's place is letting the man be the boss, and ya'll follow. Talking 'bout that independent Black woman crap. Ya'll need to read the Bible! Women were created to be man's helper, to clean house and have babies —"

"The Bible also says, if thee eye offend, thee pluck it out. Which means you need to pluck your stupid-ass tongue out!" Nandi shot back.

"Face it, men feel threatened by a woman's aspirations to be independent and self-sufficient. Strong minded Black women are tired of being used and abused by Black men that only have one thing on their minds—how to exploit a sista for what they can get." Nandi then turned and looked me dead in the face with an expression that read like she was about to deliver a cliché.

"If you don't believe in a Black woman, you can't possibly believe in yourself, because it was the Black woman that made your ass. Marcus, don't call here no damn mo', hating on the sistas," Nandi sassed, hanging up the phone.

*Click!*

We laughed, and gave each other high-five hand smacks. It truly turned out to be one of the best shows we had. We had about a half a million listeners, young and old, Black and white, which used to come as a surprise to me, but then Nandi taught me that white people have always been intrigued by certain facets of urban life. I thought about the white boys that I was starting to see with gold in their mouths.

Afterward we just sat around the studio chatting, drinking herbal tea, and enjoying each other's vibes. Nandi Shakur was by far my best friend in all the world. As much as I hated bringing back the memories of my one night fling with Life Thugstin, I had to tell her everything, well, except for the part about seeing myself on the news.

Nandi listened astutely while occasionally nodding her head, hands clasped together in her lap, eyes lidded with something I could not read, and her mouth slightly agape. Nandi's parents were both Civil Rights lawyers back in the day, and even after retiring they were still active. Her father was part of the Rodney King defense. By Nandi being the only child, in some way they breathed the fire of revolutionary consciousness in her spirits and every year they still traveled to the Motherland. She was rooted like a tree stump in her history; she wore it like some kind of badge of honor. Once when she told me that her parents were both Black Panthers in the 60s, that told me so much about her as a person, as in her upbringing. I figured that was how the show got its name, the Panther Power Hours. After I finished talking, Nandi leaned back in her seat. "Girl, that sounds like a best seller. Who is this dude? John Dillinger? And you gave him the poonany, too? Did ya'll rob a bank or something?" she teased and her brown eyes sparkled.

I made a face that said, "Hello! I am dead serious!" Her eyes narrowed, taking me in, looking for any sign that I could be joking. She found none.

"Hope!" Nandi said screeching my name the way my mother would have, I imagined, if I had one. "Please tell me that you're lying and just making all this up." I shook my head no, and looked down at the stool, wondering if I should have told her so much.

In walked the handsome brotha that came on late night. He called himself Soul Man. He hosted the show playing all the old tunes. He was also in one of my classes. I think he had a serious crush on Nandi. Whenever she walked into the room, I noticed that his face would beam and he would display that fifty-watt smile. We all exchanged pleasantries, as Nandi and I left, giving him room to set up for his show. We walked to the parking lot and

I showed her the evidence of my betrayal to Marcus, as well as myself. I showed her the car. She whistled as she looked inside as I held the door open for her.

"Well, at least you didn't give him the poonany for free."

"I didn't sell it to him either."

"Oh heffah don't be so touchy."

Looking deeper into the car, Nandi spotted more truth.

"Well," Nandi droned raising one suspicious eyebrow at me. "Tell you what," Nandi said in a conspiratorial tone. "Let's just split the money and throw the gun in the river, and we'll say that you were out trickin." I swung my purse at her. Nandi danced out of the way laughing at me. I guess she must have sensed the serious side of me, because the smile eased from the soft corners of her cheeks and concern moved to her eyes.

"Hope, you're my best friend in the whole world. There can be a thing as an intelligent fool. You read all those books, Nat Turner, Ida B. Wells, Black people that have died and sacrificed their lives, and at times I feel that you take them more seriously than the people that wrote them –"

"You're the one that gave them to me," I interrupted just as a few brothas walked by and got into a black Jeep. Nandi gazed up at the moon as people do when they're contemplating thoughts. I did too. The sky was dotted with stars. The celestial heavens in all its majesty was decorated with a crescent moon, that for some strange reason, looked out of place. It hung sideways with a shit-eating grin at my young naiveness.

"Hope, you are the most passionate person that I know, but you can't literally look at all life the same way, as to what happened to us back in slavery, or the years that we were lynched and hung."

"Why not? You said it yourself. If white folks ain't changed by now, they ain't never going to change."

"See, that's what I'm talking about." Nandi responded. "Hope, what you did was foolish. I know that you were tryin to save the brotha, but damn." Nandi made a face at me that I could not deny. Logic.

"I know," I said finally. My voice trembled. The air suddenly felt crisp and cool on my skin giving me goose bumps.

"The only lawyer you're going to be is a jailhouse lawyer if you keep making bad judgments like that." She threw her arms around me. Lord knows I needed her hug, her support. Her friendship meant the world to me. Somehow I think she knew it. In my eyes Nandi Shakur, morally, was the perfect Black woman. We sat right there under that shit grinning moon and talked until two thirty in the morning. It wasn't until I was older, years later, that I would learn just how precious my college experience, along with Nandi's helpful advice, would be.

At eleven the next day my other roommate, Roberta, woke me. She was my homegirl from Miami. On campus they call her the Mouth of the South. She could talk non-stop for hours with that big-ass gold tooth in her mouth. She often dressed slatternly, to put it mildly, with as little clothes as possible. She was over-weight and short. I don't know what she saw when she looked in the mirror, but it made her feel good about herself. So I guess that is what's important about life.

"I woke you up cause I'm finna go to the flea market and get me some shoes. You wanna go?" she asked knowing damn well how evil I get when I'm awakened from my sleep. I had trouble going back to sleep.

I tossed the covers over my head, and grumbled something about being tired and rolled over on my stomach. I heard the door shut. I lay there in the dark and could not go back to sleep. I thought about my picture being on the news, and heard Nandi's voice, *the only lawyer you're going to be is a jailhouse lawyer.*

The gun flashed in my mind. I sprung up in bed thinking about Life's sly ploy to get with me.

I took a quick shower, got dressed, did my hair, placed the gun and the money in my book bag and drove to his hotel. Today the Tallahassee heat was sweltering. I wore a pink halter top and white shorts. I drove with the windows down trying to save gas. Halfway to the hotel I was hit by the reality of what I was doing. Like a ritual of mating, boy meets girl, I was allured by this thug. He could possibly ruin my future, my life, and deep down inside, I knew that I was attracted to this man and his ravenous lovemaking skills. He was rough, but sensitive in a way that a woman could appreciate, and yet he was a damn thug that wore his pants sagging and referred to me as 'Shouty'. Yet in my mind, I couldn't help comparing him to Marcus who came up short in ways that mattered to a woman at times. Marcus was sweet, that's what I told myself. He treated me like a lady.

*****

I knocked on the hotel door. Finally he answered, wearing only his boxer shorts and his thang pointed right at me. The room reeked of weed and something that could pass for sex. I stormed in, a sista with a serious attitude.

"You're going to get me arrested! Did you see the news? And that was not cute what you did by leaving that gun in the car!" I was talking so fast that my tongue had a hard time trying to keep up with my mouth. Life was not paying me the least bit of attention. He walked over to the rug examining a certain spot in the carpet. I thought I heard him mumble something about that bitch beat me for my stash but by then, I was in his facing ranting about how he tried me. Finally, I dug in my pocket. "I don't need your money either," I said with more contempt than I actually felt. I was just trying to strike a nerve, you know how we sistas can do so well. Life completely ignored me. There was no fight in his eyes. Surprised the hell out of me. He just took the money from my hand and tossed it on the dresser with his shoulders hunched as he padded over to the bed and sat down running his fingers across the waves in his head. "Hope could you please leave now?" There wasn't an iota of fight in his voice. I swallowed the dry lump in my throat that gave birth to my emotions as I heard a fire truck somewhere in the distance. This wasn't what I expected, not from him. I found myself lost for words. For some reason I thought about the singer, Prince, and the song, "When Doves Cry." I wondered if thugs cry, too. I reached into my purse retrieving the two books that I told myself I was going to give him. Nandi gave them to me when I was lost and searching for who I was. One of the books was, *The Destruction of Black Civilization* by Chancellor Williams and the other one was *Black, Single, Absolute and Dangerous,* by M.

"I was hoping you would call the station last night," I said, looking down at him, my voice resonating into a soft cadence that moved me closer to him gnawing at his resistance. No response. His eyes looked away from me, and I swear to God it looked like that brotha was bearing the weight of the world on his shoulders. I thought about what Nandi warned me about, being too passionate. I picked up my dejected emotions and carried them to the door for the first time realizing that I felt something deep for this brotha. I would have at least liked a good-bye kiss or a hug because I knew that I would never be coming back.

"Hope." He called my name. It sounded sad coming from his lips. I turned real slow as the light from the open door beamed in his eyes and he squinted at me. "Thanks for the books Shouty, I'll read them. Um, do you know where Trina lives?" His question caught me off guard. I'll admit, I was tinged with a little jealousy too.

"I heard she lives somewhere near campus." I wanted to ask him what he wanted with Trina of all people. She was poison. Her last boyfriend was doing time in the feds. I just shook my head and walked out of the door as I heard him yell behind me, "Tomorrow I'ma go to the unemployment office."

I walked to my car with a feeling of uneasiness. Maybe it was guilt—there were all kinds of feelings going through my young mind. I mostly wondered what Trina did to him. She must have come back to his room. I thought I heard him mumble something about his stash. He sure did not argue about taking that money back. It was almost as if he needed it. *What a shame that a brotha could be so fine and sexy and be our people's worst enemy,* I thought.

\*\*\*\*\*

As scheduled I drove to the Tallahassee Children's Hospital to meet with Nandi to work with the children. I became attached to a special little girl that I really tried to give my attention to. She was 7 years old and over 90 percent of her body had been severely burned. Her mother, father and three younger brothers all died on Christmas Day due to a fire that started from a electric heater that malfunctioned. The little girl was a mask of gory pain. She had no relatives and already experienced over twenty skin grafts, and was scheduled for dozens more. The first day I met her, she held my hand while I read her stories. When it was time for me to leave she would not let my hand go. The next day, I cried for the world, and for the first time, I questioned my God. Nandi apologized, but she could not go anywhere near that little girl. The horrible sight of her charred body was hard to grasp, even for the nurses. Afterward, it made us feel good helping mostly impoverished Black children that were abandoned and neglected by their families.

*****

The days quickly turned to weeks and with it came the reality that I missed my period, which wasn't unusual because it had been late before; however, on the second week, I sent out a search party lookin' for it. I went to Walgreen's and bought one of them little test kits, you know the ones where you wait for the color to change to see if you are pregnant. School was in full blast. My roommate primped for hours in front of the mirror getting dressed to go to a club called The Moon. It was a hot popular spot where the young folks hung out on the weekends. A rap group called Poison Clan and J.T. Money were performing. I watched as Shanana got dressed hoping that she would hurry up and leave. The anticipation of taking the pregnancy test was burning me up inside. Shanana put on a tiny outfit and high heels. For the life of me I could not understand why some big people tried to wear clothes that they knew were too damn small for them.

"How do I look in this?" Shanana asked, as she paraded in front of me with one of her stomachs protruding over the other. She looked like a Black version of Ms. Piggy. However, Shanana was blessed with a congenial personality, the kind that could wring the last smile from your lips on your worst day. I just shrugged my shoulders, nodding my head as if to say, no comment. Shanana already knew how I felt about her hoochie mama dress code. Determined not to have her jovial spirits dampened, animated as usual she responded, hands on hips, "Big girls need love too," she said flippantly, and at the same time, she turned around and tooted her butt up in the air and strutted out of the door. I couldn't help but laugh at her antics as she bounced away on a mission. As soon as she was gone, I tore into the box of the pregnancy test, my hands trembling badly, my heart racing in my chest. When the test showed the results, I could not believe it. The damn thing said I was pregnant.

I was tempted to go to the store and buy another one, or better yet, go see a doctor and let him charge me to tell me what I already knew. I plunged down in my chair thinking this couldn't possibly be happening to me. Fucking men! Fucking Marcus! I was tempted to call his sorry ass and make him fork over the money for an abortion. "Shit! Shit! Shit!" I exasperated, banging my fists on the table. I was finally about to achieve my dream of entering law school, now my life was ruined. I began to sob uncontrollably. I thought about all the girls that I went to high school with that had got knocked up and were shunned in a way that society does when you're a failure. I used to feel sorry for them and in some strange way, it made me feel proud that I made the right choices and never fell victim to the lures of the streets. When I went home, all my family and friends often referred to me as "Hope, the future lawyer." This reference made me hold my head dignified. For a woman, especially a young Black woman, there can be no other personal devastation than an unwanted pregnancy, for it entails the complete solitude of misery and despair that renders a woman powerless over her own body. The unwanted burden of a life, God's bliss to a woman, is often viewed as some cruel evil curse bestowed upon her.

I had to get a grip on myself. I was a wreck. I got dressed in a daze without combing my hair and I meandered down the hall in a fugue. People stared at me openly, a few called my name, I just kept walking.

At the pay phone, I called Nandi. She answered on the first ring.

"I'm pregnant," I cried into the phone wishing that I would wake up and this would all be some bad dream.

"And I'm Michael Jackson, hee hee," Nandi sang playfully.

"Nandi, I'm fucking serious! I took the test and it came back positive."

"Lawd have mercy! Hope, girl, are you serious?"

I nodded my head on the phone like she could see me. "If I used a rabbit, they would have charged me with cruelty to animals."

"Who's baby is it?"

I could not believe Nandi would have the nerve to ask me such a dumb question.

"Who in the hell do you think it is? It's Mar-cus!" I said his name like it was some virulent disease.

"OK, calm down, calm down. We need to talk, I'm on my –"

"Talk? Talk about what? There's nothing to talk about! I'm getting rid of this bastard!" I screamed on the phone and suddenly looked around and all the girls in the dorm were eavesdropping. I glared at all of them as if I were possessed by demons ready to kick ass and take names later.

"Stay right there, I'm on my way girl. Please think, don't panic. It's not the end of the world," Nandi said with her voice filled with sympathetic overtones that made me want to cry more.

"Have you talked with Marcus yet?" Nandi asked.

"Hell naw!" I cried. "I should cut his little dick off. He did this to me on purpose." I was giving the girls in the hall an earful.

"Don't they all," Nandi responded frankly.

I ran my fingers through my hair trying to regain some semblance of my composure. I reasoned, "I don't want to meet you here, I need to get out and get some air."

We agreed to meet at Subway on Buffow Street.

As I hung up the phone, all eyes were on me. The hall was so quiet you could hear a rat piss on cotton. I walked back to my room on legs that felt like rubber. It was the longest walk of my entire life.

*****

We sat at a table inside Subway next to a window with a view to the streets. Cars passed in the night, occasionally strobbing flashes of light across Nandi's face. For some reason I was famished, and the air conditioner was turned up high enough to turn me into a human icicle. I ordered a steak sandwich with extra cheese and a Coke with a bag of chips. Nandi looked at me like I was crazy. She was a faithful vegetarian. I was too until that day.

It was about a quarter to ten and I could not believe this lady had her two bad-ass kids out this late. They ran around the place recklessly knocking over things in their path, making enough noise to raise the dead. I had a headache and they were getting on my last nerve. I could not believe this white woman would not restrain her kids, but when that little bad boy ran his egg head ass under my table and knocked my drink in my lap, God forgive me, I looked under the table and saw the malice in his blue eyes as he then ran his fire truck over my toes. I snatched his bad ass up from under that table so fast he bumped his head causing the table to rattle. He wailed, crying, as if I were torturing him. Actually, I kind of squeezed his arm too, as I took him over to his mother. "Your boy was under my table," I said jaws clinched tightly.

"She's a girl," the lady said flatly, taking her child and cooed, "Mama's baby got a boo-boo on her head."

That's when I noticed the golf ball sized lump on the child's forehead that must have come from the table. I walked away not wanting to believe I had one of them in my stomach. The other child was somewhat smaller, smarter, the sole witness to what I had done to his older sister. One look at me and the child took off running in the opposite direction, reminding me of a scene from the Little Rascals. I sat back in the booth. Nandi was curled over laughing hysterically at me.

"Did ... you ... did you see the way ..." Nandi laughed so hard she could barely get the words out. " ... that little kid ran away from you like you was the real Boogey Man." Nandi held her sides as she lost her breath in giddy laughter. Regardless of my somber mood I couldn't help but to smile at her hilarity. Finally she stopped laughing, however, the corners of her eyes still held a tinge of humor. She reached over and held my hand in a sympathetic gesture. "You're going to be OK," she assured, then leaned closer and whispered, "An abortion is out of the question."

"Shiiiit!" I lisped indignantly, looking at the white lady with them bad-ass Bebe's

kids running around. It looked like the poor woman lost her mind and got used to it.

"I ain't havin' no damn babies."

"You have a precious life within your womb. Regardless of the circumstances, you were placed on this earth to do God's will. To give life, not take it." I couldn't help it, I began to cry. Nandi had a way with words, making everything sound spiritual. I turned away from her, looked at my reflection in the window and saw facets of my life pass by me.

"At least talk to Marcus. See what the man has to say." Nandi pressed on. "The man wants to marry you, he loves you Hope." Angrily, I wiped the tears away from my face with the back of my hand.

"Stop being so mean. What's done is done, just call the damn man! See what he has to say." The moment lulled into a pregnant pause. Nandi could be so damn persuasive. The girl sounded like my conscience talking to me at times. I agreed to follow her advice.

Nandi planted a seed of determination that seemed to germinate in my mind and she knew it as she gave me a triumphant glare, the kind that a sista gives another sista that is so empowering and caring that you know, no matter what, she is with you one hundred percent. We hugged. "It's the woman that does not believe she can achieve her goals, thus she fails from the start. As long as you believe that you can, you give yourself and the baby positive energy, you'll be fine. If Marcus wants to play papa make his ass come to mama," Nandi said in a conspiratorial tone and winked her eye at me.

The next day Nandi was scheduled to fly to Atlanta to help organize a Million Youth March. That night, I drove to Marcus' apartment and didn't even bother to call. I was in a bad mood, like the fetus inside of me was turning me into the Exorcist, that girl in the movie that was turning her head all backward and puking in people's faces.

Marcus' friend Stan answered the door. I could have sworn the damn man rolled his eyes at me as he walked away without speaking. All of Marcus' buddies were kind of peculiar and anti-social. Of course, all of them attended Florida State, so naturally I figured that was where the friction came from. As I walked in, Marcus and his pals were eating pizza, drinking beer and watching the game. Their glares unnerved me. I could tell Marcus was not happy to see me. For some reason, when he got around his friends he would change just like that. They all came from aristocratic, well off families. They all drove BMWs and nice SUVs. I guess they thought FAMU college was nothing more then a welfare college for impoverished Blacks.

"Marcus, I need to speak to you," I said evenly while trying to keep my temperament in check. Without looking up from the television he waved his hand like I was some annoying fly and mumbled something about wait until half time. I thought I heard one of his buddies snicker at that.

"Marcus, it's important." I raised my voice.

He waved for me to be quiet. Stan glared at me with so much disdain, I was tempted to ask him what his damn problem was. The whole time a sista was trying to be polite but I could feel my hormones raging inside my body like a time bomb.

"Marcus, please!"

"Hope! Can't you see that it's almost two minutes before half-time in the damn game!"

*No he didn't just curse at me*, I thought as red flashed behind my eyes. Stan and the rest of his friends turned as if following his lead; they stared at me like I was an alien invading their territory. I was as close as a Black woman could get to becoming a socio-pathic bitch. Here I was, pregnant, with this man's child and don't want the bastard, and he is treating me like I am gum stuck on the bottom of his shoe. If he only knew I was thinking about killing his child, and possibly his ass too. Calmly, I strolled over to the tel-evision, snatched the plug out of the wall so hard that it sent sparks flying. Walked over to the door, flung it open with all my might, and one of the pictures on the wall came crashing down. The scowl on my face was carved like granite stone. My nostrils flared, eyes bugged, as I screamed at the top of my lungs, "All ya'll, get the fuck out!"

Marcus stood up with a beer in his hand, eyebrows knotted together in dismay.

"Hope! What's wrong with you girl?"

"Boy, I told you I need to talk to you. When you get around your damn friends you want to get all brand new and don't want to give me no respect!" I turned to one of his friends, eyes blazing with fury. "I told ya'll asses to get out!" I said belligerently. They all looked at Marcus. He slumped his shoulders. "Yo, fellas, let me holler at her." They grunted and shot me a few cold looks, but reluctantly they gathered their things and left. As Stan walked by he gave me a mean and evil look. A look that I would see again and it would cause my whole world to come crashing down around me.

One by one they left as I stood at the door. Outside, I heard Stan say just loud enough for me to hear, "You can take a nigga out the ghetto, but you can't take the ghetto out the nigga."

"Stan, kiss my ghetto ass!" I yelled and slammed the door.

"Girl what the hell is wrong with you coming in here actin' like you done lost your damn mind?" Marcus said hotly.

I stalked over to him, more than willing to engage his ass in battle. I was not myself and we both knew it. I was over the edge.

"Marcus, I'm pregnant." I threw the words at him like they were some evil curse. He considered me for a moment, eyes narrowed like his brain was trying to decipher what I just said. I could not read his stoic expression, but I will never forget it. I saw infusions of something in his eyes, like a boy not really sure of his manhood. I watched his demeanor because a woman needs the complete support of a man, not a boy unsure of himself. Then he grinned at me and that grin said I had fallen victim to his game. I wanted to slap that silly grin off his face. He smiled and had the nerve to try to hug me.

"Hope, we're having a bay-bee," he lullabied happily. I shoved him away from me.

"We ain't having shit!" I snorted.

I saw something wash over his face, something between hurt and dejection. Marcus got down on one knee. "Hope, please don't kill my baby ... our baby," he said somberly as he wrapped his arms around me pressing his face tightly against my stomach. I tried to peel him off of me but he clung to me for dear life. He dug into my resistance with his poignant pleading, "Hope, please don't kill the baby. I'll take care of it and support you while you go to law school. I have enough money saved up for a home, at least a nice down payment, plus I have nine acres of land."

"You do?" I asked dumbfounded as my mind changed lanes on a highway of life's young indecisions fueled by a new impetus to survive, the life that I now bore within me and a woman's intuitive instincts for her baby.

"Hope! Please! Please! Marry me," Marcus said sentimentally. It's amazing all the damage a penis full of semen can do. OK, I can't lie, Marcus' financial status along with an unexpected baby played a big factor in my decision to marry him.

*****

A month later, using Marcus' family's money, I had a big African-style wedding. Nandi designed all the clothes. My sorority sisters, the Deltas, were my bridesmaids. We had a ball. Even though none of Marcus' family came except his querulous-ass mother, she could have stayed home. It seemed like nothing I did was right for her and the old bat made no secret about her contempt for me. And to make matters worse, my father arrived with his young girlfriend. He was dead drunk and embarrassed the hell out of me. However, for the first time in my young life, I had some semblance of happiness. About eight months later I gave birth to a healthy six-pound baby boy. It was the most painful experience of my entire life. It felt like I had shitted out a bowling ball. It was Nandi's dumb-ass idea to have a natural birth. Hello! Girlfriend might be taking this Afrocentric thing too damned far.

Lawd have mercy, when the nurse pulled the covers back showing my son, Marcus Jr., I damn near fainted. The baby was dark as coal with a head full of hair, with them little beady eyes just like his father. I was going to have a lot of explaining to do. I had just given birth to another man's child. There was no doubt in my mind who the real father was. The thug, Life Thugstin, was a father and didn't even know it. The next time I would hear of him would be in a crowded courtroom where I would be a prosecutor and he would be on trial fighting for his life.

*****

# Chapter Seven

## "All in the Name of the Game"

### *— Life —*

Nightfall. I crept into Frenchtown on a real mission to find Nina Brown. I needed to talk to her. If she knew where Trina was I was going to force her to tell me.

I wore dark blue Dickies with a matching shirt and black Timberland boots. I had my best friend, Jesus, tucked safely in the small of my back.

Strategically, I entered from a back street not wanting to risk detection. The streets were clogged with traffic. I heard a gun shot up ahead. I stood in the shadow and watched. This place was like the Wild Wild West. A fight or something broke out up ahead in the pool hall. That's when I spotted Nina Brown. She had on the same clothes. I walked right up to her and tried to blend in with all the commotion. I made a crucial mistake. Hustlers always recognized new faces. That's part of their business. Nina Brown looked up at me horrified.

"Boy, what you doin' huh? You crazy, that's lil Stevey D over there. They been lookin' all over for you. They just jumped on a boy from Miami, damn near kilt him, took his dope and his car." As on second thought, she squinted at me, pulled my shirt.

"You shot that boy so many times, almost kilt him too, and where is my dope you promised me nigga?"

"I gottcha." I handed her the hundred-dollar bill I had for her.

"Where is Trina at?" I asked.

Nina Brown was not paying me the least bit of attention, as nervously she looked up the street to a money green Chevy doing the smooth creep in our direction. She danced her eyebrows, a warning. Four or five dudes were headed our way and they walked with a purpose. They had my full attention. Nina whispered that it was Stevey D and his henchmen. When I saw the little runt with them I knew that I was busted. "That's him," she said pointing at me, just as niggas in the Chevy piled out four deep. One thing I can say about Nina Brown, she stood her ground. I noticed one of the cats that got out of the Chevy ducked down. I couldn't see where he was, shit was happening so fast, my mind raced to keep up.

"Watch the Chevy to your right, watch the four men going up on you to your left." Quickly, I decided Stevey D was not the real threat. I needed to keep my eye on the possible shooter hiding behind the car.

"Nigga you jacked my man," Stevey D said pulling out his strap at exactly the same time I pulled out Jesus, cocked it and carefully aimed it at his chest. Shock registered in his face, I saw it in his eyes. I walked out into the streets in order to see where the shooter was. I saw him squatting down with a gun in his hand. When he saw me he stood. The other three cats were gingerly walking toward me.

"Yo, my nigga. I ain't jack nobody! That chicken head bitch lying," I said looking back and forth.

One thing about power, whether it be the United States Army or an army of thugs embattled in urban warfare, power will only acknowledge counter power, and thus, gangsters are born. I positioned myself between two cars, gun still level at Stevey D, and prepared for a blood bath. Kill or be killed. This had all the ingredients for murder and I honestly had no intention of dying alone. I was out-numbered about nine to one.

"Nigga you got a lot of balls coming in here. You could get fucked up. Lose your life," Stevey D threatened.

"Look playa, I ain't lookin for no drama," I said respectfully, but my body language made it perfectly clear I was prepared to throw some hot balls with Jesus.

"Want me to shoot dat nigga?" I heard someone say with courage that they did not feel, or else they would have shot without asking permission.

"Naw," Stevey D said, raising his hand as they inched closer trying to surround me. Shit was starting to get out of hand like I was going to have to fire a shot.

"Look man, lemme talk wit you," Stevey D said, inching closer.

"I ain't tryin to rap right now," I said easing backward. Them niggas wanted to pounce on me like a pack of wolves.

"Yo, your name Stevey D?" I asked, trying to keep the fear out my voice. He did not answer. "I'ma break bread witcha."

My voice was a plea bargin that hung in the air, as the seconds of my life tucked in the crevice of my mind. Any moment I was expecting shots to ring out.

"In a few days I'ma come back and give you something to make money off of," I said, as I eased into the streets, my gun still leveled at his chest. A car came screeching to a halt nearly missing me. Nina Brown watched me intensely, eyes glazed with suspense. Ghetto chicks see this kind of stuff all their lives, gunplay, killed or be killed. I was just trying to stay alive the only way I knew how, keeping it gangsta!

I continued to walk backward, gun pointed at Stevey D. The silent message was if I was going to die, I fully intended to take someone with me. Once I felt that I was at a safe distance, I took off into a trot. They did not pursue me, and if they did, I took so many shortcuts and back ways they would have needed bloodhounds to keep up with me.

*****

The next morning I sat by the pool in one of them uncomfortable-ass chairs, smoking a cigarette, thinking about Trina touching me for my stash and what I was going to do with her ass if I ever caught her. The whole time I was watching white folks like a hungry lion trying to get close to his prey. I was just trying to pick one to rob. I was on my dick doing bad. After paying two hundred for rent, and giving Nina Brown the hundred-dollar bill, I had less than two hundred dollars to my name.

I took a sip of the beer that I bought earlier at the poolside bar. It was hot, the sun was sweltering. I had my T-shirt wrapped around my head. I looked up into the blaring sunlight to see two gorgeous sistas strolling poolside headed straight for me. I thought I was seeing a mirage. One was wearing a leopard skin two-piece thong bathing suit. Her body was sleek, wide hips, nice ass, pointed breasts, full with erect nipples, the kind that make men dribble.

I was sitting straight up in my seat now. Her friend was just as fine. She wore a stunning white french cut one-piece bathing suit. It showed everything including her coochie lips and they were fat to death, and I stared wondering if all that was her down there. The symmetry of her body was God's gift to a Black woman. Together the two women seemed to put on a show as the entire pool quieted. The one with the leopard skin suit looked just like Lisa Raye, sophisticated and sexy. I noticed that they were holding hands, then it dawned on me that they might be lovers, a lesbian couple, as they sashayed right up to me. This was the one moment in my life I was happy to be a Black man. The one with the leopard skin suit asked if they could sit next to me in the vacant chair. I looked up into the glaring sun between her legs; the gap in between her thighs caused an eclipse of the sun, all that hair running down her thighs. Thank God for lesbians! To this day I do not know why women shave down there. If Black women only knew how sexy it looked to brothas.

"Does a bear shit in the woods? Hell yeah ya'll can sit down," I said playfully. They giggled and took the seats next to me. I was instantly intoxicated by their sweet perfume. There's something that intrigues the hell out of men to imagine two beautiful women fucking, especially these two chicks. I was feeling aroused just by their nearness and the scent of their perfume mingled with the air. We were the only Black people at the pool. I watched as little kids ran wild playing and occasionally splashing us with water. The adults lingered at the poolside covered with oil; white folks trying to get Black, torturing themselves for a suntan. I just ogled the two women like eye candy as they chatted and then turned to me.

"My name is Tomica, this is Evette," the one with the leopard skin suit said.

"I'm Leonard," I said dryly. Lust had me lockjawed so bad I could hardly lie with a straight face as I made up the fake name. I was feining on both these chicks.

The waiter came around and I offered to buy them drinks. Drinks that I really could not afford. Of course, being sistas they ordered the most expensive drinks. By dawn, I was drunk, and dead ass broke. For the past few hours the women had been acting real freaky. It was tormenting me to watch them feel on each other and occasionally kiss. My dick was hard as the concrete stairs of the swimming pool. Somehow watching them was like viewing an exotic X rated movie, only they were not naked, yet. At least that was what I was hoping.

Somehow, even in my semi-drunken stupor, I managed to keep my wits. I knew that good liquor makes for loose lips, but I had to spin my web in order for me to kick my game. I kept on talking, and they enjoyed my spiel rewarding me with laughter. The good thing about being a preacher's son is, if needed, I could drop the street lingo and talk intelligent. I learned that in private school and in Sunday School also. I gave them some lame-ass story about how I was a Florida State student that flunked out of school. They ate it up. For some reason it got quiet and for the first time, I ran out of words. They began to whisper. I heard Evette say, "Ask him." Tomica gave me the once over like she really was not sure of what she wanted to say, or just how to say it, a look that said if she could peek inside my soul to see could I be trusted, she would. I just acted nonchalant to their whispers. A lone pigeon landed on the walkway a few feet away from us. It was dark outside except for the pool lights. The bird scurried around either lost or late as hell, trying to get home. Somehow I could relate to him. He ambled over to a folding chair and watched us.

"Leonard ... Leonard!" Tomica called to me. My mind was elsewhere. I turned to her. She watched me intently before she spoke, "Evette and I have a proposition for you."

I leaned forward, craning my neck, damn near falling out of the chair. Evette erupted in laughter. Tomica just made a face that said she thought I was stupid.

"Proposition?" I repeated scratching my head. They were watching me like hawks. My mind was full speed ahead, two beautiful women and a proposition? I placed both of my hands on my lap to hide my thoughts. Not to mention, that hairy-ass bulge between Tomica's legs was driving me crazy. Lesbianism is about as erogenous as sex can get to a man's mind. Like a feminine utopia.

"Follow us to our room," Tomica said, with eyes lidded with a promise of sweetness. She stood turning her back to me. Her thong was missing somewhere in the mounds of her butt cheeks. As she helped Evette up, I watched her ass dance for me. How much torture can one man take by a twosome of scantly dressed lesbians in heat? I could see Evette through the gap between Tomica's legs. She was watching me closely.

I played it off, acted naïve. Evette ate it up. I didn't know what these two females had in store for me, but the excitement was mounting, like reading a good suspense novel.

The pigeon watched. The waiter, turned janitor, swept the deck of the swimming pool within inches of him. The women were whispering in conspiratorial tones as they walked into the lobby. I followed, enjoying the view from the back. For the first time I noticed the tiny mole on Tomica's butt as she wrapped a towel around her waist. Up ahead at the elevator door, a family of white people were watching us as we approached. They looked like the Brady Bunch on vacation. I could tell they were not used to being around Black folks. Tomica and Evette were still talking in low tones. I whistled absent-mindedly as I looked around like I was fascinated with the décor of the hotel lobby. I was just trying to blend in and not establish eye contact with the white folks that were gawking at me. I was conscious that I was not wearing a shirt, it was wrapped around my head. I was drunk and horny. A little white girl was staring at me. She was no more than 12 years old. She was looking right at my crotch. I had an erection somewhere close to my knee.

The elevator door dinged open. We entered. The little girl was still leering at me. Tomica and Evette positioned themselves on both sides of the pudgy looking white man. He had rosy cheeks with a pleasant cherub face, with thinning hair on his shiny dome with a few strings of graying hair combed over the front, the way men do when they're going bald and refuse to let it go. Just as the elevator door slowed to a stop, Evette turned and flung her arms around the white man, kissing and jabbering lunatically.

"Thank ya sir! Thank ya sir! Thank ya sir for freeing the slaves." *Kiss, kiss* ...

I watched in shock, mouth agape, but the old white dude looked to me like he might have been enjoying himself. His wife was furious as the rest of his family just looked on bemused, except for the little girl that had been watching me. She placed her hand over her face and giggled. Tomica wrestled Evette off the man and rushed out of the door as soon as they opened. Shoving Evette, she stopped and gestured with her hand, pointing her finger at her head indicating that Evette was crazy. "Excuse her sir, she's on medication." The white man just blushed like it wasn't every day he was mauled by a beautiful sista.

Even if that had not been my stop when that door opened, I was fully intent on getting off that elevator; them two broads were acting strange.

I entered their large plush hotel room. It looked like a large warehouse, it was stocked full of everything. You name it, they had it. Everything from fur coats to twenty-two inch rims. Wide screen televisions and clothes, clothes, clothes were everywhere from wall to wall. I looked around in awe trying to figure out how two women could have so much shit. Then it dawned on me, they were boosters. Professional thieves. It wasn't uncommon in the hood for women to hustle to earn a good living off of stealing clothes and things.

Evette removed a wallet from underneath the towel she was wearing. It became clear that these broads were clever, a lot cleverer than I thought. While Evette acted as the decoy, Tomica relieved the mark of his wallet. I feigned like I did not know what was going on.

Tomica counted out money. I folded my arms across my chest. The room was cold. They had the air conditioner turned up sky high. Evette must have sensed my discomfort because she walked over to the air conditioner and turned it down.

"Chang! Chang!" Tomica said jovially, holding a fist full of bills in her hand. "Seven hundred dollars, from a fat square." The women exchanged high fives and kissed lightly on the lips. Tomica winked slyly at Evette. She thought I did not notice.

"Go fix our nice friend here a drink," Tomica said to Evette. The plot was about to thicken, I could tell by the way the two looked at each other they were up to something devious.

I remarked dumbly, "Ya'll sure like to do a lot of shopping." I made my words slur like I was drunk. Evette rolled her eyes as she moved toward me gracefully, wide hips swaying. She walked like maybe she could have been a model at one time. As she passed me the drink she never took her eyes off me.

"Have a seat."

I looked around and shrugged my shoulders. There was no place for me to sit, and I couldn't even find a spot on the floor. The place was packed with merchandise. My mind was now calculating numbers, figures in my head. I watched as Evette took the clothes off the love seat. Surreptitiously, I peered down her bathing suit at her breasts. They looked firm like she had never given birth. I wondered how old she was. Twenty-five at best, I figured. Evette was the silent one, but her voluptuous body spoke a language, the kind that communicated with a man in ways that her mouth would never be able to. Some women were like that. Bodies that exuded more than charm, they asked questions, but only if a man took the time to listen to the signs.

My mind wondered again, *how could two women possibly get off on bumping and grinding pussies on each other?* In a way I felt somewhat agitated by it, like a man couldn't satisfy them. Hopefully I would be able to change all that.

Undulating, Evette sauntered by. I bit down on my lower lip as I touched myself. Lord these women were killing me softly.

There's an alluring scent that women omit that no man can accurately describe, I'll just say that it is sweet like nectar. The room seemed to permeate of it, making it hard for me to keep my composure. Inside my body, I felt wild and untamed, lewd thoughts rushed my brain.

From across the room I watched as Tomica meticulously went through the wallet as if she were looking for something in particular.

"Is everything there?" Evette asked.

"Yep," Tomica responded, the scowl on her pretty face tense with concentration.

In the mark's wallet was a Visa, MasterCard and various other credit cards and IDs. The items were neatly placed on the bed. As they worked, I watched wondering what the hell they were doing. Occasionally I would pour my drink into the carpet, fake like I was sipping something.

Poised, Tomica held the phone, sighed, took a deep breath and for the first time I noticed a large diamond ring on her pinky finger as it sparkled. Her fingernails were long and manicured. From just holding the phone she looked like one of them classy broads.

"You ready?" Tomica asked Evette. Evette nodded her head up and down, her expression intense like she was giving Tomica her undivided attention. Tomica dialed the number on the back of the Visa. I sat up in my seat trying to peek game. I could sense something was going on, but what?

"Hello! My name is Mrs. Luwinzky. My husband and I have

been robbed of all our cash and credit cards." Tomica sounded just like a distraught white woman, panicky voice and all on the verge of hysteria. I looked on, astonished as these sistas put down their hustle.

"Oooh, thank you! Thank you!" Tomica lamented dramatically.

"You can refund us with cash, and replacement credit cards? You want my husband's social security number?" Tomica said loud, as she pointed at the items on the bed. Desperately the two women went scrambling looking for the information. It was a sight to behold. They found it. Tomica recited it like she had been doing it all her natural life. This went on for a minute as the two worked in sync with each other. Finally, Tomica flashed the thumbs up sign as she smiled brightly. Shit, I took a sip from my drink, and watched as these two gorgeous women perfected their scheme.

"Yes, we're going to need ten thousand in travelers checks and a new ATM account number so that we can withdraw money," she added. As Tomica talked, Evette jotted down the information. I thought to myself, with a feeling of inferiority, here I was risking death running around robbing niggas and selling dope and these women were getting paid in full like pimpstresses from the plush confines of a hotel room.

They did the same thing with the other credit cards, this time more practiced like a well-rehearsed script. I felt like a lame for real now. Never sleep on the conniving intelligence of a Black woman. They entered the hustling arena and changed the game. In my mind I was doing figures trying to count their money. The numbers were large.

Once they were finished, their room became electrified with their hyperactive energy, laughter and giddy playfulness.

Tomica pranced right up to me, her silky black hair cascading down her ebony brown thighs. She placed her hand on her hip, her body shifting a gear, coochie in my face, and looking down at me, she said as a matter of factly, "Evette and I met in the joint."

I could tell she waited for a surprise that never came from my expression, and then it occurred to me that I was supposed to be playing dumb, so I dropped my face into a no shit scowl. Evette erupted in laughter. Tomica just continued to look at me as if I was a peasant and was about to give me a command. "She's from California, I'm from the South Bronx." The moment stilled as she considered her next statement carefully.

"Like we were saying earlier, we have a proposition for ya." *Now we're finally getting somewhere,* I thought. The liquor kept telling me to reach out and grab that fat pussy, so I did, well, kind of. I reached out boldly and caressed those silky black hairs between her thighs like it was a kitten. Halfway expecting her to purr for me, she just stood stoically still, giving me a look that said, *look at this lame.* She casually turned her head and looked at Evette. They exchanged a kind of communication that I would never know.

"You ever been with two women before?" Tomica's voice was that of a temptress, sultry like she could set me on fire with her breath. So much lust. Her tongue slowly licked at the rim of her top lip. I could hardly control myself. My hand eased up her thigh. She moaned softly and inhaled deeply like she just stepped into some cold water. My finger roamed, like an escaped convict from an asylum, until I found the soft moist opening of her pussy lips. Evette peeked our move and disrobed down to bare nudity. Hell, if I were a woman I would have been attracted to her, too. Her body was audaciously voluptuous; small waist and full breasts and free of blemishes. The beauty of them both seemed to radiate throughout the room. The small bush between her legs was manicured into a heart like an exclamation mark flaunting her beauty.

"If oh … you … you …" Tomica stammered, as I moved my fingers around inside of her, stirring her juices as cum dripped and coated my fingers.

"… we … we … we'll pay you $500 … damn that feels …" she still couldn't gain her composure.

With my free hand, I unzipped my pants, took out my dick

and stroked it like it was my most prized possession. I began to ease Tomica's bathing suit off, inch by inch, like it was the most delicate fabric in the world. I was getting ready to do some serious fucking.

*Click! Click!* Out of nowhere, Tomica came up with a pair of handcuffs, handcuffing my wrists to the wooden arm on the love seat. My stupor brought on by the alcohol made my reaction too slow, I was more drunk than I thought.

Pixilated, Tomica grinned at me as she walked backward. The rabbit had out-smarted the fox.

"Sorry, we don't do threesomes honey, besides you could stretch a girl outta place wit dat big ole dick." Together they laughed. Their cackle sounded like taunting to me. I was pissed!

"You are in for a surprise though," Evette chimed in. Her voice was hoarse; it ringed with feminine mischief. I made a futile attempt to get out of the handcuffs.

"What the fuck is dis?" I screeched. My words fell on deaf ears as I watched the two of them walk up to each other and embraced, kissing passionately like they were sharing oxygen to save each other's life. They got into the bed. Tomica positioned her head between Evette's legs. She licked pussy like she was giving me a lesson in vaginal stimulation. If I was jealous before, I was now irate. Evette was moaning and groaning like Tomica knew a trick or two with her tongue. I hate to admit this but it's true. Women know how to please each other orally better than a man could ever know. They went at it feverishly. I looked on, listening to all their moans and sighs of fervored lovemaking. There was something so erotic and sensuous about watching two women getting it on, as if they were in a zone no man could enter. Together, their bodies entangled, gleamed with a light sheen of perspiration like they were bathing in honey. I had to admire Tomica's technique as she skillfully made love to Evette's body like it was an art that was practiced by few.

After they finished, I glowered at both of them the way a man does when he has been deprived of one of life's greatest gifts—to be with two women. I decided right then, since they wanted to play a nigga like a sucker, I was going to go along with their game, and when the time was right, I was going to get that ass, introduce them bitches to Jesus, and take all their shit. Might even take a piece of ass for trying a nigga. Like a thug determined to make show of my manhood in front of women, I began to stroke myself. They watched in silence, eyes lidded with curiosity at my cameo intrusion on their freak show. Like an actor, I just stole the show. I masturbated long and hard like my hand was the most intimate creation in the universe, and they watched, fascinated. I did not know that women got off on that kind of shit, especially lesbians. I guess regardless of a woman's sexual preference, in some ways they still bonded to the laws of nature because they enjoyed seeing a well-endowed brotha's stiff penis. Evette just stared, bug eyed, licking her lips with an intent I knew all too well. Tomica snapped out of the trance that sexually forbade her to go there, and cut her eyes at Evette. Innocently, I continued to stroke myself, now enjoying each moment of it … up and down … faster … faster. There's a convulsive reaction that no man can resist when he reaches that point. The handcuff on my wrist began to rattle a rhythm that chimed as my top lip curled into a real snarl, and then I exploded in gushes of three jet streams across the room. Evette clapped and applauded excitedly like a little girl who had just witnessed her first magic act. I reclined back in the love seat still holding my erect penis like it was a dangerous weapon.

"Gosh, have you measured that thang?" Evette asked sheepishly.

"Twelve and a half inches," I lied as I wiped the sweat off. Tomica gave me a look that did not favor me. Like maybe I was overstepping my boundaries. She couldn't help but notice that Evette was attracted to me. I forced myself to calm down, but shit, these broads were looking like super models. I was drunk and trying to keep the thug desperation off my wary face.

"Stop it! Stop it!" Tomica yelled. She was on her feet, her breasts bounced as she stalked toward me. In the drunken fog of my mind I saw wide hips swaying, a gap between her legs and hair that reminded me of a small kitten.

"Put that thang up now!" she screeched. Her voice a brusque command. I placed my joint back into my pants not trusting my eyes to look up at her, for she would see the brutal reality of my soul. I had no love for hoes. I couldn't risk losing my element of surprise. For some reason Tomica continued to stare down at me, like maybe she was surprised that I would pull out a big ole dick and choke my chicken. Hell, I spent years in prison jacking off on fuck books and for me it was an honor to have two bitches to watch. I reached out to touch her, actually, I tried to grab her. With feline quickness she scratched the back of my hand drawing blood. Somehow it only seemed to excite me more.

"Evette put on some clothes," Tomica said over her shoulder giving me a look that said I had fucked up bad.

Evette walked to the other side of the room and put on a black and gold smock. I could still see the outline of her figure. Tomica put on a nightgown and drew the strings like she was forever concealing her body from me. I looked down at my lap at my penis—it had fainted in my pants. I had two gorgeous women in a hotel room and couldn't have sex with either one of them.

As Tomica unlocked my handcuffs, I fought with all my might to bridle my anger. This playing the role of a lame shit was starting to take its toll.

I rubbed my sore wrist as Tomica talked. She explained to me that they had to leave in a hurry to go clean out the ATM and take care of other matters. She detailed a plan about a jewelry store caper where all I had to do was walk into the store, holler at the top of my lungs and fall to the ground, like I was having a seizure. It sounded pretty easy to me. So I just played dumb, I shrugged my shoulders dancing my eyebrows with an idiot's smile and replied, "Okey-dokey," in my best lame voice. For the first time Tomica laughed at me, and I knew it was more of a relief that she found the perfect fool to pull off the heist.

Evette lay in bed on the satin sheets looking at me with her long legs crossed. I just stared at the carpeting, at the stain where I poured my drink, and fought with every fiber in my body to keep my composure, act like a square and play the lame game. Around this time tomorrow, the tables would turn. My plan was to rob them bitches, and maybe even out of spite, handcuff them together and grudge fuck Tomica in the ass for trying to be the man.

"What size clothes and shoes you wear?" Tomica asked, disturbing my daydream. I gave her my measurements without ever asking any questions. Afterward, Tomica walked me to the door. It hurt me to my heart to have to walk out that door not getting what I had come for. I took one last sniff of their feminine scent, and feeling like a rejected whore, I moped past her, only this time I was not faking it. I was humiliated.

I staggered back to my room, lay in my bed fully clothed, drunk and frustrated still smelling the sexual aroma of those two women's perfume emanating out of my pores. Their erotic performance still heavily on my mind. I felt my pistol, Jesus, under my pillow and smiled to myself promising that tomorrow would be my day, tomorrow the lame would turn pimp. I had a trick for them bitches and as soon as we pulled off the heist, it was on.

Puzzled, I lay in bed in the dark intrigued by the women. They pulled off the credit card scheme with ease. Then Trina's face flashed on the screen of my mind like lightning causing me to flinch uncontrollably with anger. In my mind again, I swore if I ever saw her again I was going to kill her. What I didn't know was that we were going to meet again, soon.

*****

The next day at 2:34 in the afternoon, I was startled from my sleep. Someone was pounding on the door. Hastily I grabbed my gun from under the pillow and walked over to the door looking out the peephole. To my relief it was Tomica and Evette. Tomica was beating on the door with her shoe. I had a slight hangover. To my brain it sounded like a little man was hammering on my skull with a sledge hammer. My tongue felt like sand paper, my throat was dry, I was so thirsty I needed something cold to drink. For a fleeting second I thought about opening the door putting my pistol to Tomica's temple for making all the goddamn noise on my door. Black women can be so ignorant.

I took a deep breath, opened the door, showed them my lame face, blood cracked eyes from my hangover and all. The women stalked right past me, shopping bags in tow. I shut the door, went to the bathroom, pissed like a race rose, drank water from the faucet like I had been out in the desert for weeks. Looking in the mirror I splashed water on my face and washed the dried saliva off my cheeks. I could hear their chatter in the next room. I walked in just as they were placing clothes on the bed–men's clothes. A black suit with a gray tie. Shoes, socks, shirts, even underwear for me. I had to do a second take at them. Both women were decked out, dressed to kill. Tomica wore a sophisticated, conservative brown two-piece suit with black stockings and low-heeled black pumps. Her hair was stylishly coiffured into long locks of dazzling curls that seemed to enhance her lovely face. She looked like she was ready for another day at the office on Wall Street. Evette, the more feminine of the two, wore a short mini dress showing off her long legs and nice figure. Her heart-shaped blouse exposed even more cleavage with its wide neckline and low cut, hanging off her shoulders. She wore her long hair straight and untamed like a white girl letting it cascade down her shoulders. Her face was rough with what I thought was too much makeup but some men would find it attractive in a way. Her thin Chanel gold eyeglasses set her off into that new cultured elegant beauty that was becoming vogue at the time. She carried a mystic that could make you fantasize.

OK, I'll admit, these two women so far had amazed the hell out of me. I had not seen one flaw in their game. I was in the minor league, they gave me a glimpse of the pros.

Finally I was dressed. Eight hundred dollar suit, three hundred dollar kicks, Armani shirt, gold cufflinks, the whole nine yards. One thing I can say, these women knew all the expensive clothes to steal. They dressed me sharp as a tack in the finest threads. I couldn't help but admire myself in the mirror. In the corner of my eye I could see Evette watching me, too. On my way out the door Evette passed me a leather briefcase and winked her eye.

In the car, Tomica was talking me to death, going over each and every detail of what I was supposed to do once I entered the jewelry store. She talked so damned fast. With her brow-furrowed eyes, she penetrated deep concerns of something at first I could not read, and then it dawned on me, I had seen and felt it many times before: fear. The fear of the unknown, riveting with courage, in the duel of a no compromising mind, when it was decided that there was no turning back. Even though I threw bricks at the chain gang and robbed niggas like it was a sport, I realized from looking at Tomica's face, in a sense their hustle was no different than mine. They relied only on sheer wit and cunning savvy but we shared that one common bond–the fear of getting caught.

Finally we road in silence. R. Kelly crooned something about his mother on the radio, how she was his favorite girl. As I drove, I made a mental note to call my stepmother. I glanced in the rearview mirror. Evette stared at me with eyes hooded, it was something that I would never be able to read. I told myself that after I robbed them I was going to do something special with her, some freaky shit.

The jewelry store was located in the hub of Tallahassee on Tennessee Street in a shopping mall. It was Saturday and the place was packed. Its pristine décor looked somewhat out of place. Maybe it was how white people were able to dress up places that cater mostly to the rich.

As I pushed on the revolving doors I couldn't help but admire my reflection in the glass. As soon as I walked inside my heart skipped a beat. I don't know what it is about white folk's establishments that are so intimidating. It wasn't just that, I realized that I did not have a clue as to what these women were going to do. How were they going to pull off such a heist in a classy joint like this? This was out of my league. Playing the lame game had me in the blind; however, I understood that they wanted me to know as little as possible in the event I got caught and turned snitch.

Shopping music played from the speakers as shoppers lazily browsed. With hands in my pockets, I causally tried my damnest to blend in. I checked out the palatial splendor of the joint. It was a very expensive place. Now I could see why they had me dress up for the occasion. The diamonds in the showcase windows looked unreal. So much ice, I could not believe my eyes. Every now and then my eyes would dart to the door waiting for the women to make their entrance.

"May I help you?" a genial voice asked.

I did not want to look up. Out of all these people in the store, she had to ask me. Of course, I was the only Black person. I adjusted my tie and smiled brightly.

"No thank you. I'm just looking," I said awkwardly to the white woman.

She opened her mouth to speak, but thought better of it. After she left, I exhaled deeply, adjusting my tie again, it was starting to become habit forming. I walked to the end of the counter, positioning myself so I could see the door when Tomica and Evette entered. I pretended to be interested in a pair of sunglasses. I tried them on looking into one of them small mirrors that they have on the eyeglass rack. That's when I saw him, like eyes in the back of my head. I saw the huge white man watching my every step. He had to be the store security, probably an off duty cop. I wasn't sure but I had a gut feeling. I wondered if should I warn the girls when they came in. I moved on just as Tomica and Evette came in the store. My heart raced in my chest. Should I tell them about the cop? Hell, I had no idea what they were going to do.

They wasted no time, walked right up to the clerk pointing at something they wanted in the case. I looked over my shoulder at the cop. He was still there watching me like I had already stolen something. Shit! From across the store I turned my head just in time to see Tomica give me the signal just as the clerk was passing a diamond bracelet to Evette as if it were a royal gift to a princess. Even from across the room, I could see the diamonds shimmering like celestial stars captured in a delicate hand.

"Thirty thousand dollars," the clerk mouthed.

Somewhat delayed, I went into my animated act.

"Help! Help! Oh god! Someone help me!" I yelled going down on my knees clasping my chest like I was having a massive heart attack. People rushed over to me including a few store clerks. The clerk that was attending Tomica and Evette turned her head for one split second, and that was all it took for Evette to make the switch. I dropped my briefcase to the floor in an overly dramatic fashion and keeled over.

In a frenzy, white folks were all over me. In the meantime, Evette handed the lady the fake bracelet and they walked over to me as if concerned, only they walked right out of the door. The clerk placed the fake bracelet in the display case and hurried over to me and placed her hand over her thin lips as she looked down at me sprawled on the floor in pain.

"Call an ambulance!" someone shirks.

"Are you OK?" a white woman asked, bending down, embracing me. She had the bluest eyes I had ever seen. She had blond hair, and her lips were glossed in a way that made them appear sensuous. Her forehead was creased with lines of concern. Her perfume engulfed me, fumigating my nostrils. She loosened my tie opening my shirt.

"Oh, no," I moaned pathetically. Now the entire store gathered to gawk at me. I figured about five minutes had passed of my impromptu performance. I got off the floor to the hushed drones of disbelievers as they looked at me in awe, like a dead man walking. Someone tried to grab my arm, told me I ought to try to wait until the ambulance arrived. The white lady that was trying to resuscitate me affectionately touched my arm and told me to wait for the ambulance. I thanked her and picked up my briefcase and squeezed through the throngs of shoppers that had gathered with the number thirty thousand in my mind. I smirked as I rushed through the revolving doors walking out into the scorching summer heat. The car was parked up ahead. As I walked, my mind plotted on how I was going to beat them bitches out of their riches.

Up the street, I saw them standing next to the car with its doors wide open. Something was wrong, terribly wrong. My pace slowed. As I neared, I could see Tomica's face. Her eyes tried to warn me. That's when I noticed what was wrong. Tomica and Evette's hands were in the air. It was then that I recognized the undercover cop from the store. He had his gun pointed at them with one hand, and in the other, he held the stolen bracelet. My heart somersaulted in my chest as my breathing quickened. Without thinking, I reacted like a man does in war, or a lesson taught in the ghetto, the survival instinct kicked in. Raw energy seized my body. Nothing else mattered, nothing else existed. This was the concrete jungle. In it, life was a conquest of kill or be killed. If gunplay could have earned me a medal, I would have won its highest honor. In one quick motion, I reached into my back pulling out my gun, placing it against the cop's skull. In the distance I heard screams as people scurried about.

"Move, muthafucka, and I'll blow your goddamn brains out!" In my peripheral vision, I saw a lady pick up her small toddler and take off running. Pandemonium quickly was all around me.

"Pha-pha-pleeze don't kill me," the frightful cop drawled. "I got a wife and two kids." Cars drove by with their occupants looking on in horror.

"Get his gun," I said to Tomica. Both women were frozen like statues. They were going to get me busted. I had to move fast. I heard sirens in the distance.

"Get on your knees cracka!" I commanded as I snatched his gun placing it into my pocket and then I grabbed the bracelet. Just up ahead, I saw the blue and white police car turn into the parking lot. With all my might, I hit the officer upside the head with the butt of my gun. His blood got on my suit as he fell backward onto the concrete like a sack of rocks. I was moving fast. Tomica and Evette were still in a state of shock. I jumped into the car, fully intent on leaving their so-called professional asses right there. All their sophistication, savvy and wit had failed them miserably and now when it came to the last resort, brute force with a twist of some real gangsta shit, they were just as intimidated as the victim. I started the engine and they jumped in the car. I pulled off, there was no traffic in front of me. I drove slow, as inconspicuously as possible. There was only one way in and one way out. Up ahead the police car was coming slowly toward me. I had my gun on my lap with my hand on the trigger. I smiled and moved my lips like I was heavy into conversation with my lady friends.

"There's the police," Tomica said, panic stricken.

"Bitch, I see them. Smile like you ain't tryin to go back to the chain gang," I said between clinched teeth, wondering how could she be so fucking dumb.

As we passed the police, they stared into the car. Thank God they were slowed down by the oncoming traffic. It would be a minute before they reached the unconscious cop. As soon as I turned onto the main street, police cars came from every direction, lights blaring. I punched the gas. Up a block, I turned on a side street taking the back way. I pushed the tape in on the tape deck. UGK was rapping about having a pocket full of stones. I thought about the diamonds in my pocket and drove faster. A police car raced by us. I knew where they were going, to the place I had just left. I just knew there would be an all-points bulletin out for the car.

I glanced over to see Tomica staring at me. Whatever it was written on her face I couldn't read. She had her mouth open like she had lockjaw or some shit. I needed to get back to the hotel and fast. For some reason, I don't know, I looked over at Tomica and smirked. I thought about the lame game and now who tricked who. I guess it was my manly ego, or just that triumphant feeling a hustler gets when he hits a good lick. That ruthlessness a thug feels, like liquid fire surging through my veins. Yeah, I was keepin' it gangsta!

I pulled into the hotel with my thoughts heavy on my mind. Just the fact that we had been silent all the way back from the caper gave me an advantage, a kind of leverage that I fully intended to exploit. Now it was time to execute plan B, "Big Pimpin." Break these hoes. Shit, they were going to do it to me if I let them. I knew that I still had to use some finesse but with a different technique. I spun around fast in my seat, placing my arm around Tomica's headrest. It startled her. Now they were watching me with their full attention. I knew that I held all the advantages. Actually, it was the thirty thousand dollar bracelet in my pocket.

I turned, glancing back and forth at both of them.

"That shit ya'll bitches pulled back there was not proper. Could have got a nigga kilt," I said, pointing my finger at Tomica, my voice cold, impassive. "You understand me?!" I yelled. Tomica flinched fearfully. I turned to look at Evette. She was already nodding her head up and down, starry eyes brimming with tears. *Good*, I thought to myself. Give them a large dose of fear. In my mind I wondered where they had all that money stashed and just how was I going to take it. I thought about the pussy game they played on me and started to feel sexually aroused. I thought about what I was going to do to them with those same handcuffs.

Tomica primed her lips to speak like she was considering every word carefully.

"I didn't know that you was packin' heat, that's all, but you don't have to talk to us like that," she said tentatively. She sent her words like a scout to test my temperament. It took a second for me to read into her ploy.

"Bitch! Did I tell you to talk?" I snapped.

She cringed in her seat, damn near jumped out the window. I heard every whimper in the back seat. Her mind still held the fresh memory of what I had done to the cop. Violence does that to people. With that I realized that I had more than enough persuasion to make them submit to my every whim.

I adjusted my tie, made like I was trying to get comfortable. All eyes were on me. I dropped my voice a few decibels, tried to act civil and loving every damn minute of the control I was now feeling over these women. What were they going to do, call the police on me?

"I really don't want the bracelet," I said matter of factly. I lied. Tomica's eyes got big as silver dollars. I could hear Evette in the backseat sniffing back tears.

"Just give me the money ya'll owe me and we can work something out." I smiled sincerely with my own motives.

"Let me have the bracelet," Tomica said meekly. Her words hung in the air resonating without an answer. I knew they would take the bait.

"Ya'll go back to the room, get comfortable, and I'ma get a lil sumpin' sumpin' to smoke on and we can get our drank on. I have a proposition for ya'll, and we can get our freak on."

"Proposition? Freak on?" Tomica retorted disdainfully, eyes narrowing at me. I peered at Evette in the back seat and she looked at me the way a follower does. She just wanted to be led to safety. I thought I detected a hint of something in her demeanor. Just then a blue Lexus pulled into the parking lot. I leaned forward in my seat craning my neck not believing what I was seeing. It was Trina, the bitch that stole my stash. I slouched down in my seat and watched as she parked the car. Tomica made a face at me, she was about to say something. I grabbed the gun. Just as Trina was exiting the car, I took the keys out of the ignition of Tomica's car and placed them in my pocket.

"Hey!" Tomica complained.

"Go to the room!" I said getting out of the car, my pace brisk like a stalker. Trina had not seen me yet. She wore a simple white dress with flowers, pink sandals with a Gucci ankle bracelet on her leg. She had shut the car door retrieving three large shopping bags. She looked up just as I approached. For a fleeting second, I thought I saw a smile cross her lips. I slapped her so hard her neck snapped back and she stumbled holding onto the car to keep her balance, dropping her bags to the ground.

She wiped her bloody lip with the back of her hand, looked at her blood almost examining it. She spit blood at my feet as she continued to hold her head dignified.

"You didn't have to hit me out here in the streets. I have your money, plus more." Her composure completely caught me off guard. Not what I was expecting. I grabbed her by the hair. "Bitch, I'ma kill you!" I said with my face just inches from hers and then shoved her face away. She picked up the shopping bags. I marched her right past the car with Tomica and Evette in it. Their breath fogged up the windows as they watched me abduct a woman in broad daylight. *The lame?*

As soon as I turned the corner, that's when I saw him, the white man, watching me. His face looked familiar. As I passed the car I took a closer look at him, he turned away. I thought nothing more of it, and continued to focus my attention on Trina. That white man would come back to haunt me.

*****

# Chapter Eight

## "The Ultimate Betrayal"

*— Hope —*

Three years later, life couldn't have been better. My child was in preschool, I was attending law school and my husband, Marcus, had a great job making excellent money. He was far from being perfect, but he was a good husband and father. We had a big house out in the suburbs, in a multi-cultural community. For the first time in my life, a sista was truly happy. I worked as a counselor for troubled kids for the Department of Corrections. The pay wasn't bad, thirty eight thousand dollars a year. I went to school at night to earn my law degree. In a lot of ways I knew that I was neglecting my child as well as my husband, but I was less than a year short of earning my degree and all my hard work would come to fruition. Upon my graduation I already secretly made plans to take my family to Walt Disney World and just act like one big-ass kid with Marcus. At least that was my dream.

For now, the reality was that most days when I came home, I would be so tired, all I could do was take a quick shower and collapse in the bed. Thank God Marcus was one of them fathers that enjoyed cleaning and cooking, like it was second nature to him. I could never understand it. I was just thankful. With him, everything had to be extremely orderly and neat. I wished that he felt the same way about my body and our sex life. Our sex life suffered miserably. No matter what I did, the man just did not want no nooky. I even went out and bought all kinds of expensive lingerie, read books on how to rekindle love after marriage and children. Even bought one of them lovemaking tapes you see advertised in the back of the *Essence* magazine. Marcus was numb from his brain down. I even tried to molest him, my own damn husband. I had never performed oral sex and was anxious to try it on him. He flatly refused me, saying that it was nasty and sinful. Made me feel like a slut. I went out and bought myself a woman's best friend, the ultimate toy. I named it Big Boy. All a sister needed was two D batteries and an imagination. I convinced myself that things would change, just give it time. Besides, I realized that not being at home a lot of times was placing strain on our marriage. In my heart I knew that once I started practicing law and we were able to take a long vacation, Marcus would change. In a lot of ways, like many other women, I learned to love without sex and that would have to suffice. Marcus and I lived on two separate islands. Our only real connection was our child and the sad truth about that was, it wasn't even his child. I knew that the only reason I accepted my husband's denial of my body was to purge myself from a woman's greatest sin—infidelity that resulted in another man's child. The last few years I had learned to cope with my transgressions.

*****

On September 4th, Cathy McMillan, the Judicial Judge for the Ninth District of Tallahassee Juvenile division retired. She was 62 years old. On that day the entire juvenile department held an honorary celebration. A catering service provided lots of good food, with the state footing the bill. I left work three hours early. With my son at preschool and my husband at work, I was going to catch a few Zs in my king sized bed and enjoy some peace and quiet. Something I learned as a new wife and mother, working and going to school, you slept when you could, not when you wanted to. Rest can be a commodity given away for the sake of motherhood.

As I pulled my Benz into the driveway I noticed Marcus' Range Rover in the carport. He never parked in there. *What is he doing home so early from work?* I wondered. Then I had this idea, it overpowered me. *Sex!* As I hopped out of the car my pace quickened. It felt like I was about to have a hormone attack. Sex was no longer an option, it was a demand that I was not going to compromise. Right then and there I decided that Marcus was going to give me some or I was going to turn this mutha out. A woman can only take so much. We hadn't had sex in over six months.

As I stepped inside our spacious living room, the first thing I noticed was Marcus' clothes thrown everywhere, like he was in a hurry to take them off. I thought that was particularly strange of him, since he was a neat freak. Hesitantly, I placed my briefcase and purse on the floor. My woman's curiosity piqued, my senses acute to any sight, sound or smell. I kicked off my high-heeled pumps along with my suit coat. In my stocking feet I followed the trail of abandoned clothes … up the stairs … to my bedroom door. My heartbeat was in my throat as I listened astutely. On the other side of the door I could hear panting, groans and sighs. The sound of lovemaking. My husband was in my bed, making love to another woman, on the satin sheets that he would not make love to me on, in my fucking house. I was enraged! Past the brink of no return. Insanity. My first thought was to find a gun and blow both their goddamn brains out! Then I had a better idea. Much better. I retraced my steps, tiptoeing backward.

I went out to the garage, retrieved the small gas can Marcus used for the lawn mower. It was full. On my way back in I stepped in an oil spot in the garage, tracked it back in on my eight thousand dollar Persian rug that I was still making payments on. In the living room I stopped and got the lighter out of the drawer. I walked back up the stairs, gasoline in hand, footsteps smearing my carpet with oil. At the door my hands trembled as I turned the doorknob. The hump in the sheets confirmed the nightmare. The two people did not even notice my entrance. I walked closer and closer with murderous intent. Gas in one hand, lighter in the other. I began to pour gas all over them and the bed, to set their bodies into human flames. In their fevered frolic they did not even notice me. Then, to my utter disbelief, it was Stan's hateful eyes that stared back at me. He threw back the covers and I saw my husband Marcus underneath him lying on his stomach. They both looked back at me, then to the gasoline can in hand and it took only a second for it to dawn on them what I was about to do. The fumes were a dead giveaway. Can you say, extra crispy courtesy of gasoline and fear? I flicked the cigarette lighter.

"Noooo!" Stan shrieked and stood up in bed throwing the wet gasoline covers off of him like that was going to save his ass from the fire that I was going to ignite. As he stood there, from the size of his huge erect penis as it dangled in front of my face, I realized that my husband was definitely more woman than I was to take that up his rectum.

"Hope, this is not what you think!" Marcus screeched in terror.

"Hope please don't do this!" Stan pleaded for his life.

In my mind, in that moment of insanity, it would have been better if I caught my husband with a woman. This only seemed to infuriate me more. Two men packing shit, and with Stan of all people. I reasoned all those years, that was why he hated me. He was fucking my husband and was jealous. Now as I took a step, lighter in hand, like some demon-possessed woman, I was fully intent on torching his ass. Like a trapped animal he began to plead and cry, begging for his life as his eyes frantically searched the room, looking for a way out. I stood between the door of death and his fiery hell. There was no way he was going to get past me and the wrath of a woman's vengeful anger. I flicked the Bic lighter, stalking him with my movements, deliberate, measured. Each step I took forward he took two backward. Cat and mouse. There's something so sinister about death's imminent demise, and it registered in his face. The sweat, the tears mingling with fear. "Please! Please!" Hands outreached, face scowered in painful desperation.

"I don't believe this! How could ya'll do this to me? Faggot-ass fuck boys!" I screamed, irate.

Stan was against the wall. Gasoline and perspiration gleamed off of him like shiny wax. I could hear noise behind me and turned just in time to see Marcus scrambling for the door. During his haste, he fell, slipped, tried to get up and fell again. He busted his ass. Once he was halfway steady, he hauled ass out of there. I looked back at Stan, just as he lunged forward, leaped, took flight and jumped out of my window, shattering glass. I stood there huffing full of rage. I walked over to the window and peered out. Stan was sprawled out in my driveway in obvious pain. In the fall, he had broken both of his ankles and his spine. A few of my neighbors were now standing outside their homes gawking at the naked Black man now lying face down, ass up, in my driveway.

In a fit, I ran through the house searching for Marcus. I found him cowering in the bathroom with the door locked.

"Marcus, bring your pussy ass out here. Now nigga!" Yes, I used the n-word but if you came home and caught your husband in bed with another man with a dick the size of a log shoved up his butt, you would be mad, too. Now that I think of it, maybe I should have been jealous, my husband could take more dick than me.

"Marcus, bring your faggot ass, out here!" I screamed pounding and kicking on the door like a crazed maniac. I listened. All I could hear was water running at first.

"Hope … Hope I was going to tell you," Marcus whimpered from the other side of the door. I had to strain to hear him.

"Tell me what, that you a goddamn faggot and all the grips is worn off your asshole? Muthafucka open up the damn door!" I pounded, until a few minutes later I broke down and sobbed, crying uncontrollably like a baby. This was just too much.

"Mar-cusss, Marcusss! We have a baby, a life … a family. How could you do this to us?" Right there I plopped down on the floor, my resolve shattering. I was only 24 years old and the brotha was giving me a nervous breakdown.

Marcus unlocked the door and peeked out to see if I still had the gas can. Deciding it was safe, he came out into the hall.

"Hope, I'm sorr –"

I threw the cigarette lighter in my hand at him.

"Muthafucka, you ruined everything!" I cried, looking for something else to throw at him. Marcus now had on a pair of jeans he must have gotten out of the dirty clothes hamper in the bathroom.

"Hello? Hello? Anyone home? This is the police department." Shouts rang out from the first floor.

Marcus stood rigid, eyes bulging with fear. Beads of sweat cascaded from his forehead as he whispered in a hushed tone, "What do I tell them?"

As I sat there on the floor with my eyes full of tears and emotions spilling over, for the first time I recognized something in him that I should have seen all along, femininity. It was right there staring me in the face. I raised my voice, making sure that the police could hear me. "If you don't take your punk ass down there and talk to them, I'll be more than happy to tell them what happened. That I came home and caught you with a dick up your ass the size of my arm."

Marcus took one look at me and must have decided that I would now be a good candidate for the crazy farm. As he scurried by me, I kicked him with all my might. He fell hard. "Bitch!" I cursed as he got back up. He hardly looked at me. I could tell his mind was somewhere else–probably on his crippled lover and what the hell lie he was going to tell the police. After a minute or so, I regained some semblance of my composure, picked up the lighter and ambled to my window looking out. The entire neighborhood was out in throngs; it looked like a festive event. I watched as they loaded Stan in the ambulance. He looked up at the window at me in obvious pain. With his stare fixated on me, I smiled as I flicked the Bic lighter as a friendly reminder of what could have happened, and waved at him sweetly as the ambulance drove away. OK, a sista was being a real vixen. In a year or so he would get over it, as soon as he got out of the body cast.

I heard the sporadic crackling of police radios. I spun around and there were two police officers standing in my bedroom, a place that I once held sacred in terms of its intimacy that we women have for our personal sanctuary.

One of the officers was Black, tall and strikingly handsome. He stood about six feet four, built like a football player. I realize I was supposed to be traumatized by the day's events, but I had an overwhelming desire to stand in the mirror and fix my do; officer man was fine with his wide broad shoulders and tree trunk thighs. His partner was white, older with stringy blond hair, a long beak nose and unpleasant blue eyes that looked at me with the disdain of his forefathers as he announced, "Ma'am, we're going to have to take you in, you're being placed under arrest for assault –"

"Whaaat!" I screamed. "I come home and catch my husband with another man, and you're going to arrest me?" Incongruously both officers turned to look at Marcus as he stood in the hallway.

"Get your ass in here!" the Black officer yelled not bothering to hide his contempt. "Why in the hell did you tell us that damn lie? You said she came home and just went off on ya'll," he said, while the other one had me place my hands behind my back while he read me my rights. I could tell he was enjoying the hell out of his job, just from the impressive singsong of his voice.

"Hold up, hold up Ralph!" the Black cop said to his partner. "You want to tell us what happened?" he asked Marcus with little patience in his voice. Marcus gazed at the floor. The fumes of gas permeated the room. He just shrugged his shoulders. The Black officer shook his head somberly as he picked up a picture. Our family portrait.

"This your son man?" The words came out choked like an accusation between two Black men. A silent berate that a white man would never be able to understand. Marcus swallowed the dry lump in his throat and nodded yes.

"How about we just take both of them down to the station and let the judge decide the outcome first thing in the morning?" the white cop asked. For the first time the Black cop looked directly at me.

"Ralph, let me speak to you out in the hall a sec." His voice hinted at a plea, I hoped that his plea would be for me.

"I'm going to call in and get a female officer to take her in," Ralph said on a second wind, not even paying attention to what his partner just said.

"Ralph!" his partner called again. I got the impression that they had been working together for a while. I watched as they walked into the hall, leaving me alone with a man I realized that I never knew. My husband.

"Marcus, no matter what, you're gonna hafta pack your stuff and get out of my house!" I said, feeling the blood boiling in my veins. The police walked in. My heart fluttered in my chest. I had never been to jail before.

"You come with me," the white officer said pointing. I suddenly had the urge to go to the bathroom and it wasn't to pee either.

"Me?" I asked, pointing a finger at my chest. That white man walked right up to me and continued walking. I watched as he handcuffed Marcus. Lord God! I couldn't help thinking, better him than me. Take him away. I watched as Marcus was being led out of the room in cuffs with a shocked expression on his face.

I was alone with the Black officer. His intimidating presence seemed to fill the entire room. He walked up to me and placed his big hand on my shoulder. This was not the officer, this was the brotha comforting a sista in distress. Someone raised their child with compassion for human life.

"Are you going to be all right?" His words stroked me for something I realized I had been starved for, affection. I bit down on my lower lip, held back my tears, exhaled frustration, looking away from him as I felt the tide of emotions building. A sincere man can always do that to a hurting woman. I didn't trust my voice. I tried to smile, but hurt pulled my cheeks the wrong direction. The nametag on his broad chest read "Coffee." *Damn, the name suits him well,* I thought as I looked up at him. Coffee, with a touch of cream, his complexion was smooth mahogany.

"We're going to take him down to the station, charge him with obstruction of justice for lying to us. Now, ma'am, you did say that the other guy slipped and fell out of the window, right?" It took me a second to catch on. "Ma'am?"

"Oh, uh, uh, yes, yes, he did slip and fall," I stammered with my words trying to connect. He still had his hand on my shoulder trying to coach me. When he stepped away taking his hand off of my shoulder, he offered me his card.

"If you have any more problems, let me know." I looked up into his handsome face, the man was Denzel Washington fine. Damn I wanted to fix my hair. "Call me. You know I'm here for you, to serve and protect."

I wondered, *Is it me, or is Mr. Policeman trying to flirt?* I watched him as he headed toward the door checking out his nice rear end. He turned catching me with a knowing grin that says caught you looking.

"Mrs. Green?"

"Yes."

"You know some of the best things in life are free. Call me." He smiled a one-hundred watt smile that could make a girl need sunglasses and walked away. Mr. Policeman definitely was flirting.

*****

I took all of Marcus' belongings and had a yard sale. When he came to get his stuff, I called the police on him. I drained all of the money out of our accounts, wouldn't let him see his child and when he started getting too intimidating, I had a restraining order placed on him where he could not come within ten miles of my home. Basically, I became the proverbial bitch, making his life a living hell. And the bad part was, I still loved him with all my heart. I too was guilty of committing a sin. Every day I looked at my child and was reminded of the old adage: You reap what you sow. Ain't love grand?

*****

As always, in times of need, I called my girl, Nandi. She was now teaching at UCLA as an assistant professor in African studies.

**133**

She answered on the third ring sounding winded.

"Hello, Nandi?"

"Girl, what's wrong? I know that voice," she said with concern.

"You sound like you was running or something," I said stalling for time, not sure that I wanted to tell her.

"Well, if you want to know the truth, me and my warrior were doing a little nation building in the bed." She laughed. Nandi was happy. I felt a pang of jealousy. She married an ordinary brotha. He was a carpenter, had one of them African names that was hard to pronounce. They had three kids. Her first pregnancy was with twins. More African names.

I sighed over the phone shaking my head as if she were standing there as I blurted out, "I caught Marcus in bed cheating on me –"

Before I could get the words out, Nandi was hollering, "I told ya, I told ya his sorry ass wasn't shit, too damn pretty with his conceit –"

"I caught him in bed with another man," I interrupted.

"Man? Girl tell me you lying."

"Nope, caught them in my damn bed playing hide the sausage. Child, Marcus' asshole elastic gotta be ruined. The man backed out of his ass with something as long as my arm."

"Helll naw!" Nandi drawled unbelievingly on the other end of the phone.

"Guess who he was with."

"Who?"

"Stan Johnson."

"Stan Johnson? That preppie cute guy that used to drive the nice Benz that went to Florida State?"

"That's him girl," I responded trying to carry on a conversation like it was not humiliating me as well.

"What the hell is going on with our Black men?" Nandi said exasperated. "Didn't he marry that nice girl Tonya the AKA?"

"I dunno," I said with my mind conjuring up the vivid scene of walking in on my husband with anther man. In the background

I could hear Nandi's husband calling her affectionately. Nandi always told me that she was going to have ten kids if she ever married. In my heart and soul, I honestly believed her. We talked a little while longer then we hung up. For the first time I felt worse than I actually did before I called her.

*****

# Chapter Nine

## "Starting Over"

### — Hope —

My life turned hectic fast. Being a single mother trying to raise a small child, go to school and work a full time job was kicking my ass.

I arrived home running late from picking my son up from daycare. My plan was to take him out to dinner again to McDonald's. The good thing about him being young was he hadn't mastered the art of complaining yet. We ate fast food so much, they could charge me with cruelty to children. It's amazing what you can do with a Happy Meal.

As I drove up, I noticed the police car parked in my driveway. It was Officer Coffee. He smiled that sexy smile of his as I parked. It should be a law against a man being so damn fine!

He got out of the car to greet me. I was dressed for the occasion. My hair and nails were done. I had on my favorite Italian hand-woven gabardine skirt suit with a killer eggshell, silk, nearly transparent please-don't-hurt-'em blouse. It was completely see-through except for the breast area, just enough to flirt with the imagination. With my suit coat on I looked very conservative. As I was retrieving Junior from his car seat, Mr. Policeman walked right up behind me, just as I planned.

"Mommy, mommy, po-leees," my three-year-old said, pointing his sticky fingers at Officer Coffee. I turned abruptly, catching him looking at my behind just as I did to him. He smirked, embarrassed, furrowing his brow, like a gentleman caught in the act. I couldn't help but smile, maybe showing him a little too much gum and teeth, enjoying the attention of being noticed by such a handsome man.

"So what can I do for you Mr. Coffee?" I asked, remembering his cliché–the best things in life are free. I hadn't been with a man in almost a year. His words held a special meaning to me. I held my son like he was contaminated, trying not to let him put his sticky little fingers on my $180 dollar blouse as my eyes quickly roamed the car looking for the candy apple he had earlier.

"Just stopped by to check on you. Hey lil man," he said, ruffling my son's hair. I could smell his cologne, it was a beautiful fragrance that seeped inside of me like his imperturbable masculinity. Damn he smelled good.

"I just thought I'd make good use of your tax dollars by coming back to check on you and your son, besides, you never called me."

I looked up at him with his handsome face carved out in the majestic clouds as birds flew overhead, chirping chimes of summer's reign. "You know what Officer Coffee, I refuse to answer that under the grounds that it may incriminate me."

He chuckled a good one at that. What he did not know was that I already called the number in the pretense of a booty call, and the number that he gave me was an answering service, not his home, which meant that policeman was a playa or else he would have given me his home phone number. My girl Nandi taught me that a long time ago when we were in school.

"So how are things going?" Officer Coffee asked. We both knew what he was talking about–Marcus.

"I'm taking it one day at a time. Boy! If you don't put that dirt down, I'ma knock you into tomorra. Come here!" I yelled at Junior. All the ghetto came out a sista. You know a bad-ass kid can do that to you. "Excuse me." I blushed and apologized to Officer Coffee for my language.

"So, are you two going to get back together? If not, I'd like to ask you out." The brotha squeezed a bunch of words into one sentence catching me off guard. I pondered the thought, as I watched my son meander over to the damn dirt pile again. I stared up at Mr. Coffee absent-mindedly and felt the bright sun on my cheeks.

"It's going to take time," I responded melancholically, hearing the slight tremble in my voice that usually gives rise to my emotions. Officer Coffee brought something to the surface in me that I had been trying to run from. I wanted to forget the day that my marriage went bad. In some ways I think that it traumatized me, the way that it does a lot of women.

"I'll tell you what," I said, deciding to make no secret about my attraction to him. "If I decide to play the dating game, you'll be the first on my list." Boldly, I tiptoed, kissed him on his lips and rubbed my body against his. Estrogen and testosterone pollinated the air. We had cerebral intercourse. My body just seemed to gravitate toward the man. I pulled myself away from him, walked over and snatched my little rugrat out of the dirt and took off walking like I stole some love. Actually, I was a little embarrassed by my antics. I turned and peered over my shoulder once I reached my door. Mr. Coffee was wearing my red lipstick. I couldn't help but giggle. "You need to get a real phone number. That answering service is a sure giveaway that you're a playa." Mr. Coffee's jaw dropped realizing that I had indeed called him. My son waved bye as I closed the door.

*****

For the first time in my life, I was going to have to be an independent single parent. I could not lose sight of my dreams and aspirations. I didn't just want to be a lawyer, I wanted to be a damn good lawyer and help my people as best as I could. They gave my baby brother life for a few rocks of cocaine, and white men were stealing billions from corporate America, shutting down entire cities and never went to prison. In my heart I knew this was not right.

Eventually Marcus won a court order granting him weekend

visits with his son. Can you believe I was still in love with that man? In fact, I was tempted to seduce him, just out of spite. To be truthful, it's a woman's dream to turn a gay man straight, especially if he just happens to be your husband. But in my heart, I knew that Marcus would always be damaged goods. I would never be able to forget the sight of Stan backing his anaconda out of my husband's ass. Disgusting! In some ways we were now strangers. I held the darkest secret within me–Marcus Jr. wasn't his child. In my mind I reasoned that's why I had to forgive him. We both cheated and now must suffer the consequences. I could never ask him for a divorce. For me that would be the testament to the failure of something I held very dear to me, the precious virtue of marriage. So often, I just blamed myself then got lost in my work and school.

*****

On May 28, I graduated from law school. Two months later, I passed the bar exam with one of the highest scores in the state. However, months later I was still unable to find employment. I sent my resume to hundreds of employers. One day when I arrived home there was a message on my answering machine. The United States Attorney's office for the district of Tallahassee, Florida wanted me to come in for a job interview. As desperate as I was, there was no way in hell I was going to work for them. Especially after what they did to my brother, and not to mention their so-called war on drugs, which was actually a war on Black males. Lately there had been a lot of DWB charges–driving while Black. For a Black woman, me anyway, it would feel like treason to help imprison young Black men. As it was, America was already spending more money on sending Black men to prison than the entire educational budget. My sole purpose of becoming a lawyer was to get Black men out of prison, not keep them in. I decided to call Nandi to chat with her about this latest event.

"Girlllll, you've got to be out your cotton pickin' mind!" Nandi screeched. In order to learn the enemy and how to defeat them you must first learn their tactics. Not only will it give you

**139**

valuable knowledge but will give you an advantage like being behind the enemy lines of their scrofulous ways, teaching you their strategic tactics," Nandi exhorted, and went on to regale me with one of her stories. This one was about the true story of General Hannibal and how he journeyed all the way from Africa through the Caucasoid mountains of Europe. He had over one hundred thousand soldiers and elephants and they went through the treacherous rough terrain and tempest weather. They encountered tribes of barbaric cavemen, better known as Neanderthal. By the time they reached Rome a year later, he lost over half his of his forces. Weary and fatigued, with forty thousand soldiers, a Black man conquered Rome, defeating its million-army military. Hannibal is known as the greatest stratagem of all time. He ruled Rome for many years. How was he defeated? He made the mistake of allowing a Roman to join his army. The Roman befriended Hannibal, learning of all his brilliant war tactics and defected back to the other side and defeated Hannibal in battle.

"Hope, you can learn a lot from your enemy. White folks have been doing that to us for years. Stealing our genius and using it against us."

I hung up the phone in a daze. Nandi was right. She knew one of my life-long desires was to get my brother out of prison, and one day file a class action suit against the government. I wasn't anti-government, but I was anti-discrimination, anti-racism, anti-oppressive and anti-genocide. So if the government was that, then I was against it and any act that violated human rights against human life, Black or white.

# Chapter Ten

## "A Bird in the Hand"

### — *Life* —

I shoved Trina in the room shutting the door, as I spun around realizing my blunder. She had her hand in her purse. I forgot all about the small derringer .38 two shot pistol that she carried.

"Nigga, let's get one thing straight! Don't you ever, ever, place your damn hands on me out in public." She took a step forward, and continued, "Yeah, a bitch was wrong for stealin' your shit, but I knew you would never trust me with your money." She then reached into one of the shopping bags, took out not one, but two bricks of cocaine and placed them on the table. As if reading my mind she answered, "I bought them from my cousin in Brooklyn for ten grand apiece. He gave me one for eight after I promised that I would come back and get more. I stood there rigid. I never had a bird in my entire life, much less two of them. Trina sauntered up to me real close and poured a heavy dose of herself all over me as her hand caressed my private part then unzipped my fly as she eased inside my pants. "Papi … I would never betray you … Never!" Vaguely I could hear what she said as my mind did figures, weight, dollars. There are thirty-six ounces in a kilo of dope. Two times thirty-six is seventy-two. Each ounce goes for about a grand in Tallahassee. My face broke into a shit-eating grin. Trina removed her hand and looked at me strangely, sensing where my mind was, knowing it wasn't on sex.

**141**

"Let me cook it for ya," she offered. "I can make one hundred thousand off each bird."

I looked at her like she was crazy. "You must be going to make up some fake dope -Dreams."

"No, no Papi. If you whip the dope just right, cook it slow and use just enough baking soda and water you can make three ounces out of one. My daddy taught me that. All the old heads in Brooklyn have been doing that for years. The trick is to cut dime rocks out of each ounce, that way you get more money, three grand instead of the one." I was listening to this Brooklyn chick talk and I was sucking up game like a sponge. She continued, "By selling dime rocks you keep the federalies off your ass. They're only looking for weight. Ain't no longevity in the dope game, stick and move. Get out within a year."

*****

I sat back and watched her as she attempted to make her magic. I had to see this shit to believe it. In all, she was going to take two birds and make six. I had already decided if she fucked up this dope I was going to kill her. Her face was fixed in heavy concentration. Cooking cocaine was an art, like a delicate trade, and it involved a special skill. Like a chef, every cook has his own technique, as well as formula. That day, I was learning that Trina was a pro at cooking dope. From a glance, you would think that she was fixing dinner.

"So how did you meet Nina Brown?" I asked. Trina turned and looked at me with cocaine in a pot of hot water. Then there was a knock on the door. A knock that only a hustler and his girl can describe. Scared the hell out of both of us. Quickly, I grabbed my gun. As I walked to the door looking out the peephole, Trina gave me that look that asked, *what should I do?* Someone had their finger or something over the hole blocking my vision. Police? I turned to Trina and mouthed for her to put the yae away. She scrambled around trying to hide all of the drug paraphernalia. I dashed to the curtain and looked out. "Godamnmuthafuckin-sonofabitch!" I saw Blazack standing outside the door with his finger over the damn peephole. With him was a posse of niggas from Miami's notorious set, the Oplica Triangle. "It's cool," I said to Trina over my shoulder. To my surprise, she was packing dope in her panties. I walked out of the door into the sweltering heat. Blazack and I ain't never been close. It wasn't nothing personal. It was just his demeanor, cool and aloof. Looking at all of them I had to smile. They all looked haggard and wary, like unemployed hustlers. I knew the feeling.

In the crew with Blazack were Dirty, Gucci, Mad Ball and Twine. All of us at one time or another hustled together, either in Sarasota, my stomping ground, or theirs in Miami. Basically we were tight, but it dawned on me, they could be here to kill me. The last time we were all together like this was at a strip club down in Miami called The Rollez. Coming out of the club, the police took a combined $98,000 from us and we couldn't say shit. Charge it to the game and they label us crooks.

"What the fuck you doin wit dat?" Blazack asked, pointing to the gun at my side. "We ain't drive all this way for you to be stuntin' wit your gun, wearing that Sunday School suit. What, you preachin' now too?" he joked, showing a grill full of platinum and diamonds worth enough money to buy poor folks a home. His hair was uncombed and nappy, however he wore it like the urban trend. Short and stocky, with broad shoulders the size of large watermelons, Blazack was a diminutive tank of a man. The kind of man that never accepted defeat under any kind of circumstances. He possessed the uncanny ability to display human kindness. And like all leaders, he could be very persuasive when need be. Marvin Johnson, a.k.a. Blazack, was a cold-blooded killer, at least by metro's Dade police department standards. He was rumored to have taken part in at least twenty gangland slayings of rival drug dealers and was currently the number one suspect in a double homicide of his baby's mother and her boyfriend over a dispute over custody of the child. The only evidence the police could find was spattered blood, no sign of a struggle, no bodies, no witnesses. That was Blazack's MO. Currently, Blazack's mother had custody of his three year old child.

"If I was comin' for you, you wouldn't know it until you was all wet up," Blazack said, continuing to berate me as he pulled up the towel in his hands showing me the eighteen inch double barrel shotgun pointed at my nuts. They all erupted in laughter at the dumb expression on my face as I stepped to the side, moving my balls out of the line of fire if he happened to shoot.

Dirty was the first to greet me. He was the baby of the crew, 18 years old, and had a heart as big as the Atlantic Ocean. He still had that youthful smile of innocence that the ghetto had not yet stolen from him. Next was Gucci, a fat boy. He loved to dress and eat. He was the kind of man that looked good in his clothes and ladies found him attractive. His loyalty was priceless. He once took seven shots from the police using his body as a barricade on the door during a bust, just so that the rest of the crew could get away. We did. The doctors later said the only thing that saved his life was the fact that he was overweight. Next was Mad Ball and Twine. They fam for real. The last time we were together, they were in the back seat asleep while I drove ten hours in the wrong direction trying to find a town called Stone Mountain, Georgia. When they awoke that morning to find out I was lost, we argued the entire trip. We exchanged dap. Twine grinned at me and asked, "Nigga you find Stone Mountain yet?" We erupted in laughter at our own personal joke. Blazack quickly seized the conversation. He wanted to talk about the snitch Dre' and then he added, "I got somethin' I want t'show ya in the van."

"Van?" I repeated. "I sent you money to catch a plane," I said as I followed them to the parking lot to a brand new customized black Chevy van.

"I had a change of plans at the last moment," Blazack said to me as he opened the back door to the van. The doors were the kind that slid open. He did this with a wavy show of his hand, as if opening a display case with a choice of doors. To my utter shock, there were two people blindfolded and hog-tied. I slammed the door back, scared that someone might see inside the van. As it

**144**

was, we were attracting attention.

"What the fuck are you doing man?" I snapped.

"That's Dre'. We found him in Sarasota at his dad's crib. I had to shoot the old man," Blazack said matter of factly.

"Who is the other guy wit'em?" I asked.

"Oh, dat's just a guy we hitched a ride from."

"Hitched a ride from? Nigga you done kidnapped a cracka!" I said, not believing what I was hearing. "Look man, ya'll got to get this shit out of here," I said talking fast, and walking faster, trying to distance myself from that van. I suddenly stopped and dug into my pockets. I had twenty dollars and a diamond bracelet. "Ya'll wait here. I'll be right back," I said and took off into a trot.

*****

"How much money you got?" I asked Trina as soon as I walked in the door.

"Who was that outside?" she asked, ignoring my question.

"They my boys from Miami. How much money do you got?" I repeated again, this time with a little more urgency in my voice.

"About eighteen dollars," she said looking up while measuring cocaine into a pot.

"Shit!" I cursed.

"Papi, I bought you an outfit while I was in Brooklyn, used the last bit of the money," she said apologetically.

Suddenly I had an idea. "Lock the door, put the chair under the knob, and don't open it for nobody," I said heading for the door. Then on second thought, I turned. She was wearing that *please don't leave me* sour expression on her pretty face. I walked to the table, tore a piece of paper off one of the shopping bags and filled it with about an ounce of cocaine, pecked Trina on the lips and bounced out the door.

*****

I hurried over to Evette and Tomica's room. Evette answered the door scantly dressed in a white halter top and pink short shorts with a fat pussy print like a big fist in her drawers. I looked around the room for Tomica. "Where's Tomica at?" I asked. I could see that Evette was easily intimidated by my presence.

"Sh ... sh ... she's in the shower," Evette stuttered.

"Here's the bracelet, where's my money?" I asked as I showed her the bracelet. She pointed at her purse and walked over to it.

"You got ID in there good enough to rent an apartment?"

"Yeah, why?" She looked at me like I just hit her with a trick question.

"Come go with me," I said and pulled her arm. I could tell by the frightened expression on her face that she wanted to scream. Slightly she resisted and then something washed over her face the way a mouse looks up when the heel of a boot is about to come crashing down on him, or perhaps she recalled the episode at the mall with the cop, or maybe the demonstration in the parking lot when I slapped the shit out of Trina. Whatever it was, Evette was easily persuaded. We walked out of the door with her wearing them little ole shorts.

My plan was to get Evette to rent an apartment or something until I could figure out what I was going to do with the crew. Dre' the snitch weighed heavy on my mind.

I walked fast with Evette in tow.

"Give me the money," I said, suddenly stopping in my tracks. She dug into her purse and removed a roll of cash big enough to choke a cow and counted out five hundred dollars.

"Damn girl! How much money is that?" I asked in disbelief. Evette was a little slow, but she was far from being dumb. She just looked up at me with cloudy eyes and did not answer. I thought about their caper with the credit cards and all that stolen shit back at their room and God only knows what else them two broads had been up to, driving around the country stealing. Evette must have had at least twenty grand in her purse. I grab her by the arm tightly. "Listen Shouty, whatever you do, don't let these niggas see that money. They'll slit your throat and take it!" I was taking about Blazack. She looked up at me, swallowed in her throat and looked around like this was a hostage situation. I wondered if she would take off running.

As we approached the stolen van, loud music was playing. The van rocked from side to side. Blazack was at the driver's seat smoking a blunt. Something in the back of the van had his attention. He was laughing hysterically. I peeked inside of the van. They were all piled up in there like the forty thieves. Mad Ball had a cigarette lighter out burning the white man on the ass with it. His pants were down around his ankles, booty tooted up in the air because of the way that they had him hog-tied. As soon as everyone saw Evette, the games stopped and catcalls ensued. "Look at the fat monkey on that bitch, looks like she got a boxing glove in her drawers," someone said.

I couldn't believe what I was seeing. I lost my composure.

"What the fuck ya'll doin'? Stop the dumb shit! These crackas in this town ain't playin'. This is the capital of Florida. These rednecks gonna give a nigga a life sentence if they catch us with this cracka." Blazack casually turned, looked at me and blew smoke into my face. Someone in the back of the van snickered at me. Then I heard giggles, the white man yelled again in pain. It was as if I was talking to the five stooges. So I tried my hand at diplomacy. My voice lowered a notch.

"Listen, ya'll follow me. We're going to see if we can we rent ya'll a place to stay," I said, nodding at Evette. She looked like she was about to make a dash for it after hearing the horrible sounds coming from inside the van.

*****

Five hours later, thanks to Evette and her hot pants, we were finally about to rent a house right off FAMU Campus on Stocky Street. Evette was able to talk an elderly white man into renting an older model four bedroom, two-bathroom home with a nice spacious yard. She flirted and laughed showing him a lot of teeth. With a $1,800 dollar deposit she had the keys and with them was a piece of paper with a phone number on it. The old man really liked her.

Now the problem was, what to do with the stolen van, its owner and Dre' the snitch. When I confronted Blazack about it, all he said was, "Dre' was a wrap," and signaled with his hand slicing across his throat. I walked away leaving it up to him. My conscience was getting the better of me. Call me soft, but I did not want to see Blazack kill Dre'. He was my dawg at one time, he just went bad. I know that if I tried to stop it, it would be like signing my own death warrant, like I was admitting I conspired with Dre' to set up Lil Cal. One thing was definitely for sure, Blazack had no problem making people disappear.

"Yo!" I turned as I was about to get in the car. I handed Blazack the packet of cocaine I had taken earlier from my room. A few of the crew liked to smoke Bunk–that's weed mixed with cocaine.

*****

Blazack drove along in the van with the human cargo. I did not ask him what he was going to do with it, that would have been asking too much.

I pulled out into traffic with a feeling of utter relief. I noticed Evette watching intently. For the first time I thought I detected a pleasant smirk on her face.

"Daaamn Shouty, why you looking at a nigga like that?" I asked. Evette made a face. "You're something else," she beamed. "You tricked us." Her voice chimed sweetly as she crossed her long legs, one over the other, hands snuggly clasped between curvaceous thighs, the way a woman does when she's getting comfortable and looking sexy and unconscious of it.

"Are you a pimp or something?" she asked. For the first time I gave her my undivided attention. The expression on her face said that she was dead-ass serious.

"Why you say that?"

"Cause, first you tricked us by actin' like you was a college student. Then you beat up that security guard back there at the mall and took our bracelet." Her eyes leered at me when she said our bracelet. "You jumped on that poor girl in the hotel parking lot, and you just took my money too," she said in one long breath.

"I told you I was going to give you back your money," I said.

She rolled her eyes twisting her lips to the side of her face, typical Black woman antics. Shyly she smiled, and then burst out in hearty laughter, the kind of laughter that has a soulful melody of a Black woman. It spilled on to me, and I can't help but smile back at her. "What's so damn funny?" I asked.

"You."

"Me?"

"You should have seen the expression on your face when Tomica handcuffed you to the love seat, and you pulled out that big ole dick and started wackin' off." She laughed hysterically. I think it must have been all that built up frustration stressing her over the past twenty-four hours. She wiped her eyes and her laughter subsided. On a more serious note she said, "I would have been game for the threesome ... twosome even." For emphasis she uncrossed her legs opening them like showing me the packaged goods. As I drove I had a lot on my mind. A fat pussy was not one of them. Evette sensed my mood and turned away sitting straight forward in her seat.

I pulled into the hotel parking lot and looked for any sign of anything unusual. This was not the time to get caught slipping. "Go to your room. If Tomica asks you about the money just tell her I took it, and I'm gonna pay it back," I said.

"Just give me the bracelet," Evette suggested, and made a face at me, the kind that says, *you ain't shit.*

"Go!" I yelled. She slammed the door and stalked off.

*****

I inserted my key into the door. Just as I asked, Trina barricaded herself inside using a chair and the burglar chain. She opened the door and greeted me with a hug and kiss like I had been gone for years. Inside, to my dismay, Tomica was sitting at the table cutting up dope. Her eyes flashed signals that said, *let's keep what happened in my room a secret.*

"What the fuck? What you doin' in here?" Trina tugged at my arm like a three-year-old trying to get my attention. Soft-spoken, she said, "Tomica's my homegirl. She's from Brooklyn."

**149**

"Ya'll know each other?" I interrupted, in total disbelief.

"Naw, well, sorta." Trina stuttered under the weight of my eyes boring holes through her. She was nervous. "She came here looking for you. I recognized the Brooklyn accent. This bitch is my homegirl. I went to school with her brother Rakim." Together the two of them giggled like school girls that shared a secret. Women. I suddenly had the uncanny feeling that the two of them were talking about me in my absence. I just openly stared at Tomica, wondering just how much I could trust her.

One thing about this business, there is no room for mistakes, most importantly in the judgment of people's character. Maybe Tomica was on to the scent of Trina's pussy. It's always important to know a person's motives when they are trying to get close to you. I walked up and inspected the dope. It looked nearly perfect, except for a few air pockets. Trina said that it would take longer to dry. I vaguely heard her as my mind churned numbers, ounces and prices. It was then I realized that Trina made her second biggest blunder of the day. The first was letting the dyke Tomica in the door, the second was the dope was short by my figures. This is important, very important, and not just the financial aspects of it. New acclaimed power is like an iron fist, it is meant to be challenged like all authority. People will seek out its weaknesses, especially women. It's in their very nature to find the core of a man's soft spot. I wasn't having none of that! "This muthafuckin dope short a few ounces!"

"You took some when you left, remember? Plus, I got all that left over in the plate over there at the sink." She pointed. There was a pile of cocaine there that I didn't notice. I shrugged an expression that said, *my bad*, and turned and walked over to the window peeking out of the curtains. Hustler's habit. I plopped down on the chair by the window. I was tired and wary. Over the past few days it seemed like things were moving fast, unpredictable, and now I was moving into a realm of the game that I really had no experience in. To top it off, I was in a spot that ain't never been friendly to niggas from out of town. Now, in a matter of seconds, I turned from flat foot hustlin', to dope man entrepreneur, pushing weight. The contrast of the two professions is about as different as night and day. For me to be successful it would take the cunning wit of a fox, along with the organizing skills of a crooked preacher soliciting money from his parishioners. There was zero room for mistakes. In the dope game you got leaders and followers, there is no in between. The streets keep the score: who leads, who follows. Caskets and prison cells bore witness to a hustler's timely demise. All this was in my thoughts as I plucked my last cigarette from the pack, lit it and inhaled deeply. As the smoke filled my lungs, I gazed up at the ceiling reflecting on all the shit that had happened. I exhaled, trying to erase everything from my mind. There was a spider web in the corner of the ceiling. Something about it held my attention. For some strange reason, Hope's face flashed in my mind, voice echoing, *you'll end up dead or in prison.* Suddenly I had an urge for a strong drink.

"Can Tomica have the last of the coke in the plate?" Trina asked casually as if it were a request for a slice of pie. She indeed confirmed my thoughts, the two of them were talking about more than the old days. There can be a lot of wisdom in playing dumb, my stepmother used to say. So I did my part and let her question roll right over my head. I took off my shoes, my dogs were killing me.

"How long is it going to take ya'll to finish cutting up the dope?" I inquired.

"Just about all day," Trina replied.

"Tell you what, go to the store and get me a bottle of Hennessy and a pack of smokes, stop by Popeye's and get something to eat, I'm starving, and you can have some of the coke." Tomica stood up in front of the chair, eyes flaming with anger.

"I just know you ain't finna try me like that!"

"Try you like what?" I raised my voice. Realizing this dyke was trying to show off for the benefit of Trina's presence, I prepared to bust her ass if she got out of line.

"Try me like I'm some junkie, or something." Tomica sat back down. I was eyeballing her like she went there. On second thought, I had a better idea. I stood taking the gun out of my pocket, along with the diamond bracelet and began to strip down to my boxer shorts.

"Boo, where are the clothes that you bought?" I asked Trina, as both women looked at me quizzically.

"Over there on the other side of the bed," Trina answered.

I walked over looked inside of the shopping bag, pulled out the expensive two-piece Versailles outfit—a jacket and pants in a beautiful shade of turquoise and gold, strictly a baller's style. Trina had good taste in clothes. I hurried getting dressed. Afterward, I looked in the mirror and I wanted to salute my muthafuckin' self. In the background I heard Tomica suck her teeth, hatin' on a nigga. Bitch! I retrieved the chunky iced out chain I took from Suge Knight's cockeyed twin back at the hotel. Putting it around my neck, I walked over to the table and began placing the dope into Ziplock bags. I would just have to get someone to cut up the rest later.

"What are you doing?" Trina asked.

"What it look like I'm doing? I'm getting out of this joint." Trina and Tomica exchanged glances. Actually what I was really doing was following the number one code of the game: never shit at where you got to eat. Meaning, never keep dope where you got to lay your head. Never!

"Gimme the keys to the car," I said to Trina. She hesitated with a look of despair the way a woman does when she wants to ask a question, but is unsure of her boundaries. She reached into her purse and gave me the keys. I placed half of the powdered cocaine that was at the sink into a bag, and left some. I walked to the door. I could feel their eyes boring through by back.

"Come here," I turned, talking to Trina. She walked toward me. If her brown eyes could talk, hers would have plainly begged me to stay. I spoke a whisper against her ear lobe palming her ass through the soft material of the dress. "Dig, Shouty, I'll be back in a second."

"It's going to take some hours for the stuff to dry," Trina said in her attempt to get me to stay. I could hear the somber plea in the tone of her voice.

"If you like, you can give the rest of the powder on the sink to your homegirl."

I bent down and pecked her on the lips. She reached up, lassoing my neck with her arms and kissed me like I was a soldier about to go off to war.

"Baby, don't go. I bought a nice sexy Victoria's Secret outfit I wanted to wear for you." As Trina whispered I looked at Tomica. She was watching us closely. That reminded me of something. I peeled Trina's arms off of me, reached into my pocket removing the diamond bracelet, and gave it to her. Tomica damn near fell out of the chair when she saw that.

"Ohmigod! Ohmigod! It's beauuuutiful!" Trina exclaimed after she saw the price tag and began to do the two-step like I used to see women do at my father's church when they claimed to have the Holy Ghost. As I walked out of the door, I thought I heard Tomica call my name.

*****

# Chapter Eleven

## "The Jump-Off"

### *– Life –*

Trina's Lexus Coupe was nice, real nice. The inside was handsomely designed with expensive oak wood and plush butter soft leather interior. The seats felt like I was riding in the cockpit of a jet. Yeah, I could tell her daddy was deep in the game. He spoiled her rotten. I placed the shopping bag of cocaine on the seat next to me, with Jesus on my lap, my hand resting on it in case there was any drama, and my mind on my money.

As I drove, the air felt crisp and cool. I was on a mission to stack some chips. While driving I counted out twenty ounces, my mind struggling with the mental transition of being a jackman, to not get jacked. Easier said than done.

*****

I parked down the street from the house that I rented for Blazack and the crew. I walked in the shadows of semi-darkness and hid the dope underneath a tree in a hole I dug. Afterward, I got back into the car and drove the short distance to the house. There were so many cars parked in the yard and driveway, I had to park in the middle of the street. As I walked up, people were hanging out everywhere. Females lounged out front on the porch. It's hard to believe that only a few hours ago this place was for rent. Mad Ball and Gucci looked up to see me. They could tell by the expression on my face my mood was not good. I walked inside and saw that the place was jam packed. In the kitchen, I saw Dirty throwing dice. They were gambling, playing Low. He looked at me and said something slick out the side of his mouth, something about how much money did I have, and then he threw the dice. I shot him a look that said, *don't fuck with me.* Twine walked up and grabbed my hand. He was smoking a blunt, eyes red, pants hanging off his ass.

"Nigga, you been killing 'em huh?" he said checking out my gear and running his fingers over my necklace.

"Listen man," I talked between clinched teeth fighting to control my temper. This was becoming a habit dealing with these niggas. I was trying to stop it before it started. "Ya'll didn't come down here to party, this is strictly business. Clear these muthafuckas out the house!"

I knew that there was no way that Twine was going to take orders from me, at least not at this stage of the game, but now was the time to employ my will for the sake of building a team and bleeding this town out of its riches. "Where's Blazack at?" I asked. Twine pointed at the back room giving me a look like he was trying to read where I was coming from with the attitude.

I knocked on the door. Heard a voice say come in. I walked into what looked like a gun show. "Damn it man!" I intoned. "Where did ya get all dem shits from?" There were about a half dozen AK47s lined up on the wall, a Mac-10, Mac-11, various handguns, a Thomson submachine gun with a special shoulder holster to hold three thousand rounds of ammunition. On the bed next to Blazack was his trusty double barrel 12 gauge sawed off shotgun, the same one that he pointed at my nuts earlier that day. On the bed was a book titled *The Art of War.* Blazack just lay there, looking up at the ceiling. He was the most reclusive man that I had ever known. His quiet could be disturbing at times. It gave you the feeling that he was always plotting. I hoped he was not plotting about me.

Slowly he rose from the bed ignoring my disapproval of his arsenal of guns.

"I had to use my hands," Blazack said, flexing his fingers. His hands were huge. He now examined them as if it were his first time really seeing them, their power and strength.

"What?" I asked, confused as to what he was talking about.

"He wouldn't die." Blazack continued. The scowl on his face was that of a man reliving a bad memory.

"I strangled dat nigga for damn near ten minutes. He wouldn't die."

"Who?" I asked aggravated.

"Dre'," Blazack said clinching his fist.

"Oh." The sounds left my lips, with it the grimy reality of who he was talking about. I stared, mesmerized. Once again I wondered about the mystic of life's greatest mystery—death, and if the people who kill are haunted by the very souls they stole. There was a glassy look of a madman possessed by demons on Blazack's face as he examined his hands like they were murder weapons he wished he could discard. I think that to some degree, the dead are still alive, they live vividly in the minds of the people that killed them. At least with Blazack that was the case.

"Yo, I let the cracka in the van go and tied him to a tree. Someone'll find him in a few days, maybe. But Dre'… dat nigga ain't never comin' back," Blazack said with malice as his eyes narrowed, giving me the full intent of what he meant. The moment lingered. I was lost for words. I noticed in the corner of the room there was a stick of dynamite and some other kind of explosives. Just when I was about to ask about that rat muthafucka, his statement completely caught me off guard. I knew what he was hinting at.

"My nigga, on everything I love, when the shit went down in the hotel with the nigga trying to set me up, I had to out-run helicopters and some mo shit. Hooked up with this broad, if she didn't help me, I'd be fucked up right now, that's how I ended up here."

"Uh huh," Blazack said with all the interest of a man watching paint dry. "I talked with Lil Cal's mom this morning. Told her to ask about you, since you da one that introduced us to Dre' in the first place." Blazack left no doubt in my mind his suspicion of me, as well as his loyalty to Lil Cal, death before dishonor. He would kill me in a heartbeat. The feelings were mutual. Our real common bond was only Lil Cal. I knew I would have to accept the dark cloud of treason that loomed over my head. For some reason the dope game is like that. It permeates on paranoia and fear for the lack of trust. Trust is like a good woman forced to go bad, she will always be needed and unfortunately used and abused to serve like hell in the dope game. If there were no trust, there would be no lies.

I ignored Blazack's acid remarks. The reality was, I needed him as much as he needed me.

I retrieved five ounces from the bag. His eyes lit up like novas as I passed them to him. Maybe he was thinking about searching me to see if I was I wearing a wire. He hesitated. Through the dark pools of his eyes I read his suspicion of me.

"What you want me to do wit dis?" he asked, still not touching the dope.

"Keep 'em," I replied, tossing the five cookies to him.

"Getting paper?" His faced cracked into a sinister grin.

"Jus a lil sumpin' sumpin'," I drawled slyly, as my mind deftly tried to search for the holes in his mental armor, an avenue for my sales pitch in recruiting him and the rest of them Oplica niggas.

"Dig, playa. I'm tryna build a team right here in Tally. Open up shop, drop some weight, boom dis muthafuckin town and get ghost 'fo the spot get hot. Nawaimsayin'?" As I talked, in the background I heard JT Money rapping, *Bitch shake what yo momma gave ya.*

"I want you to be my lieutenant. I'll pay you five G's a week once we get on our feet."

I waited for his response. Blazack was a natural born leader. Since his man Lil Cal was gone, he might rather rob than work for another nigga. I was aware that he could take what I said as being disrespectful on the strength of the caliber of nigga he thought he was. He stood all five feet seven, two hundred thirty pounds of brute force.

"Nigga you got me fucked up!" All that platinum and diamonds in his mouth sparkled for emphasis. I braced myself, felt my hand with a mind of its own inching toward Jesus in my drawers.

Then Blazack smiled like the sun coming from behind dark clouds. "You damn right I want to be down wit your team." I felt a wave of relief wash over me. Afterward we sat down and talked. I explained to him how we had to act like niggas on a mission, and to stop the dumb shit, as well as the partying. I didn't tell him that I had a connection so large they could use the scales for elephants to weigh the dope. In time he would find that out for himself. Trina's cousin was a major Colombian drug lord of both "Boy" and "Girl" meaning cocaine and heroin. Her cousin liked my hustle. I never looked back. My life would never be the same.

*****

That night I drove through Frenchtown. It was dark. Most of the streetlights were shot out by drug dealers for the protection of the night. A lone luminous light shined within the dense fog of smoke and air pollution. Throngs of people moved like cattle to the pulsating rhythm of the ghetto. Every Black section has one. A strip of town where everyone hangs out, flossing in their cars, clothes and jewelry, parlaying their hustle–get in where you fit in. A place where a man could lose his life over the throw of the dice.

I've learned that the element of surprise, if used effectively, is a brilliant strategy in winning over your adversaries. It could also get you shot. I made up my mind days ago that I was going to make my move, boldly. Fuck 'em! I felt like all hustlers feel when they're hungry. I needed eat!

*****

I finally spotted Nina Brown. She was in a crowd of about two or three hundred people. The scene was rowdy. I heard gunshots in the distance. I was having second thoughts about my plan. Stevey D and his henchmen were a few yards from Nina. They were all sitting in front of the pool hall. He was leaning against a blue tricked out Caddy with a ragtop, sitting on dubs. Back in the day if you had a clean caddy on expensive wheels, you was the shit. Rubbing up against him was a thick redbone. She wore skin tight blue jeans with holes near her ass cheeks. She was fat-to-death, ass for days. I drove up with Trina's system bumping Dr. Dre' and Snoop's joint talking 'bout, "If your bitch talks shit you know I got to put the slap down." I hopped out of the car, and boldly walked into the lion's den. The element of surprise, I had Jesus tucked in my drawers, made sure they could see the bulge. Niggas jaws dropped like old folks with no teeth. Stevey D shoved the girl off his lap. I could tell he wanted to go for his strap. I walked up humbly, and never took my eyes off him. The expression on Nina Brown's face was that of complete shock, like seeing a dead man walking.

"Whuz up, yo?" I said to Stevey D. He had on a thick her-ringbone, a white shirt, a pair of starched Dickies and a pair of black Nikes. The redbone was eyeballing me. From the expression on her face I could tell she could sense something was about to go down. "I told you I was comin' back ta break bread wit cha," I said, smiling with more gaiety than I was actually feeling. Stevey D bunched his face, crinkling his nose, the way people do when they smell something foul. He then looked to check both ends of the street like he was going to start blasting.

"I don't believe dis nigga," he said tensely while shaking his head at me. The crowd was starting to circle us. The tension was tight as a fat lady climbing a rope. I felt a glaze of sweat on my forehead. "You got some'tin for me."

"Sho'll do," I drawled. He laughed and looked around at his crew. They followed his lead and laughed too. He walked up and placed his hand on my shoulder in a friendly gesture, like the spi-der introducing himself to the fly.

"Let me holla at you for a sec," I said, walking to the car. I needed to get out into the open.

"Yo D, you aight?" one of his peeps asked. He threw up his

hand. "Yea, I'm aight."

I was parked in the middle of the street with the engine running. We got in the car. "Nice ride," Stevey D said, rubbing his hands on the oak wood dashboard. I ignored him and hollered out the window for Nina Brown, signaling for her to get in the car. As I pulled off I threw an ounce into Stevey D's lap.

"What you want for dis?" he asked, never taking his eyes off the dope.

"That's yours."

"Mine?"

"I told you I was going to bless you when I came back."

"True, true, true," he intoned, shaking his head.

"Bet that up my nigga." I could hear the delight in his voice. I also knew that my kindness could be taken for a sign of weakness but he had something that I wanted–this town. He extended his fist, I hit it with a mean dap.

"Let me buy some of that off ya, it's a drought in town."

Ain't no way in hell I was going to sell this cat some dope. A hustler's dream is to have a spot on lock down and be the only man holding. That's like cornering the entire market of Wall Street, having the only commodity.

"I'm fucked up right now, I can't sell you nothing, but when I get on my feet, I gotcha." He twisted his mouth the way people do when they want to say, "Don't piss on me and tell me it's raining."

"Tell me, what ya'll payin' for a bird?"

"Nineteen, twenty grand," he said, throwing numbers at me from his head.

"Tell you what, the next time I go to re-up, I'll get you one for $17,500," I said, thinking about Trina and her whip game, plus I could get them thangs for ten stacks.

"Hell yeah nigga, I want you to get me three birds!" he said excitedly. "When you leavin'?"

"I don't know." I replied, knowing you never tell a man your comings and goings in this business, unless you want to come home one day and get touched.

I bent the corner and parked at the same spot I picked up Stevey D.

"Yo, my nigga, I got a couple stones, I'ma do a little hustling with Nina Brown," I said, but actually I was letting him know I was getting ready to open up shop in his town. He said it was cool, but I could see larceny in his eyes. He knew that if I gave him a whole ounce I must have been straight.

"Where ya'll going to be serving at?" he asked. I turned to Nina Brown in the back seat. She was cleaning the brillo out of her stem, a cocaine pipe made out of a car antenna.

"Where you want to serve at?" I asked her.

"We gon' be at my house," she replied.

"Aight," Stevey D said, nodding his head. "You got a beeper number?"

"When you wanna holla at me, get in contact with Nina."

He walked away. Nina jumped her musty ass in the front seat next to me smelling like burnt motor oils and some mo' shit.

As I pulled off she asked frantically, "What you doin' drivin' Trina's car? What did you do to her?"

I turned to Nina with a dead serious expression and said, "She's in the trunk of the car."

"WHAT?!" Nina screeched. "Hell naw, lemme outta this bitch!"

I laughed so hard it hurt my sides. Crackheads are some funny muthafuckas. Up the street I saw the redbone that was sitting on Stevey D's lap. She waved at the car. When women find out a cat is from out of town and is getting money, they make themselves available. I asked Nina who she was. Nina told me she was a skeezer that sold pussy out of both drawers. I made a mental note to buy me a shot of that ass.

*****

Nina Brown lived in the old run down section of town that looked as if it dated back to slavery. Actually, they were Section 8 homes sitting on top of rotten wood and bricks. Strangely, across the street from where she lived was an abortion clinic. At the time it seemed so out of place. I parked my car up ahead at the gas station and sent Nina to the store to get me a pack of razors, two quarts of Olde English 800 and a pack of Newports. As we walked back to her place every moment so far had been carefully planned, parking the car at the gas station as well as walking back to her place, served as a reconnaissance move to survey the spot I was about to turn into a trap, a dope hole. Police are trained to associate cars with drug areas. I did not want to make Trina's car hot.

Nina Brown had not paid her light bill, so we had to use candles in the dark. Her place was eerie and damp inside with a foul malodorous smell. The wooden floors were barren and dirty. There were three rooms, a front room, kitchen and her bedroom. A worn dirty sheet served as the room divider to her room. She had a back door with a clear view to the streets. That's where I set up. I gave Nina a half an ounce, her personal stash. She pinched off a piece and stuffed it into her stem, lighting it up. The dope crackled and she sucked on the devil's dick and her eyes grew large. Once she filled her lungs, she began to get animated. She leaned forward and whistled, placing her hand above her head as if she was shading her eyes from the sun, looking at me from a long distance, she tapped her feet and blew out a cloud of smoke in my face. "Ooh wee! Dis be that good shit!" she exclaimed and began to smack her lips like she was trying to get her tongue unglued from the roof of her mouth.

"Give me a plate," I said smiling like a father who just learned that his wife delivered a healthy baby boy. Having a good product is the ultimate form of power when a hustler is trying to seize the reigns of power on the streets.

"I'ma get you some customers," Nina said like super woman. She now had a jerky movement about her.

"Hold up." I instructed her to bring the customers to the back door and to make sure she told them I ain't got no weight. She nodded her head and took off out the back door like the place was on fire. I took my gun out placing it on the table and opened up the pack of razors and began to break down some dimes. Nina was back sooner than I expected, and true to her word, with her were some customers. I served dope out of her back door. The time went by fast. I looked at my watch, it was 3:21 in the morning. The nighttime is the most dangerous time to serve stones. In fact, most successful hustlers won't do it. Too much risk. Even cowards get courage in the dark. However, at nighttime the money triples, just like the risk. As soon as Nina saw the size of the rocks I was serving, she tripped.

"Hell naw! Dems too damn big. What is this, a fifty dollar rack?" she asked, dead serious. I cut up sixteen hundred out of an ounce, but I forgot in a cocaine drought, a basehead will buy just about anything to smoke.

"Give them here. Lemme sell them," she demanded.

"Girl I want sixteen off this bomb," I said and passed her an ounce. I sat right there and watched her sell some of them little ass rocks for fifty and if a person only had eight dollars, she would take that too. I peeped what she was doing, selling half and keeping half. I looked out the window, cars were lined up and a few prostitutes lounged around. Everywhere I looked, I saw people. It was easy to tell I was the only nigga in town with a package. The next ounce I cut up smaller, a lot smaller. Nina started smoking again.

She walked in and asked to see the size of the rocks. I showed them to her. "You catch on fast," was all she said and then asked to use my cigarette lighter. Reluctantly, I gave it to her, knowing I would never see it again. Junkies could take a cigarette lighter apart and make a flame thrower out of it. She walked back into her room. I knew that was all the work I was going to get out of her for the night, but it was all good, her place was a gold mine. The money was starting to come so fast I couldn't count it all at times. Suddenly, she ran back into the room and slid across the floor, damn near falling. With her eyes bulging out of her head, panic stricken, she shrieked, "Don't open the door! Don't open the door!"

"WHAT?" I asked incredulously, hoping she wasn't starting to trip off the dope.

"Jackie Boy and T-Bone!" she exhorted. "They on their way around back. They gon' rob us. That's all they do is rob niggas!" Nina said, horrified. I watched as she then hid her money under the sink in a pot. There was a knock at the door. Nina whispered, "Don't open it." I yanked her arm so hard her neck snapped. "Just do as I say!" she pleaded.

"Them niggas ain't going to fuck with us. Who is it?" I asked with enough base in my voice to scare a small child. Nina cringed. A voice returned.

"T-Bone."

"Go 'round the front."

I knew this was it. I had a feeling that Stevey D may have sent them. Now came the risk. I grabbed my gun off the table as the candles flickered our shadow on the wall, like ghosts dancing in a gloom of a murderous reality. Tomorrow ain't promised to no one, not even a gangster in town with the odds stacked against him.

"I'ma scare 'em," I said. "Go blow out all the candles in the house. As soon as they come in I want to you to stand on the other side of the room, in the opposite direction from me. Count to ten and stomp your feet as loud as you can, and get the fuck out the room.

"Nigga, you crazy fo-real!" she said with the confidence of a woman that just had her greatest fears confirmed. What she did not understand was I had no choice in the confrontation. It was as imminent as life itself–power only concedes to counter-power when tested. These niggas had come to test me. There was little doubt in my mind that Stevey D was behind this. The only good part was cats in this town had to already know of my early record of putting them hot balls in a nigga's ass.

Reluctantly, Nina Brown answered the door as I instructed her. From the corner of the room, hidden in the darkness, I watched the silhouette of two figures enter the room. They both wore large coats. Nina closed the door. Complete darkness. I heard feet shuffling. A frantic voice called out, "Nina cut on some fuckin' lights!"

"Yeah, what can I do for ya playa?" I said.

"Cut on the fuckin' lights man!" an agitated voice sounded. More feet shuffling with the sound of ruffling clothes. *Click ... click ...* a cigarette lighter flickered. I cocked the hammer on Jesus and the sound resonated in the darkness.

"Nigga cut dat muthafuckin' light out!" I barked. The light died, along with any hope of their plan of robbery. I was aware that they pulled out their straps pointing in the direction that they heard my voice coming from. When Nina stomped her feet, it scared the hell out of me, too. I heard guns being cocked. It damn sure wasn't mine that time. I crouched down as low as I could to the floor and headed to the kitchen door. I was certain there was going to be some gunplay. I heard someone fiddling with the door, and then it flew open, clanging against the wall. The light from the street lamps sliced through the darkness as I watched the two figures scurry out of the house falling on each other. To my surprise, Nina followed suit. She reminded me of one of them little dogs that ain't going to do shit but yap.

"What the hell ya'll want anyway Jackie Boy? Don't be bringin' that bullshit around my house!" she scolded while walking up behind them.

"Tell him to come out here, we just want to talk wit him," I heard one of them say.

I walked to the door, gun in hand, making sure they saw Jesus. He normally has an instant effect on people's minds.

"Look my nigga, I'm just tying to get a toe hole, I ain't got nothin' but smokin' dimes." For the first time they looked in my eyes, nodded their heads in agreement, and walked away. I knew that the two of them were going to be a problem, I could feel it in my gut. Call it a gangster's intuition, but I felt it. Just then, three people came up complaining to Nina that they had been banging at the back door. They wanted some stones. I turned to walk back in the house. The Narcotic Taskforce car rolled through, four deep, looking out of the car window. With them is the telepathic message that they are watching me. Them white boys sent a shiver through my spine, a signal that I had to be very careful and watch out for the jackman and the policeman. The ironic part was, a dope fiend is cleverer than both of them put together, so I had to watch for them, too.

*****

I served out of Nina's house until the crack of dawn. When the sun started to rise I knew it was time to bounce. The whole time I thought about Trina waiting back at the hotel for me. She was going to be pissed. This was one of my greatest rewards–coming back pockets phat like they got the mumps. I had money in my drawers, socks and all my pockets. Twenty-two stacks, not bad for one night of hustling. Throughout the night, Nina and her elite friends of basers were in the back room of hers having the great smoke out. I was down to my last few stones. My body felt fatigued, my back hurt from bending over serving and my clothes stunk from the awful smell of crack smoke. I was about to call it a day and gave Nina the last of the rocks I had in a bag, about a hundred dollars worth, when I heard a soft knock at the door. I opened it, and there stood the cutest little girl I had ever seen in my life. She was dark as coal, with enchanting almond eyes that seemed to sparkle. I stared, mentally stung, mouth agape. I couldn't take my eyes off of her. Didn't want to either. Something about her held me spellbound. Then it dawned on me. Uncannily, she looked familiar. She looked like Hope! Holy shit! The crack smoke was starting to make me hallucinate. She smiled up at me batting her long pretty eyelashes, wringing her hands together as she danced her leg nervously. I was prepared to dig in my pocket to give her some money. As cute and young as she was I just knew she was selling Girl Scout cookies or something. My eyes trailed her body until I saw the swell of her belly. Like a basketball, she was ready to drop a load. Looked like she was about fifteen months pregnant under that dirty coat. I guessed her age to be no more than 12 years old.

"I don't have any money, but I'll do whatever you want for a rock," she said. I felt my legs wobble as I grabbed hold of the doorframe for support. "I'll suck your dick." I felt my knees damn near buckle.

From somewhere I did not know existed, I heard a voice groan, "NOOOO!!" as her little hand reached out to grab my shirt. I wanted to scream at her and ask where her family was, especially her mama, but Nina's voice broke my thoughts.

"Black Pearl, whatcha doin' out there? I thought you was still in the hospital."

"I left. I got tired of them people sticking needles and stuff all in me. Gurl, give me a bump. I need something to smoke," the little girl known as Black Pearl said. She tried to push past me. I quickly seized her arm, spun her around. She looked up at me, a face of youthful innocence.

"Nina what the fuck you doin'? You see this damn girl is pregnant! How old are you?" I asked, fuming mad. The girl cast a long glance at me shuffling her feet. I had the feeling she was asked this question one too many times. "Sixteen," she mumbled, rolling her eyes.

"Dat girl gonna smoke if I give it to her or not," Nina said. "I smoked with my first two babies, and all of them came out all right," she continued.

I turned ready to smack the shit out of Nina. She held a pipe in her hand, a rock balanced on top of it. From the look in Black Pearl's eyes, she wanted to hit that pipe awfully bad. For the first time in my life I was overcome with guilt. This little girl with Hope's eyes caused the incantation of the words to flow all over again, *you'll end up dead or in prison*. This shit was strange. One thing was for sure, this girl was somebody's child, somebody's daughter, sister and now was about to be somebody's mama. Shit! This was not supposed to be part of the game. Someone was violating the rules.

"Girl, where in the fuck you live at?" I asked her.

Nina cut in, "She lives wit me sometimes, now leave that gurl alone." I continued to stare her down, like waiting for an answer. Finally she looked up at me and blinked her eyes the way a child does when they are being chastised.

"Where your mama at ... your family ... somebody?" My emotions consumed me. I found a part of myself that I, along with millions of hustlers, find it difficult to identify with—the plight of Black life and just how destructive we are in selling poison to our people. Her bottom lip began to tremble as her delicate starry eyes began to brim with tears. Her features Nubian, like an African Princess, she possessed the kind of beauty that should be captured and placed on a poster for the world to see the destruction of Black humanity. How the ghetto chews up and spits out children like recycled waste.

Someone else was at the door, a body with no face. I was in a fog. My emotions were on my sleeve. A voice asked, "Lemme get six for fifty." Just as I reached in my pocket and passed him the last of the dope, a police car cruised by. Too close for comfort. I needed to get out of there. I tried my best not to look at the little girl, but I couldn't help it. Her ebony cheeks were streaked with tears as she cried silently. She watched me as if I were the one responsible for her tears. To the strongest of men, to watch a child cry, especially a pregnant child is truly tormenting. *Keep the babies and the fuckin children out the game!* I thought.

I heard a noise as I was about to leave. I turned around to see Nina Brown on the floor on all fours, searching ... searching for an invisible rock. The dope was starting to play tricks with her mind.

As I checked to see if the coast was clear to make my exit. I tried to shake the scene from my mind, but it was too strong, the voice in my ears was too much. The girl was now holding her stomach bent over crying. From the look on her face I did not know if she was in pain or what. My insides were killing me! I decided right then and there, there was no way in hell I was going to leave this child in this crackhouse. Gangsters have hearts, too. I reached out taking hold of her little hand and together we walked out the door.

A cool morning breeze welcomed my damp skin as we walked out of the house. It felt like I had been in a cave all night. It was the start of a beautiful morning. In the blue sky the sun strobe the clouds in search of its place in the heavens, while below in hell, I was trying to make reason for what I was doing with a pregnant child.

Once we were safely in the car, I watched her as she struggled with the seat belt. "Oh, you'll wear a seat belt but you won't stop smoking to save your baby's life," I said indignantly. She gave me a look that pleaded with me not to go there. It worked. I swallowed the dry lump in my throat. I realized that I was powerless by her stare. I couldn't help thinking how much she looked like Hope. I had to turn my head.

After I drove a few blocks, I heard my voice ask ever so gently, "Are you hungry? Do you want something to eat?

"Yes ... I'm hungry," she answered in a bare whisper. I watched as she rubbed her stomach. I imagined the life of the child in it.

"Where do you want to eat at?"

She shrugged her shoulders as if to say, I don't know. We rode in silence. Up ahead I saw a Shoney's Restaurant.

"What 'bout dat there?" I asked, pointing. She nodded her head yes. I thought I detected a sparkle in her brown eyes.

This was my first lesson in taking a pregnant Black woman to an all you can eat buffet. The sister could throw down! She ate everything in that restaurant, twice. Cheese eggs, strawberry waffles, bacon, toast–they definitely lost money that day. As I sat there watching her eat, it made me feel good, and the whole time she carried herself like a young lady, polite and well mannered. Afterward she belched and we both laughed.

I drove to a Dollar General Store and gave her a hundred dollars. We went inside and she bought panties and bras as well as scented soaps and deodorants. For the first time she looked up at me and smiled, it was the smile of gratitude, something that comes from a woman's heart that melts a man's soul leaving him powerless. Black Pearl's biggest strength—a child's smile that seemed to radiate in infusions of love—would, from that day forward, be my weakness.

*****

When we pulled into the hotel parking lot, I already knew what was on her mind. It was placed there by all the men that violated the sanctity of her chastity. Men that were sent into her bedroom in the wee hours of the night. Men that stole her virginity robbing her of a woman's greatest virtue. These men had been sent in payment for a debt in drugs owed by her mother.

"Dig Shouty, you can stay wit a nigga as long as you like, but you got to keep it real, promise me you'll stay off that shit. And once you have the baby you'll get back in school and try to do something constructive with your life." Black Pearl nodded her head. She was not much for words.

"I'ma be aiight. I only started smokin' when one of my mother's boyfriends raped me and forced me to get high with him," Black Pearl said confidently as she innocently curled her finger around a lock of hair. "I tried a few times, back there with Nina, I just wanted to fit in, needed a place to chill for the night."

"What's your real name?" I asked.

"Annie Bell," she replied.

*Annie Bell*, I thought. She's a country girl in this redneck-ass town.

"I want you to meet my girlfriend."

Black Pearl jerked her neck like she had been hit with a stun gun. "Girrrrrl friend!" she screeched like one of Grandma's old 45 records.

*****

Black Pearl and I entered the room, shopping bags in tow. The soft murmur of feminine voices filled the room, and suddenly stopped, replaced with the evil glares you give a peasant or some unwanted person. To my surprise, Trina, Tomica and Evette were in the room. The air was tainted with the sweet redolence of per-

**170**

fumes and Juicy Fruit gum. Shoes and wine cooler bottles cluttered the floor.

"I see you finally met the 'if it ain't nailed down they can steal it crew'," I said, sarcastically talking to Trina. Evette was sitting on the floor between her lover's legs, getting her hair braided. For some reason, Tomica had this satisfied smirk on her face.

"L, why you give me that girl's bracelet?" Trina asked, getting out of bed. She was talking about the bracelet from the heist that I had to knock the cop over the head for. I gave it to her before I left yesterday in front of Tomica to piss her off. From the looks of things my little ploy backfired. Trina got out of bed wearing my T-shirt. I could still see the sleep in her eyes, or perhaps it was a hangover. I noticed the bracelet on Tomica's wrist. She shots me a knowing glance, like she just scored points for the shit she had started with the bracelet.

"And where is my damn money at?" Tomica questioned, raising her voice for the sake of an audience. Those Brooklyn bitches. Tomica was talking about the money that I took from Evette to rent the place for Blazack and the crew. If I didn't know any better I would have thought they conspired against me in my absence.

"Don't get used to wearing that bracelet," I said to Tomica, hoping something slick would come out of her mouth. Trina hopped her ass out of bed, pink panties cutting in that ass. I saw Tomica's greedy eyes watching as she walked up to me and rolled her eyes at Black Pearl, with all the makings of a cat fight.

"L, I need to speak with you in private," Trina said with her jaws clinched together like her teeth were super glued. On her left cheek, I could see a small scar from where I slapped her in the parking lot. Before I could answer, she pulled my arm and led me into the bathroom.

"What the fuck you doin' bringin' that young-ass girl here?" Before I could open my mouth to answer Trina made a face and continued. "In case you haven't noticed she's pregnant." In the small bathroom, her voice carried like we were in an underground tunnel. Trina was standing close, real close. She was my boo, but that morning breath smelled like pig feet. I took a step back, crinkled my nose.

"Listen, the girl doesn't have a place to stay, she's 16 years old. What was I s'ppose to do?"

"You was s'ppose to bring yo ass home last night! That's what you was s'ppose to do." Trina sassed, shaking her neck one way, her hip another, with her hand on it, lips pouting, nostrils flaring. "Instead, you come in here with this pregnant heffa smelling like …" Trina was lost for words. She pulled at my shirt, using two fingers like I might be contaminated, she sniffed.

"… Smelling like you've been up all night smoking crack," she finally said, her voice laced with the heavy accent of broken English. A curly lock of unruly hair fell over her forehead. I could see the outline of large nipples waving at me every time she moved. She was not wearing a bra. Something about her began to excite me, perhaps it was her animus, that rough and rugged feminine part of a woman. I began to dig into my pockets and throw money on the bathroom floor, and then I took the money out my drawers and socks. Trina's whole demeanor changed. I saw a glimmer of a smile in her eyes as I stood. This, for me, was a hustler's proudest moment, this is what I did best. Some people scored touchdowns, others had their degrees for their personal satisfaction. I had the glory of the game. To be truthful, the reason why a lot of niggas couldn't do this shit was because they didn't have the balls nor the heart to keep it gangsta. I walked up to Trina, eased my hand up under her T-shirt and pulled down her panties with the other hand. She did not say a word as her eyes stared at me defiantly, like when a woman is daring you, and at the same time, I could see the surprise written on her face as I unzipped my fly and pulled out my joint. She looked down and watched it. I was on full blast and feeling freaky, the way a brotha be feeling in the mornings. I turned her around and bent her over.

"Go slow," she whispered in the echo of the bathroom.

I spit on my hands lubricating my joint and to wet the rest of her hairy bush but to my surprise, she was already wet. We got busy in the bathroom. Some of the best sex I ever had.

When I walked out of the bathroom, Tomica and Evette were gone and Black Pearl was standing in the same exact spot I left her.

"Where did they go?" I asked. I was thinking about the bracelet. Black Pearl shrugged her shoulders as if to say, *I don't know.* As I looked at her I realized that she did not want to be there. What Black Pearl didn't know was, I didn't want to be there either.

*****

Three days later, me and my crew were encroached in a fierce struggle. Like all confrontations over drug turf there were casualties. However, when you execute a proper turf take over, niggas normally catch on fast. Get shot, or get the fuck out the way–that was Blazack's motif. After all, a nigga wasn't new to this, we were true to this. Frenchtown was a hustler's paradise. After a few days of Blazack's mayhem of pistol-whipping and kidnapping niggas, we were presented with the keys to the city, so to speak. Niggas got real friendly and even started betraying their homeboys, which is normally the case. Especially with the women, when niggas come from out of town stacking paper.

Finally it happened. T-Bone and Jackie Boy caught Dirty in the projects flaunting, trying to holla at a chickenhead. They split his wig and robbed him for about three grand.  He ended up needing forty stitches in the back of his head. Blazack went on a rampage. His understanding was zero. That night, we rode back through the projects, abducted an innocent bystander and beat the breaks off his ass. Shot up the place, tried to air that bitch out. Made that AK and street sweeper sing a song of the promise of death. In the end, seven people were shot, two critically wounded. I advised Blazack to tone it down, but he seemed to be possessed with finding T-Bone and Jackie Boy, the niggas that had touched Dirty on the jack tip. I just hoped that they had enough sense to get out of town.

*****

**173**

# Chapter Twelve

## "Crooked Cops"

### *– Life –*

Blazack began to act strange, doing things that were not in his character. One of the things that caught my attention was a phrase that he would repeat over and over again. He thought it was the funniest shit in the world. "If you got a problem, ax Blazack. If your homeboy is missing, ax Blazack." For all of us it was weird, and at times, he was starting to spook the hell out of us. As a true lieutenant he handled his business. In fact, we all owed it to him for putting the fear of God in them niggas. "You got a problem ax Blazack." It took us a while to catch on to what the fuck he was talking about. By the time we did it was too late. But the mystery of how he was making people disappear was revealed.

***** 

Soon I received a message from Stevey D. One of his guys was missing. He wanted to know if we had anything to do with it. He was real humble, like he was concerned for a friend. But I know that he was really checking to see if we were beefing, too. I don't know if it was out of fear, or the coke that I promised to cop for him, probably both. When he told me that one of my homies was shaking down niggas, making them pay protection fees, I knew that he was talking about Blazack. That was the same shit he used to do in Miami. Extort niggas. It dawned on me that one of the reasons Stevey D was calling was to see if he was on Blazack's "must do list." After I hung the phone up, I was pissed the fuck off. Blazack was a walking time bomb. The shit he was doing was for his personal gain, not for our benefit. I knew that I was going to have to check his ass. The confrontation could not be avoided, I had no choice.

Tomica and Evette formed a clique with Trina and her sorority sisters, the Deltas. I found out that one of the worst things you can do is put a bunch of women together that are from New York, mainly Brooklyn. They will turn a town full of rednecks and country Black folks out. They called themselves "Thug Misses." I called them some ruddy-ass bitches. Tomica and Evette were still mad boosting, but with the recruitment of the rest of the girls, they graduated from simply stealing jewelry and clothes to stealing expensive cars. The other day I saw them pull up in the parking lot, in not one, but two brand new Benzes with the paper tags still on them. I was riding dirty. They were making so much raucous I had to distance myself. I tried to talk with Trina about it, but Brooklyn broads will run circles around the average nigga if he ain't used to the "Rotten Apple." I could understand why it took her seven years to complete a four-year degree in business. She was scheduled to graduate in a couple of weeks, the same day as Black Pearl's seventeenth birthday. I took that as a good omen, especially since the two of them had started speaking. Trina couldn't help but like Black Pearl. She was a real trooper. She enrolled in school to learn fashion design. After school she would come back to the hotel, tired, and cook a big ass meal. Sometimes there would be as many as ten or more people eating her food. Black Pearl was a country girl at heart. I was so proud of her. I think we were all a little worried about the baby, wondering if the coke she smoked was going to have an effect on the child.

*****

Two weeks, two keys and three hundred dollars later, I was out of coke and anxious to fly back to New York to meet the infamous Willie Falcon at a five star hotel called the Trump Tower. He was major. It was like the dope god had shined on a nigga. To this day,

**175**

I still don't know how my name came up in the echelons of such esteemed drug lords. I do recall when Trina and I went back to her cousin to re-up on dope, she introduced him to me. He drilled me with the one thousand question routine. Mainly he was interested in knowing how in the hell Trina and I flipped two birds and made over three hundred G's and were back wanting twenty more. I wanted to tell him to ask Trina. She was the one that knew how to stretch the coke, whipping it and then breaking it down into dime rocks, but I took the credit and wore it like all thugs do. Now word spread, young nigga on the come up, and I had their attention. I was in the minor league, and Willie Falcon wanted to draft me into the pros. Willie was a Colombian. He was also into "Boy"–heroin. He had the best heroin known to mankind, China White. A key went for four hundred G's. You could step on it thirty times, meaning, you could cut the dope and make thirty keys off of it. I did not know what the fuck I was into. You really had to know what you were doing when cutting up the dope, or you could run the risk of fucking up the product, or worse, killing niggas like roaches.

The morning I came back to the hotel it was thundering and lightning in a tempestuous storm. The canvas of the sky was black like smoke billowing. That day it rained so hard, I wondered if God was mad at the world and he was crying, pounding his mighty fist. The day before, I bought an antique '73 convertible Caddy, black with red interior. The car was in good condition. I hadn't had a chance to buy any shoes for it yet, because the roof leaked, the air conditioner was broke and some mo' shit. I pulled up in the parking lot, sweating like a nigga sitting in the electric chair. The windows were fogged. I had a shopping bag full of money lying on the passenger seat. This was perfect weather for touching a nigga, so after I surveyed the scene, the only thing I noticed out of place were a few cars. A real hustler is always going to know his surroundings. That is if he's on point. In the shopping bag I had eighty grand.

Once I entered my room, Trina's clothes were cluttered everywhere. She refused to cook or clean. She told me that's what maids were for. She and Black Pearl attended school in the mornings, and the two kleptomaniacs, Tomica and Evette, were still going about their business of five-finger discounting. For me, that morning was my quiet time, a time for me to be alone and ruminate on past events.

I took off my wet clothes, along with my gun, and placed them on the dresser. Walking over to the table, I fixed myself a strong drink and lit cigarette. I sat on the bed in only my boxer shorts and began to count money. In the back of my mind certain things about Trina were starting to gnaw me raw. Things that a man cannot escape. I was following her meticulous plan to the letter. In a sense, she was the real mastermind, and we both knew it. My male ego was killing me. Once again I thought about what she said when we first met, *to keep the federalies off your ass, they're only looking for weight. Ain't no longevity in the dope game. Stick and move, get out within a year.*

So far what she was saying was true, with her whip game plus breaking the coke down to its lowest terms, we were making a killing. I was scheduled to meet with Willie. He was going to front me a key of Boy thanks to Trina's persuasion. I did not have a clue as to how to cut up heroin but Trina did. This was around the time she seriously started nagging me about retiring. Hell, I just got started. I hadn't been in the game a hot month yet, but I knew what she was talking about. Willie would escalate profits so much; he was the kind of man who, if you made a few nice moves with him, you could retire. A year before, they found a shitload of coke in Tampa. It was estimated to be over one hundred million dollars. Everyone knew whose dope it was, including the feds. I think that's what Trina was most worried about. I propped my feet up on a chair, went a little deeper into my thoughts and inhaled nicotine like I was a fiend. I thought about the calls that Trina had asked me if she could she push "five" for. Calls from a federal prison. Her ex-boyfriend, Mike, was doing life in the joint in Atlanta. In hushed tones they would talk. With every fiber in my body, I tried not to listen to their conversations, but out of respect, she always talked to him in front of me. She told me she had no secrets, had nothing to hide. Honesty was the best policy and all that bull crap. I made the mistake of asking her if she still loved him. She shrugged her shoulders and told me she did not know. In a woman's language, that meant, "Yes, but I don't want to hurt your feelings." Damn, I hated to admit, but I was jealous. I wondered if he asked her for phone sex. Tell her to play in her pussy and moan in his ear. I was powerless. I had to respect the game, that is, if I was real. Hustlers are abnormally superstitious people. That's where a nigga's blessings come from–honor amongst playas. I knew that it could have been me on the other end of the phone. As I sat there thinking, raking my mind, I detected some movement in my peripheral version. Something caught my eye. I was not alone in the hotel room. Then I heard the all too familiar sound of a bullet being engaged into a semi automatic. For some strange reason, I held my breath and waited for the inevitable, my brains to be spattered across the wall. The sound of thunder resonated outside and in the dark crevice of my mind, Blazack's face flashed like some evil troll, he was here to do me. My gun was out of reach on the dresser. I got caught slipping.

"Place your hands were I can see 'em!" a hoarse voice commanded. I raised my hands fully prepared to accept the consequences of my blunder as I thought about all the cars in the parking lot that I should have paid more attention to.

"So we finally meet, boy," a voice said, dripping with all the Southern hospitality of a Klan redneck. From the corner of my eye, I watched as the white man stepped from the shadows of the closet. His complexion was a sickly pale white. He had a long beak nose that pointed downward like a hook. His beady eyes were set far in the back of his head, and appeared to sit too close together. His hair was dirty blond.

I could feel my heart racing in my chest as something stirred in the pit of my gut–fear. I knew his face from somewhere, then it hit me, Spitler! The crooked cop that Nina tried to warn me about. Damn, how could I have been so fuckin' blind? It suddenly occurred to me that I saw his face in different places, just never took the time to focus on him. He always blended in perfectly with all the white folks. The police always get credit for being clever whenever they capture a criminal, but nine times out of ten, it's a hustler's fault for thinking too slow and moving too fast.

"Life Thugstin." He called my name. Like in all the cops and robbers games, he was letting me know that he did his homework on me. He probably got my prints off the car and ran them through NCIC, the National Crime Information Center.

"In my eighteen years on the force, I have never seen one boy cause so much havoc in this town as you son," he said and walked so that he was standing in front of me. His Southern drawl made the hair on my neck stand up. Florida crackas are the most evil, treacherous men the United States had ever bred. In fact, that's where the name "cracka" came from. The hot Florida sun bakes their white skin making it look like old cracked leather. When I was a little boy, my stepmother told me stories about how the slave masters used to hang pregnant women upside down and took a knife and butchered the baby out of their stomachs and when it hit the ground, they would stomp it. She told me this was done to implant fear in all the slaves. And even after Lincoln had so called freed the slaves, Florida crackas would rather kill theirs than let them be free.

I had no intention of ever going back to prison. As he talked, I measured the distance to my gun. Desperation will make a man do some suicidal shit, like leap for a gun when he really doesn't have much of a chance.

"You shot that boy in Frenchtown and robbed him after he wouldn't buy your fake drugs."

"That wasn't me!" I quipped, easing closer to my gun. I could feel my palms sweating.

"Shut up! And keep your hands where I can see them," he snorted, as he continued to brag about himself, how brilliant of a cop he was to be telling me of my track record in his town.

"You robbed that jewelry store and knocked the snot out of the security guard." Someone once said that ignorance is bliss, so I did what Black folks are famous for whenever they were caught, cold busted. I played dumb and looked at that white man like he was speaking a foreign language.

"Where did you get the money from?" he asked, nodding at the pile of money on the bed.

I didn't ever answer, just looked him in his eyes, and thought about prison bars and caged cells not big enough for dogs much less a human being. That desperate voice in my head was telling me, *Try him! Go for your gun.* Then something dawned on me, where was his back up? Something was out of place.

"Today's your lucky day boy," he said mockingly. "I'm not going to turn you in, but I am going to help myself to some of this money here. He started stuffing his pockets with my money. He was robbing me. I jumped up from the bed taking a step forward.

"Wha  da fuck you doin'?!" I was enraged. This is why you only see white cops killing Black men in cold blood. In their eyes Black men were powerless against the system.

"You make a move like that again, and I promise you boy, I'll blow your goddamn brains out." There was no doubt in my mind that he meant what he said.

"Sit down!" he barked. My eyes shown optic slants of hate that back in the days of the slavery of my ancestors, he would have had me lynched for. Reluctantly I sat back down. My breathing was labored and I could feel my heart pounding in my chest. I was sick and tired of white men constantly taking from me. If it wasn't my freedom, it was my money, and as I looked at that white man with blood in my eyes, I realized that it was just the principle of the thing. Even so-called criminals respect each other.

"I'm here for a good reason," he said.

"What, to take my muthafuckin' money?"

"No, to make you money."

"Huh?"

"As long as you're selling drugs and killin' each other in that jungle ya'll call Frenchtown, I ain't got no problem with that."

"I can't muthafuckin tell! You come in here actin like John Wayne takin' my muthafuckin money!"

"That's because crime does pay. It pays the judges, the lawyers, the FBI, CIA, the DEA and you just paid me." With that, he smiled like Lucifer in the flesh. My blood boiled in my veins. Only history knows best the relationship of the white man stealing from Blacks in the name of the law. He continued, "America has built illegal drugs into the most powerful institution the world has ever known. Like the prisons, legalized slavery, check the stock market." As he talked, I had no idea what the hell he was talking about, and didn't care neither.

"But on the other hand, I like you, you remind me of your so-called black leaders of today. You're in it for the money, them boys back in the day ..." Spitler stopped to think, and suddenly snapped his finger like he had a bright idea. "Martin and Malcolm X, all they did was stir up trouble, wasn't no good to black folks. Now you, you think like a white man. You know how to take advantage of your race. From here on out you can sell all the drugs you like, just keep it out the white folks' neighborhood. Them white kids is America's future. You hear me?" He raised his voice. Something about what he said hurt me to the core, made me feel less than a man, less than human. White people have this uncanny way of making Black people feel awkward in their presence and all the time he talked, smiled, looking like a Catholic priest.

"This is my cut," he said stuffing more money into his pockets.

"HELL NAW! FUCK DAT!" I stood up fast, stiff like a human rocket. "Listen, cracka, I don't fuck wit no muthafuckin police, period!"

"Sit down!" he commanded, pointing the gun at my head.

I guess this is the way Black men get shot, because all I could see was red. Spitler provoked me, pushing me over the edge.

"If you're gonna shoot me, shoot me now! You ain't finna come in here, take my muthafuckin money, telling me how to run shit!" I said, standing my ground, fists clinched at my side. We stared each other down. I knew it was foolish of me to do what I was doing.

"For two thousand dollars a week you can sell all the dope you want. Just keep it out the white neighborhood. Hell, it would be like you have a license. I can make sure you and your people never get caught, as long as you're working out of a house." Spitler was talking a mile a minute, non-stop. "I'll actually be working for you."

I sat back down on the bed, rubbed the waves in my head, thinking about what he said. I knew I had no out with him; I was in a no-win situation in this deadly game of crooked cops. One thing was for certain, once a hustler had a cop in his pocket, that changed the whole game. Things could turn from sugar to shit. I took a chance and tossed a gambit at him. "OK cop you work for me now." He smiled like he had just sold me a comfortable cell in Sing Sing prison. "That money that you just took off the bed, that was your first month salary and I'm payin ya one grand a week, not two," I said as the smile died on his face.

"I'll take fifteen hundred a week or I'm taking your black ass down to the station."

*He took the bait*, I thought as I tried to my best to look disappointed, frowned like he was taking advantage of me. I looked at him, saw all the greed of his ancestors in his little beady eyes. I went for the evident, this white man wasn't no earthly good.

"You got a deal," I said, and looked at the bed at the pile of cash. For some reason he did not take all of it; that only meant that he was serious about wanting to be on my payroll.

There was a knock at the door. Startled, he flinched. *Scary-ass cracka*, I thought to myself as he waved his gun and told me to answer the door. I walked to the door, and while I tried to keep my eyes on him, he picked up my gun emptying the bullets out on the rug. I looked out the peephole and saw Black Pearl standing there. She looked worried, and continued to glance over her shoulder. I opened the door. Spitler rushed by me out the door, damn near knocking Black Pearl down. That white man scared the hell out of her. She walked with one hand on her stomach, the other over her heart. She grabbed my hand holding it tightly.

"Lawd have mercy! Pah-leez tell me that was not that nasty-ass cracka police, Spitler," she said, exasperated. I could feel her hand trembling. "Look outside the window," she said. Her voice was barely above a whisper as her starry eyes searched mine asking me what was going on. I pulled the curtains back in the window just as a huge bolt of lightning lit up the sky. Eerily, I saw my reflection, jagged edges of a man. Down below in the parking lot, six black unmarked police cars sat idling. I watched as Spitler scurried out into the pouring rain and signaled a thumbs up and dashed into the car. One after the other, the cars trailed out of the parking lot.

Black Pearl tugged my shirt. "You're going to have to leave here. I know a place you'll be safe." To the average hustler, a pregnant woman is about the purest form of good luck a man can have. So as the thunder and lightning clapped, I was listening to this pregnant woman like Moses did the Ten Commandments.

We packed in a hurry. Jumped into the hoopty and drove forty-five minutes outside of Tallahassee to a small rural town called Quincy. For me it was love at first sight. As country as you can get but the town had a serene peacefulness about it. As I continued to drive, I was overcome by the beautiful landscapes, like the ones you see on a postcard—peaceful and serene with a dazzling sun that bathes the scenic green pastures. In the distance, I saw an old mansion with plantation style shutters and sprawling green landscape that must have dated back to the seventeenth century. I slowed the car down, looked at the "For Sale" sign hanging askew in the wooden fence. It said, "Twenty acres for sale." I turned to Black Pearl and dreamed out loud.

"I'ma buy that place, fix it up real nice, name it Chateau G.P., short for Gangsta Paradise."

In response, Black Pearl hitched a ride to my dream and asked excitedly, "Oh please! Please let me do the decorating and interior design." She was a true-to-heart sixteen-year-old. Anyone else would have told me I was crazy. The place was not worth a rusty nickel.

*****

I drove back to town and rented two rooms, one for myself and the other for Pearl. Dirty hit me on the hip. I checked my beeper, 911. I called him and he said it was an emergency, something to do with Blazack. I agreed to meet him at Denny's Restaurant. When I got there he was seated all the way in the back. He looked like a nervous wreck, chewing on his fingernails. As I approached, he smiled up at me wearily.

"Whuz up yo?" I said, sliding into the booth with him. A waitress with a foreign accent and a nice figure gave me a menu and said she'd be right back. I watched her hips as she walked away.

"Man, you gotta stop this fuckin' nigga Blazack! He done lost his fuckin mind and some shit," Dirty said. I sat there and listened to a horror story about how Blazack murdered both T-Bone and Jackie Boy in cold blood. In the early morning, Blazack went to Jackie Boy's mother's house and shot him in the head right in front of her and two younger brothers. That same day, the entire crew abducted T-Bone from the work release center and took him down to the basement of the house that we rented. To everyone's utter shock and dismay Blazack appeared with an ax and made T-Bone bow down to his knees and began to hack his head off with the ax. Afterward, Blazack threatened all of them, if they told, they would be next. Then he showed them how to cut up a body. The art of making people disappear. Now for the past few days Blazack had been driving through Frenchtown with T-Bone's head in a bag showing it to all the hustlers, not just as evidence of revenge for robbing a member of his crew, but also a means to intimidate drug dealers for their money. I was reminded of Stevey D's earlier call. Blazack had him shook, scared to death.

Now shit was starting to make sense, the mystery phrase, "Your homeboy missing, Ax Blazack." For the past few years,

**184**

secretly, Blazack had been making people disappear, including his own baby mama and her boyfriend. Now as I sat there in the booth, it dawned on me like I'm sure it must have dawned on the rest of the heads of the crew, I was going to have to step to him. I knew that I could not underestimate him, but there was one thing that stood out in my mind back there in his room when he described having to kill Dre' with his bare hands. All killers have a weapon of choice. Knives, guns, axes. As I remembered, Blazack was not good with his hands in battle, at least I hoped in preparing for the confrontation.

Perplexed, I frowned and asked Dirty, "Damn, you don't think the nigga smokin' or sometin' do ya?"

"Hell yeah he smokin'," Dirty shot back.

"Huh, smokin' what?"

"Smokin niggas wit dat 12 gauge shot gun," Dirty retorted. "Man you ain't hearin' me! Dude out there on a killin' spree. When you find him have your burner witcha, I ain't one to be startin' shit, but not just dude, but the whole crew been grumblin' bout all that fuckin money you been makin'." With that, Dirty raised his chin like it was connected to his pride, his way of telling me he too was pissed about the money I was paying him. I walked away from him wondering when the shit went down between Blazack and myself, just whose side would the crew roll with.

*****

# Chapter Thirteen

## "A Deadly Confrontation"

*— Life —*

As soon as I walked into the house, I knew that something was terribly wrong. All I saw were somber faces. Gucci, Mad Ball and Twine. The kind of faces you see at funerals. Twine looked up at me as he stopped rolling a blunt.

"Why the fuck ya'll niggas ain't at work?"

"Ain't no work!" Gucci shot back in disgust, throwing up his hands frustrated. "Cats been coming out of town to buy our shit and taking it back and reselling it. The dime bags of powder, too. Shit selling like hot cakes my nigga."

It was Trina's idea to sell the dime bags of powder. On just a Friday alone, we could sell five bricks or more. That was over a million and some change.

The vibe in the room wasn't right. I reflected back on what Dirty warned me about at the restaurant, the crew being unhappy about the chips I was paying them, so I tried to read each man's face, and they all looked the same, like mutiny waiting to happen. Then I heard a blood-curdling scream come from the basement.

"What da fuck was dat?!"

"That's crazy-ass Blazack!" Gucci said. "Look man, shit getting crucial. We thinking about bailing back to the crib, a nigga ain't making no money and Blazack runnin' round here actin' like he psycho, cuttin' muthafuckas up with an ax and shit."

"Where in the fuck he at now?" I asked.

"Down in the basement, he got Major down there, said he stole a bomb of rocks from him."

I took off in a hurry down the stairs to the basement. Major was our all-purpose man. Every crew had one. If it was broke he could fix it, whether it be a motor or installing a car stereo system. I had a lot of respect for Major; even though he smoked he still carried himself like a man, always wore clean clothes and took care of himself.

As I walked down the darkened stairway, I felt for the .380 pistol in my pocket, thought about what was about to go down with my confrontation with Blazack as the smell of death and Pine Sol reeked in my nostrils. It kind of made me want to vomit. At the bottom of the stairs in the dimly lit loft I saw Blazack standing over Major holding a hot iron, one of them old fashion kinds used for ironing clothes. Major's shirt was torn off, he was bleeding badly, his face was discolored and bruised. Blazack had him tied to a chair. I walked up without either of them hearing me. I was fully prepared to kill Blazack. I had to be, because I knew without a shadow of a doubt, he would kill me just for the sport of it, if the time suited him right.

"Yo, that's enough Blazack! Untie him!" Blazack spun around to face me. I saw something in his eyes, wild and untamed.

"Fuck dat! Dis nigga done fucked up a package. I'ma havta make an example out of him, too!"

"L, pleeeese man, stop him," Major pleaded through swollen lips. His skin was pink and red from the burn marks from the hot iron.

I walked up to Blazack. "Let him go!" I said louder this time.

"What part of no you don't understand?" he asked with in venom in his voice. I was conscious of him swinging the iron at me. In my mind I was thinking, *this nigga ain't never been known to be good with his fists*. I thought about how he damn near cried when he was telling me about how he had to kill the snitch Dre' with his bare hands. Take away his gun, he probably wasn't shit. It was plenty of cats like that, real gorillas with a gun, but hoes when it came to their fist. Major whimpered again for me to help him. I bent down to untie him. Blazack dropped the iron and grabbed my arm, I shoved him. My instincts told me to go for my heat.

"Don't make me havta bust your ass in here nigga," I said, feeling the  adrenaline rush of a fight.

"My nigga you really ain't tryna see me," Blazack's mouth said, but his body spoke a different language as he took a step back, sizing me up, his eyes registering the surprise of my boldness. From the corner of my eye I saw the rest of the crew, watching, waiting. I guess the jury was still out with them in choosing whose side they were on.

"Yeah, you right, I ain't trying to see you. You need to go! I ain't paying your bitch ass five G's a week to be runnin' round here torturing and killin' niggas," I said, pointing a finger in his face. I went to finish untying Major, at the same time, I kept my eyes on Blazack.

"I'ma be the muthafucka putting the fear of God into these niggas," Blazack shrilled angrily. "Nigga, you couldn't sell a fuckin' bird until I got here!" With one swift kick, Blazack sent the chair with Major still in it toppling over onto the floor. Major got up and ran to the stairs. I told him to meet me at my car. He needed medical attention. There was no way in hell I was going to let him leave looking like a creature from the horror show.

"You think we don't know how much money you makin' and that Brooklyn bitch breakin' ya. Trina playing ya like a sucka. While you paying us fuckin' pennies, you got the bitch pickin up the drop off." I held my temper in check while Blazack vented. As he talked, I was surprised to learn this was some shit he wanted to get off his chest.

"Every day, I give that bitch five or six hundred G's, and some days more, and you trustin' a bitch like she sincere."

A sacred rule of the dope trade is to never let the right hand know what the left hand is doing. They didn't know that it was because of Trina that I was not only locked in to a major dope supply, but she organized and carefully set everything into to motion, including her advice on how much I should pay my workers. I wasn't going to tell him that.

Right then as I looked around at the crew watching me, waiting for my reaction, I could smell the larceny simmering in the air like a hot pot of treason about to boil over. Also I understood where Blazack was coming from, but I could not let him get away with all the senseless shit he had been doing.

"Yo, you gotta to go, or stop the dumb shit," I said coldly.

"Dat nigga beat us for ten G's in dope," Blazack said, disgruntled.

"Naw he beat you for ten grand in dope. You knew the nigga was a smoker in the first place," I reasoned, took a step closer and dropped the bomb on him. "Beside, you been taxing niggas. I believe you been servin' my dope and the dope you takin' from niggas, too."

Blazack just looked at me as he ran his tongue around the diamonds in his mouth like he was searching for the right words. I caught him off guard. But now he knew that I knew he was playing both sides of the street. From the look in his eyes, I could tell he was trying to figure out how in the hell I found out. The room became quiet. This was a standoff.

From there on out, the events that took place in that basement would seal my fate. I tried to let my mind catch up with my thoughts, appraise the situation for what it was worth. Quickly, with Blazack staring me down, my assessment went to damage control. My ship with a small crew of niggas was taking in water like the Titanic with a hole in it. I had to plug the hole, fast!

"The reason that I came here was to give ya'll niggas a big raise in pay," I lied. The whole time I kept my eyes on Blazack. I went on and told them about the plan I had for operating out of safe houses. Each one of them would be assigned a house with a crew under them that they would be responsible for. When I told them I had the cop, Spitler, in my pocket, they were all happy to hear that. Spitler could be a royal pain in the ass for a dope boy. With some of the tension gone, I turned to Blazack.

"Dig yo, you can bounce my nigga if you got a problem with what I'm asking you to do. But if you do decide to get your shit together, you get ten grand a week."

It wasn't no military secret, Blazack was the glue that held us together. Every team had to have an enforcer, a man that didn't mind getting paid in blood. Blazack smiled at me.

"However." I continued, "You're suspended for two weeks with no pay." The smile died on Blazack's face as his eyebrows knotted together.

"Gucci, you're going to take Blazack's position until ..."

I let the word hang in the air as I gave Blazack a look that came with a silent threat.

He cursed. Called me a bitch-ass nigga under his breath. I acted like I didn't hear him.

That day when I walked out of that basement, for the first time in my life I won the entire respect of the crew, including Blazack's.

*****

"What do you want to drink?" I asked Major, trying not to look him in the face as we got into my car. He looked like he stood in front of a train.

I knew he was in great pain as he mumbled, "Whatever." I saw the tears in his eyes. Eyes of a defeated man. A mere husk of his former self. Major had not one, but two college degrees. He was in the Marines and had the pleasant demeanor of a soft-spoken Southern gentlemen with manners to match. I knew how bad he wanted to get off the dope, but the demons wouldn't let him. He talked to me about it on several occasions.

We drove through Frenchtown, the place looked like the walking dead. Junkies tried to flag down my car hoping to buy some dope. Nina Brown stood in the middle of the street like she had an 'S' on her chest looking like a zombie. I almost ran her over. I knew if I stopped they would rush my car like starving Africans do missionaries.

As I drove, casually I asked Major where was the dope was that he stole from Blazack. I didn't really expect for him to be truthful with me. When he told me that he had it stashed over a female's crib, and the only reason he did not tell Blazack was because he was afraid Blazack would kill her, too. We stopped off and picked up the dope. I took half and gave him the rest. I pulled into a drive-through liquor store, bought a bottle of E&J, a bag of ice and coconut cream to cut it with. I flirted with a sexy redbone cashier that looked like Sade.

Drinking and driving, sipping on juice with my system booming, I pulled into the mean strip on FAMU College campus. Even though it was raining a light drizzle, females, honeys galore, were jocking my ride. College girls be on dope boys like groupies on rappers.

At 11:04 a.m., I was looking for Trina's car. It was still raining. I found her car in the parking lot. Moments later, as scheduled, she came out of the building wearing blue jeans and a gray FAMU sweat shirt with a black leather jacket that had NY stenciled on the back in big purple letters. She wore my Chicago Bulls baseball cap pulled down over her eyes as she walked to her car with umbrella in hand. I honked the horn. As soon as she saw me her face lit up and she gave me a mischievous grin. I know what was on her mind. Sex. Occasionally I would pick her up from school and we would go back to her place right off campus and have sex. She hardly ever stayed there, so I also thought it was an ideal spot to hide the money since it was her job to pick it up daily. Trina could get so animated when she was happy, maybe that was the Spanish side of her. She approached my car like she was dancing in the rain. The bounce in her step had her ponytail swinging like a devious kitten. With all the vibrance of a young woman ready to set out to conquer the world, no one would have ever thought she could be the brainchild to a million dollar drug ring. A Brooklyn chick.

I rolled down the window and she kissed me with enough tongue to hang a man with, she then looked in the car at Major.

"Ouch, what happened to him?" she asked. I shrugged my shoulders as if to say, *I dunno.*

I got out of the car and walked under her umbrella to her car. We sat inside. I told her about our new living arrangements in Quincy. I talked as the rain pelted the car windows like soft music to my monologue, a conspiracy between lovers. I told her about the plantation mansion I was going to buy and remodel. She listened intently. Afterward, she asked about Black Pearl, I detected a real bond of sisterhood there. We both knew that Pearl was due to have the baby any day now.

Ever so gently, Trina leaned over and kissed me passionately, sucking on my bottom lip as her fingers walked down my thigh until she reached my fly. She eased her hand inside. "Papi," she crooned breathily as her hand stroked me. I closed my eyes just as the windows in the car began to fog.

"Papi, I want to go to Freak Nic in Atlanta, me and the girls," she said as she licked my neck with hot saliva and took my joint out of my pants. I was about to say yes, and then she added, "I'm going to stop by the prison and visit Mike." Right then, for a fleeting second, I saw a gleam of something in her brown eyes. She was talking about her ex-boyfriend. My instincts tried to tell me something, but jealousy was a barrier as I thought, *damn, this nigga in prison, but he's out here in my girl's mind.*

"No." I answered Trina's question flatly. She looked up at me with optic slits that were hard to read, but the message was conveyed, she still had feelings for him, and I was jealous and seething with the rage that came with it.

"That's your fuckin' problem, you and your frat sistas party too damn much," I snapped. Trina shook her head and craned her neck the way a woman does when she is trying to understand her man.

I tried to soften the blow, hide my feelings like a fire under the bed, but the smoke was smoldering in the dark recess of my eyes. "Ma, this weekend we s'pposta fly out to meet wit yo peeps, remember?" I said with the timbre of my voice softening. She didn't answer, she just stared at me for all it was worth as my joint went soft in her hands. She pulled away. I adjusted my fly, taking the opportunity to navigate my thoughts, it was an awkward situation. The last thing in the world I wanted was for this chick to know that I was getting emotionally attached to her.

"I'm sending Tomica to Chicago and Evette to Baltimore. From here on out, we movin' weight."

"But I thought you said we was never going to sell weight to keep the feds off."

"No! You said we were never going to sell weight. I'm changing the game plan, flipping the script. It takes too damn long to move a key of Boy in this country-ass town," I said. For some reason I was angry, hurt. It felt like she betrayed me.

"Papi, why you into your feelins?" Her words chimed. I just looked straight ahead, watched the rain dance off the windshield, thought about all the cash I had stashed at her place, duffel bags full. I couldn't even count it all it was coming so fast.

Like round two, Trina's whole demeanor changed. She placed her hand into my lap. Her index finger gyrated a figure eight motion on my thigh. I turned and looked at her, for the first time I saw Trina Vasquez, the actress. She was as fake as a three-dollar bill. I thought about what Blazack had said back there in the basement, "that Brooklyn bitch playin' you like a sucka."

I hopped out of the car into the pouring rain, heard her shout as she called my name. Emotions spilling over like some volcanic reaction. That was the day that I decided to buy a money counting machine, several of them.

I drove back to Quincy with Major as my sidekick. We drank E&J bumping Too Short's "The Ghetto" on my Alpine system. I fired up a blunt, reflected back on my life. Trina's words were haunting me. I knew it was time to start thinking about getting out of the game, but hell, I was just getting started. Besides, Trina's people had me hooked.

Two days later Black Pearl gave birth to a healthy baby boy. When she came home from the hospital, the girls decided to give her a baby shower. I had never seen so many ruddy females in my entire life. They even hired male strippers. I noticed that a few of Trina's fraternity sisters brought rulers with them to use on the strippers. When dude showed up at the door wearing a cowboy suit I knew it was time for me to get the hell out of there.

*****

It took me a few weeks, but I was finally able to purchase the land that Black Pearl and I dreamed about. The old guy thought I was crazy, so did everybody else, except Black Pearl. She had been talking to decorators and architects about building a stylish mansion just like them white folks have out in Hollywood, so I flew in decorators from California and paid out the ass for it, too.

*****

Trina finally graduated from FAMU after being there seven years, majoring in a four-year course in Business Management. On the same day Trina graduated, Black Pearl turned seventeen, so I did the damn thang! We partied lavishly. I rented five stretch limos and filled them with cases of Moet and Alize. The next day I paid for thirty-eight tickets at eight hundred a pop, plus airfare, to go see a Mike Tyson fight at Madison Square Garden. The fight only lasted thirty-seven seconds. We still had a ball. For the first time I saw Blazack with a smile on his face that wasn't from mischief, but the pure joy of being a big baller. The next morning we flew back to Florida. We were tired, hung over, pooped and partied out. I had another surprise for Trina. In the parking lot of her building complex off campus sat a top-of-the-line Mercedes. One of them big body Benzes. I even had it customized with a special stash spot and some other nice amenities. We decided to give Black Pearl Trina's Lexus to zip around town in.

The most amazing thing happened. Something that a man will never fully be able to understand, the metamorphosis that a woman experiences with her body after childbirth. Keep in mind, Black Pearl was like my baby sister, or for that matter, my daughter. After she had the baby she blossomed into a drop dead gorgeous beauty. Her hips spread wide, her butt got big like Wow.

**194**

One of them ghetto booties with a small taut waistline, punctuated by the symmetry of her figure like a deformed Coke bottle. Lord, I tried not to look at that child's rear end. If Trina, Tomica and Evette were dime pieces, then Black Pearl was definitely a twenty piece with her dark features, deep chocolate skin, perfect white teeth with a dazzling smile that could make a man blush from standing too close to beauty, not to mention body. She named her son Shawn L. The L was named after me. I thought that was kind of dope.

Shawn L. was a cute little booger. Looked just like his mama. As soon as he started walking we called him Lil Man. The first words that came out his mouth were "muthafucka" and "money." I taught him that.

*****

Two months later the remodeling of the Chateau was going lovely and I was bringing in so much money that I had to hire more workers. August 26, 1992, Lil Cal was found guilty. He was sentenced to life in prison. I immediately hired attorneys to work on his appeal. The last time we talked he sounded distraught, that was my nigga, and with all my newly achieved wealth, there wasn't a damn thing I could do to help him other than send him money.

*****

May 1994, two years later, I was still in the game, only then, I wasn't a playa, I was coaching from the sidelines, doing big thangs. Moving major weight. Tallahassee was small to me, so I gave Blazack the entire operation. That way officially it looked like I retired, but actually I graduated into the Ivy League right up there with the rest of the corporate American thugs. I was doing all the things that I promised Trina I would not do. Only now, I kept her out of my business. We were starting to grow apart. Money can do that to a relationship. I knew of her disdain for me selling dope. Even though I promised her I would get out, I couldn't and sometimes I wondered if her cousin, Willie Falcon, would let me. I knew too much.

To everyone's delight, Pearl and I remodeled the old mansion into grandiose elegance with sprawling manicured landscaping of picturesque green pastures surrounded by a white picket fence that gave the estate the appearance of the White House. In the driveway and in the garage sat ten luxury cars including my two prized possessions, his and hers Rolls Royce convertible Bentleys sitting on dubs. We spent close to three million on remodeling the place. I named it "Chateau G.P."

For me, this was the testament of a hustler's grind from having a team of niggas with one common interest: money. Outside, I lived lavishly. There was a waterfall connected to the swimming pool, and of course, a basketball court. Inside was sixteen thousand feet of nothing but plush luxury. Black Pearl had everything decorated white with sparkling crystal chandeliers, which accentuated the marble floors. There was even a white baby grand piano that sat in front of the picture window that overlooked the swimming pool. I installed a state-of-the-art security system with cameras set up so I could see any part of the house I wanted, both inside and out. I even had a secret passageway built in behind the bookshelves in my study, just in case I needed to make a quick escape if them folks came looking for me. About a year ago, Willie Falcon got nabbed in New York. The media had a frenzy. His bust made world news. The papers dubbed him the second biggest drug lord in the world. They said his empire was worth billions. So I continued to make moves with his backing, only now since his arrest, for some reason, more trust was bestowed to me. My millions were crumbs compared to his billions. So I moved weight, occasionally I would fly over to Colombia. The job was risky as hell, but the rewards were great. I'd never seen so much coke in my life. The last time I flew over there, the National Guard with the help of the DEA tried to shoot our plane down. Scared the shit out of me. That was the last time I flew to Colombia.

*****

# Chapter Fourteen

## "Gangsta's Paradise"

*– Life –*

I pulled the old Cadillac off the shoulder of the old dirt road onto the spiraling landscape of my estate as Lil Man sat on my lap. He liked to play drive with the steering wheel. Now, at 3 years old, he was a bundle of joy. I remember when I was a shorty, my old man used to do the same thing with me.

It was one of them lazy Saturday mornings. I was just returning from the Mom and Pop grocery store up the hill. I was driving the first car that I purchased from back in the day when I first came up on the grind. The '73 Caddy was in mint condition. I made it a point to never let anyone see me drive my new whips. They were like awards given to the most valuable playa. Besides, Trina shined for the both of us. There is something about New York chicks. Trina drove around town in a customized white Bentley on dubs, she and her wild-ass homegirls.

As usual, as I approached the security gates of the Chateau, with its large embellishment decorated in brown stone and white marble. Looking at this filled me with pride. I noticed that the gates were wide open and thought that was unusual of Major to leave them open like that. As soon as I turned into the circular driveway, I saw trouble, six unmarked police cars lined up. Spitler was standing next to the statue with the waterfall. For some reason it made him look small. My heart skipped a beat as I frantically stashed my heat under the seat. I saw Trina and Black Pearl watching from the doorway of the mansion. I got out of the car with Lil Man in my arms. I was trying to act nonchalant, but I could feel my leg shaking.

Spitler walked toward me gingerly. I tried to read the expression on his face, but didn't want to look him in his eyes. I learned long ago that white cops are easily intimidated by that. Spitler's brown suit was wrinkled like he slept in it for days. His eyes were red with dark circles underneath them. A tuft of unruly blond hair hung over his left eye. Trina rushed out of the house, the sound of her slippers racked the concrete like a woman on the verge of panic. She took Lil Man out of my arms and looked at me and asked was everything all right. I told her to go back inside. She walked away with the baby on her hip and glanced back over her shoulder. In the distance, I saw Major grooming a horse watching me carefully.

"How in the fuck did you get through that gate?" I asked pointing a finger at him.

"I had one of my men take a sledgehammer to it," he said.

I turned, and vaguely I could see the face of a Black man sitting in the front seat of one of the cop cars.

"What, you come to arrest me or sumpin?"

"Maybe. I thought I told you not to sell that stuff to the white kids!" he said angrily jabbing his finger into my chest. I took a step backward and braced myself. In the background, I heard the sounds of police car doors opening.

"Man you know damn well I don't fuck around in Frenchtown no mo."

"Yeah, but your gang does, Blazack and his crew."

"Then that's who the fuck you need to be harassing! He's the one payin you now, not me. I'm outta the game." I lied, and we both knew it. It was just that I graduated to selling weight, a hustler's dream. Ten keys or better and most of my clients were Willie Falcon's people.

Agitated, Spitler spoke through clenched teeth. "You're not listening to me. Someone is flooding the town with high quality heroin called China White, now we got white kids dying too," he said, walking up to me getting all in my face. I could smell his fetid breath. There was something about what he said. Maybe it was the way that he said it all in my face. I just lost it.

"I don't give a flying fuck about no white kids! All my life niggas been dying around me like flies and no one cared about them, but the moment white kids start dying there is a problem with that."

"It's you! And I know that it's you flooding the town with dope. Look how you're living." For emphasis he turned and gestured with his arms doing a half circle. I saw his cheeks flush red with envy. He walked over to my black Bentley and spit on the ground in disdain.

"We're going to have to make other arrangements."

"Arrangements!?" I retorted.

"Yep. Arrangements for you to start paying me."

"Payin' you. I told you, I'm out of the business."

"And I'm telling you, you're going to start paying me again since you violated the terms of our agreement."

"What fucking agreement? I don't know what the fuck you talkin' bout."

"Keep the fucking dope out the white com –"

I lost my temper. "I don't give a fuck about you and no cracka-ass kids. If I give you one fuckin dime, it will be over my dead mama's grave. Now get the fuck off my property!" I turned and walked away.

"You're going to regret you ever laid eyes on this town … you fucking nigger!"

I stutter-stepped in my tracks. His words stabbed me in the pit of my gut. I had never been called a nigger by a white man in my entire life, for some reason the shit hurt, those words would always have an humiliating affect on Blacks. The voice in my head told me to keep walking. Spitler was trying to bait me.

*****

That night I held an emergency meeting at my estate. I summoned everyone on the carpet. The two lesbians, Tomica and Evette were the first to arrive. Trina greeted them at the door. The atmosphere suddenly turned festive. I watched them on camera from the palatial confines of my study. As soon as Black Pearl walked in with Lil Man the rest of them women showered them with affection. I could hear all that damn commotion. Women!

Later the rest of the crew arrived, Gucci, Mad Ball, Twine and Dirty. Everybody was driving New Benzes or BMWs, except Blazack, he was driving a big-ass Hummer. Trust me when I say that he gave new meaning to the term, "body space" that was usually meant for luxury.

I invited everyone into my study. They walked in, in awe over the elegant beauty and décor, soft mahogany colors, lots of leather and leopard skin. A lion's head adorned the wall to my left. Also on the wall were pictures of African women, warriors, nude, captured in battle at war.

I sat behind my desk smoking a Newport cigarette. Lil Man ran in and dived on my lap playfully, forcing me to break my train of thought. I cuddled him in my arms. He was like my adopted son.

With everyone seated except Blazack, I looked around and it kind of choked me up. I built an empire, and these was my niggas, common everyday folks.

As I talked Trina came and stood by my side like the First Lady.

"I called ya'll here cause we got a problem." I went on to explain to them the situation concerning Spitler. Even though I did not have my hands directly in the mix of things, other than supplying major weight from time to time to the crew and letting the girls do some trafficking, whatever Blazack and his crew decided to do with their profit was their business. In a lot of ways I was an outsider. I just wanted them to be on guard. Needed them to know and understand that we were still family.

There was one more issue, Tomica and Evette were working

independently of each other trafficking Boy to three major cities: Chicago, Detroit and Baltimore. I tried to separate Tomica and Evette as best as I could to stop them from stealing my shit. There was a guy in Baltimore who just happened to be where Evette delivered. He owed me a hundred grand. He called to tell me he couldn't come pay me my money because he was sick and that the only way he felt safe that I would get it, was for me to personally come pick it up. Not. Dude gave me a bad vibe. After arguing with him over the phone, I had a migraine headache, plus it wasn't the first time he tried a stunt like that with my money. I knew that he had a bad gambling habit and liked to spend money on pussy. I decided to let him keep it, fuck it. Charge it to the game. I just threw it up in the air for the head to chew on. I guess to test my judgment.

Surprisingly Evette raised her hand. As usual, she was dressed to impress. She wore lots of jewelry and a light brown miniskirt with a matching see-through blouse and high heels with her toes exposed. She wasn't wearing a bra and showed lots of cleavage, enough to capture a man's imagination.

"If I go get the money can I have it?" she asked, hesitantly.

"Naw girl!" Tomica was on her feet. "I don't trust that skinny-ass nigga from B-More further than I can throw him. About a year or so ago didn't he leave his Cadillac in pawn to you?" Evette asked me. I thought about it.

"Yeah." I nodded my head as I thought about what she said.

The two women began to argue back and forth.

Mad Ball said, "Something don't smell right with dude all of a sudden wanting you to come pick up the money."

Just then Trina bent down and whispered into my ear, "Don't let that girl go get that money. I thought you called everyone here to officially let them know that you were out the game."

"Shut up!" I yelled at her causing everyone in the room to turn and look at us. For the past year or so Trina had been bugging the hell out of me to get out the game. Often she would plead with me to the point of tears. What she didn't know was her cousin placed so much faith in me, I felt a sense of loyalty to him. Hell, the man made me what I was. From the federal detention center in New York, he was still making major moves, placing me in key situations of certain operations. He never forgot about me, the young nigga that came up on the grind. Two weeks in the game and I made two million. He thought I was smart, told me so often. He thought it was me that called all the shots, made all the major moves. What he didn't know was that Trina was the real mastermind. She always played her part, stood in the shadows and gave me that credit like I was the genius. I never knew that one day I would realize just how much I underestimated her intelligence. Only then it would be too late.

"I'm going to pick up the money," Evette said as she nervously rubbed the palms of her hands on her thighs as she walked over to my desk. "I'ma be on the first thang smokin to B-More in the morning." With that she strutted out of the door.

Tomica came and leaned on my desk with her jawbone showing from failure of controlling her anger in losing the battle of temperament. She spoke, "You greedy ass bastard! All that fucking money we made you, and you're going to let that girl take a risk like that?"

Tomica bit down on her lower lip fuming with anger. She continued, "Word is bond! You better hope that nothing happens to her."

"Is that a threat?" I asked, tempted to get out of my chair and slap the taste out of her mouth for disrespecting a nigga.

"Naw, it's a fuckin' promise!" she shot back, turned and abruptly stalked out of the door. I knew that she was headed to try to change Evette's mind. Just that fast the atmosphere changed. Talk about a fucking bad apple, them New York bitches keep some shit going. I was denied what I had been trying to deny, the price that came with riches: mo' money, mo' bullshit.

The room suddenly turned quiet, the kind of silence that comes with the chaos in the aftermath of upheaval that people and their problems make.

Finally I said, "Fuck dem bitches! They been stealing my shit anyway, think a nigga don't know, I just can't prove it," I reasoned out loud. I wanted Trina's wannabe slick ass to know that I was talking about her, too. Trina's body flinched like she had been hit with a body blow as she took a step back from me. I could feel her eyes burning holes in me. Lil Man was fast asleep on my lap. All of a sudden, everyone was talking at the same time.

"Hold up! Hold up!" Blazack shouted above the voices, getting everybody's attention. As he took the toothpick out of his mouth, the diamond pinky ring on his finger sparkled an array of brilliant red and blue colors, flickered images of his baller lifestyle.

"I'ma bust dat cracka's ass if he try to stop us from getting our hustle on. Besides, I'm already paying his punk ass two grand a week. What the fuck he sweatin' you for? Something ain't right."

In so many ways Blazack said what I was already thinking. Something wasn't right with that cracka. I had a gut feeling.

I lit another cigarette, inhaled deeply, as Trina continued to give me a disgusting scowl. Finally, she took the baby off my lap, rolled her eyes at me and walked out of the door. I made a mental note to have a few choice words with her afterward.

"Twine, how many people you got on line workin' for you?" I asked. I watched as he thought for a second, did some quick math with his fingers.

"Seventeen, if you want to count Nina Brown smoke up all the product ass," he said. Someone in the room snickered.

"What about you, Dirty?" I asked.

"About the same."

When it finally came down to it, everybody in the room had enough employees to open up a chain of restaurants. They all had traps bringing in major cash.

"Ya'll gon' to have to step it up and grind hard, cause I think the spot done got too hot. I'ma give ya'll some extra cushion on each bird, then we move out." With that said, I searched the faces of each man. Everyone in the room nodded in agreement, except Blazack. That's what annoyed me about him most, I could never get a feel for his real sincereness. I couldn't help thinking, *what is wrong with this nigga?* I knew for a fact that he had more than a few million stashed somewhere. To be truthful, I ain't never trusted that nigga. How could I? He was a cold-blooded killer.

After everyone left, Trina eased into the room. I sat in front of the fireplace drinking Hennessy with my thoughts weighing heavy on my mind. I had a bad feeling about Spitler, something he said about me regretting I ever laid eyes on the town.

"I'm leaving you." Her voice was soft and mellow like an Anita Baker song. I didn't even turn around, just watched the security cameras and heard the crackle of the flames. However, something did dawn on me. I was in love with Trina, at least something in my thug's armor was telling me so.

"When we first met, we had plans, dreams. We had a goal. Get out of the game after a year. Now look at us! Look at you!" Trina raised her voice, I could hear its tremor with emotions.

"How much money is eee-nough!?" she screamed and began to sob uncontrollably with a Black woman's scorn. I cringed. Over the years Trina learned how to get to me. In my heart and soul, I knew she was right. Intuitively, all hustlers know when it's time to get out, like some damn premonition. That day I could feel it in my skin. The only problem was, I couldn't get out of the game if I wanted to. Hustlers are just as addicted to the game like the very fiends we serve, only worse. The money and the power was the real addiction.

*****

Stressed the fuck out, I decided we needed a vacation. Actually, I was looking for a way to persuade Trina to stay, at the same time, trying to act hard like I wasn't in love with her. Call it my thug ego, but that's how real gangsters roll. Feelings and emotions ain't part of the game. At least that's what I kept telling myself.

I broached the idea to Trina and Black Pearl as they were going over some clothing designs. Lately, Trina had started to see the brilliance in Pearl's creativity. And it wasn't just her, Pearl had been offered a scholarship to go to college to design clothes. Now, she and Trina were going to start their own clothing line. To be truthful, I wasn't feeling none of that shit, in fact, I was starting to feel threatened by Trina's business savvy. I had no idea that she learned so much in college with her degree in Business Management. She had invented a phony corporation to wash millions of my money, as well as placed liens on everything we owned in case the feds started catching feelings for a nigga's riches and wanted to seize our assets. With everything having a hefty lien on it, if the feds wanted to take anything they would be forced to pay off the liens, which amounted to millions of dollars. Plus, Willie Falcon showed me how to hide money abroad in Swiss bank accounts.

Reluctantly, I was able to talk Trina into staying. Actually, I swallowed my pride and begged my woman to stay. I went out and bought an eight carat Marquis diamond ring. Enough ice to make her brain freeze about leaving me.

*****

The day before we were scheduled to leave, Trina decided we should go shopping for vacation clothes and Louis Vuitton luggage. Later on that day, Major pulled me to the side and pointed to one of the security screen cameras. A yellow van was parked across the street from my estate, directly overhead was a white man wearing a construction hat. He sat perched on a telephone pole.

"That yellow van been parked there every day now for the past three weeks," Major said with his voice filled with concern. I shrugged him off; thought about asking him to go on vacation with us, poor soul, the game had him paranoid, too.

"Lemme find out you still smokin," I joked, and playfully patted him on the shoulder as I smiled. Major didn't smile back. He had not smoked a rock since that day I saved his life from Blazack.

*****

May 26, 1995 there wasn't a cloud in the sky, just a magnificent day. I was driving Trina's Benz, headed for the Tallahassee Shopping Mall.

Trina sat next to me in the car and for the past few days, she had been aloof and distant. In my heart I knew that I was losing her. She just stared out the window like a beautiful caged bird wanting to fly away, I imagined. Pearl sat in the back seat going over clothing designs. Lil Man sat between Trina and me. Playfully, he tried to take hold of our hands and place them together, like he knew there was disharmony between us.

"Aunty Trina, give me yo hand."

Trina couldn't help but to give him her hand as she smiled allowing Lil Man to connect the three of us together. I don't care what anyone says, children are angels. By the time we reached the mall, Lil Man had all us singing merrily, "Old MacDonald."

I found a parking space. Lil Man quickly climbed into my lap and nestled, clasping his arms around my neck. His way of saying he wasn't going nowhere without me.

I looked up just as a dark shadow casted ominously on my window, a black SUV with smoked windows pulled up to the side of our car. From that point on everything began to move in an slow, surrealistic motion, as I stared up at the vehicle. It wasn't until I saw the masked gunmen dressed in all black leap out with them tens—meaning AK47 assault weapons. Holy Shit! They caught me slipping. Metal and glass exploded as my body experienced a burning sensation like I was on fire. Trina's blood curdling scream only seemed too intensify, witnessing the horror of the assassination on my life. Someone had sent professional killers at me. Who? As best as I could, I tried to shield Trina and the baby with my body. Just as quickly as the shooting started, it stopped. My ears were ringing. I could feel the blood rushing from my veins. I was hit several times. For some reason Trina stopped screaming as I lay on top of her. In the distance, I heard one of the gunmen say, "Shoot him in the head and let's get out of here!" I played dead. Prayed like a muthafucka. Someone walked up and snatched the iced out platinum chain off my neck and then placed the AK47 to the back of my head and pulled the trigger. *Click . . . Click . . .* The gun misfired.

I heard an urgent voice say, "Let's go! Let's go! Let's go!" with the sound of footsteps retreating. I just lay there numb, scared to death, soaking wet covered in blood. I could feel Trina shaking underneath me. *Lil Man?* I thought. He was wedged between Trina and me. My right arm was barely attached to my shoulder. Them AKs ain't nothing nice! Somehow I managed to pull myself up off Lil Man and Trina. The gory horror of what I saw tormented me more then the pain that raked my body. The right side of Lil Man's face was completely blown off. All that was left was skull with his brains spewing out. As I held him in my arms my eyes filled with tears. His handsome face was gone, only to be replaced with blood and brains. Then I remembered. Black Pearl. I turned to look in the back seat. She was motionless, keeled over on her face, crimson blood stained the interior. With it was an awful smell that I will never forget.

DEATH. With my vision blurred, I looked over at Trina as she got off the ground. A crowd of white people were starting to gather around the car. Trina was crying hysterically as her hands trembled, her face was spotted with blood. I could tell she was fighting to take back control of what the armed gunman had nearly stolen from her, her sanity.

"Are you hit?" I managed to ask her. She shook her head no, and reached out to see if Lil Man had a pulse. I passed out to the sound of sirens in my ears, thought about all the niggas I touched on the jack tip and now it finally came back to haunt me. *You'll end up dead or in prison,* the intrusive voice said inside my head.

*****

# Chapter Fifteen

## "Game Over"

### — Life —

I woke up in a hospital bed. My body was riddled with bullets. I never experienced so much pain in my entire life. It even hurt to breathe. My mouth was dry, and my tongue felt like sandpaper. I saw Trina sitting next to me. Her face was swollen and scarred, I guessed from all the flying glass from the gun blast. I could hardly recognize her.

"L, you aight?" Twine asked. At first I did not see him standing over me. His eyes were red and bloodshot.

"Where is Lil Man at?" My voice creaked barely above a whisper. Twine looked away and wiped at his eyes. In my mind I prayed, *Lord, please let this all be a dream.*

Twine turned back toward me, "They kilt Lil Man." His voice cracked. I closed my eyes and felt a piece of my soul die as I felt Trina's eyes bore through me. Her reservoir of love was gone, only to be replaced by hate.

"L, Pearl is down the hall in a coma. I hope your ass is happy," she said and began to cry, the tears streaked her cheeks.

"Somebody robbed Gucci's trap last night, and kilt his twins," said Lieutenant.

He managed to get away by jumping out the window and crawling under a car."

"He jumped out the third floor window?!" I yelled and tried

to raise my head in disbelief, as pain ricocheted throughout my body.

"Where in the fuck was Blazack at!?" I yelled at Twine.

"I dunno."

Lucky for me, I had only been hit three times, mostly flesh wounds, one in the ass and thigh. The most serious injury was to my shoulder. A short Chinese doctor entered the room followed by two huge burly white cops that looked like linebackers for the Pittsburgh Steelers.

"My name is Doctor Wong," the doctor said, his voice was laced with a heavy foreign accent. He glanced at the clipboard in his hands. "Your injuries are very serious. We're going to have to operate to repair your shoulder."

As the doctor talked, I tried to listen, but like the rest of us in the room, I couldn't help but focus most of my attention on the two cops. Finally, the doctor said the police wanted to talk to me. With that he bowed his head slightly and left the room.

"Mr. Leonard Smith?" The plain-clothes detective asked as he took a step toward me. His skin was pale white, eyes were piercing and he wore an expensive suit. Everything about him told me that I'd had better be careful of what I said.

"Yes, I'm Leonard Smith," I said, acknowledging my fake name.

"I'm investigating the homicide and attempted murder of three year old Shawn L. Bell and his mother Annie Bell."

He was talking about Lil Man and Black Pearl. If I could, I would have bolted from the room, from that place that I had created, my own man made hell, from the grim reality of what was happening to me. The detective turned to Twine and Trina and asked, "Do you mind if we speak to him alone?" All I heard was the scuffle of chairs moving and feet shuffling distancing themselves from me. Twine and Trina hauled ass out of that room!

The two detectives played cat and mouse with me for nearly an hour. I adamantly continued to tell them that I did not know what happened. They let me know of their suspicions and promised to come back and arrest me once they found out I was lying. They knew that I lived in Quincy at the Chateau G.P., that told me a lot, the spot was getting hot.

*****

Later on that night I got into a wheelchair and strolled down to Black Pearl's room. She was connected to so many wires and contraptions. An episodic beep chimed in tune with wavy lines, her lifelines. She wasn't even breathing on her own. I fought to restrain my emotions as I looked at her beautiful face and saw Lil Man's eyes. I would have given anything in the world to have both of them back. What kind of monster could do such a thing? Blazack's face flashed in my mind. *Ain't no longevity in the dope game, stick and move, get out within a year.* I thought about what Trina first warned me about that night in the hotel when we first met. And now, for the past year or so, she had been begging me to get out, and now ...

After I left Pearl's room, I called the Chateau and told Major to come and get me. Later on that day to the disagreement of the entire hospital staff, I checked out of the hospital on crutches.

I was a sight to behold with all the stitches and bandages; I could make a mummy jealous.

The first stop we made was to the liquor store. The whole time Major just looked at me like I was crazy, but he kept his fucking mouth shut. He too didn't agree with me leaving the hospital in my condition, but he also knew what was on my mind–187, murder!

As he drove I was in agony. The pain was excruciating. A few times I almost fainted. I rode in the car in a very awkward position due to the gun shot wounds in my ass and hip, all on the same side. Blood was starting to soak through my shirt from where my shoulder was nearly torn off. The liquor helped a lot, but not nearly enough.

I had Major drive to the house that I first rented for the crew back in the day. Now it was nothing more then a stash spot or a place to cut, get laid.

Dirty's brand new BMW was parked in the front yard. I sent Major inside to ask about Blazack's whereabouts.

I watched as Major walked inside. Someone left the door ajar. Moments later Major reappeared, running like he was being chased by the devil himself. He got back into the car, his words inaudible.

"W-W-We gotta get the hell outta here. Dirty and some broad are in there dead as a muthafucka!"

"Are you sure?" I asked grabbing his arm and wincing in pain. Major turned and looked at me the way people do when they're being annoyed.

"Look, I did a tour of Vietnam, I done seen mo' dead muthafuckas than you have seen livin'!" Major had the old Caddy in reverse burning rubber out the driveway.

"You bring my pistol wit cha?" I asked as suddenly the image of the black SUV and armed gunmen jumping out flashed before my mind. Major reached underneath the seat and passed me Jesus. I took a long swig from the bottle of Hennessy and asked Major if Blazack owned a black SUV. Major thought for a second and then answered yes. He turned and looked me directly in my eyes and asked if I thought Blazack had something to do with it. I didn't answer, just took another long swig from the bottle and caressed Jesus in the palm of my hand praying that I would have enough strength when the time came.

As we approached my estate, the same yellow van that Major had expressed suspicion to me a few days ago was still parked across from my security gates. The guy wore dark shades. I thought that it was odd for a man that worked out in the sun to have skin as white as chalk. As we passed, I could have sworn he looked at me and smiled.

Major had to nearly carry me inside, I could hardly walk. At the top of the stairs Trina stood stately, poised as if she had been waiting for me. The way that she looked down at my pathetic body was humiliating for me. She wore a long gown with a reveling split up the front. Her right hand was posed with a Black and

Mild cigar smoldering. As soon as she spoke I knew that she had been drinking heavily.

"I'm leavin' you, BITCH!" she cursed, slurring her words miserably. Wobbling she began to walk down the stairs, one step at a time.

Major gave me a knowing look. "I'm going to check the grounds, make sure that everything is aight." With that he left.

"You fucked it up! What you thought you was Scarface or some shit, L? We had it all, money, clothes and fine cars. Five or ten millions dollars wasn't enough for you?"

I raised my hand to slap the cowboy shit out of her. Once again, I had underestimated her and before I knew it, Trina reached into her bra and pulled out a small pistol and fired at my head.

"You put yo muthafuckin' hands on me and I swear to God, I'ma send you to your grave next to your dead-ass Mammy," she said coldly with the gun still aimed at my head.

"Girl, what da fuck wrong with you?" She just looked at me dead serious, and then on a second thought she just shook her head and walked away. I followed her to our bedroom. Louis Vuitton bags sat in front of the bed. This time Trina was fully prepared to leave me.

She whirled around to face me, her eyes optic slants of contempt.

"I let you be the man with your balls and super ego while I sat in the background and played my part, let you get all the credit for being the brains —"

"Trina let me —"

"Don't fuckin' interrupt me!" she said pointing the gun at me. "When you first started out hustling, in the first two weeks you made millions. I made that happen. And when you couldn't find a supply for coke, I made that happen, too. I bet your punk ass didn't know that it was I that went to my uncle and got you put on. I made all of this happen!"

Perspiration was starting to form on my forehead as I listened to Trina, a woman I realized I never really knew.

She continued, "I let you be the head, the lead, because a real thorough bitch knows the neck moves the head." Then in one of her mood swings Trina lowered the gun, her eyes cast down at the floor. "Lil Man is dead. DEAD!" She screamed at me. "... And his momma is in a fuckin' coma about to die, and Lord only knows where the hell poor Evette is. She never made it back from Baltimore."

I hobbled over to the bed and lay down on my stomach. I was in too much pain to talk. Trina came and stood over me with the smoldering Black and Mild in her mouth, gun in one hand, and a large suitcase in the other that looked big enough to put a small body in.

"Just so you know, I've already drafted the paperwork to have the Chateau, cars and jewelry placed into a shell corporation in the event that the feds come at you. I'm outta this bitch."

With all my meager strength I reached out and took hold of her hand with the luggage in it. She pulled away, the contents of the luggage spilled onto the floor. For a moment we just stared at each other. I could not believe what I was seeing. Money. Lots of it! Nicely wrapped hundred dollar bills in bundles of twenty-thousand dollars. Finally she said, "See what you made me do?" For the first time I heard the panic in her voice, saw the fear in her eyes as the guilt was written all on her face. All those years she had been stealing money from me. Fifty thousand here, ten thousand there. Trina, the Brooklyn chick.

I watched as she bent down and retrieved the money. Her eyes darted from me and to the door like a thief making a hasty get away. It felt like I was being robbed.

"Bitch! You been stealin' from a nigga," I said and tried to get up.

"Naw trick, I been preparin' to do me, ME. You think I'm gonna let you bring me down cause you don't know when the games are over?" Trina spat the words at me as I watched her tote that heavy-ass suitcase to the door. I couldn't even get out the bed and we both knew it. Opening the door she turned and called my name.

"L."

"What?" I answered disgruntled.

"Nigga I loved you with everything I had. We had the Bonnie and Clyde chemistry but not enough for me to do a lifetime in prison for you." She began to cry from deep within. "I tried to tell Big Mike the same thing, like you, he wouldn't stop." Trina wiped her face with the back of her hand and for some reason smiled at me through her tears. "You were a better hustler than Mike. You knew how to listen to me." Then she added, "A better lover, too. Bye." She mouthed the word with no sound and closed the door on our lives forever.

*****

That night I was awakened in the still of darkness by a soft rap on my bedroom door. My entire body was covered in perspiration and blood had soaked through my bandages. I tried to move from the fetal position I was sleeping in. "Oooh, oooh!" I shrieked in pain. That AK had torn chunks of flesh from my body and now I was feeling it big time. The medication that they gave me had finally worn off.

"Come ... in," I groaned.

The door opened and the silhouette of a woman appeared. In the backdrop of the hallway a luminous light shined making it hard for me to see who it was.

"Trina! Trina? I need a doctor. I'm fucked up bad!" I croaked. No answer.

The feminine figure approached me, slowly sashayed and turned the wrong switch on the wall panel causing the surround sound system to my stereo to come on. Keith Sweat's song with the girl group, Kut Klose "Get Up On It" filled the room. An exotic light shinned. She walked up to me, close. Wiped at the sweat on my brow affectionately and cooed in my ear. "Poor baby, let me help you," she said in a sultry voice and licked my earlobe. Instantly I recognized that voice. It was the lesbian Tomica,

**214**

Evette's lover. At that very moment I tried to shake the wary cob-
webs from my head, but with it came the relentless pain. Too
much pain no human being should ever have to endure.

"How ... did ... you ... get in here?" I asked.

"Major let me in sweetie," she said and held a white Walgreen's
drug store bag in front of my face.

"I'm gonna take care of you."

"Where is Trina at?" I asked, my voice sounding like a small
child.  Pain can make a man talk that way.

"You don't need that bitch! That's why I'm here to warn you.
She wanted us to help set you up with the feds so she could get
Big Mike out of prison. Evette and I turned her down. Trina got
scared and left town."

"WHAAAAAT!" I screeched. "What about Pearl –"

"Shhhh," Tomica interrupted as she placed her index finger
over my mouth.

"First thing's, first. Now baby, relax and let me make you feel
betta," she said seductively.

My mind was boxed in with dilemmas that ran the length of
my confused brain. The only thing that was for certain was that
my world, as I once knew it, was crumbling around me. My nigga
Dirty was dead along with Lil Man. I couldn't help but wonder,
*why would Trina turn me in and where in the fuck was Blazack at?*

Tomica removed all my clothes and bathed me with a soft
sponge, as she grimaced at the horror of my scars. At the time I
was in so much pain I honestly thought I was going to die.

Suddenly Tomica stopped and removed her blouse and then
her bra. The lights played off the sensuous curves of her body. She
watched my reaction. I could tell it was not what she had been
expecting. The very last thing in the world I wanted was some sex.

She reached inside her purse and removed a small white package of a powdery substance and dug her long fingernail into it.

"Here, snort this, it will make you feel betta."

"What is it?"

"The same thing they gave you at the hospital, only this is

purer. China White," she said and watched me as she held it up close to my nose. Probably the same way Eve did Adam with the apple. "This will make you feel betta, handle your business, get you out of bed, no mo' pain. Take it!" she cajoled. With all the pain I was in I would have snorted horse shit if someone would have told me it would make me feel better.

I snorted from the tip of her finger as she smiled down at me, in a strange kind of satisfaction. Before I could hardly inhale she shoveled another toot into my other nostril. Within moments I was overcome with a pleasant euphoria that sent me sailing out of space on cloud nine. The pain instantly vanished. I was high as a muthafucka. *So this was the world of China White,* I thought as Tomica got me high on my own supply. Dope she had been stealing from me for years.

With half lidded eyes, dreamily I smiled up at her. Watched with the amusement as she began to take off her skirt and then wiggled out of her panties like some exotic snake shedding its skin. She stood in front of me completely naked. Pubes of silky black hair cascaded down her brown thighs. My manhood stood up with enormous invigoration. Like a long pole, it waved at her. I could feel my body experiencing a sensation I had never felt before. The swells of her supple breasts came into view. Her erect nipples were tiny like luscious strawberries, hardening into fine points that complimented the symmetry of her hour glass figure. Tomica's body was bodacious in all the right places. She reached out and grabbed my joint with both her hands, it twitched and throbbed pulsating in the palm of her hands as precum glistened from the head like a volcano about to erupt.

My body was on fire, I wanted to fuck this lesbian. She smiled at me devilishly, sensing my wanton lust. Tomica dropped to her knees and began to feverishly wax my pole with the palms of her hands causing my toes to curl as my back arched to meet her. She bit down on her lip with a purposeful scowl, that of a seductress determined to get what she came for. Slowly ... slowly ... she took me into her mouth and gobbled me up as best she could with my great length and size. "Oh, shit! Oh, shit!" I moaned in ecstasy fighting the urge not to close my eyes. I wanted to see what the lesbian could do with all this dick. I whispered her name, caressed her head as her lips skillfully moved up and down, up and down the long sleek surface of my manhood. To my amazement she had me all the way in the back of her throat. Once or twice she gagged, but never missed a rhythm, bobbing her head up and down, deep throating me like it was art practiced by many but understood by few. Tomica made loud slurping sound as she sucked greedily, without coming up for air. Each woman's intimacy of love making is in essence a part of her virtuosity. An identity given like a birthright that makes each woman unique in her own right.

Finally, I exploded deep in her mouth, down her throat. I took hold of her head forcing myself deeper in her mouth. She looked up at me without panic and swallowed every last drop and licked her lips.

Afterward, I sat up in bed with the feeling of a man that has just been resurrected from the dead. Tomica stood a few feet in front of me. My dick was still hard and throbbing. I could see her clitoris through the mounds of her hairy bush as she stood, long legs parted. I reached out and took one of her strawberry nipples between my thumb and index finger and pinched it, hard.

"Ouch!" she whined. With my other hand, I reached between her legs and stroked her kitten, made her purr for me until she started to hump my hand. I stuck my finger inside her moist opening. She was tight. The kind of tight that came from not having sex with a man in a long time. I pulled her to me, she gasped. I could smell the humid scent of her sex. With a deft finger I began to stroke her faster, roughly. She cried out in pain. I sucked on her nipples and she tried to push my head down. I was high, but not high enough to eat her pussy. Soon her juices dripped from my fingers. I stood and she looked up at me in shock, tried to read my mind. I spun her around and bent her over the bed. Tomica had a beautiful Black woman's ass, round and fat with a slim waistline of a model. I spread her butt cheeks with my hands.

As I entered her, I thought of one of the verses from the Bible my Dad use to say in church, "It was easier for a camel to go through the eye of a needle than it is for a rich man to enter heaven."

Trying to get my dick into Tomica was like going through the eye of a needle. Painful! She began to buck and resist, at one point she even tried to fight me. I enjoyed every moment of it. Finally she gave in, and it was easy, long strokes from the back. I ignored her crying sobs and enjoyed one of my dreams, to punish that ass, the bull dagger that was stealing my shit and was known to have a slick mouth from time to time. Then suddenly the dope started to talk to me. Some of the world's smoothest hustlers have been dope fiends. *Something about this bitch ain't right. Don't trust her, L!* It was then that I started pounding away inside her body. She screamed. The dope was making me crazy. She continued to beg for me to stop. I couldn't stop if I wanted to. It was all hard and brutal on her. After about an hour and a half of marathon fucking with a malodorous funk to match, I finally took it to the hilt, grabbed her hips and the sides of her ass, spread her cheeks as far as I could, and with one hard and long thrust, I exploded a shattering climax deep within her. With the last drop of my semen deposited in her, I pulled out and watched as it ran down her inner thighs. I looked down at my dick and to my utter shock, there was blood on me.

"Are you on your period?"

"No, but you hurt me." She looked back at me and tried to smile. She looked like a sad clown with her mascara all ruined from the tears she shed. I wiped at the dribble of saliva that had started to form at the corners of my mouth. The dope had me drooling.

"With Trina gone, I'ma be your number one," she said like she was asking for confirmation if she had passed the dick test.

"Number one what?" I asked incredulously.

"Lady," she replied as she wiped her swollen clitoris with a towel, I noticed the blood in it. She made a face at me.

"What about your girl Evette?" I asked, catching her off

guard.

"W-W-What about Evette?" she stuttered. And now as I looked at Tomica with her fake-ass smile and mascara running, I realized that she just took all the humiliation and for what? I thought about what Trina said before she left. Evette went to Baltimore and was missing. I know that Tomica would never turn on her girl unless, something bad happened. But what? The dope was telling *me this bitch setting you up!* So I did my part, I smiled and acted like I was going along with her ploy. I knew that the first chance I got, I was going to have to kill her.

The phone rang, Tomica flinched, startled.

"Yeah."

"We got trouble." It was Major on the other line.

"What?" I asked with concern. The whole time, Tomica watched me suspiciously.

"Blazack is at the front gate wanting to get in."

I hobbled over to the console with all the television security screens and sure as shit, there was Blazack at the front gate parked in his Hummer. The ominous fog of the night seemed to cast him in a mysterious gloom.

"L? L? L! You still there man?" Major asked from the other end of the phone. I could hear the fear in his voice.

"Yeah, yeah, I'm here. Let him in the inside the house and get the fuck out the way!" I said and hung up the phone. I had Tomica help me get dressed. Even though the dope helped a lot, I was still only about 35 percent of myself in terms of strength.

"What's going on?" Tomica asked.

"Bitch you gon' help me make it down the stairs." I reached out and grabbed her by the hair, leading her toward the steps. The packet of Boy was on the vanity next to the bed. I poured a mountain in my hand, snorted it and rode the rapturous wings of a black stallion named "H."

Naked and crying Tomica helped me down the stairs. I was sure this was not what she was expecting, not part of her devious plan.

At the bottom of the stairs Major stood looking at us in awe with his mouth forming an O. My face was covered with powder, a gun dangled from my right arm and the other arm slung over Tomica's shoulder. Major had a shotgun at his side, it looked as old as the mansion.

The doorbell chimed. I shoved Tomica away and braced myself against the brass stair rail.

"Open the door!" I barked at Major waving the gun.

"L, man, you ain't in no condition to be –"

"Open the fucking door!" I yelled again only to lose my balance but regained it.

Major opened the door. Blazack stood there formidable as usual. He looked weary and haggard, he took one look at me holding the gun and his eyes bucked wide open like he was seeing a ghost.

"Welcome to Chateau Gangsta's Paradise, nig-gaaa!" I drawled, high as a muthafucka, dead serious on killing his ass.

He walked in taking in the scene shaking his head, not believing what he was seeing. He made a face at Tomica, turned and gritted on Major standing in the hall with the shotgun aimed at him. Finally he turned back to me and looked sorrowfully.

"Wha da fuck you call yourself doing nigga?"

I cocked the gun and aimed at him. He continued to look at me defiantly right in my eyes.

"Dirty is dead man. Lil Man is dead, Gucci is lying up in the hospital with two broken legs and internal bleeding."

"Bitch ass nigga, you had something to do wit it! Where you been the last few days, huh?" I hollered. I felt my hand anxious to pull the trigger.

"Been in jail!" Blazack said angrily. "That cracka Spitler had me locked up. Wouldn't even let me make a phone call. If you don't believe me, call our bail bondsman Fletcher, I swear to God he be my witness." Blazack was talking fast. He knew at that moment and time I was dead set on doing him.

"Let me call the bail bondsman," Major cut in, possibly saving Blazack's life. I nodded my head for Major to make the call.

Sure as shit, Major came into the hall and said that Blazack was just bonded out of jail.

I sat down on the stairs, cupped my head in my hands as I thought about the cop Spitler, and how he threatened me. Damn, I should have figured it was him and his crooked-ass cop friends doing the killings.

Blazack walked up to me. "Man, you gotta let me Ax Blazack that cracka." That was Blazack's code word for murder. "He's all yours," were my final words before I passed out on the stairs.

8:18 the next morning as planned, Blazack made arrangements to meet Spitler for his weekly payoff. There was no reason for the cop to be concerned. He nor his men would be suspects in the spree of murders. They were the police. They were above the law, or so they thought. Wrong!

As usual, they met at the Holiday Inn on Tennessee Street off Lake Bradford.

As soon as the cop entered the room he knew he had walked into a trap. Blazack put a gun up to his head, relieved him of his weapon, and handcuffed him to a chair. Spitler, the racist cop, had too much pride to beg, so he tried to bribe Blazack with money. It didn't work.

Blazack began to brutally pistol-whip Spitler to a bloody pulp even knocking one of his eyeballs out the socket. The cop fainted. Blazack threw cold water in his face to wake him back up.

With a gun pointed to his head Blazack forced him to call the police station and tell all his buddies in the narcotic division that were down with the murders to meet him outside the police station at midnight. After the phone call, Blazack, in a manic frenzy, began to hack away with the ax on the cop's body. *Wack!* "This is for my nigga Dirty." *Wack!* "Dats for killin' babies." Afterward, with Spitler barely alive, Blazack shoved a stick of dynamite up his ass.

\*\*\*\*\*

Midnight, the cops arrived as scheduled. They saw Spitler sitting in his car. They all approached in jovial spirits, which was always the case whenever they were going to share some dirty money. As the first cop reached the car and looked inside, he saw the bloody stump of half a body. Desperately, Spitler frantically wiggled his head no but the cop opened the door. The wired dynamite of one hundred pounds of explosives detonated. *Kaboom!!*

*****

I lay in bed sipping on Hennessy, snorting my medication with my dick in Tomica's mouth. I was numb all the way down to my toes. Tomica came up for air. She had dark cycles under her eyes.

"What time is it baby?" she asked. A secretion of cum dangled from her lower lip.

"8:25 in the morning. Why the fuck you keep askin' me that?" I asked, annoyed. She smiled up at me from in between my legs and reached over and dug her long fingernail into the powder and placed it under my nose. Right then I saw it, felt it, knew it. I saw her treachery disguised in her eyes and she tried to mask it with a smile. I blew the dope off her fingers and sighed as I lay back on the pillow with my eyes closed. There isn't a hustler alive that can honestly say that he did not hear the voice in the recess of his mind, pleading, begging with him to get out the game. *Ain't no longevity in the dope game,* Trina's voice. *You'll end up dead or in prison,* Hope's voice. It's always the woman that warns us, and almost always we never listen, but we hear.

Tomica must have thought I had passed out. Now that I felt her trying to ease out of the bed, I played sleep, but I had one eye open. I watched her tiptoe over to the window and began to wave the curtains like she was giving a signal. My heart damn near burst out my chest, when I realized what she was doing, setting me up! I got out of the bed and stood behind her. Feeling a presence, she turned around startled. On the security screen I saw all the white vans marked FBI and ATF. It must have been over a hundred vehicles, the entire estate was surrounded. Major burst into the room.

"The police breaking down the front gate, L, we gotta go!"

Tomica just stood there in the window nude with her arms crossed over her breasts. I picked up the gun as Major grabbed my arm.

"The bitch set me up!" I said as Major walked up and placed his arms around me. We headed down the stairs.

In my study behind the bookshelf was a tunnel that lead to the sewer system. As we reached the bottom of the stairs I could hear the police pounding on the door with a battering ram, overhead I heard helicopters along with the frantic banter of shouting, "FBI."

We made it into the study just as the front door came crashing in. I stashed the gun in a Bible as Major turned the candleholder that opened the secret compartment to the door behind the bookshelf. I was barefoot as we escaped into the darkness of the tunnel. I had it all planned, leave the country. I had millions of dollars in escrow in Brazil. All I had to do was step foot on the soil.

Up ahead I saw a bright light. It beamed on us like the morning sun, and then I heard the sound of guns being cocked.

"Freeze! FBI!"

*****

# Chapter Sixteen

## "Against all Odds"

### — *Hope* —

Nine months after federal agents raided Life Thugstin's mansion in a long, drawn out operation titled Operation Thug-Sting, federal agents seized more than ten million dollars in assets, cars, jewelry, not including the four million dollars that was discovered hidden in the mansion inside secret compartments in various parts of the floors.

*****

The sound of my heels could be heard scrapping across the meticulously buffed marbled floor of the Federal Correctional building. For me, the sound only seemed to heighten the urgency of my arrival, Hope Evans, the Bureau's Assistant Prosecutor for the United States Southern District of Florida. And still with my title of elitism and all its accolades, I knew that I could never be comfortable with my job. The job of imprisoning Black people with such a high degree. I was sure that America could be charged with the cruel and inhumane act of genocide. That day I walked down the halls, it felt like I was walking down the gallows to hell. However I was determined to do my best to try to change all of this. The same dreams that I had when I was a little girl growing up, I wanted to help my people, help my brother, I still clung to, only now my convictions were stronger, more dedicated and determined.

That day I was going to do my damnest to help Life Thugstin. I was risking all I had. I came to warn him of the insidious trap that awaited him if he intended to go to trial with his team of high powered lawyers. I overheard his attorneys conspiring with my boss, David Scandels, the head prosecutor and a very ambitious attorney that would stop at nothing in order to win a conviction. To date this was by far the biggest case of his entire twenty-year career, and he had no intentions of losing it.

The federal government had a 98 percent conviction rate, which means an innocent defendant had about a 2 percent chance of success if he was going to trial. Life Thugstin was facing a life-time sentence, plus thirty years if he was convicted. My office was prepared to offer him a thirty-year bargain and a ten million dollar fine. I took a deep breath as I waited with my briefcase in hand outside a steel door marked SHU, Segregation Housing Unit.

In my career as a prosecutor and going inside prisons I quickly noticed a distinctive odor that omitted from the inside of prisons. It smelled like generic Pine Sol and semen, marinating in fear. About a month ago, Life was placed in SHU for the assault on a confidential informant. He assaulted the inmate with a ten-pound weight on the recreation yard. The inmate nearly died. He received over two hundred stitches. The informant's name was Steven Davis, a.k.a. Stevey D, a small time drug dealer turned informant. He was amongst the 78 inmates that were scheduled to testify against Life Thugstin; in return they would all get significantly reduced sentences. Some would be immediately released if Life were convicted. Only one or two of the people actually knew him and the government was aware of the fact that most of the people testifying were lying, but that is how the system worked with its 98 percent conviction rate.

Finally the steel door opened and I walked inside the vestibule. I had the jitters; my stomach was in knots. The hum of the air conditioner droned, and in the distance I could hear the staccato of a steel cell door slamming. I was thankful I wore my suit coat.

"May I help you?" a deep baritone voice asked from a speaker above my head.

I flashed my ID with its gold star and announced, "Hope Evans, the United States Prosecutor's office. I'm here to see inmate Life Thugstin. My office made arrangements earlier," I said with authority. Silence. I waited patiently. In the dim of the booth inside the officer's station flickered lights illuminated an array of bright colors that looked like the inside of the bridge of the Star Ship.

*Click!* "You may go inside. Someone will be there to assist you in a minute," the voice said from the speaker.

I walked through the door into another world. A world within a world. A world where 88 percent were of poor impoverished Blacks and Spanish decent. The federal prison institution used to be a predominately white man's institution in terms of incarceration, until corporate America discovered astronomical profits that could be made of cheap slave labor. Politicians and federal judges had financial investments in the cheap labor. Thus, harsh sentences were given out, as a way to insure their investment. One only had to go check the Wall Street stock market and he would find prisons are amongst the best investments for wealthy white men.

The cacophony of loud voices hollering and screaming roared in my ears like a million angry Black men chanting, begging to be let free. I thought about my brother, my own flesh and blood, living in one of these dungeons. I thought about how my ancestors were packed on slave ships like sardines in a can. This was no different than a slave ship. Even though I had been here before, it always felt the same, cruel and inhuman.

Directly in front of me was a line of cells. Men ogled me. It felt like I was at center stage at the Apollo Theater. I heard a voice say, "Hey, Dirty! Hey Dirty! Come to the cell door. Look at dis bitch here'rr! She fine as a muhfa." Then suddenly a frantic banter of voices echoed, signaling my presence, like a ship being sighted by men marooned on an island.

"Hey! Psss. Damn, she thick." Catcalls ensued. I tried my best not to look, not to stare. Directly across from me I detected a jerking motion. *I know damn well this negro ain't doing what I think he's doing,* I thought as a large burly officer approached. He had a grin on his face, the kind men wear when they're being mischievous.

I guess he too must have been enjoying himself at the expense of my arrival. After giving me a quick once over, with gaiety he said, "Follow me." I walked down the long narrow corridors as Black men stared behind caged bars, open mouths with their faces pressed against the steel. With each expression, invitation, flirtation, masturbation, I regretted wearing my high heels and tight-fitting skirt. We approached a door. The officer pointed and I looked inside. Life sat in a chair wearing an orange jump suit and leg irons. His right leg was shackled to a steel rod in the wall. All of a sudden, the realization of what I had come to do dawned on me, and for the first time in a long time I was scared to confront a man. Not just any man, but the father to my child. I needed him to know this. I needed him to know that I was going to quit my job and help him. I was here to help him.

I turned to the CO, "I will interrogate the inmate alone." His eyes narrowed and looked as if he wanted to say something, but thought better of it.

As I entered the room, Life looked up at me. His hair was matted. It looked like he hadn't shaved in weeks and most of all, the expression on his face said that he was not too happy to see me, at all. The room was small. His presence was large, he actually was intimidating me with his stare. In the room was a dilapidated old desk and a crumbled Coke can that someone used for an ashtray. There were two chairs, the metal folding kind. He sat in one and the other one was a few feet away from him. The man just continued to look up at me with my son's eyes. Call me sentimental, but I wanted to break down and cry. But I didn't, I had come to warn him, protect him. I sat down next to him tried to smile at the same time, taking the opportunity to compose my thoughts. I could feel my heart pounding in my chest trying to find its way out. My tongue searched for the words that wouldn't come out. The moment was awkward, like his stare seemed to pin me to the wall. I was here for my own personal redemption, the female version of Hannibal. I was here to betray my government for the sake of the love for my own people. God help me!

"Life, I come to help."

"Listen, you Uncle Tom-ass bitch." His voice was low, guttural, like he had been saving up all his agony and pain for me. "If you wanna help me, get a fuckin' razor and let me slit your fuckin' throat," he said and leaned forward and hunked up a large wad of spit and spat in my face. A trickle of saliva dripped from my chin onto my lap. I just stared at him stunned, shocked beyond belief.

*Lord have mercy this can't be happening to me,* I thought. I was here to help him, save him from this racist system that intentionally set out to destroy Black men.

"All that Black conscious shit ya'll be talkin' bout, first chance you get you sell a nigga out. Now here you is, a fuckin' slave catcher fo' Massa. All you niggas and so-called leaders is nothing but fuckin' sellouts!" he yelled at me, and for a moment I was sure that he was going to kick me. I could see large veins pulsating in his forehead and neck. In the distance I could hear frantic laughter, or perhaps it was a cry. I opened my mouth to speak, but no words came out, just a pained expression. He continued to berate me. I just sat there like a child being chastised only this was worse, much worse, as saliva dripped off my chin and for some reason as a Black woman, all his anger, all his rage found its way inside of me and nestled in a place that has been pre-conditioned to take abuse from Black men. His refuge. My reservoir, a vacuum to my soul that stored pain. I just sat there determined to weather the storm.

I willed myself not to cry as I heard a shallow voice say, "I only came to help you." Then a whimper that gave way to a sigh that lost its way down my throat.

"Help me! Wasn't it you that said that I'd end up dead or in prison? I didn't think that you'd be the one to help put me there, you and 'bout ninety other hot-ass muthafuckas about to take the witness stand against me and lie just to get their time cut and your pussy ass is down wit this shit?" Life was now screaming at me, with spit spewing out of his mouth.

"Your lawyers are conspiring with my boss. They're going to sell you out, try to make a good show of the trial for the sake of all the worldwide publicity. A guy by the name of Calvin Sweeny, you may know him as Lil Cal, he's the government's star witness," I blurted out talking so fast that I could hardly catch my breath. I wiped at the saliva on my face with my hand as I watched the expression on Life's face change from anger to disbelief, then hurt. I wanted to say more, plead with him, and let him know that he had a son that looked just like him and a woman that was willing to do anything for him. All this may have sounded insane, but I wanted to help. Suddenly, something washed over him, like the calm after the storm. He could no longer look at me. I saw him gaze up at the ceiling and saw his left eye twitch as he spoke.

"Bitch, you think I believe you? I know them crackas sent you to set me up. What they offer you one of dem house nigger jobs? Mo' money? Bigger office? You're a sell out, you and the rest of your Uncle Toms." His expression was sour, but I could read the confusion in his eyes–to believe me or not.

I rose from the chair determined to keep my composure. This was so unexpected, so unreal. It couldn't be happening to me. I reached into my briefcase and placed my new business card on the desk. I wanted to tell him that today was my last day working for the bureau but instead, I said, "Call me." I heard my voice crack with emotions. It took everything in my power to keep a straight face. Life took one look at the card and laughed derisively causing the shackles on his legs to rattle.

"Them crackas taught you well. Hope, how can you sell your own fuckin' people out?" he asked as the CO came and opened the door. I walked out the door and was once again welcomed to the raucous applause of whistling, catcalls and some of the most vivid descriptions of my butt that I had ever heard. I briskly walked down the long corridor at nearly a jogger's pace with my briefcase held tightly as if it were a shield. All of Life Thugstin's preliminary hearings and evidentiary proceeding had run the course of time. Within a few days, one of the biggest trials the State of Florida has ever known was set to begin. What Life Thugstin didn't know was the stage had already been set, rigged and arranged, like 98 percent of Federal cases. I knew this because I had taken part in more than a few legal lynchings. And every opportunity I was given, I tried my best to intentionally sabotage a trial, or a court proceeding.

I remember one particular case, the girl's name was Keychia Moore. She was 18 years old and the mother of three kids and pregnant again. Her boyfriend, a small time drug dealer, sold small amounts of coke in powder form, dime bags. A petty offense that carried, at the most, probation and a small fine. Her boyfriend made a sale to an undercover federal agent. The next day the undercover agent came back wanting to purchase crack. The boyfriend informed the agent that he did not have any. The agent propositioned the boyfriend with a deal; he would purchase a thousand dollars worth of the dimes if the boyfriend could cook it up into crack. The boyfriend agreed. They cooked the dope up in Keychia's Section 8 apartment. Federal judges and prosecutors are aware of this scheme, where urban Black men are tricked into selling crack and then given life sentences.

After the boyfriend made the sale, federal agents stormed the house. The boyfriend was shot and killed as he tried to escape out a bedroom window. Keychia Moore was arrested and charged with the sales to the undercover agent and her three kids were taken away from her and placed into foster care. The ratio between crack cocaine and powder cocaine is 100-to-1. Now instead of facing probation and a fine, she faced a lifetime in prison. I was assigned as her prosecutor. There was no way in hell I was going to help send this young woman to prison for life, and all she merely did was open the door for the undercover agent when he came to buy the drugs. Her lawyer, an old public defender, had hardly any interest in her case, heck, the same people that signed his check signed mine.

On the day that she was scheduled to go to trial, I sat at the prosecutor's table, painfully frustrated. Keychia and myself were the only Blacks in the entire courtroom. I felt so uncomfortable. Keychia, like most young Blacks had no relatives and friends to come to the courtroom to support her. Her pensive sobs rocked the courtroom. I lay awake in bed trying to figure out a way to sabotage the trial then it hit me. A plan. I would have to take a great risk, but I had to do it.

On the day of the trial, I casually opened up the case file on her and in a mock display of shock at what I was looking at, lawyer turned actor, I looked up at the judge in confusion, and asked him could I approach the bench. He stared at me quizzically over the rim of his glasses.

"Your Honor, I'm afraid the prosecution is forced to drop the charges, due to the fact the statute of limitations has expired in this case," I said, as I tried to look flustered.

The judge looked at me with dismay as he removed his glasses.

"What do you mean you're going to have to drop the charges?" he asked, disgruntled. His skin turned beet red.

"The defendant filed a motion for a speedy trial, evidently it was in oversight at my office, and just now discovered this." I passed the motion to the judge. The night before, I drafted it and forged Keychia's signature and post dated it. As the judge looked at it, I prayed that Keychia's lawyer would go along with it. Last night the idea seemed like a brilliant plan, however, this morning with the judge peering down at me, I realized just how stupid and dangerous the idea was, I could lose my job, and possibly face charges.

The judge massaged his face with a hand and sighed as he began to rub the bridge of his nose the way people do when they are having a long day.

"Counsel, what do you mean, oversight? This is plain and simple incompetence, and not in accordance with the jurisprudence of law that I practice in my courtroom," the judge spoke sternly, and then looked over at the defense table and shook the paper in his hand as he pointed at Keychia's attorney.

"Why am I just learning of this ... this so called oversight?" he asked, and glared at me. Right then and there I wanted to run out of the courtroom as I watched Keychia's lawyer stand and look at the judge in consternation as he responded, "I am not aware of such motion your Honor."

"Yes you is!" Keychia interjected indignantly.

Keychia's lawyer approached the bench giving me a look that said he was on to me and my scheme.

"Your Honor, someone needs to be investigated and disbarred and maybe even arrested. This is a travesty of injustice," the lawyer said angrily as he pointed an accusing finger at me, and then added, "I want my client released at this very moment, or else I'm filing for prosecution misconduct."

The judge looked on and shrugged his weary shoulders.

"This has been a long day for all of us," he said as he looked at me and shook his head, like he could not believe that I could be so stupid. I glanced over at Keychia's lawyer and I could have sworn that old white man winked at me. One thing was for sure, he had just proven to me that he was a better actor.

"Will the defendant please rise," the judge said. I watched as Keychia struggled with the armrest on the chair to stand. She was a very pretty girl with a light complexion and long wavy black hair. With her enormous stomach, she looked like she was carrying twins.

"Young lady, I want you to consider yourself very fortunate. Today, due the circumstances that would have violated your constitutional rights, I have no other recourse but to drop the indictment against you." After the judge made his ruling, it was hard for me to hide my delight. I turned my back and smiled as I walked back to the prosecutor's table.

\*\*\*\*\*

On the day that I visited Life Thugstin in SHU and he spit in my face, that pushed me over the edge in leaps and bounds. So much hurt and pain, and yet, I had no choice but to turn the hurt into motivation to propel myself forward. Life actually thought I had sold him out, betrayed my own people, like so many others had done. I wished that I could let him know, make him understand me, the woman that only took the job for the government in order to learn its legal tactics so that I could go back and help others. If I were to become the female version of Hannibal I would have to learn how to defeat these people at their own game. War. The logistical kind you find in the courtroom. The battle of the minds. When I had no way of possibly knowing, it would be a lot sooner than I thought that I would find myself entrenched in war in a crowded courtroom fighting for my client's life.

*****

As planned, that was my last day working for the government. I had "take this job and shove it" written all over my face. Well, at least in my mind.

I walked up to my boss' secretary, Joan Fiest. She was a pompous overweight woman that wore too much make-up. Her eyeliner made her look like a witch. She had a personality of a shark with a wide mouth to match.

"Hi, Ms. Fiest. Is Mr. Scandels in his office?" I asked. She was the gatekeeper to his office and loved the job. She turned and looked at me with a gaze that left no doubt of her disdain for me.

"Hope, you know that David does not like to be disturbed while he's enjoying his morning coffee." With that she gave me one of her shark smiles with all eighty teeth. One tooth was stained with red lipstick. She turned her back on me.

I stood there all of ten seconds counting backward, trying to calm myself, trying to reason with my brain. *Why does this woman dislike me so? I've had enough of her bullshit,* I thought as I decided to walk into my boss's office unannounced.

I stormed by the gatekeeper. She looked up at me with rouge cheeks, mouth agape.

"Wait!" she hollered. I passed through the door without even knocking. He was reclined in his chair, feet propped up on his desk with a simmering cup of coffee in his hand, pinky finger extended. A man caught in the solitude of his thoughts. Ms. Fiest rushed in behind me. She was winded like she had just run a marathon. "Mr. Scandels, I tried to stop her."

"Excuse me sir, but I need to have a word with you. It's important."

I watched as Mr. Scandels waved her away. After his secretary had left, he cocked his head to an angle furrowing his brow in concentration at me in wonder, what could be so important to make me barge into his office unannounced?

"What can I do for you?" he asked. Today he wore a starched white shirt, with a brown tie. His hair was thinning and this morning it looked wet. He had a strong angular jaw line with a deep dimpled chin that reminded me of a cartoon character. His demeanor was always poised like a man used to giving orders. He had this uncanny way of making you feel uncomfortable, the way powerful people do. And in his own right, he was a powerful man. The head prosecutor for the Northern District of Florida carried a lot of weight. I'll be the first to admit it, being a Black female in the predominately white man's world can be intimidating.

I stood in the middle of his office. On the wall I saw a picture of him and President Clinton. On his desk were more pictures, family, I guess. His office was huge, it made me feel small. I took a deep breath.

"As of today I am resigning," I said flatly, and walked up to his desk and placed my resignation letter on it. He shot forward in his chair as he removed his feet from the desk and knocked over a picture in a gold frame in the process.

"Resigning?" he retorted.

"Yes."

"But you haven't even given me a two week notice. We're already under-staffed and overloaded with cases." I just gave him a look that said, *that's your problem.*

"I'm afraid that it will not be possible for you to resign at this present time until we can find a suitable replacement for you."

"No, I have had just about enough of this. I think this entire criminal justice system needs to be overhauled. I sincerely thank you for asking me to stay, bu –"

Scandels was on his feet. It startled me for a man his age to be able to move so fast. "You cannot leave now!" he interrupted pointing his finger at me. This was the other side of the man not used to having his authority challenged and rejected, especially by a Black woman. I stood my ground, Lord knows I wanted to avoid this confrontation, yet in my own feminine solace I was delighted to badger his male ego.

"David." I called him by his first name just like everyone had been doing me since I first started working in the office. He jerked his neck narrowing his eyes at me letting me know that he did not appreciate me calling him by his first name the way he does me. White people. The nerve.

"It's a done deal. I'll be sending the movers for the rest of my things in my office." Saying that, I turned to walk away.

"Hope! I can assure you, if you try to play hardball with me, you'll end up being blackballed. If you walk out that door, I can promise you, you will never find a job in this town practicing law, even if you wanted to work for free."

His words stung me. I stood rigid and stared at the man who went out of his way to give me all the low profile cases, cases that no one else wanted. I couldn't help but smile at that white man, either that or curse him out. My daddy did not raise me that way, so I just smiled at him as I walked up and placed my business card on his desk. "This is my new employer," I said pointing at the name on the card. It read "Hope Evans, Attorney at Law" and for some reason, that name instilled a kind of courage in me, the kind that made a sista feel proud. "Feel free to use your power and prestige to blackball me if you like, but from here on out I ain't working for no one else but my damn self!" With that, I stalked out of the door leaving him staring at my card.

*****

I was getting ready to make my entrance into the world of corporate America, an independent Black woman. I was 25 years old and wet behind the ears, but determined to do my own thing. Inside my heart and soul, although I would not admit it to anyone, I was scared to death!

I left the building shortly after my confrontation with my ex-boss with most of my office material in a box. As I walked across the parking lot in the sweltering heat, with each step that little voice in my head barged its way in, the fear of failure announced its presence like an angry troll.

*Hope, you damn fool! You shouldn't have quit your job. Who's going to feed the baby?*

The diction of voices echoed in my head acrimoniously. I thought about my brother on crack, my other brother doing life in prison and catching my husband in bed with another man. I had enough blues in my life to sing a sad song, and to think, I had just quit a sixty five thousand dollar a year job. God help me, now I was going to try to make a career in a male dominated world. As I was opening the car door, I could feel sweat cascading down my back. I got in the car and tore my stockings on the door, ruining them. "Damn it! Damn it!" I screeched as I pounded my fist on the roof of my car, with it came a surge of emotions that I never knew existed. For the past year or so, I had been holding so much inside, trying to be strong, determined. I was a single parent trying to raise my son. My marriage was a failure, not to mention my husband was a homosexual. I was so filled with grief that I began to weep openly. I noticed that a car pulled up waiting for my parking space. The driver was an elderly Black lady. She watched me cry for a moment. Then she got out of her car. Age had stooped her body but she was still very attractive. I could tell she was once a very beautiful woman. She wore her hair styled and colored in a lovely shade of blue. She wore black slacks and white shirt.

"Child, are you OK?" she asked sympathetically as she lightly caressed my back with her hand. Lord knows it felt like I was having a nervous break down. I wanted to tell her no, everything wasn't OK, my life was a joke, and my real baby daddy had spit in my face and called me an Uncle Tom, and I had this stupid dream of helping my people so I quit my job.

"Yes ... I'm OK," I finally said as the tears ran down my cheeks, I cried openly.

The old woman grabbed my arm forcefully; I was surprised of her strength for a woman of her age.

"You will be all right, you hear me?" she said passionately, but there was something in her eyes that moved me. "You must never give up!" The old woman raised her voice. I nodded my head, swallowed the lump in my throat, breathed in air like it was new found courage. I met her motherly gaze and felt like she was trying to tell me something that I all ready knew.

"Thank you," I said softly as I looked away from her, embarrassed, this old Black woman that I did not even know. There was something in her warmth, her touch, and her eyes. She watched me closely as I got into my car.

"If you're not willing to sacrifice, maybe even die for your purpose, what are you living for?" The old woman yelled at me as I drove away. That was the day that my life would be changed forever. There would be no turning back.

As soon as I arrived home I checked my answering machine. One message was from Stan, the man that I caught in bed with my ex-husband. I thought that was very strange for him to call. Three other messages were from Officer Coffee. I was avoiding him after I found out he was a playa, besides, the man was too damn fine and I didn't trust myself.

I changed into my running clothes and went for a jog. I did five miles in record time, 45 minutes and some change. Afterward, I felt energized and aching in all the right places, a runner's high.

At 2:15 in the afternoon, I decided to pick my son up early from the daycare center and we would do the family thing–go see a movie at the mall.

I arrived at Saint John's Daycare Center, an ancient building that also served as a Catholic church run by elderly nuns. I paid a hundred and fifty dollars a week for Marcus to attend the school.

As soon as I walked inside I was pleasantly reminded of how it felt to be a child at heart. I smiled as I watched all the children frolic in a game of musical chairs. A child's laughter is addictive. I looked on as the music stopped and the children scurried for chairs. A little girl with blue eyes and long locks of blond hair that made her look like a beautiful baby doll stood motionless as it dawned on her that she was the last person standing, eliminated from the game. I noticed that my son, Marcus, was nowhere in sight. I looked around for him. One of the nuns, Sister Mary, approached me. I could tell from the expression on her face she was trying to remember my name.

"Hi. I'm Hope Evans, Marcus Green's mom," I said politely with a smile.

Sister Mary extended a bony hand. She wore a silver ring of a crucifix on her middle finger. Her handshake was cold and calloused.

"Where is Marcus?" I asked as I looked over her shoulder. The amiable expression on her face froze only to be replaced with a blank stare.

"Marcus is in the Time Out room. Sister Grace placed him there this morning."

"This morning!" I repeated indignantly looking at my watch. "What did he do?" I asked in a high-pitched voice causing some of the children to turn and look in my direction.

The nun sighed taking a deep breath, "Marcus curses like a sailor and fights with the other children."

"Why wasn't I informed of this?" I asked, disgruntled.

"Well, we thought that it was more than likely a bad influence coming from the household."

I listened, not believing what I was hearing, but knowing what she was trying to insinuate, that I was a bad parent.

"We've talked with the school's psychologist. The child is problematic, hyperactive and we believe that he has a learning disorder and —"

"He is 3 years old." I said cutting her off, not believing what I was hearing.

She continued, "The doctor said that he wanted to place Marcus on a drug called Ritalin. It's very popular with dysfunctional children." All I could do was shake my head at this woman that was supposed to be a servant of God.

For the second time that day I counted backward from ten. That's when I heard the little girl say, "I fucking quit, I don't want to play no more of your stupid game." The nuns must have heard too, but chose to ignore it.

"Where is my son?" I asked through clinched teeth. The nun pointed to the other side of the room. There was a large picture of Bozo the Clown along with other cartoon characters, a chalkboard with letters of the alphabet, ABCD, big enough for the seeing impaired to read. I saw my son huddled in the corner with his face up against the wall. I walked over there in a hurry, almost ran. "Honey, are you all right?" I asked affectionately.

He turned around and looked at me with almond eyes, face streaked with dried tears, his eyes the window to his soul. I saw something worse than hurt as my son looked up at me sniffling back his tears, "Mommy, I don't like it herrrre." He was trying not to cry. His little chest just heaved. The only thing I could see was his father's face, and a young Black man being subconsciously trained by the system to put his face up against the wall. I picked him up in my arms and he latched onto my neck. "Mommy take me with you."

"Mommy surely intends to take you with her," I reassured him as I caressed his head.

I looked up to see the two nuns whispering as I approached. For the first time, I took interest in the other children, and I noticed that only two children out of about forty were African American, at least from what I could see.

"I will be removing my child from this school as of today," I said curtly, while fighting to keep the anger out of my voice. Sister Mary stepped forward with a look of dismay on her pale face.

"Ms. Evans, that wouldn't be a good idea. Your son is suffering from hyperactivity along with –"

"Whaat? My damn son is not suffering from anything, but white people syndrome. When did our society start giving three-year old children drugs because they were hyperactive?" I screeched.

"And another thing, if my son learned bad behavior it was from right here. I just heard that little girl curse." I pointed at the girl. "And you heard it, too. Why is she not in the corner being trained on how to put her hands against the walls?"

The nun craned her neck backward with a look on her face like she smelled something awful, her cheeks flushed red.

"That's preposterous," she scuffed, turning up her long nose at me.

"No ma'am, what is preposterous is this school and the way it is run. Let me remind you of something, I'm a lawyer. If I find out that this school has a contract with a doctor and he is peddling drugs for profit outside the guidelines of the requirement of the AMA, I will personally have both of you placed so far under the jail, that the devil will be the only one interested in hearing your prayers." Silence. Both nuns stared at me as if I were the great white hope. Marcus retrieved his book bag and the little white girl with the foul mouth said something to him.

Once Marcus and I were in the car, I placed him in his car seat and with a moistened thumb, I wiped away the shadow of dry tears from his handsome face.

"Marcus, what did that little girl say to you before you left?"

My 3-year-old child bunched his lips together and batted his eyes looking away from me. A child's way of pleading the fifth.

"Mommy isn't going to spank you." I prodded, "Tell me."

"She said ... she said ... fuckin A."

"Fucking A?" I repeated my son's words. "'Is that what the nuns heard you say at school?" I asked. Marcus nodded his head up and down. Just like I figured.

*****

Life Thugstin's trial loomed heavily on my mind, most importantly, the cutthroat lawyers that he had spent all those millions on. The media labeled his defense team The Dream Team 2, only I knew better. One day I overheard my boss talking, actually, I was eavesdropping on my boss while he was in conference. Mr. Scandels called me into his office to get some case files for a court proceeding because one of the lawyers had taken ill and I was assigned to fill in. I lingered at the file cabinet. Once I heard the name Life Thugstin, I was all ears. After all, he was the father to my child and the master to my most deepest, darkest secret.

"With all the fanfare and media attention we're getting, this should be a piece of cake, the trial shouldn't last longer than two months. He has about as much chance at winning as an ice cube in hell." Mark Buckly, the famous trial attorney, was talking to my boss. Buckly was Life Thugstin's head attorney. Scandels cut in.

"I sure would have liked to nail his ass for tax evasion, but someone in his ring did a good job of organizing the operation. We think it's Willie Falcon and his organized crime family." Tom Braxon was another famous attorney hired on as part of The Dream Team 2. His career dated back over four decades. Tom had not tried a case in nearly three years, but still enjoyed the reputation as one of the best trial lawyers in the nation. However, like his partner, Mark Buckly, he was in it for the money. As far as Tom Braxon was concerned, Life Thugstin was guilty as sin.

"We'll put up a good show at the trial," Mark was saying. "But by the end of the trial, we'll make sure that you have your day."

I listened, not believing what I was hearing. I could not believe that they would talk so freely in front of me. Maybe it was because I was a United States Prosecutor, a part of their elite team, or maybe it was because I was a woman. That day I played the part of the proverbial fly on the wall.

"Hope!" Mr. Scandels called my name. I flinched and moved as I turned away from the file cabinet. A woman knows when it's time to take advantage of her charm, especially when she's in the company of a room full of men. I gave them my hundred-watt smile, the one that Black women invented solely for the benefit of white men. I saw how they ogled me when I first came into the office. On the inside I was infuriated, on the outside I had to play the part that was handed down to me by generations of people that learned to survive by outwitting the man. It was right then that I had made the decision that I was going to warn Life Thugstin.

"Yes," I responded to my boss.

"Are you having trouble finding the Johnson file?" he asked.

"I have it right here," I replied as I held the folder up in my hands. I had also come up on something else of interest, the witness list of all the people that were going to testify against Life, including confidential informants. With my heart racing in my chest, I walked out of the room feeling like a spy behind enemy lines.

*****

# Chapter Seventeen

## "The Ultimate Betrayal"

### — Hope —

On the day of Life Thugstin's trial, I was still brooding after the way he treated me when I risked everything to warn him that his lawyers were going to sell him out. I told myself that I would not attend the trial, but I could not help myself. The event itself was a spectacle, with media from all over the world. That was mostly due to Life's connection with the drug lord, Willie Falcon.

As I pulled into the courthouse parking lot, the media sensation was like a wild frenzy. The young thug, Life Thugstin, turned drug King Pin, with his aloof air of power and stoic thug appearance was handsome and charismatic. The media loved him. Somehow they came upon some pictures of him and Willie Falcon together on a yacht with a beautiful model. The paparazzi in England and Colombia ran full page articles on how Life Thugstin was being groomed to take over the throne of the multi-billion dollar empire at the time of his capture.

What made the case so interesting to the public was that it was alleged by the media that Thugstin had recruited all women as his lieutenants. The pictures of Trina, Tomica, Evette and Black Pearl made the front pages of the USA Today. The case was truly amazing. The government estimated Life Thugstin's wealth at over a hundred million dollars because of his association with the infamous billionaire cocaine baron.

The Thugstin case, with all its intrigue and mystic, seemed to take on a life of its own. I illegally parked in one of the prosecutor's parking spaces. I exited my car and waved through the throngs of media and ordinary people that just came for the attention of the hype, including groupies that came to watch what would one day be labeled the trial of the century.

As soon as I entered the courtroom I took notice of all the heavy security. I sat in the last row to make sure I was inconspicuous as possible. I wore my hair in a different style, I also donned a pair of Channel glasses. So far so good, no one noticed me.

I waited for the proceeding to begin. Sitting in a spectator's seat was a change for me. I tried a few cases in this very same courtroom, and was more than familiar with the judge, William Statford. He was on the bench for over thirty years and was known as a no nonsense judge, that openly displayed no mercy for drug defendants. It was rumored that his daughter overdosed on heroin. My old boss, David Scandels, sat at the prosecutor's table. Next to him were his assistant prosecutors, Brian Smith and Susan Swaltz. The prosecution motioned to have cameras allowed into the courtroom, but lost. The word in the judicial arena was that the United States prosecutor, David Scandels, was desperate. His political ambition ran as high as a seat in the Senate, but time was running out, and he was getting old. The Life Thugstin trial, and its connection to the infamous Willie Falcon cartel, would be just the stepping stone that he needed, once he made a show of defeating some of the best lawyers in the United States, The Dream Team 2. America was going to have to applaud his genius, and thus open the door to his political career.

Across from the prosecutor's table was The Dream Team 2: Tom Braxton and Mark Buckly along with a host of assistant lawyers. There were only two key participants missing, the judge and the defendant.

On the first day of any criminal trial the anxiety runs high, like watching two opponents getting ready to battle.

As I waited for Life Thugstin to enter the courtroom I reflected back on everything that happened the last nine months after his arrest. Three different branches of federal agencies orchestrated the arrest, the FBI, DEA and ATF along with the local and state authorities that raided the Chateau. Inside the authorities discovered a treasure trove—money, jewelry and expensive antique cars. The ironic thing was none of the property was in Life's name. It was in the name of a young girl, Annie Bell, who was also known as Black Pearl. Miraculously, she survived after being shot during an assassination attempt on Life. She awoke from a coma a few weeks after she was shot and learned that her three-year-old son was killed. Federal authorities placed her under arrest in a three-count indictment.

What fascinated me most about the case was how intricately designed the money trail was in concealing the assets. It led to stockholders that anonymously withheld their names, all accept Annie Bell. The shares of stock were in a corporation of investors. Under federal law it was all perfectly legal. A lien for a large amount of money had been placed on all the assets. If the feds confiscated the property they would also be held responsible for paying off the liens. This was nothing short of brilliant, and the feds quickly abandoned their pursuit to seize the assets, at least until they could figure out a way to get around the paper trail. I never would have imagined that dope dealers could be so sophisticated. And still I could not believe that this was the same brotha that I drove into town, and all he had were big dreams, big guns and a large heart. I thought about how I was the one who personally introduced him to Trina, my frat sister.

When I heard that Life could have connections to Willie Falcon, I knew it was possible.

Life entered the courtroom escorted by U.S. Marshals. The soft murmur of voices rose like the ocean tide.

Life wore a black Armani suit, gray shirt and alligator Stacy Adams. With his chiseled dark features he was by far the most handsome man in the courtroom; with his briefcase in hand he could have easily passed for a lawyer. His eyes scanned the courtroom, taking in every face, including mine, causing my heart to stir. He waved at an elderly Black woman. "I love you son," the woman said loud enough for the entire courtroom to hear. As soon as Life sat down, the artists from various media affiliates, including CNN, began drawing courtroom scenes. Since Judge Statford barred all cameras this was the next best thing.

As I looked on, once again I thought to myself, I knew why Johnny Cochran, one of the best lawyers in the world, refused to do federal cases against the government. Like myself, he knew the deck was stacked.

Life was talking with his attorneys. They appeared to be arguing. Adamantly, Life shook his head in disagreement, indicating he was not happy about something. I leaned forward just like the rest of the courtroom trying to hear bits and pieces of what was being said.

"All rise!" The bailiff bellowed. In walked Judge Statford, an elderly rotund man with a large head that appeared to be too big for his small body. He had droopy hound dog eyes, and sagging cheeks, that of a man that never smiled.

With everyone seated the clerk handed the judge court papers. The courtroom was now electrified with suspense.

"The United States of America versus Life Thugstin," the clerk announced over the clamor coming from the defense table.

The judge glared at the table over the rim of his half spectacles.

"Hmmm, hummmm!" The judge cleared his throat in an attempt to get the defense's attention. Life and his attorneys ignored him, until finally the judge banged his gavel.

"Is there a problem?" the judge asked.

Tom Braxton, the lead defense attorney, stood nervously. Even with all his polished epicure and professionalism, I could hear the tremor in his voice, "Hmmm, err, my client has just informed me he no longer wants me or my staff to represent him."

The judge pushed his glasses up on the bridge of his nose and leaned forward as if he were seeing counsel for the first time.

"No longer wants you to represent him?" the judge intoned. "You've been fired?"

It took only a few seconds for the rest of the courtroom to realize what was happening. Then, slowly, the monotone of voices signaled like a silent alarm, something about the courtroom proceeding was askew. A few reporters dashed out of the courtroom door to call in their scoop of the day, *Life Thugstin, Lieutenant of the Willie Falcon Colombian drug cartel, fires defense team, The Dream Team 2.*

Tom Braxton turned his head to watch all the commotion as the reporters left, he turned back facing the judge with disappointment written all over his face. I looked over at the defense table and Life moved his chair as far away from his attorneys as possible, his way of showing his parting of their association.

The judge arched his bushy eyebrows at Life.

"Mr. Thugstin, am I clear on this matter, you want to fire your attorneys?" the judge asked followed by a drone of whispering that sounded like a tiny roar from little people. The judge pounded his gavel and glared out into the courtroom. Life slowly rose from his seat. From the angle I was sitting all I could see was the side of his handsome face.

"I'm on trial today fightin' fo my life. I feel these men," Life turned and gestured pointing, "are not in my best interest."

"Why is that?" the judge asked.

"Well for one thing," Life sighed and looked over at his ex-lawyers, "I don't feel these men are in it to help me. I see them more on television doing interviews than I do in person." The judge shook his head in disproval at Thugstin.

"First off, let me admonish something to you. In America we have a system of democracy, and in this democracy there are servants of the people, such as lawyers. In our society, lawyers are for the benefit and best interest of the people."

While the judge talked, Life just stood there looking helpless. I glanced over to the prosecutor's table, Mr. Scandels sat in a chair, looking flabbergasted. He held onto the arm of the chair so tight,

I thought he was going to break it off.

"Why do you want to dismiss your lawyers at such a critical stage of the proceedings? The day of the trial?"

"Yo Honor, as I said earlier, I'm fightin' fo' my life. The only time these men come to talk to me is about more money, legal fees and whatnot. No one told me about a strategy, I ain't even seen the discovery list." Life was talking about a motion called a discovery, where the government is supposed to present all the evidence it intends to use at trial.

"Yo Honor, I've learned more 'bout my case from jailhouse gossip than from my so-called paid attorneys. Where I come from you don't call yourself a team and then go against the grain."

The judge had enough. "Fortunately we're not where you come from. You're in my courtroom, which just so happens to be a federal courtroom. In the federal system we do things different-ly!" Threat.

Tom Braxton was still standing. He looked over to the defense table as if to say, *what do I do now?*

"If I let you fire your attorneys how do you intend to defend yourself?" the judge asked.

"I'ma go pro se."

"Pro, se?" The judge retorted.

"Yep."

"You want to defend yourself?" the judge asked with a smirk on his face about as close as he would ever be at smiling. "How much education do you have?"

"The last time I was in prison I got my GED," Life responded.

Someone in the back of the courtroom giggled. For the next thirty or so minutes the exchange of words went on, until finally the judge granted Life Thugstin's permission to fire his lawyers. The judge said he would need a week to decide if he would allow Life to defend himself.

After court was adjourned, I walked up to the woman that called out to Life in the courtroom. Just as I suspected she was his stepmother, Brenda Thugstin. I gave her my card, told her I was a lawyer interested in the trial. She took the card, looked up at me and smiled brightly with weary eyes. I could tell that she had been crying. Gray hair ringed her temples. The wrinkles in the corners of her eyes said she was much older than what she appeared. I couldn't help but wonder, *where is her husband, the famous preacher, Freddy Thugstin?* As I recalled he had taken ill. Diabetes. One thing was for certain, Life and his father could never seem to get along. As we talked, a herd of anxious reporters spotted her and we were swamped. With microphones being thrust in her face, timidly Mrs. Thugstin began to talk, "My baby ain't done nuttin ta nobody."

I backpedaled away from that scene and all its madness, the courtroom hall filled with all them white faces. As I walked away, I made a quick glance over my shoulder. Mrs. Thugstin's fearful eyes followed me like a child standing in front of a train. This was too big, too powerful. The magnitude of it all was like a grip of a tight fist. Drug lords, money, murder, mayhem, the young Thugstin from rags to riches, I was overwhelmed. Now the only thing I wondered was, *what is he going to do next?*

*****

Later on that day, I picked my son up from the babysitter. He was asleep on the couch with his favorite stuffed animal, Barney, in his arms. *Finally at peace with the world,* I thought as I carried him in my arms to my car. God forgive me, but at 3 years old, my child was bad as hell. I guess when God was giving out intuitive curiosity he must have given Marcus an extra dose.

"Mama, what color is the sky?"

"Blue," I would answer.

"Why is it blue?"

"God made it blue."

"Why he do that?"

*****

I sat at home reading the newspaper, looking for cheap office space to rent. Marcus sat in front of the television watching "The

Cosby Show". The doorbell rang. I looked at the clock on the wall, it read 8:40 p.m. *Who could that be?* I wondered.

"I'll get it Mommy!!" Marcus yelled and raced to the door.

"Marcus! Boy, don't touch that door," I said as I walked up and peered out the peephole. It was Officer Coffee wearing a pair of jeans and a sweatshirt, and a shit-eating grin plastered on his face. Apparently, he was off duty, and as far as I was concerned, out of bounds for showing up at my home this time of night. Now it was my turn to read him his rights. I barely opened the door just enough to get my head out. "Mr. Coffee, I think it's very disrespectful for you to be at my door unannounced." Marcus popped his head between my legs.

"Mistah Coffeeee," he sang happily as he shuffled his feet from one leg to the other.

"I just came to check on you and the kid," he said uncomfortably.

"Yeah, I bet you did," I said sarcastically.

"Mommy, let him in."

"Hi, little man!" Officer Coffee started to reach down and pat Marcus on the head but thought better of it since Marcus was between my legs. Instead, from behind his back, he produced a pizza and smiled for the first time.

"Bribery will get you nowhere," I gibed.

"It's only bribery if you accept." He smiled, knowing he got me on that one.

"Mommy he got pizza! He got pizza!"

It felt like my son was going to plow my legs right from under me. All I could do was shake my head. "See what you did?" I scuffed as I relented and opened the door letting him in. He walked in, a mountain of a man. His cologne would forever be a signature on my feminine loins. He smelled like something good enough to eat.

"I apologize," he said, his thick baritone voice dripping with seduction.

He bent down and pecked me on my forehead. We were

standing too close. The man was too damn fine, and he knew it. The moment lingered like fog evaporating, lust titillating. In the background my son danced to a song he created about pizza.

I pulled my eyes away from Mr. Coffee shamefully, like maybe he could read my thoughts. "Have a seat, I'll get some plates." Before I knew it, Marcus was swinging on the man's arm. "Marcus! Stop that." Mr. Coffee tossed him so high in the air I thought he was going to bump his head on the ceiling. Marcus shrilled with joyful glee.

"It's OK, I love to play with children, wouldn't mind making a few myself," he said and winked at me flirtatiously and tossed Marcus up in the air again. The two of them were having a ball and I realized just how much my son missed the companionship of a man.

While we were munching on pizza and drinking Cokes, the phone rang. I picked it up, it was a collect call from a federal institution, Life Thugstin. I sighed deeply over the phone. In my heart I wanted him to call, didn't I?

"Ma'am will you accept the phone call?"

"Yes," I finally said and braced myself like a boxer preparing for a body blow.

"Hope? Hope! You there?" He called my name like it was the day we first met.

"What do you want?" I said acidly.

"Hope, I called to tell you that I'm sorry. I heard that you quit your job wit them crackas. I guess you were serious, huh?"

"What do you want?" I repeatedly, coldly.

"Hope, I'm under a lot of stress. Can't trust nobody, this shit big, ya know."

As Life talked, in the background it sounded like he was calling from an insane asylum. I could barely hear him "Hope, I need your help. Please?" All I could do was roll my eyes up at the ceiling. *Black men,* I thought. I noticed Mr. Coffee watching me closely.

"Evidently there's nothing I can do for you," I said curtly. I was talking about the stunt he pulled back at the SHU where he spit in my face.

"Hope, I said I was sorry."

"Uh huh," I grumbled.

"Tomorrow visiting hours start at 8 o'clock in the morning. I'll make it worth your while if you —"

"I don't need your money!" I screeched.

"Please, let me —"

"I don't have time." I hung the phone up and walked over to the couch and sat down.

"You OK?" Mr. Coffee asked.

I tried to smile, but it felt like my face hurt, actually it was my heart. I gave the man my phone number and then hung up in his face. A sista can be vindictive.

I lost my appetite along with my mood for any male company.

"I'm just tired, overworked and underpaid," I said, forcing my cheeks to form a smile. He just looked at me. I could tell he wanted to ask about the phone call. A portion of cold pizza sat on the table. I looked at Marcus, he sat nodding his head like a yo-yo, fighting sleep. I faked a long drawn out yawn like I was sleepy, too. Mr. Coffee smirked at me as if to say, *I can take a hint.*

I walked him to the door. He turned and tried to kiss me and at the same time, cop a feel. Mr. Man was smooth, but a little to slow. I ducked my lips giving him a hug. He caressed my backside and for a fleeting moment, I thought about letting him take me upstairs and rock my world. In the end, I ended up shoving him out the door. From the look in his pants he was going to have to take a cold shower when he got home, if that's where he was going.

Early the next morning, I awakened my son. He was not an early person. If this was any indication of his disposition as an adult, some woman was going to be in trouble.

I smothered his tiny face with kisses. "Wake up Pookie," I cooed in his ear. Both his mouth and his nose crinkled into a sleepy grimace. My child's rebuff with his eyes still closed, I smothered him with more kisses against his weak resistance until finally I was rewarded with a protracted yawn and a whimper with petulant lips. The sound that he made is what I imagined what doves sound like when they cry.

"Noooo Mommy," he crooned as his beautiful long eyelashes fluttered like butterflies. Afterward we took a bubble bath together, my son and I. We were both unemployed. I was out of work and he was out of school. For that day I decided that we would just have to be inseparable.

*****

I drove to the 7-Eleven and bought some breakfast. While I was in line with the rest of the early morning commuters, I couldn't help but notice the magazine rack, *Newsweek, People, Ebony, The National Enquirer*. Holy cow! On the front page of *Times,* was a picture of Bill Clinton with a background silhouette of the White House. The title of the article was, "*WAR ON DRUGS, Is it working?*" and in the left hand corner was a picture of Life Thugstin and Willie Falcon. I scooped up the magazine and started reading it right there in line.

Back in the car I pulled over to the side of the gas station, forgetting to pump my gas. In the magazine were pictures of Life's estate, along with pictures of Trina Vasquez, Tomica Edwards, Evette Keys and a young beautiful Black girl by the name of Annie Bell. She miraculously survived after being riddled with bullets in a botched assassination attempt on Life Thustin. Unfortunately her 3-year-old son died. I was already familiar with the case and all its gory details. Still I was fascinated. The authorities were still searching for the lieutenants. They were known only as the Miami Boys. They seemed to have disappeared as quickly as they appeared.

It was alleged that Life and his crew of hoodlums were responsible for hundreds of brutal assaults and murders. In some instances, body parts were found missing, such as heads and arms. One of Life's lieutenants had been murdered, a man by the name of Johnny Davis, better known as Dirty. I knew him from my neighborhood in Miami, the Pork and Beans Projects.

*****

I finally found the appropriate office space. It wasn't much bigger than my walk-in closet at home, but it was mine, and this was where I was going to make my start. I signed a lease. They wanted a thousand dollars a month for rent. I planned to buy used office furniture, start from scratch and work my way up. I will never be able to explain why I made my next move. Maybe it was just an overwhelming impulse. On the same day that I rented the office I still had Marcus with me since it was our day together. In a semi-trance, I drove straight to the Federal Detention Center. I couldn't walk away from that man if I wanted to. Believe me, I wanted to.

On the drive there, Marcus was starting to get cranky and restless. He had so much pent up energy, but not enough to want to place him on drugs. I was thinking about the nuns back at the school.

As I drove up to the FDC building there were still a few media vans and trucks still scattered around the place. I knew that if it weren't for Life's association with Willie Falcon he would not be receiving all this publicity.

With suitcase in one hand and Marcus in tow, I entered the building as my mind wrestled with what I was doing,

"Mommy, where we going?"

"To see a man about a dog."

Instantly a few of the correctional officers recognized me with a few raised brows.

Finally, after I went through all the procedures that are designed to make people not want to visit their loved ones, like waiting well over an hour and the search of my person, I was finally accepted into the visiting area. I sat in one of these terribly uncomfortable chairs. The building was cold, the air conditioner was turned up high. A few rows down from us, an obese Black woman with orange hair weave in her head sat eating chicken wings that came from the vending machine. In the distance I heard the PA system call a name. My mind was in a blur.

"What am I doing here?" Marcus sat next to me his legs swinging from the chair. He spotted the vending machine with the candy and pointed.

"Candy, Mommy."

"Not right now sweetheart."

I exhaled and re-crossed my legs. Already the chair was starting to hurt my behind. I looked up to see the large woman walk over to the vending machine again just as three visitors entered, two young girls in their early teens and an elderly woman who must have been the Grandmother. In my peripheral vision, I saw Life enter the room. My breath got caught in my throat. For the first time I noticed his limp and the way he carried his arm. I thought about the attempted murder on his life. He came and stood in front of me. I could smell soap and something else, cocoa butter? I got the impression he wanted me to stand and hug him.

"Sit down," I said rudely, giving him a once over and then glancing at my watch. He sat across from me. It felt like I was hyperventilating. I forced myself to look into his eyes, and searched his soul for some vestige of sincerity. For some reason he and my son just stared at each other. It was bizarre, like two people that knew each other but couldn't remember the other's name.

I looked between the two of them and damn near fell out my seat. Marcus looked identical to his father like he was a miniature copy, dimple and all. The scene was eerie. They continued to stare at each other like two people stuck in a mirror. For the sake of talking I started a conversation, just as a CO walked by.

"As an attorney I would advise you not to represent yourself at trial. In fact, I would advise you not to go to trial, period." No answer, just the two of them staring at each other. I was on the outside looking in. To my utter shock, I watched as my son climbed out of his chair and ambled over to where Life was and leaned against his knee. This was totally out of character. My son is shy of strangers.

"Hope, I can't believe this," Life said. His voice was hoarse. I thought I detected anger. It was a big mistake to bring my son there. *Life figured it out, the child leaning against his knee is his son,* I thought as I waited for him to speak. He licked his lips and peered closer at Marcus.

"He looks like ... he looks just like my father," Life finally said. The frown on his face was that of a man trying to understand fate, strange happenstance, or maybe why I never told him he was the real father to my child.

"Marcus, honey, go sit back in the chair," I said sweetly. My child ignored me.

"No, please. Let him stay." Life's words were soft and sounded like a plea. Still neither of them took their eyes off each other.

"What's that?" Marcus asked innocently, pointing at the prison tattoo on Life's forearm. It looked like it was recently done. It was a picture of a child's face beneath a tombstone. It read, "Rest in Peace" with the name Shawn L. Bell inscribed on it.

"That's a picture of my son, Shawn L., he went to heaven."

Life spoke as if the gruesome scene was still fresh in his memory. I found myself leaning forward staring at the tattoo with my son.

"Why he die for?" Marcus asked.

"Boy get over here!" I screeched. Life picked Marcus up in his arms holding him affectionately, and at that time the two of them looked at me accusingly. Lawd have mercy! It felt like a double dose of regret. It suddenly dawned on me if the media, or anybody else saw us together like this they couldn't help but noticed the comparison.

"I dunno what he died fo'," Life answered somberly and then his whole demeanor changed. He tickled Marcus' sides. They laughed together with the same smile. I was forced to look away. Again I was tormented about why I came in the first place.

"I saw you in the courtroom the day I fired my lawyers."

I just looked at my watch, no words, lots of body language. My intention was to get out of there with the least conversation possible.

"My stepmother told me that you gave her one of your business cards."

"She remembered me?" I accidentally blurted out not meaning to break my silence.

"Yeah, you're the only person that gives out business cards with no address on them." He smiled, all dimples, and then added, "Naw just playin'. She remembered you cause you was the only Black woman that approached her. She said it was hectic. White folks can be so rude." The moment stilled. I watched his large hands as he played with Marcus, teaching him how to make a fist to throw a punch, using the palm of his hands for punching bags. "Harder! Harder!" he instructed.

Life persuaded Marcus to swing, until finally Marcus missed and fell on his butt. My mask was unveiled. As much as I didn't want to, I couldn't help but laugh. In fact, all three of us got a good roar out of that. The CO walking by laughed, too. I guess we must have looked like one big happy family. Before I could, Life picked Marcus up and dusted off his pants and placed him on his lap and they played horsy. I looked at my watch, determined to make my exit. Suddenly Life stopped rocking Marcus and just held him in his arms. "Hope, I'm concerned about the case." He couldn't look me in the eyes, didn't want to either, just stared above my head like it was a clock up there or something. I tried to read his mood, the thug nobody knew. I looked under all that brazen gangsterism, underneath all that toughness and I saw a lonely man with dark circles under his eyes. Gone was the glory of the game, only to be replaced by concrete, steel, mail call and the same weekly three course meals. He was still not looking at me, just rocking back and forth with Marcus in his arms.

"I came to this town with a big money scheme. I should have left a long time ago." I didn't know if Life was talking to me or just pondering his thoughts. He paused and looked at the child in his arms.

"My stepmother doesn't trust white folks. Neither do I."

"It was good you fired your lawyers," I said. Marcus was

falling asleep in his arms.

"Yeah, I fired them because they were greedy, I could sense that sumpin' wasn't right wit them."

"I came to tell you that the day you took your anger out on me."

"I know, I know. I figured that out after you left. When I heard that you quit your job, I realized then that I made a big mistake," he said apologetically as his voice softened.

"I overheard my ex-boss, Scandels, talking to your lawyers. They planned to rig the trial so he could win, and at the same time, bleed you for your money while enjoying all the free press." I don't know why I was opening up to this man; perhaps it was because he was the father to my child. Maybe it was because he was a brotha.

"You said somethin' bout Lil Cal."

"Yes, while I was working for the government I stole your file. In it was the discovery papers of all the people that planned to testify against you at this trial." Life raised a suspicious eyebrow at what I just said. "Lil Cal is in Leavenworth Federal Penitentiary doing a life sentence. He agreed to come back and testify against you in return for a reduced sentence. His real name is Calvin Johnson. You know him?"

"Yeah, I know 'em," Life said, his eyes cast to the floor, hurt written all over his face. "That was my nigga. I bought his Mama a big-ass house, kept his inmate account phat." I looked away, didn't want to wallow in his sorrow. Suddenly our little space, our little world inside of a prison visitation room was filled with silence louder than any words that two people can share.

"Hope, I want you to represent me! Be my lawyer!" Life said it like it wasn't a question, it was a demand. He completely caught me off guard. The moment lulled. I was sure he was trying to read my expression. Finally I chuckled a strained laugh as fake as the fruit on Grandma's dinning room table.

"You can't be serious." I gestured. He made a face that said, *do I look serious?*

"First off, I don't have the experience for a case of this magnitude, and more importantly, the prosecution is going to file a motion for conflict of interest just to get me off the case because I used to work for their office." To me it sounded like a lame excuse.

"You must try," he said with conviction.

I'll admit, I had thought about it. What would it be like to represent a client in one of the biggest drug cases the state of Florida has ever seen?

"I'll pay you double what I paid The Nightmare Team 2. Hope, if I'ma die like some fuckin' caged dog, then at least let me be able to fight back."

His words hit deep to the core of my soul, making me feel kind of high, like an adrenaline rush that comes with a fight, a fight for a Black man's life.

"Do you know what you're asking of me?" I asked sternly.

"Yes I do," he shot back.

"If I decide to take your case and they let me, it's not going to be like your last defense team. This is nothing short of war, and it's dirty and corrupt. I'm going to have to hire attorneys, investigators, legal specialists such as psychologists and other legal experts, and most importantly, Life?" I called his name with all the sincerity that I could muster and I looked him in the eyes with a cold stare. "If you lie to me, I promise you, I promise you, I will drop you like a bad habit." He just looked at me as he switched positions moving Marcus from one arm to the other. My child was fast asleep in his arms.

"I'll send you a check for a mill."

"A mi ... mi ... million dollars," I stammered.

"That's not enough?"

"That's too much. What about taxes? The feds are already trying to nail you for tax evasion."

"The money will come from a corporation. It's all perfectly legal, the same way white folks do it," he said, as I listened and learned.

I thought about the billion dollars that Willie Falcon was

worth. I thought about Trina Vasquez and how two weeks after Life's arrest, she was arrested at the New York International Airport with four million dollars in her luggage.

One thing was for certain, Life definitely had the finances to buy the best defense that

money could buy. I did recall reading in one of the confidential dossiers while I was working for the federal bureau, Willie Falcon paid each of his lieutenants 10 percent of each shipment of coke. Each shipment was always valued at over a hundred million. The bureau had an inside informant, a man by the name of Carlos Menendez. He was going to testify that he personally took part in at least five different operations where Life Thugstin imported large shipments of cocaine from Colombia to the United States. About a month ago, Carlos and his family were murdered execution style. Both of his eyes and his tongue were savagely cut out, a warning to future snitches. His wife and two daughters, ages 5 and 3, all had their throats cut.

I warned Life not to get into any more trouble at the FDC building. He already had been in several fights and assaults. I knew that he wouldn't listen. I jotted down the address of my new office just as the CO announced the end of the visitation. Maybe I should have hugged him, whispered words of encouragement, but I felt that it was important for me to keep our relationship strictly business. But once again, a nod of the head, a shrug would have to suffice. I took my son out of his arms, and marched out of the door to the sound of my heels on the cold linoleum floor. If knew then what I was getting myself into, I would have never taken the case, United States of America versus Life Thugstin.

*****

# Chapter Eighteen

## "A New Beginning"

### — Hope —

The next day I was at my new office. The movers arrived around 10:30 in the morning, with the used furniture that I bought from Goodwill.

It was one of them hectic days, hot and sweaty. Of course, my air conditioner was not working, and there wasn't enough space in my cramped office for all of these huge men to be maneuvering around me. Someone bumped into me and I turned around to see a handsome guy in a Federal Express uniform. He smiled and began to apologize for accidentally touching me from behind. I shrugged it off because one of the movers mistakenly pushed him into me.

"You know who Hope Evans is?"

"That's me." I signed my name on the dotted line. He passed me an envelope marked American Yacht Association. I opened it and there was a check for one million dollars in my name. I sat down on a box and heard something break. The guy in the uniform looked at me like I was crazy.

*****

The next morning, bright and early, I arrived at the Federal Building downtown. I went inside the clerk's office and filed a motion that I would be representing Life Thugstin. At the time I thought I was fully aware of the repercussions of what I was doing.

The only real bright spot was the judge would be relieved to learn that Life was trying to hire a lawyer. Whenever a defendant represents himself, it's always a sure debacle, and I was sure the Honorable Judge Statford was not about to let that happen in his courtroom. The major hurdle now was my ex-boss down at the United States Prosecution's Office, David Scandels. If he decided to file a motion citing conflict of interest, more than likely I would be thrown off the case. This was too much to bear. Maybe I was stressing, but for the last few weeks I had been feeling ill, could hardly eat and didn't get much rest. Not to mention the nervous breakdown I had in the parking lot a few weeks ago.

At last, I arrived home. Crowds of media were camped out in my front yard. I had to honk my horn just to enter my driveway.

"What the ...." Microphones were thrust into my face as I exited my car. Too many cameras and too many faces. A sea of people surrounded me, instantly I thought about my hair, my makeup. This was the last thing I needed. *How did they find out so fast?* I wondered.

"Ms. Evans, will you be defending Life Thugstin?"

"No comment," I responded, as I attempted to trudge through the herd of media.

"Ms. Evans, with your prior experience with the prosecutor's office, what made you want to switch sides and go against your old office?"

"No comment."

"Ms. Evans, you're young, barely in your mid 20s with hardly enough experience to go up against your old boss, David Scandels. What kind of defense do you plan to use?" a reporter asked.

I ignored him and stepped over a thick television cable cord. I saw a reporter standing in my garden. Cordially, like every day I was used to coming home finding a herd of anxious reporters standing in my yard, I said with a straight face, "I will be more than happy to talk with you guys, but until something breaks and I am assigned the case it would be inappropriate and unprofessional for me to discuss the case with you." I then pointed to the reporter standing in my garden, he was short and round like maybe doughnuts were his first love. "Sir, if you don't posses a degree in agriculture I suggest you get off my Magnolias before I have you arrested for plant homicide." The reporters roared with laughter as the he stepped out of the garden like a fat kid that just got caught with his hand in the cookie jar. I couldn't help but grin at his antics as blue skies and camera lights flashed, bathing my body. I finally managed to make it inside my home. Shutting the door, I just leaned against it. Lord, I was so tired. I knew I needed a check-up and I promised myself as soon as I got caught up on everything I was going to see a doctor.

The phone rang, eyes bulging I stared at it as if it were a time bomb. *Reporters.* I thought. I placed my briefcase on the couch and removed my shoes. On stocking feet I padded over to the phone.

"Hello?"

"Hope?"

"This is she. May I help you?" I said recognizing the harsh tone of the voice instantly.

"This is Mr. Scandels, your former employer. What's this about you taking the Thugstin case?" There was a pause, my heart skipped a beat, it felt like the wind was sucked out of me. For the life of me, I did not know why this white man intimidated me so much.

"Yes, it's true," I heard my voice respond timidly as I gripped the phone

with both hands balancing my fortitude. Yet from somewhere in the back of my mind a voice said, *Hope you have spent your whole life preparing for this, the little Black girl from the Pork and Beans Projects. You're a fighter, fight back!*

"Hope, I suggest you withdraw from this case if you know what's good for you!" Scandels threatened. Silence, as I grasped the phone so tight it felt like I could have crushed it.

"David, I have no intention of withdrawing from the case."

"David?" Scandels repeated, not believing I would have the

gall to call him by his first name the way that he has always done me.

"I can have you removed from the case. As you are aware of, this is a matter of conflict of interest –"

"Whose interest, yours or the court?" I asked, raising my voice.

"You are not familiar with the logistics of federal law, but I'm known for

my shrewd courtroom skills."

"All I know is that in our last conversation, before I left your office, you threatened to blackball me, so if that is any indication of your courtroom skills, you're not playing fair, you're taking me back four hundred years," I said sarcastically. I heard the harsh rustle of air through his nostrils as he breathed his rage into the phone. Apparently I had struck a nerve. I was trying to play on his psyche, to bait him, use a strong dose of psychology.

"Are you implying that I'd rather blackball you than face you in court?" he shouted. I took the phone away from my ear.

"I'm only stating the facts as to how you related them to me, David," I said feeling my confidence building as I realized I might have found a hole in his armor. My rival, a man. His weakness, his ego. A smart woman has always been able to exploit that to her advantage.

"I'll tell you what Ms. Evans," Scandels said calmer, with more threat in his voice.

For the first time ever he addressed me by my last name. "I'll look forward to seeing you in court and making you the laughing stock of the town."

"Mr. Scandels, the feeling is mutual."

He slammed the phone down. I beamed with pride as I turned and peeked out the curtains. The reporters were gathering their gear to leave, thank God.

*****

Afterward I called my girl Nandi Shakur. She was now Dr. Shakur, a professor and pioneer in the study of socioeconomics. I called in a debt of friendship and asked her to be one of my expert witnesses. She told me that she had been following the case in the news. For the first time in my life she let me do all of the talking. She had no choice. Now I was a professional and this was my field, criminal law. This case, this trial, was larger than life, bigger than the both of us. I told her about one of a kind strategy that had never been used before. I was going to build a defense on what I was calling a Social-Economic crime, meaning that oppression and environment, along with the fact that drugs were placed in the Black community, were factors that had to be taken into consideration. Nandi agreed to help me.

*****

# Chapter Ninteen

## "Time To Get Ready for Trial"

*— Hope —*

"Hope! Hell naw! Have you lost your fuckin' mind?"

"Just hear me out."

"I've heard enough. I ain't pleading guilty to nuttin'."

"Five hundred grams of powder or less carries a sentence of five years, but due to your past criminal history they're going to add a few more years. The government is asking for a life sentence," I shouted, grabbing his arm. Our eyes locked like in a mental standoff. He pulled his arm away from me. I watched as he caressed the neat crop of waves in his head with his hand, eyes downcast. A week prior to my visit Judge Statford granted me permission to take the case. The only catch was I was only given three weeks to prepare for trial. A week had already passed and I was still trying to prepare a defense that even I had doubts about. And Life Thugstin was stubborn as hell, just like the rest of the brothas caught up in the system. They just did not understand the real dynamics of law.

I opened his folder and passed him a copy of his indictment, along with the discovery, a thick folder with all the evidence the government intended to use against him, including all the witnesses.

"You're charged with CCE, Continuing Criminal Enterprise. In order for the government to prove its case against you, the government must prove, without a shadow of a doubt, that you took part in a continuing series of violations in which you," I pointed a finger at him for emphasis and was surprised to see that I had his full attention, "were the leader. The government must prove you worked in concert, with at least five or more other persons, and obtained a substantial income for over a year. By pleading guilty, merely selling cocaine powder, the most time it carries is five years, most importantly, it knocks all the air out of the government's case and establishes a leeway to counter attack all 78 witnesses that are scheduled to testify against you for a reduced sentence." Silence. I could tell he was pondering what I said.

"What about my co-defendants?" Life asked.

"Annie Bell, the young lady you know as Black Pearl, is walking now. She has a slight limp and she lost a lung but she's doing a lot better. They moved her from the hospital to the FCI holding facility for women up on the hill. The government gave her a deal to testify against you." I let the words hang in the air, watched his reaction, felt his anxiety.

"What happened?" he finally asked leaning forward in his seat his brow furrowed with concern.

"Your friend Annie Bell is a trooper. She told them to kiss her ass." Life erupted in laughter as he threw his head back and slapped his thigh, all I could do was shake my head.

"What about Trina?" he asked after his laughter subsided. At that moment I saw something on his face, like maybe he had asked a question that he really didn't want an answer to.

"Trina and Annie Bell are cellmates. Both of their lawyers told me they're ready to go to trial," I said. Life was looking at me with an expression of disbelief, like he was sure that Trina was going to rat on him.

"How much time are they facing?" he asked somberly.

"Thirty years if they are found guilty. All charges dropped if they agree to testify against you." Life sighed a whistle through his teeth. I continued, "A woman by the name of Tomica Edwards, the woman that set you up at your estate, plans to testify against you in order to get a lenient sentence for herself and a friend by the name of Evette Keys. However, Ms. Keys has sent word by her attorney that she has no intention of taking the stand against you. I'll be honest, I think my staff of attorneys can crush the majority of the government's witnesses once they take the stand, but Tomica Edwards and Calvin Johnson are going to be difficult witnesses to crack." Life just looked at me with a blank stare. I said, " The reason why I want you to plead guilty to the sales of cocaine is because in law there is such a rule as buyer-seller relationship. Meaning just because you sold someone drugs doesn't mean you employed them making you guilty of CCE kingpin status of running a continued criminal enterprise." Suddenly a light bulb went off in his head as it dawned on him what I was trying to get him to understand.

"By pleading guilty, I won't be denying I sold drugs, but only that I shouldn't be charged with CCE."

"Exactly. Most importantly, everyone that is testifying against you says you sold them cocaine, or they know you from selling it. In a sense we could use their testimony to help you."

"Yo, that's brilliant, but I have one problem with that."

"What's that?"

"What about the conspiracy charge?"

"What about it?" I said making a face. "Under federal law, it takes two or more persons to conspire."

"Uh huh, so you're saying that Tomica and Lil Cal are the only two people that seem to be the biggest threat to my case?" I nodded my head. Life sat the folder down and looked at me. His entire demeanor had changed. I could tell he wanted to ask a question, but thought better of it.

"How are you and your father getting along?" I asked. Life looked at me and frowned as if to say, *what does that have to do with my trial?*

"Dig, we don't get along. As far as I'm concerned I don't have a father."

"They did a story on you the other night on ABC's Nightline.

They said your father was ill, in the hospital with diabetes."

"Fuck him!"

"What about your relationship with your stepmother?" I asked, intentionally ignoring his attitude toward his dad.

Life arched his brow, "Hope, what are you getting at?"

"Life you're going to have to trust me on this. I have a plan. I want you to tell your step mom to bring the church here, in a show of support for your trial."

"Whaat!"

"Listen, you have to trust me on this. By nature Black people are spiritual people, soulful people. Whites have always been intimidated by this."

"Hope, what da fuck dat gotta do wit my damn trial? If you're finna try some bullshit —"

"No hear me out!" I said, slamming my fist down on the table and standing up, wearing my frustration on my face. "As a Black woman, I have always been hated, discriminated and severely underestimated for my intellectual talents, told what I can't do because I was a poor Black girl from the Pork and Beans projects. Now I have the knowledge and the wherewithal to beat these people at their own game." Life just looked at me, mouth agape at my uncharacteristic outburst.

"These white folks are going to do like they have always done. They're going to underestimate us and our strategy, and that is our sole advantage." I walked over to the window with my back to Life. We were in the private section of the facility, a small room designed for attorney/client visits. Today I wasn't feeling too well, and as of lately, I had been wearing my emotions on my sleeves.

"So, you're pretty sure about this, huh?" he asked evenly.

I turned facing him and said, "The only people that we have to make an impression on is the judge and twelve jurors. From what I've heard Judge Statford is a very conservative judge, sometimes that can be good. So far I've hired experts to come testify on your behalf. One of them is a professor at UGA. She will testify that people are influenced by their environment." What I didn't tell Life was Dr. Nandi Shakur was my girl and we devised a strategy. I knew that we only had a 2 percent chance of winning, but we had a chance.

*****

The first day of the trial was eventful. The media was there in full blast. The place was a frenzy. My staff and I had to be escorted through the rear entrance of the old court building. The day before, I did an interview on BET and ABC. I was caught up in a whirlwind of media and its hype. Most days I would be so exhausted that I couldn't even eat and I lost a considerable amount of weight.

On the first day of the trial, I wore a stunning two-piece black and gold suede Armani skirt suit. I made sure I dressed to impress and the media quickly took notice. In fact, one of my pictures appeared in the best-dressed column of the Enquirer. In the paper I was standing next to Marsha Clark, the prosecuting attorney that tried the O.J. case.

By the time my staff and I entered the courtroom, it was jam packed. The section behind our defense table was mostly Black folks, with only a sprinkle of whites and they were the media, and I guess a few FBI agents. I could hear a soulful melodic hum, voices, soft like a gentle breeze. As I sat down I turned my head all the way around and saw all the elderly Black folks swaying back and forth, some of them had paper fans fanning themselves. For some reason the courtroom was hot, the air was stale. This was the atmosphere I wanted. I asked Life to send his father's church parishioners, and that he had done. Too many old Black folks will turn an old courthouse into a church house. Life entered the courtroom, smiled, as the U.S. Marshals were escorting him. He pumped my hand, I could feel the raw energy. With his cute dimples and sexy smile, he was the most handsome man in the entire courtroom. He wore a beige two-piece suit like he was modeling it.

After we said a few words in hushed tones, I surreptitiously looked over at the jury, six women and six men, all white and they

**270**

varied in age. In my peripheral vision, I saw Mr. Scandels. He sat at the prosecutor's table with his assistants. The expression on his face was nonchalant and unconcerned; in fact, he was reading the sports section of a newspaper.

I had the nervous jitters as I spoke with my assistant staff, Taya Baker and Adrienne Greene, two older women that were instrumental in my educational development, and not just as a lawyer, but in sisterhood. At one time they both taught at Spellman College and they always invited me to Atlanta to attend their seminars. This they did for free and paid all my expenses. Needless to say, I hired them at $200 an hour apiece.

"All rise! Court is in session. The Honorable Judge William Statford presiding."

The judge entered the courtroom. He was short and rotund with chubby cheeks and a large round bald head. Once he took his seat he placed on a pair of half glasses and began to read from a document on his desk.

"Errr, huh, here ... we are here on the matter of United States of America versus Life Thugstin." With that he looked glaring down at the defense table as if he wanted us to feel the weight of his statement. "Counsel for the defendant, will you please state your name for the record?" the judge asked. I rose from my seat in unison with my associates. Three Black women taking on the most powerful government in the world.

"Hope Evans, your Honor. Assisting me will be my associates, Taya Baker and Adrienne Greene," I said and watched as prosecutor David Scandels spoke introducing his staff as I had just done. Afterward the judge went on to give his lengthy instructions to the jury, and admonishing warnings there was to be no talking to the media nor was the jury allowed to watch the news or read any papers that he felt could influence their decision. He went on to explain the nature of each count in order for the defendant to be found guilty of the CCE.

After the judge finished with his instructions to the jury, I stood and prepared to give my opening argument. In the background all I heard were the soulful melodies of old Black folks droning, humming segued with an occasional, *Thank you Jesus . . . Amen.* It was all so soft, soft like the wind.

I spoke to the judge, "Good morning your Honor." Ostensibly I nodded my head at the prosecution's table, a gallant show of courtroom etiquette. Then I went into action. I strode right up to the jury box, up close and personal. I had to make a profound affect on the jury, a man's life depended on it. With a manicured hand I caressed the mahogany wood. Let my hand sail along its rich smoothness. Just as I rehearsed, I recited each juror's name like I had known them all their lives. Some looked up at me in admiration, others in awe.

"Today, ladies and gentlemen of the jury, you will set a precedence like never before, for it is solely for the betterment of mankind, humanity, to cast out the atrocities, injustice that besiege all walks of life. Today we're going to deal with urban life and this so-called war on drugs and what it is doing to our Black community." As I talked my passion grew. I thought about not just my brother, but also all the brothas in prison that were doing life sentences for $20 worth of crack. I saw my girl, Nandi, in the front row, as I heard the shrieks of my ancestors' cries. As old folks hummed a mournful dirge it felt like I was in another place, another time. The judge cocked his head to the side and frowned at the courtroom. I pushed myself forward like diving off a cliff, this was my opening argument. I had to make an impression on the jury.

"Today my client is being charged with CCE. The rule of federal law, Title 21 USC 848. It means in essence to run a Continuing Criminal Enterprise with five or more persons for a 12 month period or more. My client is being charged with being a kingpin," I said and suddenly turned and spun on my heels to elicit the dramatics. All good lawyers must be good actors first and possess a theatrical power to get the jury's attention. I walked over to the prosecutor's table, felt a million eyes on my face and heard a litany of prayers. "This man right here," I raised my voice with a strong cadence, pointed a deft manicured finger in his face. Scandels tried to smile, but he looked about as comfortable as a man standing in front of a firing squad. "He would like for you to believe that my client is the sole reason for the drug epidemic. The only problem with that is logic. He would like for you to believe that my client is a drug dealer. The only problem with that is, it's merely myth, sprinkled with speculation and false accusations. He is the one that is guilty and needs to be placed under the jail." A wave of clamor rose from the courtroom. Judge Statford banged his gavel down. I looked over to the elders and senior assistants, they both gave me a satisfied nod. Part of our strategy was to rattle the prosecutor with an aggressive attack.

The judge arched his eyebrows at me threateningly. "I suggest you tone it down." I continued to stare at Scandels. This was my stage, the jury and the media were my audience. "You're wasting the taxpayers' money, not to mention their patience," I said as I pointed to the jury box and made a face like that man should be ashamed of himself. "Today ladies and gentlemen, you will not be shown one piece of evidence. Allow me to repeat that," I said and walked up closer and looked each juror in the eye. "You will not be shown one piece of evidence. The government's case is based on what is known in the legal academia of law as circumstantial evidence. To a law professional, it means they have nothing, NADA!" I turned around to face the courtroom. I saw Life with his hand cupped under his chin watching me intently.

"Seventy eight witnesses will be paraded before you to testify against my client. But you, the jury, don't be fooled. I want you to think critical, logical, to be rational, as well as objective. Ask yourselves, what are these people, so-called friends, associates of the defendant getting in return for their testimony? Is their testimony sincere? Are they doing this out of the kindness of their hearts? Their need to help justice prevail, or are they getting paid in some other way?" With that I walked across the courtroom floor and stood in the middle.

"When I worked as a prosecutor for the government, there

were people that we referred to as paid informants. Men and women that could manufacturer a story as quickly as you could recite your phone number. These men and women are known to you and I in the real world as rats —"

"Objection!" Scandels was on his feet, face beet red, fuming mad. "Your Honor, Ms. Evans is trying to make a caricature of the government's witnesses, notwithstanding she is outside the scope of argument."

The judge turned and looked at me with an icy glare.

"Sustained. The jury is instructed to disregard the last statement. Ms. Evans you know better than that," the judge scolded.

I continued, determined not to let Scandels break my rhythm. "As I was saying —" I cut my eyes at Scandels, and turned back to the jury, heard the soulful murmur of old Black folks, a chant like a solemn hum with an occasional "Thank you Jesus." I felt the hair on the back of my neck rise as the jury looked at me transfixed. "Today you'll learn that inmates in federal prison routinely buy, sell and steal narcotics, concoct testimonies, then share their perjury with federal authorities in exchange for a reduction in their sentence. Often, these inmates testify against people they've never met. They corroborate on crimes they've never witnessed. They lie with virtual impunity, often with the government's blessings. They act as modern day slave catchers in the inhumane brutalization of Black people. These federal agents and prosecutors have been accused of helping move the scheme along and in most cases they provide convicts with information in order to help them fabricate their lies."

"Objection! This is ridiculous. The defense is mounting a vicious attack on the government and not the case."

"Your Honor, I intend to show that the government is also at fault and as much a culprit in this case and that is part of my defense."

"Overruled. The defense is entitled to present its case even if it intends to make accusations against the government."

I crossed my arms over my chest and shook my head. I had the jurors' attention now. So I plotted deeper.

"How can you have a drug case based on lies and innuendos, rats testifying–oops, excuse me," I said just as Scandels was about to rise from his seat to make another objection. The judge rubbed his baldhead in frustration. "The defendant is estimated, by the government, to be worth over two hundred million dollars and trafficked in the billions of dollars in cocaine, but yet has no real evidence. I snapped my finger. "Which raises doubt." I slammed my hand down on the jury box hard. "The law says you have to convict him without a shadow of a doubt. If there is an iota of a doubt in your mind, you have to set him free. All I ask is that you humbly study the evidence, don't be fooled by the smoke screen of lies and deceptions. Make your conclusion based on facts, not fiction." With a strong feminine baritone I exhorted, "If the evidence doesn't fit, you must acquit." I repeated over and over as I walked up and down in front of the jury box, making sure to pound it into each one of their heads. I had to get into their psyche, use words like a chisel to cut away at the stereotypical views that all white folks harbor about Blacks and they're not even conscious of it. I learned a lot from the Rodney King trial. You can brainwash a jury into believing what you want them to believe, but first you had to get inside their heads. Psychological warfare.

An hour and twenty minutes later I was finished. The courtroom was buzzing. I thanked the jury and repeated one more time. "If the evidence doesn't fit ..." I watched as the jury and the courtroom returned a chant to my surprise.

"YOU MUST ACQUIT!" I looked over at the prosecutor's table. Scandels was pissed.

David Scandels rose from his chair. I could see he was trying to mask the shock of my opening argument. He adjusted his tie, a tuff of salt and pepper hair hung over his left eye, and gray hair ringed his temples. At 55 years old, he still possessed the American golden boy image. He represented the epitome of patriotism. He served in Nam, was awarded a Purple Heart for being wounded in duty, and came home a hero. With his opening statement he went straight for the heart with a dagger.

"What is our country coming to when common criminals, thugs come in here and try to derail justice? The defendant here today is on trial for being one of the biggest drug lords the state of Florida has ever known. He has ties with organized crime. His deadly crew of henchmen, known as the Miami Boys, are known to be responsible for more than over two dozen assaults and murders just within the last two years alone." Scandels turned to the jury and spread his arms as if he were making a plea, "This is simply about law justice, equity and fairness. I intend to prove to you within the next few months of this trial that the defendant, Life Thug-Stin ..." Scandels intentionally lisped Life's name, "is a menace to our society and I intend to put him away for the rest of his natural life." In the corner of my eye I saw Life's body flinch as the formidable Scandels' presence seemed to fill the entire courtroom. Disturbing quiet set in. It was then that I realized he was good, real good and he avoided the main issues, like the government not having any real evidence. At the end of his opening argument, Scandels turned to face the courtroom; this was done solely for the benefit of the press.

"There's a war going on in America, and it's a war on drugs and the people that sell them to our children and family members. The defendant Life Thugstin is one of the reasons I'm fighting this war, and I intend to win."

Forty five minutes later Scandels was finished. I tried to check of the pulse of the jurors', a few were nodding their head in agreement. That wasn't a good sign. Taya Baker, my assistant, sat to my left with Adrienne Greene next to her. Life Thugstin sat perched in the middle of sisterhood.

"The prosecution calls its first witness, Steven Davis." Stevey D was a diminutive man, barely five feet six, slight in build with almond skin. He wore a large gauze bandage on his head that strangely resembled an oversized turban.

"Could you please state your name for the record?" Scandels asked and leaned against the witness box resting his arm on top like he was about to have a conversation with an old friend. I had been observing Stevey D since the bailiff had sworn him in. He had a jerky nervous motion about him. I could see Scandels trying to make him comfortable on the stand. It wasn't working. His beady eyes darted all around the courtroom like he wanted to bolt for the door. The bailiffs hovered near by, just in case.

"My name is Steven Davis," he said priming his big lips with a moistened tongue craning his neck forward trying to speak into the microphone.

"Would you mind telling me how you suffered the injury to your head?" Scandels asked.

"I was hit upside da head wit a ten-pound weight while I was doing bench presses on the rec yard." A slight gasp rushed through the courtroom and Scandels played out the moment for what it was worth, with a grimace, he shook his head.

"So you were attacked as you worked out. Is that safe to say?"
"Yes."

"Objection." My assistant Taya Baker was on her feet, a deep chocolate woman with a complexion so smooth it made you want to touch her. Her eyes were large and penetrating. With her short locks of black hair and slender figure of an athlete it was hard to believe the woman was 52 years old and an experienced warrior in the courtroom.

"There is no relevance in this line of questioning. I don't see where the prosecution is headed."

"Your Honor, the prosecution intends to show the relationship between this assault and the hideous acts committed by the defendant, to establish a criminal pattern of behavior."

"Overruled. Counsel I suggest you make your point and move along," the judge said to Scandels.

"Mr. Davis do you see the man in this courtroom that assaulted you?" Scandels asked. Stevey D's arm bolted straight forward pointing a finger at Life Thugstin. A slight rustle of noise came from the courtroom. I looked at a few jurors' faces and they looked visibly uncomfortable.

"Bitch ass nigga," Life said loud enough for the entire court-room to hear. I wanted to climb under the table. The judge banged the gavel and glared in our direction.

I reached under the table and squeezed Life's hand.

"Shhh," I whispered under my breath and looked up to see the satisfied grin on Scandels' face. His demeanor shifted like some wild animal that was onto the scent of blood, I saw it in his blue eyes.

"Could you tell us about your relationship with the defendant, Life Thugstin? Have you ever bought drugs from this man?"

"Yes," Stevey D said.

"How many times?"

"Two, three hundred times," Stevey D responded. Looking around the courtroom, his fidgeting appeared to be getting worse as he folded and unfolded his hands.

"What sort of drugs were they?"

"Cocaine."

Scandels rubbed his hands together and began to stroll away from the witness box. Stevey D's eyes followed him like a lost child.

"How much drugs do you think Life Thugstin distributed throughout the community?"

"Objection!" Taya Baker was on her feet. "Your Honor, that calls for speculation."

"Sustained. The witness is required to testify only to what he knows to be a fact." Scandels apologized to the court and continued with the witness.

"Approximately how much drugs did you buy from the defendant?"

"Two or three hundred keys."

"Bitch ass nigga tellin' a damn lie," Life mumbled next to me.

Scandels walked back up to the witness stand being sure to handle the nervous Stevey D with kid gloves.

"Other than him assaulting you with the weight, have you ever known him to be violent?"

"Yes," Stevey D answered a little too quick for my liking. Now I was sure that they rehearsed this whole thing, and now Scandels was coaching him along.

"Could you please explain to the court?" Stevey D batted his eyes, craned his neck forward and looked out into the audience.

"Life had a son by the name of Shawn L. He was about 3 years old, somebody tried to rob him at the mall or sumpin'. Afterward, him and his men went on a killin' spree killin' three cops and shoving a stick of dynamite up one of the cops' anus."

"Objection! Objection! Objection!" All three of us rose in unison. This was the precipice of disaster. The witness' inflammatory statement was past damaging; it could be the coup de grace to our case. Adrienne Greene spoke vehemently. Her large breasts heaved up with each pronounced word. She, like the rest of us, was angry and made no secret of trying to hide it.

"Your Honor! This is outrageous! My client is not on trial for murder. The prosecution is intentionally trying to soil the minds of the jury by tainting my client as a murderer, thus severely prejudicing him with the inference that he is responsible for other crimes. Your Honor at this juncture the defense has no other recourse but to ask the court for a mistrial," Adrienne said brusquely as a stir erupted throughout the courtroom. The judge removed his glasses. With a weary hand he mopped at his bald dome and glared at the prosecutors.

"The jury is instructed to disregard the prosecutor's last statement. The defendant is not on trial for murder; therefore, any implications of such can't be used in this courtroom against him. I will be more than happy to consider a motion for mistrial," the judge said. I'm sure at that moment I was not the only one at the defense table that felt a ray of hope, and then the judge added, "However, I will make my ruling depending on the outcome of this trial." My heart plummeted when I heard that. I wanted it to end then. The damage was done irrevocably, like slapping each juror in the face giving them a black eye, and then telling them to forget about it. They would never forget about the black eye that

Scandels had just slandered Life with. I wanted to kick myself. Shrewd like a fox and conniving like the devil, Scandels had just outwitted me. I would have to lie and wait to entrap him, but how?

*****

# Chapter Twenty

## "The Lion's Den"

### — Hope —

Judge Stafford called for a recess for the remainder of the day. Life looked over at me with a somber expression that stopped my heart as the bailiffs led him away. I saw it in his eyes like my reflection in the mirror, fear. Stevey D's statement was damaging. We both knew it.

It was Friday and Adrienne Greene, the more experienced of our defense team, was scheduled to cross-examine the witness Stevey D on Monday morning. I secretly wanted a piece of him, to make him squirm on the stand. But the last few weeks I had not been feeling well, I was just not myself. The weight loss, fatigue and the preparation for the trial in such a short time had really taken a toll on me.

*****

The prosecuting attorney held a news conference on the courtroom stairs and did a long drawn out statement about the war on drugs. He enjoyed the press and played every minute for what it was worth. He made a promise to send a message to all criminals. He also made a promise to send Life to prison for the rest of his life.

My associates and I squeezed through the crowds of reporters and spectators and into our waiting limousine. "No comment," was my response to the bombshell Scandels had just hit us with.

Life Thugstin, the cop killer? That would be the headlines in the morning newspaper.

*****

As soon as I was inside my house, like usual, I checked my messages on my answering machine. My brother in prison called. Shit! I forgot to send him his money order. It was right there on the kitchen table. I checked the other messages, one was from my Dad. Normally I would have called him to make sure he was taking his high blood pressure medicine but all of my energy has been depleted. Another message was from Stan, my ex-husband's lover. I thought that was strange as I reflected back, he had been trying to get in contact with me for the last few weeks and I never returned the calls. I decided to call my Dad and then maybe Stan, my way of keeping tabs on Marcus. Funny as it may have seemed, I still loved the man.

"Hi baby girl!" My dad sounded excited to hear from me. "We've been watchin' the case on the news and in the papers down here. They ran an article in the Miami Times about you being the little girl from the Pork and Beans projects. Baby I'm so proud of you." I heard my Daddy's voice quiver. "I don't like that white man the media say you used to work fo', what his name?"

"David Scandels," I responded.

My Dad went on to tell me that my oldest brother had been arrested again for drugs. He had a bad drug addiction. I just prayed that the media would not get wind of that. God knows I love my family, but now I found my family background extremely embarrassing.

"Baby girl, I'm so happy you done made somet'in' outta yo life. I love you sweetheart."

"I love you too, Daddy," I said and hung up the phone and wept a lone tear as I tried to force the thought of the long trial out of my mind. Today, like the rest of the days, I was so tired.

I decided to go ahead and call Stan. I knew that one day I was going to have to put my differences to the side. I took a deep breath and made the call. He answered on the third ring.

"Hello?"

"Hello, this is Hope Evans, you left your number on my answering machine." Silence.

"Hmmm, ah, yes." Stan stuttered nervously. "Hope, we need to talk."

"That's why I called," I said sarcastically. "Whatever it is you have to talk about we can discuss it over the phone."

"This is important, I don't feel it would be appropriate to talk over the phone."

"Hell, was it appropriate to come into my home and use my bed? Whatever you got to say Stan, please say it over the phone." I scuffed rudely, not realizing I was so bitter.

"Marcus is in the hospital. He is dying."

"What!?" I screeched. "What's wrong with him?" I heard my voice say in a high pitch that seemed not to belong to me.

"Marcus has AIDS," Stan said ominously.

I sat on the floor and looked at the tiny blemishes that started to form on my arms like tiny rashes. Was it possible that I too, was dying from this virulent disease? Oh God! I burst into tears and began to cry on the phone. "See what you have done! What about you? Do you have it?"

"Yes, the doctors think he contracted it from me. I am what is known as a carrier. It could be years before I start to show any signs."

"God help me! If I had a gun I would come over there and blow your fuckin' brains out."

"Hope, I'm so —"

*Click.*

I hung the phone up in his face. Quickly, I undressed, examining myself in the mirror, my hands trembled, it was then that I realized, if I did have the disease, I did not want to know. But that weekend, I made an appointment to see my doctor, he did some blood tests and said that he would let me know in the coming weeks. I never told him about my ex-husband and the deadly disease.

The entire weekend I was a wreck, but I found a way to relieve stress by working on the case. My staff and I worked feverishly going over all the documents and many depositions taken from the witnesses that planned to testify against Life. The entire time, in the back of my mind, I knew that there was a chance that I wouldn't test positive for AIDS. I was going on 26 years old, and a single parent with my whole life ahead of me. I would just have to wait for the test results to come back from the doctor's office.

*****

On Monday, the day the trial was to continue, Adrienne was scheduled to cross-examine the witness. She showed up at my office sick and cramping so bad that she could hardly stand up straight. So at the last moment it was decided that I would be the one to cross-examine the witness, Stevey D. Secretly I loved the opportunity to have the rat on stand. I knew he was a liar. Now all I need to do was catch him in a lie and prove it. I had a plan.

*****

As usual, the courtroom was packed to capacity and the media was there jocking for the scoop of the day. Also were the members of the church and I saw my girl Nandi. For the sake of all the media attention we thought it was best to not be seen hanging out together, so while she was in town for the trial she stayed at a hotel. When she saw me she saluted me with a clinched fist. Black power! Next to her were some of my Delta sisters looking dignified and proud.

By the time we arrived at the defense table, Life was already there. As usual he was dressed immaculately with his Brooks Brothers suit on. It made me want to drool all over him. And for the first time since the bombshell had been dropped on me, I smiled at the man with my child's eyes, as I thought about all the sexual fantasies I'd harbored for this brotha. Just being near him made my panties wet. I decided if we beat this trial, I was going to confess everything, he being the father to my son and the fact that I loved him with my very last breath. Now two things hung over my head like a dagger about to drop, one, to lose the trial and two, the very real imminent threat of my death.

I knew I had to take the witness apart on the stand. He was what we lawyers call a hostile witness. Life must have sensed my concerns. He leaned over and whispered in my ear, "We gon' be OK as long as we keep fighting back." I could smell cocoa butter and something else sweet emitting from his body as his lips brushed against my earlobe. Charge! At that moment in time, I could have rushed to the witness stand and fought like hell for Life Thugstin's freedom. And now like lioness, my staff of all Black females sat huddled around him, perfumes mingling, campaigning a strategy to champion a cause to defeat our all white adversaries. In essence, we were the female version of Hannibal. I looked over to my right, I could see that Adrienne was in pain but still determined to support us with the resilience in the face of adversity.

*****

After the prolonged ritual of introducing the judge and swearing in the witness, I was finally able to cross examine the witness. My mind was on attack mode. That day Stevey D was his same nervous self. Eyes darting all over the courtroom. Today he wore a black shirt and gray slacks. The gauze bandage around his head looked to be soiled with blood. I approached the witness stand gingerly and wore a broad smile, the kind we women use to flirt with, to give him a little dose of female charm. I needed to loosen him up, to make him vulnerable to entrap himself. I unbuttoned the first two buttons on my blouse, leaned closer out of the view of the jury and the audience. The only two people who could see what I was doing were the judge and the witness on the stand.

"Please state your name for the record," I said smiling, exposing as much cleavage as I could get away with without being seen.

"Steven Davis." He smiled back at me nervously while taking the liberty to peek down my blouse. I knew that he had been in the FCI holding facility for nineteen months snitching on all his buddies. I also knew the disposition of Black men that languish in prisons too long, if given the chance they would gladly make love to a hundred and ten year old woman in a wheelchair as if she were God's gift to man. I knotted my brow with sympathy, spoke with empathy. I leaned on the witness stand up close, making my breasts strain against the soft fabric of my blouse so that he could spy on my nipples.

"Mr. Davis you said that you were assaulted." I crinkled my forehead and leaned forward. More cleavage. I looked up and caught the judge's eyes all in my blouse too, like maybe he was into jungle fever at one time or another. With the question, Stevey D looked past me and directly at Scandels, like maybe he was asking for permission to answer the question. I knew for sure right then and there that the prosecuting office had been coaching him right along. I intentionally blocked his view by positioning my body so that he could not see the prosecutor's table.

"Could you please tell the court again what happened on the day that you were allegedly assaulted?"

I took a step back at the same time I buttoned up my blouse. It was time for me to mount my attack.

"I was on the recreation yard lifting weights and Life crept up behind me and hit me wit a weight."

I frowned as I turned and cast a look at Life as if to say, *how could you do such a thing to such a nice person?*

"So you were on the rec yard minding your own business and pow!" I gestured with my hand in a mock blow. "So after you were struck, what happened then?"

Stevey D shrugged his narrow shoulders and said, "The next thing I knew I woke up in the hospital a week later with 188 stitches in my head."

"You woke up in the hospital? Why didn't you fight back?" I said, stabbing at his male ego. This was my bait luring him into laxity, to cause a slip of the tongue.

"He crept up behind me. I never saw him comin'. My homies told me he did it."

"So, you never saw him hit you?" I asked, making a face.

Stevey D cut his eyes away from me and tried to look at the

defense table. I blocked his view. "But I know it was him."

I moved in for the kill. "Answer the question!" My voice echoed in the courtroom. "Did you, or did you not, see the defendant Life Thugstin hit you?!"

"Objection!" Scandels was on his feet. "Your Honor, Ms. Evans is badgering the witness."

"Your Honor, I simply want the witness to answer the question," I said curtly. The judge turned to the witness. "You are to answer the question, either yes or no. Objection overruled."

"No ... no, I didn't see 'em hit me," Stevey D said reluctantly.

I turned to the jury with a sour expression, waited a second to let the fact sink in. He didn't see who hit him. I turned back to the witness.

"How much did you make Mr. Davis, during your drug selling endeavor?"

Stevey D narrowed his eyes at me suspiciously and then answered, "A lot." Someone laughed in the back of the courtroom.

"How much is a lot?" I asked walking up closer to him.

"Eighty ... ninety thousand," Stevey D said with his hustler's bragging face on. The one thing about some hustlers I learned while living in the projects, they would never miss an opportunity to shine. "I once made a hundred grand."

"Wow!" I gibed and made a face like I was really impressed. I walked over to the other side of the witness stand to make sure that the jury could see me. This was important. I had to drive home my point to convince the jury that the witness could not be trusted. With a mock show of confession I furrowed my brow with disdain for the witness and went for the kill. With all my might I slammed the writing tablet I had in my hand down hard on the witness stand causing one of the elderly jurors to jump in her seat. Stevey D flinched nervously.

"Last Friday didn't you testify right here in this courtroom that you bought two to three hundred keys from the defendant? Each purchase was ten to fifteen keys at $20,000 a piece, but today you're testifying that the most money that you've ever made was one hundred thousand dollars. Mr. Davis, that would make it impossible to purchase fifteen keys. Mr. Davis, I think you're a liar and the truth is not in you."

"Amen; the truth shall set you free," a few members of the church were saying while others applauded. I looked over at the jury and saw faces of comprehension.

"Objection!" Scandels shouted from the other side of the courtroom as he spread his arms, palms open making a face as if to say, *your Honor, you see what she is doing to the witness.*

"Sustained. Ms. Evans, you will refrain from such an aggressive style of cross examining the witness." Judge Stafford glared at me and then at the courtroom audience. I saw a sheen of perspiration starting to form on Stevey D's forehead and his jittery movement was starting to get animated like a man sitting on a hot seat. Pressure.

"Mr. Davis, could you tell the courtroom what it is you intend to get in return for your testimony here today."

"Objection! Your Honor, the government has not promised the witness anything in return for his testimony."

"Ms. Evans, I hope that you are going somewhere with this line of questioning," the judge said impatiently.

"Your Honor, we intend to show that the witness has a motive to make him risk perjury on the stand in the form of a significant reduction of sentence."

"Overruled. The witness shall answer the question."

"No, I was not promised anything," Stevey D said, moving around in his chair like he was going to pee in his pants. I could tell that he and Scandels had gone over this. So I tried another approach, more tactful. Casually I strode over to the defense table and retrieved a piece of paper from a folder. Life was watching me with his hand posed under his chin. From the expression on his face I could tell, just like the rest of the courtroom, he wondered what the hell I was doing. After all, he had good reason. The man had placed a million dollars in my bank account. I walked back over to the witness stand, looked at the paper in my hand, frowned at Stevey D and then looked at the jury.

"I have here in my hand an arrest report. On April 10th it says here you were arrested for conspiracy to traffic in cocaine with the intent to sell to undercover agents while in possession of a firearm. Mr. Davis, you're a convicted felon, aren't you?" He nodded his head nervously. "You'll have to speak up."

"Yes," he answered. He was now sweating profusely.

I looked at the paper and looked at him again. "You're in a lot of trouble. Life plus three hundred months in prison." Stevey D continued to squirm in his chair folding and unfolding his arms. I leaned against the witness stand, up close and in his face.

"Mr. Davis, are you aware that this court can charge you with perjury if you get caught in a lie?"

Stevey D nodded his head up and down and croaked a hoarse, "Yes ma'am."

"It looks to me like you can't afford to do any more time, can you?"

"No," he said somberly, making a face that looked to me like a silent plea.

I raised my voice. "Mr. Davis, I'm going to ask you again and you be very careful how you answer this question so that you don't perjure yourself and get more time in prison. Do you, or do you not, expect to get anything in return for your testimony?" I asked threateningly, the lull and the suspense built with it. All in the courtroom anxiously waited to hear the answer. I could hear the old folks humming penitent mantras in the Lord's name, a baby cried in the distance. I watched as Stevey D's eyes skirted across the courtroom in search of Scandels. I saw fear, panic and uncertainty in the dark pools of his eyes. All informants are like human rats when trapped in a corner—they don't care who they bite.

"M ... M ... Mr. Scandels told me that if I testified against L, he would reduce my sentence to five years," Stevey D stammered.

A cacophony of voices rose from the crowded courtroom. The judge banged his gavel. I looked over at Scandels. He ran his hands through his hair in frustration, his once aplomb demeanor now exposed to agitation as he looked up at the ceiling with an expression that read, *what else can go wrong?*

I turned and mouthed to the courtroom, "If the evidence doesn't fit …"

Vociferous voices returned in singsong chorus, "You must acquit!"

I turned to the judge, "No further questions Your Honor." As I strolled back to the defense table I gave my Scandels a triumph glare. Taya and Adrienne stood to great me. I noticed that the older women were careful to mask their excitement, but I could see in their eyes, for a young inexperienced attorney, I did good. They were proud of me.

I sat down next to Life. He said, "Hope that was very powerful, praise Jesus. One down and 77 to go." I had to do a second take with Life, lately he had been talking this religious Jesus and God stuff.

"Your Honor, I would like to request a sidebar," Scandels blurted out. The judge removed his glasses and massaged the brim of his bulbous nose and looked at Scandels annoyed.

"What is the purpose of this sidebar?" the judge asked, disgruntled as he looked at his watch.

"Your Honor, it's a rather sensitive matter."

The judge shook his head dismayed. The judge called for a sidebar. We all approached the bench, both parties, defense and prosecution, jocking for a position. I noticed a few reporters careening forward to hear a bit of juicy gossip. In hushed tones Scandels whispered.

"Your Honor the press, along with the unusual crowd of spectators in the courtroom, is interfering with my case. It's like I'm in one of them Black folks' churches. I can hear them singing and moaning in the background."

Judge Statford silenced Scandels with a wave of his hand. Fuming mad, he spoke to Scandels through clinched teeth, the way a father chastises a son.

"You of all people have let this woman come into my courtroom and make you look like a fool." In the judge's rage, he let it be known his prejudice for me and my staff. "You need to find a way to win this case, your very future may be relying on it counselor, and furthermore; let me worry about my courtroom and the spectators. This young woman has just handed you your ass on a silver platter." With that said, the judge reared back in his chair. End of discussion.

One of the government's star witnesses, Tomica Edwards, was scheduled next to testify.

*****

The following morning as the trial was scheduled to begin, the courtroom was packed to capacity as usual. However, that day, I saw a woman that I have always admired, Sister Souljah. She and Nandi were sitting together talking. As soon as they saw me they waved. My heart soared. Sister Souljah is my girl! I can't remember a moment in my life I was more proud of being a Black woman handling my business. I guess that was around the time Life really started acting strange with this religious thing. He told me that he was giving his life to the Lord, but would then ask me to smuggle him in some Hennessy and something to smoke. I did it on a few occasions. I knew the man was a thug and he may have been running game on me, but I loved him. Besides, I think he was starting to take religion seriously. I knew just as I had planned, Life's father's church was having a subliminal effect on everybody like some magical spell. Black spirituality is one of the most powerful forces on this planet.

As Tomica Edwards entered the courtroom, all eyes turned to her tall and regal beauty. Her amber complexion with long black hair, green cat eyes ensconced in high cheekbones, gave her the kind of exotic loveliness that makes one question the ancestry of her linage. She moved with the graceful confidence of an experienced runway model. However, Tomica Edwards was living proof that looks could be deceiving. I spent many nights going over her criminal records. What I found interesting was she was a lesbian and that she hated men with a passion. Her specialty was boost-

**291**

ing everything from fur coats to eighteen-wheelers.

Once Tomica took the stand and was sworn in, the hateful looks that she exchanged with Life made me want to ask what had he done to this woman to make her harbor so much animosity for him. The crux of this case was just how much did she know about Life? Because indeed, if she did know enough, she could by herself put him away for the rest of his life. For the defense she would be difficult, because normally with a lengthy police record like hers you could use it against her. But in this case it would only serve to give credence to her testimony. As I looked on, it was evident from the scornful look on her face, she had a debt to settle against Life and fully intended to.

Scandels approached the witness stand cautiously, careful not to lose this witness like he did the last one. My assistant Adrienne was to cross-examine her. Earlier that week she confided to me that Tomica's testimony was going to be the most damaging. The woman simply knew too much about the inner workings of Life Thugstin's enterprise.

After a few introductory prologues, Scandels got right to the point. "Do you see the defendant, Life Thugstin, in the courtroom?"

Before he could get the words out of his mouth, Tomica pointed. "That's the bastard right there!" I saw Life's body stiffen with her words. Scandels turned and smirked at me. I noticed the judge smiled, too.

Scandels had Tomica on the stand for three straight days. She told all. It appeared as if she knew all. She told of how she first met L as he was notorious by his peers, his rise in the dope trade from selling dime rocks to keys. She testified that at one time Life Thugstin had over two hundred people working for him in six different states. At the time he was grossing anywhere from one to two million dollars a day. She told of his lavish lifestyle. He could fly to Colombia if he wanted to in his private jet. He had villas in Brazil, Costa Rica, he owned Lamborghinis and Ferraris. She claimed that the real mastermind was not Life Thugstin, but Trina

Vasquez. Tomica's testimony was devastating. Often I would look over and see Life with his head down praying.

Afterward, on our turn to cross-examine the witness, Adrienne Greene did everything in her power to crack the imperturbable calm of Tomica. One thing the press and the jury could easily see, this was past a legal battle, this was personal, and for four grueling days Adrienne went at Tomica often to both the objection of Scandels and the scrutiny of the judge's reprove. With the judge making his intentions known, he was siding with the prosecution. The beautiful Tomica, her stoic demeanor, a lesbian that felt superior to all other women, was too much for Adrienne, and to this day I am sure that was what went through the jurors' minds. Life was a small time hustler, turned multi-millionaire, that deserved to spend the rest of his life in prison, at least that was the message Tomica was sending to the jury. Once again I couldn't help but wonder, *what could he have possibly done to this woman?*

I glanced over at Life. It was the last day of Tomica's testimony. He had his head bowed in prayer. For the first time, in what felt like ages, I prayed, too, for both of us.

*****

I arrived home late that evening after picking my son up from the babysitter across the street. I found an urgent message on my answering machine. It was from my doctor concerning the blood test. He said that he needed to see me immediately.

# Chapter Twenty One

## "We Die Hard"

### *— Life —*

I'm locked up and they won't let me out! I remember sitting in a federal holding cell, wearing a thousand dollar Armani suit, seven hundred dollar Stacy Adam shoes and the weight of the trial weighing heavily on my head. I remember always hearing rappers and wanna be gangstas saying they'd rather be judged by twelve than carried by six. That's bullshit. You'll never find a federal convict agree to that, in fact, it's the opposite meaning; they'd rather have trial on the streets. That's keeping it gangsta. Besides, in the federal system if you have a life sentence your paperwork release date simply states, "DECEASED."

About the only bright spot in my trial was the fact that Trina and Black Pearl beat their trial and got all the property and cars back at the Chateau G.P. The feds gave them everything but the money they found hidden underneath the floors. My right hand man, Major, was in the same unit with me. His attorneys were waiting for the outcome of my trial, so they continued to find ways to delay his. I told Major to go on ahead and testify against me, hell, 78 other niggas had done it for a time cut. Major flatly denied my offer, said that this was just the other part of the game and it felt too much like betrayal. Besides, once you start working for the government, it's a full time job, you become a government rat.

There was no doubt in my mind that after Tomica's tell-all testimony, I was going to prison for the rest of my life. I had to give Hope her props, she and the rest of my all female attorneys fought for me. Hope even had a few specialists come testify on my behalf. Black Pearl started writing me as soon as she got out. I never heard from Trina's punk ass. She got ghost on a nigga.

One of the specialists that testified on my behalf was a beautiful redbone sista. She seemed to radiate on the witness stand. Her long locks of hair were flowing down her back. Her name was Nandi Shakur. She and Hope were good together, natural. If I didn't know any better, I'd swear they were friends. When Dr. Shakur spoke she commanded an aura of authority. I noticed a few of the jury nodded their heads in agreement on the theory concerning socioeconomical crimes and about the environment that was intentionally created by the rich in the exploitation of the poor. She explained how drugs had been placed in the Black community and the fact that whites use more drugs but Blacks are the ones targeted for arrest. Most important, federal judges, prosecutors and some politicians have investments in stocks on prisons. Some of the jurors started taking notes. I didn't know if that was good or bad. I knew the next day *USA Today* ran an in-depth article with Nandi's picture in it.

*"The Life Thugstin Defense takes a gamble by using a one-of-a-kind defense never heard of before—the socioeconomical crime theory and how the environment can play a factor in crime."*

The paper went on to give a detailed synopsis of the trial and just how prudent the theory is. The young Hope Evans was however hailed as an young up and coming legal prodigy. The newspaper compared Hope to Johnny Cochran in his early years.

*****

With each day I found it getting harder and harder for me to concentrate on the trial. Hope looked like she was starting to deteriorate right before my eyes, and the media took notice, too. They claimed in one of the tabloid magazines that she was about to have a nervous breakdown due to the lengthy trial.

*****

# Chapter Twenty Two

## "Change"

### – Life –

Like so many young Black men that find themselves trapped in America's penal system, I was determined to find a way out, so I reverted to my old ways. They say one of the most dangerous things you can do is to lock a man up and for him to have nothing to do all day but think. And that's what I did in my cell each day after trial. I found God in my cell and started praising Jesus, too. I knew what I had to do.

\*\*\*\*\*

Holding cells are like New York train stations, only worse. You get in where you fit in. You got dudes sprawled out on the pissy floor, sitting on steel toilet stools and hard benches as well as sleeping under them. The clamor of loud voices is maddening like listening to every scream at the same time. Cigarette smoke bellowed to the top of the ceiling, thick enough to obscure the crude graffiti written on the walls as well as satires about the judge's mother.

Finally, the door leading to the holding cells opened, with it came a punctuated pause as deep as a bottomless pit, a protracted silence, the practiced unison of prisoners listening, waiting to hear their name called, as if God Himself were standing at the door choosing who will make it into the gates of heaven. In prison, lawyers are like Gods that work for the devil, only worse, considering a prisoner is dependent on them as the intermediate. That's where the problem starts. Like being in a foreign country without speaking the language. Many a man has signed his name on the dotted lines, after paying a king's ransom for what he thought would secure his freedom, only to find he has paid a price to do a lifetime. Lawyers are the biggest crooks God ever created.

We all listened for our names to be called by our attorneys. In the distance the metallic sound of chains, shackles dragging across the cold concrete floor, signal the arrival of another prisoner, another destitute agony to mount in the chaos of madness. Everyone in the cell listens. I strained my ears. Two cells down, I thought I heard my name in hushed tones. I bolted to the cell door accidentally stepping on two people.

"Shh," I hissed gesturing with my finger over my lips. Of course they all complied. Over half the federal system is full of informants, snitches eager for a free ticket out of prison.

I had the most famous case that the State of Florida had ever known. So of course cats in the cell were quiet, acting like it's respecting me, but I know that they were really ear-hustling for information on my case to get a time cut. In the feds they have an old saying, "You got two kinds of people, those that told, and those that wished they had told." Those that told will never stop telling even for the sake of their moral integrity. Those that don't staunchly refuse to compromise their code of ethics, for it is intrinsically embedded in their virility. Real men do not tell on their best friends, family members, wives and kids. They die for what they believe in.

I peered between the cell bars down the hall. I saw Scandels in a heated conversation, all agitated and animated, talking with his hands raised in the air trying to argue a point. Then I heard another voice that sent chills down my spine. It was a voice that I had not heard in years. It belonged to my nigga Lil Cal. He came back from the penitentiary to do me, to take the stand and testify against me. His testimony would be the coup de grace sending me to prison for the rest of my life. I remembered Hope showing me

Lil Cal's name on the discovery sheet, but I just never thought he would actually rat on me. Shit! I made the crucial mistake of telling him too much, doing too much. I bought his moms a big house, took care of his baby mama and put thousands of dollars in his inmate account. In the process, I left a paper trail that even a blind man could follow.

Scandels stormed by the cell door without even seeing me. I'm sure he didn't know I was in the very next cell close to his star witness. This would not be the first time the feds had blundered like this. They have been known to place the rat and the accused in the same cell with the rat ending up getting killed as planned. I stared at the naked light bulb hanging from the ceiling outside the cell, lost for words, my feelings and emotions stuck in the back of my throat. There was an ancient-looking fingerprinting station in front of the cell.

"Yo ... Cal ...?" I heard my voice carry down the hall as I felt my hands gripping the bars tightly. At the other end of the hall, shackles rattled, feet shuffled. "L? L? That you man?"

"Yeah, nigga it's me aiight. Wuz up?" I said acidly.

"Man pah-lees! You gotta help me. Pah-lees!" Cal shrieked. I stepped back from the bars full of rage. I turned around and looked at some of the faces in the cell, read the deceit in their eyes like the graffiti on the wall. By the time our conversation would be over there would be a mad stampede to the prosecutor's office. Everybody trying to get a time cut.

"L ... L ... You gotta help me!" Cal continued. His voice was panic stricken, like he was on the verge of delirium. Just the way the feds will make you when they break you, when you sell your soul for another man's life. I listened to Lil Cal, careful not to get caught up in another indictment. "Both my grandma and her husband are missing." I could hear Cal crying as he spoke, "Somebody ran up in my moms' crib, snatched up my mama and my oldest brother Rob. Then yesterday, somebody mailed my brother's head to the institution with a note, '*If you're lookin' for your brother, Ax Blazack, oh, and don't worry about your Grandma*

*and Pops. They were old anyway.'* L man, I never would do you!"
Cal pleaded. His voice had taken on a feminine whine, that of a
broken man. Of course he was also lying. All I could do was shake
my head. Damn Blazack put in major work, the real menace to
society. I hurried away from the bars, away from a conspiracy to
murder and the kidnapping of Cal's family. I talked solely for the
audience of snitches and microphones that I was sure were in the
cells.

"Yo! My nigga, I'm telling you what God love, the truth. I ain't
got nuttin' do wit dat. I'ma just pray to God and let Jesus, my
Lord and Savior help me through this."

"Nigga, who you think you talkin' to? I know you and Blazack
are behind this."

I walked to the corner of the cell, lit up a smuggled cigarette
rolled in toilet paper wrappings and tried not to listen to Lil Cal's
plaintive cries about murder and kidnapping. *Don't worry about
your Grandma and pops. They was old anyway.*

*****

As I entered the courtroom it dawned on me, that even after
almost two months I was still not at ease with the media and all
the attention. As usual, my stepmother called out my name along
with her declaration of love. Strangely, no matter how bad my day
was, she seemed to always get a smile out of me. In the back of my
mind I worried about the conversation I just had with Lil Cal back
in the holding cell. The feds are notorious for entrapment. I wondered if they were using him to set me up with a new indictment.
I pondered, maybe Scandels did know I was back there next to Lil
Cal in the holding cell all the time, and it was just an act. About
the only thing for certain was that Scandels saved his best for last.
Lil Cal was the last to testify against me of the 78 informants. So
what the hell was going on if Cal said he wasn't going to testify?

After I greeted each of my all-female legal team and was seated next to Hope, she crinkled her nose up at me playfully, said I
smelled like smoke. Her beauty, along with her body, was seriously starting to deteriorate. I could see her cheekbones, the shallow

**299**

husk of flesh that covered her face. Her eyes looked to be too far back in the sockets. She was tired and wary. Uncannily, I could still see the impeccable courage in her eyes. She would not accept defeat. Never. Despite being the youngest amongst the entire group of lawyers, there was no doubt in anyone's mind, she was the brainchild and our leader. Just about every petition, every motion, and every strategy, she had prepared it.

I looked over at the rest of my attorneys. Today they looked stone faced, staring straight ahead at the judge. The entire scene was bizarre, like I was living in a dream. My defense counsels, Adrienne and Taya, continued to stare straight at the judge, as if they were somehow beckoning him, willing him, in some kind of way. Maybe that was their plea, as only Black women knew how to plead, a desperate attempt to save a Black human life. They failed.

*****

The proceedings were underway and Lil Cal was seated at the witness stand. For some reason, Scandels looked very uncomfortable. The prosecutor fumbled with his suit coat buttons as he asked, "Mr. Johnson, do you see Life Thugstin in the courtroom?" Cal looked over at me with piercing eyes, brows knotted in contempt. I tried to match his stare, as I held my breath, and felt my heart beating in my chest in a way that makes it hard for a man to breathe. That very moment felt like a showdown. Time was infinity that lasted ... lingered on forever.

"Naw, I don't see him in the courtroom," Lil Cal answered and turned his chin back to the prosecutor with his head held high. Scandels flinched uncontrollably. It looked like his feet came two inches off the floor like a man that just had the biggest surprise of his life. It showed on his face.

"Are you sure you don't see the defendant, Life Thugstin, in the courtroom?" Scandels asked, raising his voice, making his question sound like a command.

"No!" Cal answered without even looking at me.

Scandels turned beet red. Through clinched teeth and angular

**300**

jawbone protruding in an irate temperament, Scandels looked like he wanted to yank Lil Cal off the witness stand and beat him to a pulp. Again, I was reminded of the old saying, *a rat don't care who he bites when trapped in a corner.* All Cal wanted was to free his mama and not receive another Ax Blazack letter. Scandels fumbled with some paper. "Are you aware of the statements you made, in the form of over a one hundred page deposition, where you alleged you and the defendant, Life Thugstin, sold drugs?"

"Objection!" Adrienne Greene was on her feet, her large breasts heaved forward pronouncing her point for added emphasis. "Your Honor, the witness has already stated he does not know the defendant. The prosecutor's only purpose is to badger the witness with hopes to illicit anything incriminating."

"Objection sustained," the judge said like he was not all too impressed with having to take orders from the defense.

Scandels tried another line of approach. He looked over and smiled at the jury, wiped at a tuft of unruly hair on his forehead nervously and walked up closer to the witness stand.

Genuinely he asked, "Do you remember talking to me for hours in my office?"

"I would like to plead the fifth," Cal said smugly with his thick lips bunched together as if to say, *I will not be answering any further questions.* There was a buzz in the courtroom. I have never been good at reading people's hearts, but growing up in the ghetto you had to know how to read people's minds. So I looked at all twelve of the white jurors' faces, faces that our society says are my peers. But I knew then what the verdict was going to be. Just like I knew what I was going to have to do to cheat life and win my own trial. I can't lie. The broad, Tomica, and a few of the other witnesses that testified against me hurt me bad! Now the trial was almost over, nearly two months of verbal gymnastics of what is termed law. I would've rather gone out in a hail of gunfire. At least that way it would've felt like I was fighting back. For any Black man being on trial and having to be forced to be judged by an all white jury is truly a humiliating experience. Then as I thought about the dope game, and all its street fame, I can bare witness, it's two sides of the game. The other side ain't nothing nice and it comes with a hell of a price. Right there in the courtroom, I opened my Bible. Secretly I enjoyed the way the media always took note of every little thing I did. If I dozed off or laughed, it would be in the next day's newspaper. Reading the Bible made no difference. They quickly took notice of that too, just like I wanted them to. I remember my stepmother always telling me when I was a small child and been bad, to pray to Jesus. So that's what I did, I read my Bible and prayed to Jesus.

*****

# Chapter Twenty Three

## "The Verdict"

### *– Life –*

At the end of all trials, the defense and the prosecutors are allowed to present their closing argument. This, in legal terms, is known as summations.

Hope went first. Wary and fatigued she spoke passionately, exposing all the key points where the prosecution had blundered. Dramatically she exhorted the jury to see the logic in her argument and the flaw in the prosecutor's case. As I looked on, she really touched my heart, because to me with all her big words and drawn out statements, she looked like a Black woman pleading for a Black man's life. I wondered, *how many times in history has that happened?* I felt bad and ashamed of myself. The dope game was not worth this. For two hours, Hope's voice carried like the wind. The church played their part with reverent hymns to Jesus with enough fervor to get God's attention. I'm sure to this day the imperial heavens must have peeked down in wonder at what was going on in that old courtroom.

Hope ended her summation with a standing ovation. All Black folks clapping their hands with the commotion, I looked around the courtroom as the judge pounded his gavel. Most of the white faces in the courtroom looked uncomfortable. I watched as Hope held on to the rail next to the jury box for support. She was coughing violently in spasms; she looked so weak, faint. Taya and

Adrienne had to help her back to the defense table, they damn near had to carry her. I turned my head as Hope sat down next to me coughing in fits. She was sweating feverishly and was having a problem breathing. For the first time it truly dawned on me, something was terribly wrong with Hope. I reached out to grab her hand, this Black woman, the warrior that was fighting for me. Her hand was moist, hot. Hope was on fire, a feminine inferno. The judge

looked over at her. "Would you like to take that out of my courtroom? If you're ill we can stop the trial for recess." Hope rose, weary on her feet, balancing herself by holding onto the table edge.

"Thank you your Honor, but I'm fine. I welcome the opportunity to engage the prosecution in this case with hopes that justice may prevail," Hope said magnanimously, and then smiled at the jury and began to cough again. She sat back down and closed her eyes as if to gather strength. I wanted to reach out and hold her close to me, to shield her, as I realized I never wanted to hurt a Black woman again as long as I lived, only now it was too late.

David Scandels was next with his closing argument. For three hours he ranted and raved in his theatrical epilogue. Occasionally he used the words "Black criminals" and "war on drugs" like they were some kind of code words to the jury. I read the faces of the jury while he talked. Most of the all white jury nodded in agreement. These people were supposed to be impartial, they were supposed to be a jury of my peers, but as I sat there on that hard wooden chair staring them white folks in their faces, I saw something else. I was forced to admit, Scandels was good. After he finished his summation the reporters made a mad dash to the door. One of the biggest trials of the century was over. That was around the time I really started to take notice of the exultant praise like a slow mournful hymn. The jury looked startled, so did the judge. Black folks worshiping God the only way they knew how. I looked over at Hope, she still had her eyes closed, lips moving, she was humming with them too in a silent benediction for God to do his work. I looked over my shoulder and saw a sea of Black faces, mostly old folks. All the way in the back, to my surprise, I saw Black Pearl seated next to Blazack. I had to do a second take.

They were both dressed conservatively. Blazack wore a suit and tie with a pair of rimless glasses that made him look anything but gangsta. Black Pearl shyly winked her eye and blew me a kiss. I also saw the woman known as Sister Souljah; she was sitting next to Dr. Nandi Shakur, the expert witness that testified for my defense.

It was over and vaguely I listened as the judge admonished the jury that they were not to talk to anyone about this case. They were to base their decision solely on the evidence. I watched as the judge talked, a few members of the jury would furtively glance at me. I pretended not to notice, but I felt their stares. I felt them in a way that prods a man's consciousness, my own fate was no longer in my hands; it was in the hands of twelve white people. I'd rather be flipping burgers at Burger King than have the seat I was sitting in.

I looked up at the clock on the wall, it was past lunchtime. I wasn't even hungry. One of the benefits of going to trial when in federal custody the U.S. Marshals let you eat restaurant food. In my case, he let my defense team bring me food. Let me tell you, Black women knew how to throw down when it came to good old-fashioned soul food.

*****

Hours later I was seated in a conference room with my lawyers. The tiny room was nothing more than a holding cell with a small barred window. A few rays of streaming sunshine piped in the room. All three of my lawyers sat huddled around me as an assortment of spices, feminine enticements, the sweet allure of perfumes mingled with my starved loins. It felt so good to be so close to what we hustlers take for granted, our women. In that room, that tiny cage, we discussed everything but my case. For me, their laughter was intoxicating, inebriating. I wished that the moment would last forever. We were no longer in a cage, this was the lion's den, and they were the lionesses and I was the lion, and all was secure from the hunt. These same women that just valiantly fought for me were now trying to comfort me, placate me with the nurturing instincts that women have. It's all so natural, all so beautiful, a Black woman's love. One of the U.S. Marshals rapped on the door and walked in. On the table was Bar-B-Q ribs, macaroni and cheese and peach cobbler. He licked his chops as he stared at the food. From the somber expression on his face I knew what he had come for. We were informed that the judge wanted us back in the courtroom. That could only mean one thing, the jury reached a verdict. About eight hours passed since they went into deliberations. Each one of my counsels hugged me. Hope was the last. She did not want to let me go, that really touched me, told me a lot. She continued to hold me even as the other women looked on. I was confused, didn't know how to react. Throughout the entire trial, Hope never dealt in emotion and feelings, just logic and sagacious strategies. I could feel her fragile body trembling in my arms. The other women walked out and the Marshal looked on. Hope pulled away from me and made a feeble attempt at gathering her emotions. I watched as she nervously pressed the wrinkles out of her dress with the palms of her hands. "I'm sorry." She looked up at me and whispered as she walked of out the room.

"Sorry about what?" I asked myself as she walked away.

\*\*\*\*\*

Moments later I was being escorted by four U.S. Marshals down the long direful hall of the Federal building. I couldn't help but wonder, *how many other Black men took this long desperate trek to a destiny unknown?* For me the walk was long, I can't say what anybody else has felt, but for me, them crackas had me scared to death. I was at the mercy of the court. Normally the Marshals would be congenial and talkative, but that day I was met with stoic faces and cold stares.

As we entered the courtroom everyone turned to look in my direction. I felt like a condemned man. The courtroom was eerily quiet except for the herds of reporters. Like flies, they never seemed to go away. Most of the seats were vacant. I sat next to Hope. Looking straight ahead she held my hand. In walked the foreman along with the jury. They all piled into their seats. None of them could look me in my eyes. The foreman handed the judge a piece of paper. The judge read the paper and looked in aghast. "Hmmm, errr, I have just been informed that the jury has reached a deadlock." His breathing was heavy, not concealing his disappointment. He, like myself, was shocked that the jury had not returned with a guilty verdict. He raised his hulked eyebrow over the rim of his glasses. "It says here that the jury would like to review the portion of the trial transcripts of the testimony of the expert witness Dr. Nandi Shakur and her terminology of socioeconomic crimes," the judge said with disdain and jerked his neck at the foreman. "This is preposterous! You and the jury are to go back in there and reach a verdict!" Adrienne shot to her feet.

"Your Honor, it is my understanding that the jury can take as much time as they want to reach their decision and if they want to review all records and evidence that may be of relevance such as the court transcripts, they are at liberty to do so."

The judge removed his glasses and glowered at Adrienne. "Counsel is that all you have to say?"

"Yes."

"If you, or any member of your staff makes an outburst like that again I will charge you with contempt of court. Is that understood?" Adrienne's eyes turned to optic slits as she defiantly looked at the judge.

"No it is not understood! My client is entitled to the full use of his constitutional rights as it relates to the jurisprudence of law, if the jury wants to hear —"

"I am warning you to sit down or I will charge you with contempt of court." I could see a vein protruding out of the side of Adrienne's neck, she was fuming with indignation. Hope gently took her arm, and with a silent command of her head, she nodded for her to sit down. The older woman complied. I wasn't sure what was going on; however, the judge did state reluctantly that the jury would be allowed to review the transcripts. He also stated that he wanted to see my counsel in his chambers after the proceeding. I wasn't sure if it was good or bad that the jury wanted to go over the transcripts of the professor's theory about socioeconomic crimes. This was all Hope's strategy. One thing was for certain, the judge sure as hell was not too pleased about it.

# Chapter Twenty Four

## "All Eyes On Me"

*— Life —*

It was Friday and we were all tired. I watched as the judge mopped his face with a weary hand and admonished to the jury, once again, they were not to read any newspaper reports about my case, watch the news, or talk with anyone outside of the jury about the case. The jury was sequestered in a hotel and ordered to hurry up and reach a verdict.

On the ride in the van back to the FDC building it was one of the most beautiful days I had ever seen, at least that's how it will always look through the eyes of a man that has lost his freedom. I remember sitting in the back of the van in chains and shackles feeling like a caged bird. The officious U.S. Marshal tried to talk me to death. The van rode through Frenchtown. I searched for Nina Brown. She was nowhere in sight. I saw a few rock stars. I thought about Black Pearl and Blazack showing up at my trial. I had to smile. Blazack was past keeping it gangsta. He was on some guerilla G-Unit shit.

*****

By the time I changed clothes and made it back into the unit I was so fatigued that my brain even hurt. I needed a smoke bad to get my lungs out of pawn. As soon as I walked into the unit, all eyes were on me. In the distance I could see that most of the prisoners were watching the news. I had the uncanny feeling they already learned from the television about the proceeding of my case. The first lesson a true convict learns in prison is, if you want to enhance your chances of waking up in the morning without a shank stuck in your back, keep your mouth shut. See nothing, but at the same time, see everything. Being anti-social is the key to survival. I learned that from my first bid in the joint.

I walked straight to my cell, opened up a pack of Newports had in my locker and went and sat in the smoking range out in front of my cell. Major walked over and sat down next to me. He too was into the church lately since we caught our case. I inhaled deeply on the nicotine. Irately, Major fanned the smoke away. I could see all the faces watching us. Curiosity did not just kill cats, I knew a few niggas that got killed, too. So I mean mugged a few niggas as if to say, *what the hell you looking at?* Ever since I cracked Stevey D's cranium with the swift demonstration on how to punish a rat, I was respected by all. I've never been one to adopt the fear factor of influence because I don't care what anyone says, both fear and love will produce illogical results when pushed to the brink of precipice.

As Major and I talked about our cases and his lawyers decided that they would wait for the outcome of my case before going to trial, so I thought. However when Major expressed to me that he was going to cop out to ten years my heart sank. I tried my best to keep a straight face as I blew smoke up at the ceiling. We both knew that if he wanted to testify against me they would let him go home. For him that was out of the question. We just mellowed in our own silence, the way people do when they're heavy into thought. Finally, I said "Whatever you want to do my nigga, I'm behind you one thousand percent. You or your family will never want for anything." With that, I gave him my word. Major was still lost in thought. I surveyed the scene. Directly to my right was a water cooler. I noticed this big dude spying on me. In fact, ever since he first got here I caught him looking at me like he knew me or something. It dawned on me he was the same dude a few weeks ago who made a testimony at church saying his Lord and Savior

Jesus Christ told him to come back from the penitentiary and testify against his homies. He said that he had his life sentence taken off and reduced to five years. Everybody in the church hooped and hollered praising the Lord, all Black folks and a white preacher. I had to walk out of there. I was sick to my stomach. I knew that the life of a Christian was going to be hard work for me, but damn! I asked Major about the dude and I could tell from the look on his face he did not want to tell me who he was. In fact, Major began to stir uncomfortably in his seat. All major said was the dude was once one of the biggest drug dealers in Tallahassee, then he quickly changed the subject. We continued to talk, just shooting the shit. Occasionally I would see the big dude glance our way. I made a mental note to step to the big dude as soon as the opportunity presented itself. Major was holding something back. I wondered why?

At lockdown, I got into my hard-ass bunk, and for the first time in almost a year, I slept peacefully.

Early the next morning I was awakened, someone was yelling my name. "Thugstin, you got a visitor!" I quickly took a shower and got dressed in my prison jumpsuit. Whoever designed them was playing a cruel joke on convicts. The CO checked underneath my nuts and all in the crack of my ass. To this day I still haven't figured out what they were checking for.

I bounced into the visiting room halfway expecting to see my stepmother, but I was instantly greeted by the jubilant frolic of small kids scurrying about. Scooby Doo was on the television, the acoustic volumes turned up loud enough to hide the humiliating whispers of crestfallen men, gangsters, thugs, desperately trying to hold onto a man's most prized possession, his family, the jewels, the cars, the money.

The delicious aroma of buttered popcorn and pizza delighted my sense of smell. I approached the desk and gave the CO my ID card just as a little brown girl ran into my leg at full speed ahead. She bounced off my thigh and fell on the floor. She was about 3 years old. I resisted the urge to reach down and pick her up. She was as cute as a baby doll. She got back up and continued to play with the rest of her new friends. The place was crowed. It was Saturday morning. The CO seated me all the way in the back. As I walked to my seat people pointed and whispered. My face had been plastered on the television and newspapers so long that I'm sure these people had me on celebrity status.

I sat in my chair and tried to look as inconspicuous as possible as I occasionally spied the front door waiting for whom it was to arrive. Finally, I looked up to see Black Pearl and Trina stroll through the door looking like sophisticated chicks the way broads start looking when they get used to spending another nigga's money. Trina had her hair piled high on top of her head in some kind of French bun with embellished designs. She wore painted on black Guess jeans that showed off the curvaceous symmetry of her God-bless-the-world Black woman's thighs. She also wore enough jewelry to make an Egyptian jealous. The diamond baguette earrings with an iced out Cuban link chain thick enough to pull a train. She wore rings on just about every finger and each one of them was laced with diamonds. Opposite to her was Black Pearl, unadorned, unpretentious. She wore a simple white sundress and sandals with her manicured feet showing. Unlike Trina, Black Pearl's hair was real thick and natural and it cascaded past the middle of her back. Her sable velvet complexion seemed to radiate in hue in contrast to the white dress that strained against the sensuous rondure of her curves. At 19 years old, Black Pearl was still blossoming into one of the most stunningly gorgeous Black women that I had ever seen. Trina looked somewhat generic standing next to her. From the look on both of their faces they did not look too happy to be visiting me. As for myself, I couldn't help but to smile a shit-eating grin. I thought back to the time I first met Trina and she had stolen my stash and came back and blessed a nigga with two bricks. I then wished I married her like she wanted.

Still with a goofy-ass smile on my face, my delight in seeing this gangsta bitch, I thought about all the millions she had stolen from me. Wondered how she was going to dazzle me this time with her return. Maybe she bought a nigga a yacht. That was the one thing I did not have. Giddy, I laughed out loud throwing my head back. A few people glanced over in my direction. I watched as Trina approached the CO's desk. He pointed in my direction. More goofy-ass smiling. She walked toward me. The sway of her wide hips, ass so fat that you could see it from the front, then my smile died in a carnage of burning betrayal. I watched as Trina made a left at the next row of chairs and walked right up to another man, she extended her arms. I could hear the bangles on her wrist chime as she hugged him. He kissed her passionately while palming her ass. I was blinded with rage! All I could see was blood behind my eyes. Murder, murder, murder! I breathed in fitted sips of air like sipping oxygen through a straw, I was desperately fighting for control. I could feel my blood, a rivulet, rushing through my veins.

Timidly, Pearl approached. Subconsciously I stood rigid. She tried to speak but no words came out of her mouth. The brim of her starry eyes were filed with tears. I remember feeling uncomfortable, ashamed and embarrassed. Pearl hugged me in a way that felt like she latched on to my body. Her pungent sobs rocked us both. I looked up to see the CO giving me the evil eye. I could get my visitation terminated for "Unauthorized Touching." The entire visiting room was watching, including Trina. I had to wrestle Pearl off of my neck. We sat down. I tried to smile, I'm sure my face looked like cracked glass in the mirror in her eyes as she cried openly for everyone to see.

"Girl, what you cryin' fo?" I asked with a frown on my face.

"I ... miss ... you," she wailed, wiping her eyes with the back of her hands. The little brown girl that ran into my leg earlier meandered over, with her index finger in her mouth, the expression on her face said she was in awe at seeing the big girl cry.

It had been about a year since I last saw Black Pearl. I sat right there in that chair and reminisced about how a dreary past had run me down and pounced on me. I thought about Lil Man.

Shamefully, I cast a glance down at the floor and looked at the ankle bracelet on her leg.

"L, when I was 16 years old, pregnant, strung out on crack with no place to live, you took me in, fed me, gave me a place to stay." Pearl painfully swallowed a sob inhaled a sigh. The little girl tentatively took a step closer.

"Nigga you picked me up out of the dirt, made me go to school, made me the woman I am today, and the only reason I'm saying this is because I love you and it hurts." She cried some more. I looked over at the little girl, she was about to cry, too. I remember a feeling of despair like I have never felt before. And for the millionth time, I wished that I were someplace else. Black Pearl continued. "Trina knows just how much I love you. She knew it from the very first day that you brought me to that hotel." I just sat there in the chair like a deaf mute soaking in her poignant words. Pearl furtively glanced in Trina's direction and whispered. "Don't be mad at her. When she found out Big Mike was coming home –"

"Big Mike!" I repeated, taking a closer look at the dude she was talking to.

At first, all I could see was the side of his face, and then the face turned.

Goddamnit! Big Mike was none other than the big dude that made that testimony at church talking about his Lord and Savior told him to come back and snitch on his friends and family. I thought to myself, *no wonder he was watching me the whole time.* And to think, Major knew it all the time, but did not want to risk telling me so there would be no drama. Because of all the anger and frustration, all I could do was laugh a mirthless chuckle, for the sake of my ego and the fact, all eyes were on me. With a plastic smile on my face, all I could do was think about Trina going for the okey doke. I thought about the lives this rat ass nigga must have had to sacrifice at the expense of gaining his own freedom. OK, I'll admit, I was jealous as hell too. I knew one thing, I could not wait to step to dude. As Black Pearl talked I really didn't pay much attention to what she was saying. A woman with a bad case of acne came and picked up her child. I took the opportunity to make the bold leap of no return. This is the hardest part about going to prison, you have to let go, not just of life and liberty, but love and affection, or else it will come back to haunt you. No man can remain immured in concrete and steel for too long and not suffer the pain and anguish that a woman can bring. A man can't expect for his woman to be stronger than he is. In essence that is what he is asking her to do when he expects her to wait for him.

I took hold of Pearl's hands and forcefully looked into her big brown eyes pulling her close to me, her sweet perfume engulfed me. "Baby girl, I'm no good for you! I'm an illusion, these crackas have created a game with our lives. That's what the dope game is. I want you to sell the Chateau, all the cars and go far away from here, find you a square and marry him, not some thug. We're destined to destroy some shit, and sometimes even ourselves. I've fucked up, it's a wrap with me, my life is over."

"No, what about the trial? The jury didn't reach a verdict yet." People in the visiting room turned and looked in our direction, including the CO.

"I was with you when you were on the grind, when we didn't have shit, we dreamed together, lived together and if we have to, we'll die together. I don't want to live my life without you. I love you L." A lone tear distilled down her ebony cheek. Through teary eyes, she tried to smile, and at the same time, keep the panic out of her voice. Her fear of the inevitable, even to the end, I was going to keep it gangsta. I saw her bottom lip trembling. This shit was getting too emotional. With my mind made up, I knew what I had to do. I rose to my full height towering over her.

"Go to the Chateau, get my Bible and bring it to my lawyer, Hope." Pearl tried to grab me and I pulled away and saw the hurtful scowl on her face. "I never want to see you again! You have to promise me you'll never come back here again."

With that I walked off, my legs felt like rubber and my heart was hemorrhaging a trail of blood behind me. Black Pearl had always been like a little sister to me, there was no way I was going to fit her in with a ball and chain around her neck and expose her to my own self induced torture. She was too young and she didn't know what she would have been getting herself into, the misery and hurt that destroys a woman within, like some virulent disease. A woman that waits on a phantom lover that will never come. Always waiting, always hoping until she finds that time is her enemy, too.

My pride wouldn't just let me walk out of that visiting room no matter how hard I tried. Maybe it was my sweltering ego or even Trina for that matter; whatever the case, in passing I could not resist stepping to Big Mike. I had to. I walked right up to him like I knew him. I secretly enjoyed the terror stricken scowl on his mug when he looked up and saw me. I glanced over at Trina. A million episodic memories flashed on the screen of my mind. Trina, the Brooklyn chick, who stole me blind. I thought about the luggage full of money she walked away with as I lay in bed writhing in pain, body riddled with bullets. I thought about the woman that had introduced me to a game bigger than life, the real mastermind behind a million dollar plan. *Ain't no longevity in the dope game, stick and move. Get out within a year.*

I felt my top lip curl up as I looked down at the both of them. The only thing missing was the gun in my hand and I would have put both their asses on fire with them hot balls. On the inside I raged with violence. I wanted to take the crime to dude bad! "Wuz up Trina?" I said coldly. She rolled her eyes at me, turning her head she sucked her teeth disdainfully. I felt my hand coiling like how it feels when you're about to slap the shit out of somebody. "How is the good Christian brotha doin'?" I asked sarcastically. With a mouthful of pizza, Big Mike looked up at me in between bites. I could see the puzzled look in his eyes, the way people look at you when they're trying to assess your motives.

"I'm aiight," he grunted. I could tell he was trying to act hard by his demeanor. He had a mouthful of gold that looked like chipped old pennies. He wore his jumpsuit about two sizes too small, showing off his huge arms.

"So dis the muthafucka you was waiting on? Had me acceptin' his collect calls and shit. Huh bitch?!" I said stepping closer to Trina getting ready to swing. Her eyes bulged at me in frightened disbelief.

"L, man you wrong! Nigga if you got beef wit me you could have waited until we got into the unit," Big Mike said and stood up.

"Nigga it didn't start in the unit. You been grillin' me with the screw face ever since you got here," I said. I created a scene as I continued, "And you, bitch ass nigga, I ain't got no respect for a nigga that snitch on his friends and family." With that Trina's jaw dropped as she looked at him. I took a step closer hoping to get off a punch first. I really wanted to punish dude and get one of them gold trophies out of his mouth. The CO started to walk in our direction. I played it off and whispered as I smiled. "My nigga, I'm tryna holla at you when we get back into the unit." With that said I strolled off. My life trying to serve God was going to be difficult. The old folks had a saying, *what would Jesus do?*

*****

I waited in the unit for Big Mike, strapped with my joint in my pants, a box cutter stolen from the R&D department. By the time the 4 o'clock count came around, he still had not shown up. A sexy female CO with fake European hair and nails approached me. She wore her pants tight with ass for days. She had ghetto written all over her, and for some strange reason, it made her appealing. Twice I already offered her some money to let me hit it. Playfully she would always ask me was I serious, and laugh hysterically when I replied, "hell yea! Does a bear shit in the woods?" So when she sauntered up to me at count time with a dead serious expression on her face, that fat ass spread eagle on my bunk flashed in my mind. At count time everyone would be locked into their cells, that would be a perfect time. I touched myself as my eyes roamed over all the curves of her body, she was jet Black. I watched her sexy mouth as she talked—there was something about women with big lips that turned me on. She had about two or three shades of lipstick on her large soup coolers. Sexy.

"Thugstin, they want you in the LT's office," she said and shrugged her shoulders to answer the question that she knew was coming next.

"Shit!" I cursed and took off to my cell. I had to get rid of the knife. While I was there I stashed some cigarettes in my drawers.

Four deep, all rednecks, they escorted me to the LT's office. Once there, I was informed that I was being placed in SHU for my own protection.

"That's bullshit!" I protested to the redneck. They wouldn't even tell me why. I could tell they were hoping I tried to buck so they could kick the bone out of my ass and say I fell down some stairs. I had my suspicions that maybe Big Mike had something to do with it.

They placed me into a cell with a Mexican that smelled like he wanted to be left alone. He was locked up for murder. We got along fine, chain smoked all night, while I talked about my upcoming trial. The Mexican could speak no English.

The next day bright and early, the CO kicked on the door. Scared the shit out of me. He called my name and opened the little slot in the cell door handing me an envelope. He informed me that I had a visit from my lawyer, Hope Evans, but once she learned that I was in SHU again, she became upset stating that she could not bear coming back there again. I looked at the neat woman's handwriting and opened the letter:

*Dear Life,*

*I see you still have the propensity to find trouble or trouble always seems to find you, even when you're in prison. Don't tell me you didn't do anything wrong ... I've heard it all before. Whatever the case, I apologize, but I could not muster the courage to drag myself back there to see you with all the chaos and madness, it's too much like touring a slave ship, only worse!*

*Anyway, I just came to update you on your case. I can't lie to you, this is a rough one. Jurors are a strange group. About as unpredictable as the weather and need I mention Judge Statford is highly pissed to say the least. So I must warn you of all the obstacles, in the event of a hung jury. The government, with its unlimited resources of money and paid informants will go to great lengths to try you again at the cost of millions of dollars. Life, I'm sorry to tell you this, but I don't think I can make it through another grueling trial, but we'll just have to cross that bridge when we get to it. Right now, all we can do is be patient.*

*On a brighter note, boy, I want you to know that I fought for you with every fiber of my being, every sinew of my strength. One day after all of this is over, regardless of the outcome, you and I will sit down and I'll tell you about the birds and the bees, the lies and deception, the birth and the death. I'll tell why I fought for you till my very last breath. Time is now a thief in the night; he waits for both of us, but only if we lose.*

*Emphatically,*
*Hope Evans*

Frustrated, I must have read Hope's letter a hundred times. What was she trying to tell me? What was she saying? My hands began to tremble and then the rest of my body began to shake involuntarily. I balled up the letter in my hands and threw it into the toilet. What the fuck was she talking about? The birth ... the death ... time was a thief.

I walked over to the window and looked out through the steel bars. The sun felt hot on my skin. The Mexican lay in the top bunk snoring with his mouth open. An angry fly buzzed against the windowsill. I watched him. He was no different than me, he wanted to be free. About the only thing that a prisoner has that the system can't take away from him is his memories. Mental mementos, everlasting reminiscence like old currency. Cherished times will always retain their value to a prisoner by casting in on all the vivid pictures that will forever be captured on the screen of his mind. I thought about all my luxury cars, the clothes, the bitches, Black Pearl, Trina, Lil Man, Blazack, and always for some reason, the woman, Hope Evans' face flashed in my mind. Instantly, I regretted taking her through this. Anyone could see the trial was taking a toll on her body. She was thin as a rail and her once beautiful complexion now looked ashen. Once again I cursed, shit! I should have had trial on the streets. I turned to the sound of the food carts. It was brunch time. The Mexican awoke from a dead sleep giving me a startled expression, the kind that said I was standing too damn close. I made a face and tried to smile as if to say *my bad.* I walked over to the door as the CO put the food trays through the food slot. I gave my food to the Mexican. His long scrubby hair hung askew in his face, for the first time he smiled at me, I noticed his teeth were rotten. I lit up a cigarette and walked over to the window and looked out at the world. I decided right then and there, I'd rather be carried by six than judged by twelve. Come court day I had a surprise for the world!

*****

# Chapter Twenty Five

## "The Day of Judgment"

### – Life –

Tuesday, November 11, two days after receiving Hope's letter, the CO hurried me to get dressed. Again the U.S. Marshals rushed me to the back of a van. They were taking me to the courthouse. To this day I have no idea how the media got wind of my court appearances before my counsel and me.

As we pulled up to the federal building, I noticed the streets were littered with media vans, trucks and a few huge trailers. Cameras flashed, microphones were thrust into my face, my hair was nappy and I hadn't brushed my teeth or washed my face. An attractive white woman with a microphone shoved it in my face as I walked past.

"Your boss, Willie Falcon, was convicted yesterday. If you're convicted today, do you intend to file an appeal?"

Momentarily stunned of learning of Falcons' conviction, I replied, "Lady, I don't have a boss." I tripped over the curb, the Marshals stopped me from falling just as cameras flashed. I grimaced in pain as the shackles bit into my ankles with shark's teeth.

Five minutes later I was seated around my attorneys. Their smiles looked wry, but yet they welcomed me with warm embraces. I could tell they were having a hard time trying to conceal their fear. That day the courtroom was eerily quiet and nearly vacated. There were none of my father's parishioners there; in fact, the only Black faces I saw were my defense team. Then it dawned on me, that was the way they planned it. That's why the judge had them rush me here at this hour without all the fanfare, like some modern day legal lynching. I looked over at the prosecutor's table, Scandels winked and waved at me. I will never forget that face. I knew right then and there, the fix was in.

Hope leaned over and whispered into my ear, "The jury has reached a verdict." Her voice cracked so bad I wondered if it hurt for her to talk. She had a small rash on her bottom lip for some reason and the makeup only seemed to make it look worse. Her face was ashen and looked shrunken. She looked twice her tender age of 26. I tore my eyes away from her. It hurt so bad to look at her, instead I glanced over at the Bible on the table. Black Pearl did as I asked of her and delivered the Bible to Hope. I sat there uneasy as vaguely I could hear the murmur of voices around me. I could feel Hope's eyes boring holes through me. Finally, I reached for the Bible. She grabbed my wrist, I pulled away and turned a few pages. To my right I could see Scandels watching me intensely. I found Jesus on page four hundred in Psalms. The pistol was just as I had left it. It gleamed in the light. Now it was time for me to serve my God. To serve the Lord in the only way I knew how. I had found God in a prison cell. My God was the will to want to survive, the kind of God that governs self. As I touched the gun I felt that surge of power, that raw energy. If you're going to die, you might as well take somebody with you. It sounds crazy to the average person, but unless you've faced a life or death situation you would never understand.

Hope tugged at my shirt. I turned and looked at her. Her eyes were tearful. She gulped air and spoke barely audible, "Life ... I'm dying." She blinked her eyes, a tear fell. "I have no choice in this matter, but you do. The only reason I brought you this Bible is because, whom am I to deny you your freedom when I know the criminal justice system is corrupted, besides what can they do to me, but please, don't do it." I could hear the tremor in her voice. Just then the jury foreman entered the room. The judge smiled.

"Have you reached a verdict?"

"Yes," the foreman responded.

As I sat there in that wooden chair, it felt like a noose was being tightened around my neck, I was having trouble breathing. The jury entered taking their seats. I turned my head to see Black Pearl and Blazack enter the courtroom.

"Will the defendant please stand and approach the bench." As I slowly rose, I looked between Hope and the Bible hesitantly, my God, Jesus. *Please don't do it,* Hope's voice played in my mind with a continuous echo *Life ... I am dying.* I swallowed the lump in my throat disregarding the gun and looked at Hope. She's dying? I walked up to the podium feeling like a slave about to be sold.

The judge snarled, "Today justice will finally be served and you young man will either pay a debt to society with your life or be set free. I personally have my doubts about you and your character. I will say this, there is a place for you and your kind." The judge did not disguise his prejudice. "And for the record, the motion you filed for prosecutorial misconduct against Mr. Scandels is being denied, with it goes the motion for mistrial," the judge said with humor in his voice as he looked over at the prosecutor's table. Adrienne Greene was on her feet fuming.

"Your Honor! Under the rules of Federal Procedure you cannot address that issue at a federal sentencing."

"Sit down and shut up! If you don't like it bring it up on appeal with the Eleventh Circuit."

"Appeal?!" She scuffed indignantly with her eyebrows knotted in anger. Right then I think it dawned on all of us sitting at the defense table, if the judge was talking appeal, then it meant that I was going to be found guilty. I heard my stepmother's voice. I turned around to see all the people from the church. The old Black folks piled into the seats, with them came their humming. The judge made a face that usually comes with a curse word. Right then and there I decided, if they were going to take my life then I was going to take somebody with me, that was if I couldn't escape. I glanced at the back of the courtroom, Blazack shrugged his shoulders as if to say, *whatever.*

"Your Honor, may I please get my Bible?" I asked feeling my palms starting to sweat. The judge chuckled like the devil. I'm sure he thought he read fear into my actions, just like the thousands of impoverished Blacks that are paraded in front of him for selling small amounts of drugs and given large amounts time.

"Yes, you may go get your Bible," the judge said and then added, "I have a feeling you're going to need it."

I walked toward the defense table. Hope placed her hand over her mouth as if willing herself not to scream at me to stop. I grabbed the Bible and with it came the feeling of power, like an adrenaline rush, for me the kind that only Jesus can bring. As I walked back to the podium I glanced at Blazack. He nodded at me, *whatever.*

*****

The jury foreman began to read the verdict. I opened my Bible. The old folks were humming the gospel. My heart raced at an accelerated pace. Like I said, I'd rather be carried by six than judged by twelve. I'd rather be dead than spend the rest of my natural life in prison. For me, that was not living. So if it meant shooting the judge in the head in cold blood and taking the jury hostage, so be it. At least I was going out my way, on my terms, and there was the slight chance that maybe I could actually get away.

"On the first count, conspiracy to traffic cocaine, we the jury find the defendant, Life Thugstin," as the foreman spoke I slightly aimed the Bible at the judge. "We, the jury find the defendant." I looked over at Scandels, felt like my hand had a mind of it's own. My hand was itching to shoot him first.

"We find the defendant ..." the foreman dropped the paper he was reading from. I had my hand on the gun. Finally he picked up the paper and read, "We find the defendant, Life Thugstin, NOT GUILTY." The entire courtroom erupted in pandemonium. Black folks acting like Lincoln had just freed the slaves. The judge pounded his gavel frantically. I stood there as if frozen and then

**324**

glanced back at Hope. The weary corners of her mouth tried to smile but her eyes warned me. This thing was far from over.

The foreman cleared his throat, looked around the courtroom nervously. "As of count two of the indictment CGE, Criminal Enterprise." This was the most serious charge–it carried life. The foreman continued, " NOT GUILY." Again the courtroom erupted. I closed the Bible and along with it a chapter of my life. I looked over at Scandels, his face was red, he was overcome with grief, like he needed to be placed on suicide watch. The judge pounded his gavel so hard it broke as Black folks ran around celebrating, hooping and hollering. The few reporters that arrived late could only look in. I weaved through the crowd with fake Bible in hand. Someone was trying to hug, touch me, and shake my hand. I searched for Hope. She was nowhere to be found. Finally I was able to reach the table with my lawyers. I saw Taya and Adrienne bent down looking at something on the floor. I walked over and to my utter shock it was Hope lying on the floor with a smile on her face, her ebony eyes were glassy, distant, as if she were looking at something we could not see. I dropped to my knees cradling her frail body in my arms. Taya screamed as she held Hope's wrist, "Ohmigod! She doesn't have a pulse!" I gently wiped a tuft of hair from Hope's face. She smiled up at me, tried to laugh. She coughed. I yelled to the top of my voice, "Pleeeze! Pleeeze! Somebody call an ambulance!"

As I rocked Hope's body in my arms tears spilled down my cheeks falling onto her face. "We ...won," Hope said in barely a whisper.

"No Hope! No Hope! You gotta stay with me. I don't want to live without you. I can't win without you. Noooo!" I wailed as the tears streaked my face.

"Don't cry," she cooed. "Don't think of it as death. Think of it as life. I did what God intended of me to do. I gave you life, twice ... this trial and bearing you a beautiful son."

"Son?" I repeated as I cried.

"Yes, Marcus is your son," she said and reached up and feathered my cheek with a delicate finger. Promise me that you will take care of him."

"Okaay, okaay," I droned as I wept sorrowfully. The pain in my chest, I couldn't describe, it hurt so bad. Why couldn't God take me? I would have gladly given my life for this woman.

The entire courtroom had taken on a still quiet. Through blurry eyes I looked up to see Black folks in a circle around me swaying and humming an old dirge. Hope took a deep breath, her very last breath, "I love you," she said and closed her eyes. She died right there in my arms, in them white folks' so-called courthouse. She had a victorious smile on her face.

The medics arrived. Blazack and my stepmother had to wrestle me away from Hope's lifeless body.

*****

# Epilogue

## "The Beginning"

### *– Life –*

A year later, I married Black Pearl on August 21. Life is strange. I am still trying to get to know my son. However, Black Pearl and Marcus are inseparable, mother and child. She calls him Lil Man. Black Pearl and Trina are still friends as well as business partners. They design clothes for many companies. One of them is a company called Phat Farm. Blazack is doing time for manslaughter. Ironically they found no body and no evidence, just an eyewitness that saw him abduct a man in broad daylight.

Tomica, the lesbian that testified against me at my trial—I guess God don't like ugly. The last I heard, Tomica was strung out on heroin somewhere in New York, in a place called Hell's Kitchen. Evette, her ex-lover, is still in prison. She calls the house from time to time to gossip with Pearl. Gucci and the rest of Miami's notorious Oplica Triangle crew went home. They now own a chain of car detail businesses. Major, my all-purpose man that was on the case with me, is doing time in a federal prison in Edgefield, South Carolina. Two months after Big Mike was released from prison, someone caught him at a red light and pumped 41 bullets into his body. One for each person that he testified against. As for myself, I started a non-profit organization called The Hope Evans Scholarship Foundation. It's designed to help impoverished young Black children make it to college.

Hope's death taught me a lot. I no longer refer to Black women as bitches and whores. One of the world's best kept secrets is, a Black woman gave birth to humanity, and historically, she had been used and abused, history stolen and relegated as just a woman, when in all actuality she was the first "Womb-man." To date, AIDS is the number one killer of young Black women. Black women are 25 times more likely to be diagnosed with AIDS than white women. The leading cause of HIV among Black men is having sex with other men. The leading cause of HIV among black women is having sex with men.

I'm still trying to survive with this thing called *Life*.

**THE END!**

# ORDER FORM

## Triple Crown Publications
### 2959 Stelzer Rd.
### Columbus, Oh 43219

**Name:** _____

**Address:** _____

**City/State:** _____

**Zip:** _____

| | TITLES | PRICES |
|---|---|---|
| | Dime Piece | $15.00 |
| | Gangsta | $15.00 |
| | Let That Be The Reason | $15.00 |
| | A Hustler's Wife | $15.00 |
| | The Game | $15.00 |
| | Black | $15.00 |
| | Dollar Bill | $15.00 |
| | A Project Chick | $15.00 |
| | Road Dawgz | $15.00 |
| | Blinded | $15.00 |
| | Diva | $15.00 |
| | Sheisty | $15.00 |
| | Grimey | $15.00 |
| | Me & My Boyfriend | $15.00 |
| | Larceny | $15.00 |
| | Rage Times Fury | $15.00 |
| | A Hood Legend | $15.00 |
| | Flipside of The Game | $15.00 |
| | Menage's Way | $15.00 |

**SHIPPING/HANDLING (Via U.S. Media Mail)**    **$3.95**

**TOTAL**    **$_____**

**FORMS OF ACCEPTED PAYMENTS:**
Postage Stamps, Institutional Checks & Money Orders, all mail in orders take 5-7 Business days to be delivered.

# ORDER FORM

Triple Crown Publications
2959 Stelzer Rd.
Columbus, Oh 43219

**Name:** _____

**Address:** _____

**City/State:** _____

**Zip:** _____

| | TITLES | PRICES |
|---|---|---|
| | Still Sheisty | $15.00 |
| | Chyna Black | $15.00 |
| | Game Over | $15.00 |
| | Cash Money | $15.00 |
| | Crack Head | $15.00 |
| | For The Strength of You | $15.00 |
| | Down Chick | $15.00 |
| | Dirty South | $15.00 |
| | Cream | $15.00 |
| | Hoodwinked | $15.00 |
| | Bitch | $15.00 |
| | Stacy | $15.00 |
| | Life | $15.00 |
| | Keisha | $15.00 |
| | Mina's Joint | $15.00 |
| | How To Succeed in The Publishing Game | $20.00 |
| | | |
| | | |
| | | |

**SHIPPING/HANDLING (Via U.S. Media Mail)**          $3.95

**TOTAL**          $_____

## FORMS OF ACCEPTED PAYMENTS:

Postage Stamps, Institutional Checks & Money Orders, all mail in orders take 5-7 Business days to be delivered.